Beware False Profits

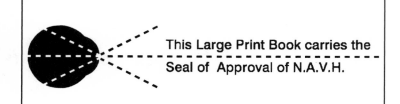

This Large Print Book carries the
Seal of Approval of N.A.V.H.

BEWARE FALSE PROFITS

EMILIE RICHARDS

THORNDIKE PRESS

An imprint of Thomson Gale, a part of The Thomson Corporation

Detroit • New York • San Francisco • New Haven, Conn. • Waterville, Maine • London

THOMSON
™
GALE

LIBRARY OF CONGRESS CATALOGING-IN-PUBLICATION DATA

Richards, Emilie, 1948–
  Beware false profits / by Emilie Richards.
    p. cm.
  ISBN-13: 978-1-4104-0396-4 (hardcover : alk. paper)
  ISBN-10: 1-4104-0396-3 (hardcover : alk. paper)
  1. Spouses of clergy — Fiction. 2. Missing persons — Fiction.
3. Politicians' spouses — Crimes against — Fiction. 4. Female impersonators
— Fiction. 5. Large type books. I. Title.
PS3568.I31526B49 2008
813'.54—dc22   2007042581

Published in 2008 by arrangement with The Berkley Publishing Group, a member of Penguin Group (USA) Inc.

Printed in the United States of America on permanent paper
10 9 8 7 6 5 4 3 2 1

BEWARE FALSE PROFITS

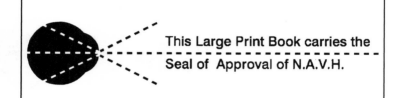

This Large Print Book carries the Seal of Approval of N.A.V.H.

BEWARE FALSE PROFITS

1

For a minister's wife I spend too much time in bars.

Okay, maybe "bars" isn't exactly the right word. Sure, Don't Go There, in Emerald Springs, Ohio, is a working-class, slugfest, "Daddy won't you please come home," semi-biker bar. And yes, despite the inherent warning in the name, I've "been" there a few times too many. Just asking questions, of course.

Technotes, farther afield, isn't really a bar. It's a dance club with enough blinking lights to trigger seizures and enough taut, gleaming skin to make me sadly aware that my vegetarian diet isn't a diet at all. I've had reason to go there, as well.

But the Pussycat Club in Manhattan's East Village, with a fifteen-foot pink cat blinking above the marquee? This one is new to my radar, and it's going to be hard to top. No pun intended, but judging from

7

some of the photographs in the glass case at the entrance, Saturday at the Pussycat is a drag queen review with ladies who are weightier on "top" than I. And I'm often forced to resort to Frederick's of Hollywood for a bra that fits.

I'm getting ahead of myself, of course. Ed and I did not come to Manhattan to inspect, spectate, or even speculate at the Pussycat Club. We came for a much needed romantic weekend, something that hasn't happened in years.

This all began when my mother, Junie, decided to call Emerald Springs her home, too. After decades on the road between one craft or Renaissance fair and another, Junie decided that hanging her hat, not to mention her quilts, in one place was a treat she deserved. She bought an old Victorian house I was flipping with my friend Lucy Jacobs, and moved in, lock, stock, and barrel.

With us.

The problem is that the Victorian still needs a lot of work, and Junie can't live there yet, much less turn the bottom floor into the quilt shop she envisions. Although we're working on fast-forward now, Lucy and I had more or less been taking our time until Junie signed the contract. Lucy works full-time as a Realtor, and I, well, I work full-time at being a mother to two daughters, a wife to Ed, and inoffensive to the congregation.

This last role is the hardest.

I wasn't born to be a minister's partner. I'm not sure anyone is, of course, but truly some people seem more inclined toward this job than others. I was raised to be as Bohemian and freethinking as my mother. My two sisters and I traveled coast-to-coast with Junie, attending school here and there, calling new members of Junie's Husband-of-the-Year Club "Daddy" until the next meeting of Junie's Divorced-but-Dear Club. Junie has been married five times, and Sid, Vel, and I each have a different father. Despite our upbringing or because of it, no sisters are closer.

But back to Bohemian. On the religion scale Junie's friends ranged from shamans to charlatans, Spiritualists to skeptics. When we went to church as a family, we only went to churches with names that intrigued my mother. The Holy Raiders Revival Church. The Sect of Secrets and Signs. The House of Heavenly Harmony.

Normally we breezed in and out. As a teenager my personal theology grew to include the following: There may or may not be a God. He or She may look like Lord Ganesh, the Hindu elephant god, or perhaps some amalgam of an elephant as described by three mythical blind men who are touching either a leg, a trunk, or a tail.

Then I met Ed Wilcox, seminary student and devoted attendee of the Unitarian-Universalist Church. They were a tad more orthodox than I was, but I did immediately feel at home.

Cut to the twenty-first century and the Consolidated Community Church of Emerald Springs, Ohio, where I update the archives, throw rip-roaring holiday open houses, and find naked bodies on the parsonage porch.

You have to remember, I came to this job without a resume.

Now that Ed has served three churches, one of the things I've learned is that congregations take up most of our waking hours, and sleeping hours aren't sacred, either. Ed and I have learned to steal moments for conversation and intimacy whenever we can find them. Unfortunately, sneaking around gets wearing. When Junie moved into the parsonage, and we had one more person in the house to contend with, things began to deteriorate.

So when a Harvard classmate of Ed's suggested we come to the Big Apple and stay in his apartment some weekend while he was off on sabbatical, we bought tickets on the first cheap flight out. And here we are. Standing at the entrance of the Pussycat Club in the East Village on a chilly spring evening, looking at the lineup for the night's entertainment.

"We wouldn't be here if you hadn't given your cell phone number to Norma," I reminded Ed, yet again. "What were you *thinking?*"

"I was thinking there might be an emergency." Ed hadn't come to New York with appropriate Pussycat clothes. He was wearing a pinstripe dress shirt and pleated khaki pants. He'd planned to ward off the chill with a monogrammed wool crew neck his mother gave him for Christmas, but I'd reminded him we weren't having tea after a cricket match and made him leave it at the apartment.

"For pity's sake, Ed, you knew Norma would give out your number if a parishioner's dog got fleas. You might as well have published it in the *Flow*." Norma: our garrulous church secretary. The *Flow:* our Emerald Springs daily.

"In this case Norma gave it out because we have a missing person," he reminded me.

11

Yet again.

I watched Ed shiver and felt a smidgen of regret that I'd denied him the crew neck. Had it only been black. Or fraying at the cuffs.

I stepped aside so that two guys in their sixties, one with a parochial school plaid skirt over dark trousers, could get through the door. "I really can't believe Joe Wagner is missing. And I really can't believe he was ever *here*."

The Wagner saga started this morning. Just as Ed and I were getting out of bed after a spectacular marital booty call, Ed's cell phone chirped Beethoven's Fifth. We'd been planning to find a local deli where we could buy lox and real bagels, spread the *New York Times* from one end of the table to the other, and drink quarts of strong coffee. The rest of the day was filled with glorious possibilities. But the call changed everything.

I only heard Ed's end, which went something like: "Uh-huh. No. Of course you're upset. I can't imagine."

I nearly fell back asleep, but when Ed put down the phone, I recognized the look on his face. The sweet afterglow of sex, untarnished by the soundtrack of Saturday morning cartoons and Junie's morning mantra, was no longer reflected there. This was unmistakably the look of a minister with another problem to worry about.

"Don't tell me," I said. "Oh, please don't tell me we have to go home before tomorrow night."

"That was Maura Wagner."

Maura, her husband, Joe, and son, Tyler, are members of our church, although of the three Wagners, Maura is least often on the Tri-C scene. Joe's a big, handsome guy, the director of Helping Hands, the local food bank, and everybody's friend. Need tables set up for a potluck supper? Joe will come early to help. Need somebody to count the dollar bills in the collection plate? Joe's the man. Need a chairman for the annual pledge drive? You get the picture. Joe is one of those people who keeps churches healthy. He shakes hands and gives out orders of service. He gives laughing toddlers rides on his strong shoulders and assures teenage girls that the male of the species can eventually grow up and clean up spectacularly.

Maura Wagner is Joe's opposite. She is small and fragile, with Easter egg blue eyes and a halo of curly blonde hair. If Maura stubs her toe, she calls Joe and asks what profanity she can use. She's weak to his strong, unfocused where he is forceful.

The roles seem to suit them both, because from the outside their marriage looks happy. Seemingly the only real bump on their road to marital bliss was the discovery that Tyler, now twelve, was diabetic. But even this was a bump, not a mountain they couldn't scale. Between Joe's attention to proper doses of insulin and Tyler's resilient spirit, Tyler's life has been for the most part normal and happy.

Maura Wagner was one of the last people I expected to bother Ed when we were off on a holiday. I wasn't even sure she knew how to dial a telephone.

"Did somebody die?" I asked, afraid I already knew the answer.

"No, but it's not much farther down the list." Ed ran his hand over his chin. For months there's been a beard there, not a very successful one. Last week he disposed of it, leaving chin pallor and a small scar on one cheek. He still forgets it's gone.

"Please don't make me guess." I could envision all manner of crises. I've had too much experience with crises lately, and wasn't longing for more.

"Joe's disappeared."

"Disappeared is a big word. Is he late coming home from the grocery store? Sitting through a twelve-inning game at Jacob's Field? Or did he make off with their entire bank account last week and she's only just noticed?"

"No, he was here, in the city, for a meeting. And he didn't come home."

"Joe in New York?"

"Supposed to be." Ed rubbed his hand over his hair, which was still, fortunately, intact. It seemed to calm him. He dropped down to the bed beside me. "He was supposed to be home last night, but he didn't show. At first Maura thought maybe his plane was just late."

"Then she knew what flight he was on?"

Ed looked at me as if my IQ had suddenly dropped into an unacceptable range. "Aggie . . ."

"So okay, Maura isn't a detail person. But knowing Joe, he left all the information. He probably laminated copies and posted them all over the house. He probably made Tyler memorize arrival times and airline phone numbers to repeat back to Maura at hourly intervals."

"Maura says Joe goes to the same meeting in Manhattan every month and has for over a year. He leaves on the first flight out of Columbus on the third Thursday and comes home at the same time on the third Friday evening. And that's all she knows."

"Only this time he didn't come home? And he didn't call her?"

"That's the strange part. Apparently she did get a call. She has caller ID, so she knows it came from Joe's cell. But the call was garbled, the way they are when the tower's too far away, or the caller's inside a building. She thinks it was Joe on the other end, but she's not even sure of that. And she couldn't understand a word."

I could just imagine how frustrating that had been. But Joe *had* called home. Maura knew he was alive and probably just held up in New York. Why had she bothered Ed?

"Did she call his hotel?" Ed gave me the "look" again and I narrowed my eyes. "You're telling me she doesn't know where Joe stays when he's here?"

"Apparently he moves around. She says he shops for the best deal every time. She doesn't keep up."

This didn't sound believable. "Joe knows Tyler could have a problem while he's away. He would never leave without telling Maura where he's staying."

"That's why he carries the cell phone."

"So, has she tried to call him back?"

"She's not that helpless. Repeatedly, apparently. Through the night and all morning until she called here."

"How did she know to call you?"

"The whole church knows we're in New York this weekend, even Maura."

"Can't she just wait and see if he shows up today on a later flight? It's a weekend. Maybe Joe just figured he'd take a little time for himself for a change."

"You're forgetting something."

I racked my brain, then I realized what Ed meant. "Mayday!"

"You got it."

Mayday!, complete with exclamation point, is the Helping Hands yearly fundraiser on the first Sunday afternoon of May. It's a big deal for Emerald Springs. Unless you've lived in a small town, you can't understand how important an event like this one is in community life. We don't have a symphony or ballet — unless you count the annual spring recital of Bela's Ballerinas, featuring seven-year-olds wearing tutus and lipstick. There's no auditorium for fifty miles that's large enough to showcase touring companies with third-rate casts of old Broadway musicals. So for the most part we entertain ourselves. And each year Mayday!, a spring carnival with pony rides, games of skill, and more junk food than you can shake a corn dog at, is happily anticipated.

Planning for Mayday! takes all year, and

dozens of people spend the whole weekend doing the necessary physical labor. Last year I spent an entire day setting up and taking down tables in the food tent. I'll confess removing myself from table duty was one of the joys of coming to New York this particular weekend.

"Joe told me once that they raise more than a quarter of their yearly budget at Mayday!," I said.

"So Joe would never willingly miss it."

"But what does Maura expect you to do?" I saw the answer in Ed's eyes. "No, Ed. We aren't going to spend our only Saturday in Manhattan looking for Joe, are we? Please tell me we aren't."

But of course we did.

Now, after a day of following clues, here we were at the Pussycat Club on a borderline seedy East Village street. There had been compensations. I've done a lot of detective work on my own this year, and this was the first time I hadn't been forced to shield my activities from my husband's suspicious gaze. Today Ed and I were a team, albeit a reluctant one. And even if our activities weren't as much fun as a leisurely stroll down Fifth Avenue, at least we were together.

"Let's go over what we know one more

18

time," I said, "and maybe we'll have a great idea, which will include hopping in a cab and going somewhere else. Like out to a great restaurant for dinner."

"Repeating the facts won't change them."

I repeated them anyway. "Joe was supposed to be in the city at a meeting of an organization called Funds for Food. He told Maura he came here to attend a similar meeting every month."

"And now we know there's no organization in New York called Funds for Food, and that nobody at any of the local food banks has heard of an organization by that name." Ed glanced at his watch.

Behind us, the perpetual serenade of police sirens and honking horns crescendoed. I spoke louder. "Our repeated calls to Joe's cell phone have gone unanswered."

Three guys pushed past us. One was dressed as a cowboy, the second a cop, and the third was unmistakably an Indian chief with a headdress that almost didn't clear the doorframe. They were three guys short of the Village People. I stifled the impulse to raise my arms and make the letters *YMCA* in salute.

Apparently Ed had no such impulse, because he was still listing facts. "Unfortunately, just as we were about to give up and tell Maura we'd hit a brick wall, you had to try one more time."

I wrinkled my nose in apology. "Sorry, I get going, and I just forget to stop."

"Whoever picked it up —"

"A guy with a gravelly voice," I reminded. "Said there was nobody named 'Joe Wagner' there."

"But just before Gravel Voice spoke, I heard —"

Ed sang the finale: "Pussycat, pussycat, I love you. Yes, I do."

"Welcome to the East Village's own Pussycat Club," I finished on an exhale.

"See any good reason to hail a cab?" Ed glanced at his watch again.

I opened my mouth to say no, that it looked like we were stuck with paying the cover charge at the East Village's own Pussycat Club, and trooping inside to see what we could discover. But as I avoided eye contact with my significant other, my gaze fell on the photos displayed in the case just in front of us.

"Ed . . ."

"You know, we could be in and out of there in minutes, Aggie. But first we have to go *in.*"

"Ed" — I took his arm — "I, well . . ." I turned him a little. "Look at these photos and tell me what you see."

I didn't want to influence him, so I forced myself to watch as three heavily made-up women in sequins and fishnet stockings sauntered into the club.

Ed sounded tired. It had been that kind of a day. "I see what I'd expect to. The Pussy-cat Club's a no-holds-barred kind of place. Old-fashioned burlesque on Monday and Tuesday, vaudeville on Wednesday and Sunday, female impersonators on Thursday and Saturday. Something for every —"

He stopped. I let my gaze drift back to the photos. "That's some coat, isn't it?" I said.

Ed leaned closer. But I didn't have to watch to know exactly where his eyes were riveted. He was staring at the gorgeous dame, third from the left, posed in a stunning full-length fur coat, with just enough shapely leg peeking out the opening. How many animals had gone to the happy hunting ground to provide enough pelts for that number? Because the gorgeous dame had to be six foot three in her bare feet and was broad shouldered to boot. She had straight black hair and thick bangs, like the younger Cher, and the toothy, flirty smile was Cher's as well.

But the face was not. Nope, under the false eyelashes, the layers of foundation, the close, close shave, the face was even more familiar.

"Maybe we've been working on this so many hours we're just seeing him every-where," Ed said at last.

"Or maybe we're looking at the real reason Joe Wagner comes to New York once a month."

We both stared at the photo a minute longer. Then Ed sighed. "Exactly what are we going to say to Joe if we find him in there dressed like that?"

I took Ed's arm and pulled him toward the door. " 'I Got You, Babe'?"

2

Dorothy Gale wore the requisite ruby slippers, although this particular pair looked to be a size twelve. She also wore lace-trimmed ankle socks and a blue gingham dress and accessorized with a brown terrier named Toto who thought I was the Wicked Witch of the West. Toto hadn't stopped baring his sharp little teeth in my direction since Ed and I accepted the invitation into Dorothy's dressing room. Growl rumbling, beady eyes narrowed, Toto was plotting how to rid the Land of Oz of another interloper. And not with a bucket of water.

"Oh, he's just too sweet, isn't he?" Dorothy cooed, rubbing noses with her pet.

Ed was trying to look comfortable. He was finally warm, which was a good thing. The dressing room was maybe seven by eight, minus two feet of metal clothing racks and another three of table jutting out along the longest wall. The stained white Formica surface was flanked by mirrors and over-flowing with what looked like Macy's entire range of cosmetics. Dorothy, Toto, Ed, and I were sharing body heat, and Ed was beginning to sweat. Although the reason was up for grabs.

"Tell the dog I have no intention of siccing my flying monkeys on the pair of you," I told Dorothy.

"Oh, little Totes is *so* not violent." Dorothy rubbed her nose with Toto's, then straightened. She held the little dog out to Ed. "Here. He'll love you."

Ed had no choice but to accept. Had Dorothy been standing she would have loomed over us. Ed is tall, but Dorothy had inches on him, about six foot four, with shoulders that suggested when she wasn't skipping along the Yellow Brick Road, she was working construction. One whack of her punching bag hand, and Ed — no slouch in the physical department — might end up flying through the dressing room door to sprawl on the stage twenty yards away, where a trio of drag queens in skintight sequined dresses were lip-syncing the old Pointer Sisters hit "I Want a Man with a Slow Hand."

Ed might have a slow hand, but I don't think he's willing to demonstrate for this audience.

Toto licked Ed's beardless chin. The dog's beady little eyes were now a liquid, adoring brown. I kept my distance, which meant I edged ten inches away from my husband and his new canine groupie.

"I've got to finish getting ready," Dorothy said in her gravelly voice. "You can stay if you like."

Having never in my unusual life watched a man change himself into a woman, I was fascinated. Ed, for all the predictable reasons, seemed less so. But he was also a guy who spent his life fighting stereotypes. He stood his ground and didn't even pull his collar away from his neck when sweat began to trickle in that direction.

"Thanks for letting us be here," Ed said, as if he meant it.

"No problem. I've been worried about Josephine. I'm totally thrilled somebody else is worried, too."

I shifted my weight, lurching an inch toward Ed. Toto growled menacingly.

Shifting back, I beamed at Dorothy as if I wasn't about to be shredded by pointy little teeth. The stage manager had been less than thrilled to let us backstage, but Dorothy had overheard our questions, interceded, and led us through narrow winding corridors to her dressing room. Unfortunately, it all happened too fast to suit me. I missed an on-stage rendition of Madonna's "Material Girl" performed by a guy whose ice-cream cone breasts made the real things, well, im-material. And when would I ever have a chance to see anything like this in Emerald Springs?

"We're glad we found you. Were you the one who answered Joe's cell phone earlier?" Ed asked.

"I feel like such a fool." Dorothy smiled ruefully. She had a wonderful voice, rich, deep, and simpering. I was really hoping we could stay long enough to hear her warble "Over the Rainbow."

"So it *was* you?" I asked.

She shook her pigtailed head sorrowfully. The pigtails were luxuriant, as long as my arm, and sticking out of hair that was teased into cottony poufs. Had I tried this with my youngest daughter Teddy, she would have asked her father to remember me in his prayers.

"I forgot the phone was here," Dorothy said. "Isn't that silly? I guess I dropped it back on the table Thursday night."

"I'm confused. Why did you have it? It belongs to . . . Josephine, doesn't it?"

"Oh sure, it's Josephine's. He was just *so* upset that night. He came off the stage and

26

made a call to somebody, then I guess he came back in here and changed. By the time I finished my act he was gone. Like the wind — and without his phone."

Dorothy swept a bejeweled hand in a graceful arc. "I saw the phone and picked it up. I tried to return it, you know, but no such luck. So I put it back where he dropped it, in case he came back. And this dressing table is just *such* a mess. I guess I forgot about it. I guess none of the other girls saw it, either."

"I guess nobody heard it ringing. Because people have been calling Joe." I didn't say the "wife" word. I wasn't sure how that would go over here.

"The phone was set to vibrate. I only heard it because it rattled the bottles in front of it this afternoon. I was here practicing my new number."

Dorothy flipped open a case and took out a false eyelash as thick as an Ohio woolly caterpillar. She dotted glue along the edge, then waved it in the air. "They go on better this way, you know. What girl needs glue in her eye? Right, sweetie?"

I didn't know. My own average eyelashes have to suffice, although now I felt a sting of jealousy, compounded by the flawless red nails on the hand that was holding the lashes. When was the last time I had enough time for a manicure?

Clearly Ed was as confused as I was. He tried for clarity. "So you answered today . . ."

She carefully attached the eyelashes to her lid, then repeated the ritual for the second lid before she answered. "I did. Then I got up to close the door so I could hear whoever it was, and by the time I got back to the table, the phone went dead. The battery, of course. Gone with the wind." She smiled shyly. "I guess you can tell I'm Scarlett O'Hara in the final revue of the evening. You should see me in a hoopskirt."

"I'd like to," I said. "What color is your dress?"

"Aggie . . ." Ed frowned at me, and sensing his annoyance, Toto made a lunge in my direction. I shrugged as Ed jerked him away.

"We don't want to take up a lot of your time," I said. "Here's the thing. Joe seems to have disappeared. His wife" — I paused, because now that secret was out — "He has a wife."

"He wouldn't be the only one. A man's gotta do what a man's gotta do." Dorothy winked. At Ed. The new lush eyelashes created a much needed breeze, although the sweat seemed to trickle faster.

I went on. "The thing is, nobody at home

knew about, uh, this part of his life."

Dorothy rolled her eyes. "See my last statement."

"Okay. Well, can you maybe tell us how long he's been performing here?"

Dorothy pursed her lips and stared at them in the mirror. Either she was thinking hard or about to touch up her lipstick, which, I might add, was already perfect. I was hungry for lip liner tips, but with Toto and Ed menacing me, I knew better than to ask. In extreme circumstances I was afraid Ed was capable of setting the dog loose.

"I've only been here about six months," Dorothy said. "I came up from New Orleans. Before Katrina I was a star on Bourbon Street, and afterwards, well, it just wasn't fun anymore. Josephine was already here. See, Pussycat has this contest once a month. We take men in the audience who want to transform and make them stars for the night. The audience votes for their favorite and she gets a prize. A facial, makeup tips, you know."

I didn't, but I was learning fast.

"And Joe . . . ?" I asked.

"I'm pretty sure that's how Josephine was born. He was such a hit, he got a regular gig as his prize, I guess. You never heard him sing?"

"In our church choir. Baritone. He gets all the solos."

"Oh, such a voice. Lots of us lip-sync. But not Josephine. His tone is so gorgeous. When he sings 'Gypsies, Tramps, and Thieves,' I get all choked up." She put her fingertips to her cheeks and swallowed hard. "That poor girl in the song, left alone and pregnant by a cad. Men!"

Now Ed did pull his collar away from his neck. Me, I'd always felt the same way when I heard the song. I couldn't help myself. I sang a little. "I was born in the wagon —"

"Of a traveling show . . ." Dorothy joined in. Then she shook her head. "Oh stop, I'll cry and mess up my eyeliner."

For Ed's sake, I did. "So Joe performs regularly?"

"I don't want to get him in trouble. The girls and I stick up for each other. He's one of us."

"Nobody's trying to hurt Joe," Ed promised.

Ed has a wonderful voice, too. Deep, resonant. He's mesmerizing from the pulpit — and that's coming from the woman who washes his dirty socks. The voice and the inherent sincerity seemed to soothe Dorothy and make her decision easier.

She started dusting sparkly powder over

her cheekbones. "He came in on Thursday, like he was scheduled to do. He's just here that one day a month, although he could be here more if he wanted. He's *such* a favorite. Anyway, he opened his set the way he always does, with 'If I Could Turn Back Time.' He brought the house down."

She put down her brush and stood. "Let me show you what he wore."

We didn't exactly have to follow her anywhere, so Ed didn't protest. Dorothy took four steps and started rummaging through the rack. She paused, swept some more clothes aside, then she pulled out a dress I would have given a year of chocolate chip cookies to own. It was silver lamé, with a plunging neckline, rhinestones and pearls, and a hemline slit to eternity.

"And that's not all," Dorothy said, shoving the dress at me.

I grabbed it. I couldn't help it. I held it to my nose and sniffed. I'm not sure what I expected. A whiff of testosterone? Old Spice aftershave? Chanel? But it smelled a little like sweat, a lot like a cheap Halloween costume. I was disappointed.

"Here." Dorothy whirled, holding the fur coat I'd seen in the photo out front. She cuddled it against her, clasping the bottom of the sleeves with her fingertips.

31

The coat was gorgeous. I'd never seen anything quite like it. It was made from strips of fur of all colors and types. Silver, gold, ebony, spots . . .

"Leopard? That's against the law." I threw back my shoulders and narrowed my eyes. "For that matter, every bit of it should be against the law. That's not the Joe I know. He'd never wear that coat."

"Oh sweetie, relax. Take a deep, cleansing breath." Dorothy demonstrated, and I was vaulted back to Lamaze class, training for the first labor pain.

"It's not real fur," she said after the long exhale. "It's fake, every bit of it. He had it made out of scraps Larry — he's our manager — found in the garment district. But you better believe every girl here wants it. Every girl!" She held it out for me to feel. "See?"

I did. The coat felt lush and silky, but it was clearly not real.

"The coat is a problem," Dorothy said. "Josephine is *such* a star. A lot of the regulars don't like him. But they're just jealous old biddies. He gets a lot of perks for a part-timer, you know. He shares this room with me when he's here. He makes a suggestion, Larry says, 'Fine, do it.' He's the favorite, that's for sure. But hey, he's here one day a month. I always say, 'Get over it,' you know? Marilyn, she's the worst. She actually clapped her hands when Josephine left early on Thursday. And when she performed later? She was better than usual, although 'Diamonds Are a Girl's Best Friend' still sounds like rhinestones to me."

Ed's eyes were glazing over. Maybe it was the hot little room or the fragrance of a vat's worth of cosmetics. Maybe it was his hypnotic stroking of Toto's fur. Or maybe, heck, it was a guy having trouble with another guy's lifestyle. A liberal guy.

"Can you tell us more about Thursday?" Ed didn't add *quickly,* although I knew it was on the tip of his tongue.

Dorothy seated herself on the bench again, squinted at her face in the mirror, then began to stroke a soft brown powder under her cheekbones. "Well, he came backstage after he finished the opener, and he looked radiant. I mean Cher never looked that good, if you know what I mean. His hair, well he has the most incredible taste in —"

I interrupted. "Did something happen after that first number? Does he normally do more?"

Although Toto snarled, Dorothy didn't hold my rudeness against me. "His set is usually about five numbers." She counted silently on her fingers. "Six. He always does a quick change after the first one. Hangs up the coat until the finale, wraps a gold shawl around his shoulders for the second number. He seemed just fine. He got ready and went out. He sounded great. He sang . . ." She thought a moment. " 'Bang, Bang'."

I'm a big Cher fan. I knew the words to this one, too. But I was fairly sure Ed might pass out just to avoid hearing it. "And then?"

"Well, I was standing in the wings when he walked offstage. They were cheering out front. He'd given it his all, although it's not his best song by a long shot. But when I saw his face, I knew something was wrong. He was as white as a geisha. Just so pale you couldn't be sure he was still breathing. I asked him what was wrong, and he said he was sick. Then he ran to the loo and locked himself inside."

"Wow." *Wow* is my fallback word. I didn't know what else to say.

Dorothy shook her head. Then she leaned forward and peered at her face. Seemingly satisfied, she uncapped what looked like eyebrow pencil and began to dot more freckles on her cheeks.

"When he came out, he really looked bad.

He told me he was done for the night. I told him the show must go on and all that garbage, but he just shook his head. Said he was making a phone call, and I should tell Larry he wasn't going back onstage."

Dorothy stopped dotting and turned to look at me. "You can guess what Larry said, right?"

"I'm pretty sure I can. What happened next?"

"I went on instead. And I really had to work up some enthusiasm, you know? I mean, was I in the mood to sing 'Ding Dong the Witch Is Dead?' I didn't even have my freckles."

I clucked in commiseration. "But I meant what happened to Joe?"

"Well, I guess he made that phone call."

I pondered this. "You were out on the stage."

"Well, I was, yes. But Marilyn wasn't. She told me everything."

Ed pulled himself together. "Do you mind filling us in?"

"She said that Joe went out in the alley for a few minutes, then he came back inside and changed his clothes and scrubbed his face. She went in to see if he needed anything. Of course that's not why she *really* went in. I think she was hoping she'd catch him at something that would get him thrown out for good. She's all about herself, our Marilyn, and just between us, she wants that coat. Anyway, she said his hands were shaking. She said she was afraid he might pass out, but he said he didn't want any help. On the way out Larry tried to talk to him, but Joe brushed him aside and took off through the alley door. Larry said he wasn't steady on his feet. And that's all I know."

Even though we knew a lot more now, I was afraid what we did know was something of a bust. We knew once a month Joe performed as a female impersonator. That was a bombshell with all kinds of implications, but it didn't begin to explain where he was at the moment. He wasn't here; he wasn't at home. How many secret lives did this man have?

"You mentioned something about trying to return the phone," I said.

"That's right. After I finished up for the night and changed out of my hoopskirt" — Dorothy winked at me — "blue, almost a turquoise. With a neckline cut right to here" — she demonstrated with index fingers — "Ecru lace trim. I have a matching hat with more feathers than Vivian Leigh *ever* had. I'd show you, but it's hanging in the wardrobe room because it takes up *so* much

36

space. Anyway, I found the phone on the table. I knew where he usually stayed when he was in town, so I went over there to check on him and return it."

"Where?" Ed asked.

"A small hotel on Seventeenth. The Chelsea Inn. There's a bar in the neighborhood where we go sometimes after we finish here. You know, to eat and let off steam. Nobody looks twice. Splash is that kind of place. I'd walked with Josephine back to his hotel a few times on the way to my apartment. So I knew where he liked to stay. But by the time I got to the Chelsea Thursday, he was gone. Checked out, and they wouldn't give me an address so I could send him the phone. You'll take it back to him?"

"Sure, only we don't know where he is. But we can give it to his wife." I imagined that conversation and winced.

Actually, I'd been steadily wincing inside since the story began. The thing is, Joe Wagner is one of my favorites in our congregation. Not everybody sees me as a person in my own right. Joe has always made it clear he's interested in Aggie Sloan-Wilcox, human being, and not Aggie Sloan-Wilcox, ministerial appendage. And by interested, I don't mean "interested." Not in a sexual way. Just interested, as in he likes my sense of humor and brain. It endeared him to me right from the beginning.

There were too many parts of this saga that worried me. First and foremost, Joe was missing and possibly lying ill somewhere or worse. I couldn't think about "worse" right now, but the possibility wasn't going to disappear until I knew he was okay.

Second, at the very least Joe had a double life. He left Emerald Springs every month, lied about his reason for leaving, and came to Manhattan to perform in a drag queen revue. Some people might be worried about that last part. I was worried about the first. Joe was not a man who would lie easily. I suspected this was not an easy deception to maintain, not logistically, and not emotionally.

Third, I didn't think we were any closer to finding Joe than we'd been this morning. Yes, we knew more details about Thursday night, but how could we follow up? We would certainly check the hotel, and maybe the bar Dorothy had mentioned. But I was pretty certain this trail was going to go cold quickly.

Of course there was one more thing we could try, although the thought gave me shivers.

"We have to call all the hospitals in the

city." I wondered who we should ask about, Joe Wagner or Josephine Fairheart? Would each hospital require two phone calls or just a long explanation?

Ed gave Toto one last stroke, then held the fawning dog out to Dorothy. I leaned as far from the transaction as I could. Toto gave the air between us a ceremonial nip.

"She's really not a bad person," Ed told Dorothy, inclining his head toward me. "Most dogs tolerate her pretty well."

Dorothy nodded gravely. "It's a guy thing."

Ed turned to me. "That's a lot of hospitals."

"I guess we'd better get started."

Dorothy deposited Toto in a basket, then walked us the three steps to the door. Ed thanked her. I thanked her with a wary eye turned toward the dog. The door was already open when my curiosity overcame me.

"Dorothy?"

She looked expectant, a hulking Judy Garland with the same dewy-eyed intensity. I was really sorry we were going to miss her gig. I had a feeling she was one heck of a performer.

"Here's something I noticed. You referred to all the other . . . performers as 'she.' But whenever you talked about Joe? Well, you referred to Joe as 'he.' Would you mind telling me why?"

Dorothy leaned closer. I noted that the freckles looked real. This time she was all set for her trip to the Emerald City. "You noticed that?"

"Uh-huh. I was wondering if there was some kind of message I can't decode."

"Like if Joe's different from say, me or Marilyn? You really want to know if he's gay or he's not. Does it matter?"

Ed clarified what I hadn't been able to ask. "I think Aggie's wondering if Joe might have a special friend here in town. Somebody he's staying with? Somebody we could check with?" When Dorothy didn't answer, he went on. "Maybe one reason Joe disappeared is that he's tired of pretending he's something he's not."

"No, you'd be barking up the wrong tree looking for another guy in the wings. Josephine liked to strut his stuff on the stage, but when he walked off? Nobody had any doubts, and nobody ever tried to push him on the subject."

"You're saying Joe's not gay? That he's straight?"

She smiled. "There's no requirement. Nothing in our contracts. You'd be surprised. Lots of guys like to hang out in their wives' clothes once in a while. But they also like being married and going to bed with a woman. Joe's just a great performer. Me, I wish he'd been different."

"Gotcha. Um, any idea why he'd perform here?" I tried not to stress the last word, but that turned out to be impossible.

"Don't know and don't care. I just hope he's okay and plans to come back. There was this moment at the end of his set, when he'd come out in a white jumpsuit all spangled and sparkly wearing a long white wig. The crew would flood the stage with color, and he'd sit on a trapeze. They'd crank it up and he'd swing over the stage out into the audience and sing 'Believe.' I get shivers thinking about it. I don't know if I want to live in a world where I don't have that to look forward to."

Dorothy looked so crestfallen I considered giving her a hug, but decided against it. Toto looked like he was ready to leap out of the basket.

She pointed us toward the exit door, and we took off as somebody on stage crooned "Stormy Weather."

Outside on the street Ed pulled me against the building and we stood quietly a moment.

41

"So . . . what do you think?" I asked at last.

"I think this is going to be one of those ministerial moments I don't look back on with pleasure."

"You mean telling Maura?"

"Among other things. Finding out what's happened to Joe isn't going to be much fun, either. Whatever it is can't be good."

"I guess at this point we go back to the apartment and start making calls."

"Ag, unless we discover something that keeps us here, I think we have to go home on the first flight in the morning. Maura has to know what we discovered as soon as possible, and I can't see keeping her waiting or explaining something like this on the phone. She's going to have to figure out what to announce at Mayday! Joe's always such a huge part of the celebration."

I'd thought the same thing, although rebelliously my mind had skated through other possibilities first — just in case there was some way to salvage our romantic weekend together. No such luck.

We walked toward the front of the club in silence. A platinum blonde in a raspberry miniskirt and a sweater tight enough to diminish lung capacity gestured at one of us. I wasn't sure which, and it didn't matter, because as if he'd been born to it Ed quickly hailed a cab. He was so comfortable in the city, I wouldn't have been surprised if he conversed with the driver in his native language.

I settled on the bumpy seat while Ed gave directions. In English. Then when he sat back I tapped him on the shoulder. "The Plaza Hotel?"

"I thought we'd take a carriage ride through the park, then find a nice place to eat, if it's still possible to get a table on a Saturday night. But we'll try."

I didn't know what to say. As our cabbie sped into the heart of traffic, Ed shined his sexiest smile on me. I even forgot to be terrified.

"I'm sorry," he said. "I really am. I know you were looking forward to this time away. But we'll have the rest of the night to make calls to the police and the hospitals. Let's take a little for ourselves, okay?"

I leaned over and kissed him. I barely noticed when the driver stomped on the brake, and the resulting snap of my seat belt launched me backwards.

I'm married to a great guy, and when he has time, he can be wonderfully romantic. I was delighted we were going to be spending a few hours doing what we'd come to New

York to do. But I wondered, even as I kissed him again, if either of us would be able to put the saga of Joe Wagner, alias Josephine Fairheart, behind us tonight.

3

Maura and Joe Wagner live in a perfect Cape Cod on a perfect street in Emerald Springs. Using *perfect* twice in the same sentence doesn't begin to point out the, well, picture-perfect, storybook setting for their lives.

The Wagner's neighborhood, Essex Village, is just old enough to have towering trees and homes built when quality and individuality were valued. Luckily, the neighborhood isn't so old that houses are being torn down to make room for more contemporary specimens. Maybe the houses don't have today's recreational bathrooms, or media rooms where moviegoers can park a fleet of Hondas drive-in style, but they have class. It's even possible to walk into town without packing a lunch. Of course it's easier to drive the family Volvo or Saab, which is more often the case.

If I was going to buy a home in Emerald

Springs, I would first look in "The Village," as locals call it. An area has arrived when it coins its own nickname. Although real estate in general sells slowly in our little burg, houses in the Village are snapped up immediately. Our richest citizens live in the modern, pretentious homes of Emerald Estates, but young professionals with luck and taste congregate here.

The Wagners' house is white frame, with slatted spruce green shutters and a mulberry front door. The windows are multipaned and double-hung, and three dormers nestle into the roof. A cupola with a rooster weather vane graces one side, a fieldstone chimney juts from the other, and a wide front porch looks over the neighborhood. The yard is surrounded by a picket fence corralling displays of herbs and perennials, flowering shrubs, and a superb rose garden. I know from attending a Valentine's Day brunch here last year that one of the two flawlessly proportioned wings holds a parade of bedrooms. The other contains the garage, master bedroom, and bath. Maura is only too delighted to show guests through her pride and joy.

The term *housewife* has gone out of favor, but Maura is more or less married to her house. I'm convinced she thinks of her charming little Cape Cod the way some of us think of best friends or lovers. She never seems happier than when the two of them are alone together. She gifts the house with precious finds, fusses over it until it's in peak condition, and murmurs sweet nothings when no one is around to hear them.

Okay, so I've never really "heard" her murmuring sweet nothings to the family room fireplace or laundry chute. But some things are obvious without a shred of proof.

When Ed and I drove up, the lilacs stationed at the entrance to the driveway breathed a sweet welcome. I could smell them before I opened the car door, and once outside, the fragrance was enough to root me to the spot. On one side of the yard a crab apple flowered in cotton candy puffs, and underneath it, drifts of daffodils outlined the walkway to the porch. Beside the front door a deacon's bench sported two life-sized rag dolls dressed in Amish clothing and posed back to back.

I know from my tour that Maura changes the dolls' clothing whenever she feels the whim. She has an entire guest room closet filled with everything from yellow rain slickers to a ball gown and tux. The day of the brunch they had been dressed as Romeo and Juliet. Today the dolls looked as if they were about to head down to the barn for the morning's milking. Mama would come back with enough cream to churn the day's butter.

"It's all just so strange," I told Ed as reluctantly, I lifted the pineapple door knocker and let it fall above a shiny brass plate that said The Wagner Family.

"I know."

"How do you get from this to belting out 'Dark Lady' at the Pussycat Club?"

"One agonizing step at a time, I guess."

The door opened, and Maura stood at the threshold. There was no sign of emotional trauma. She looked much as she always did. Maura is slender and small, with pert features offset by amazing blue eyes. Her naturally curly blonde hair was neatly combed, each curl a shining tribute to the masses. She wore a pale blue twinset and camel-colored slacks. I was most impressed that under the circumstances, she had still found the presence of mind to add a gold chain, small hoop earrings, and an impressive watch.

"It's bad news, isn't it?" She looked vaguely puzzled, as if hearing bad news was so far from her universe that this moment was akin to preparing for an alien invasion.

"We haven't found Joe," Ed assured her,

"but we need to talk to you."

"Of course." She stepped aside and gestured us in. "I have a fresh pot of coffee and a cinnamon coffee cake."

Had my own husband disappeared, I probably wouldn't think to break out the lemon Pledge. But the telltale aroma proclaimed that Maura had just polished the furniture. In one glance I could tell the house was spotless. She could serve us coffee cake on the foyer's maple floor without concern. As we passed the living room I was fairly sure that the needlepoint pillows on the sofa and love seat had been recently plumped, and the collection of antique mantel clocks had all been wound.

In the blue and yellow kitchen she gestured us to the table by a bay window and without speaking set botanical-themed dishes in front of us.

"Maybe you should sit down, too," Ed said gently.

"Oh, I will in a minute. Just let me get organized."

Organized meant five long minutes, a silver tea tray with a coffeepot and all the accoutrements, the aforementioned coffee cake, a vase with one fragrant narcissus to adorn the center of the table, and napkins straight from Provence. By the time she joined us, I had taken stock of everything in the room and was fighting back the urge to report Maura to some higher female authority. Not a thing was out of place. No keys on the counter, no newspapers on the table, no dishes in a drainer. No drainer, in fact. I suspected she washed, dried, and put away every single dish without the need for one. Next to Maura, the Stepford wives were slobs.

Everything in plain sight had been placed there with care. The walls were embellished with cheerful embroidered sayings augmented by kittens or cherub-cheeked children. Shining red apples filled a pottery bowl. From an uncapped crystal jar, potpourri added its rose scent to the lemony air. I had a sneaking suspicion Maura had spent more time folding and ironing her dish towels than I had spent remodeling the parsonage.

We were both relieved when she finally sat. Me because I could stop imagining how often she cleaned out her refrigerator, and Ed because he needed to get Joe's story out in the open.

She sliced the cake and we accepted pieces. She poured coffee, then cream. I stopped her at the sugar cubes. It was time to move on.

"I didn't know you would be here so early, or I would have sliced some fruit." She lifted her cup gracefully and took a dainty sip. "It was kind of you to come." She could have been thanking a neighbor who had brought her a piece of misdirected mail.

"Where's Tyler?" I asked, hoping Joe and Maura's twelve-year-old son wouldn't walk in as we were describing Joe's slinky silver gown.

She gestured vaguely. "Oh, upstairs I think."

It was eleven o'clock, and had Joe been home, Tyler would have been sitting in Sunday School. But even if Maura hadn't been worried about her husband, she probably wouldn't have brought him to church. Joe was the parent who rounded him up and herded him there.

"Can we speak privately then?" Ed asked.

"I doubt he'll be down anytime soon. He's probably working on a model. That's what he and Joseph normally do on Sunday afternoons."

I picked up my cup. Of course the coffee was exceptional. "I imagine he's worried."

"Tyler?" She looked vaguely bemused. "I haven't told him anything. Why would he worry?"

"Wasn't he expecting Joe to come home

Friday?"

"Well, yes, but he just thinks his father was delayed. I didn't tell him differently." She looked at Ed's plate. "You aren't eating, Ed. Please go ahead."

Ed reached across the table and rested his hand on hers for a moment. "Here's what we discovered. Joe's trips to New York haven't been for business, Maura. There is no Fund for Food."

"But of course there is. That's why he goes." She was wide-eyed and not one bit petulant. She was sure that Ed had simply made an error.

He picked up his fork, but the coffee cake remained untouched. "No, he's been going for another reason."

Had this been me, I would have immediately guessed my husband was having an affair. What woman, even a minister's wife, wouldn't jump to that conclusion first?

But Maura shook her head. "What reason could there be?"

"He's been performing once a month at a nightclub in the East Village, a place called the Pussycat Club."

"What a silly name." She murmured this into her cup, just before she took another measured sip. "That doesn't sound like Joseph."

I wondered if Ed was going to skip the part about Joe being a once-a-month drag queen. We hadn't discussed how he would tell Maura, and I wondered if he would spare her.

But of course, he couldn't. Joe was missing, and every clue to finding him was an important one.

"The Pussycat Club has a variety of acts," he said slowly, clearly feeling his way. "And Joe entertained the audience by impersonating Cher."

"Cher?"

"That's right."

"Like Sonny and Cher?"

"That Cher, yes."

"But Cher is a woman."

"Joe dressed up like a woman, like Cher, and sang her songs."

"And people came to see this?"

"They did."

"People will pay to see a man dress like a woman?"

Earth to Maura. I could see that Ed hadn't had a clue she would be so completely unprepared. I took over. "The thing is, he's been doing this for some time. It started as a joke, but he was so good at it, they asked him to come back. And apparently he enjoys it."

Maura nibbled at her bottom lip. It was the first real sign she felt anything. "He does have a good voice."

Now *I* was speechless. I glanced at Ed. He was looking at his coffee cake longingly, as if he wanted to shrink to ant size and escape into yeasty oblivion.

Maura shook her head. "It just doesn't sound like something Joseph would do. Are you sure?"

"You haven't noticed anything different about him in, oh, the past year or so?"

"No, he's just the same as always."

"Maybe there were some physical things?"

"Like what?"

"Like maybe he was shaving more than his face?"

Her eyes widened, and this time she nodded. "Only he told me he had developed some dermatological problem and all the hair on his legs had fallen out. Just sometimes, though. Then it would grow back."

Again, I was speechless.

With team spirit Ed took over. "Maura, Joe performed last Thursday, but we were told he left before his act was over. That's when he must have called you, but he left his phone behind."

He pulled Joe's phone out of his coat pocket and handed it to her. "People there thought maybe he was sick. We checked with the hotel where he was staying, all the hospitals in the city, and the police. We couldn't turn up anything. He just disappeared."

She took the phone, then she nodded. "Well, okay."

"This must be hard on you," I prompted. "Finding out Joe had a secret, kind of an unusual secret at that. And now, still not knowing where he is?"

"I don't know what I'll do without him."

I had been uneasy. I was hesitant and sorry to be the bearer of bad news. But now, for the first time since she opened the door, I felt a rush of sympathy. Despite my feminist leanings, I felt the same way about Ed. I couldn't imagine what I would do if he disappeared from my life. I put my hand over hers, as Ed had done.

"This must be hard," I said.

"Joseph does so many things for us. I don't know how we're going to manage. He makes sure Tyler's eating right and testing his blood and managing his shots. He pays all the bills and watches our investments and cuts the grass." She looked up. "And it's May, the grass will need to be cut regularly, won't it?"

I pulled back my hand.

Ed took over again. "You can pay somebody to do that, Maura."

She couldn't pay somebody to be the love of her life, her partner, her best friend. But those weren't the things that seemed to concern her. I told myself I was being unfair. People react differently to bumps in the road. Maura was trying to be practical. Perhaps she wasn't a woman who showed her feelings. And even though Ed was her minister, we were really little more than strangers. She might be saving face.

I realized how upset she was when she got up and started to clear away our dishes, although we hadn't touched our coffee cake and our cups were half full. "What about Mayday!?"

Ed looked at his watch. "It starts in about two hours, right?"

"People are still expecting Joseph to be there. I've had to field so many phone calls. He should have been there all morning setting up, and everybody wonders where he is."

"What have you been telling them?"

"That he was called out of town on an emergency, and I'm hoping he'll be back in time. Hazel Kefauver is the worst. She keeps calling, like I can magically transport him to the grounds of the food bank if she just calls here often enough."

Hazel Kefauver is the wife of our mayor. She and her husband are akin to Jack Sprat and his nameless wife. Brownie is a little, bow-tied man whose hours in office are spent currying favor with the town's elite. Hazel is beefy and forceful, a descendant of an Emerald Springs founding family and not one bit shy about using her heritage to shake down anybody who gets in her way.

Hazel is also the chairman of the food bank board. I'd heard she was a thorn in Joe's side, and now, apparently a thorn in his wife's.

"I'm not a fan of lying," Ed said, "but for now, you might want to stick to that story. No one will fault you, even if a different story eventually unfolds."

Maura stopped clearing long enough to wring her hands. "They'll ask me what kind of emergency."

"You can say it's personal," I coached.

"No, that won't do. It'll sound like I'm hiding something. It has to be something good." She looked up. "I know, I'll tell them his mother is dying."

Ed took his turn. "Maura, that could come back to haunt you. What if everything gets straightened out with Joe, then Joe's parents show up for Christmas or Tyler's birthday?"

"Oh, they won't. Joseph's an orphan. His parents are dead."

"That's a shame," I said, getting up to help her clear. "But if they lived in this area, won't people know that?"

"They lived in New Jersey. I never knew them. They died before I met Joseph. Car accident I think."

The "I think" part amazed me. Apparently Maura was even more clueless than I'd thought. The slightest things, even something this important, seem to have alluded her.

As if she read my thoughts, she shook her head. "It's not that I don't care, Aggie, it's just that Joseph doesn't like to talk about the past. He's a private person." Her eyes filled. "More private than I knew."

Guilt descended. I'd come into the pristine Cape Cod with an immediate bias against Maura, counted the dust-free surfaces, added up the regiment of sharply creased dish towels, and decided that she was incapable of feeling what any normal woman would. I had leaped to judgment and not given her the benefit of the doubt.

"It might not be good to compound a lie," Ed warned.

"No, I have to say something, so that's

what I'll say." She blinked back tears and squared her shoulders. "Joseph will come back, and we can work this out. He won't stay away long. He would never leave Tyler alone this way. He knows I'm not good with the medical stuff. He knows he's needed here."

Guilt was still a thick curtain, and I refused to jump, even silently, on the fact she'd said Joe wouldn't want to leave *Tyler* alone and hadn't mentioned herself in the equation. Maybe Joe and Maura were having problems, and maybe Joe's little rebellion included performing at the Pussycat Club, but people had worked through worse. Maybe Joe would come back in a day or two. Maybe Maura could learn to sing backup.

"Good for you." I handed her a tissue from a handwoven reed basket on the counter. "Take the high road, and let's see where you end up, okay?"

"There's just one thing." She sniffed and dabbed at her eyes. "Joseph is supposed to be the fortune-teller again today. It's the biggest moneymaker at Mayday!"

I've only lived in Emerald Springs long enough for one Mayday!, but even so I remember the line outside the fortune-teller's booth last year. I didn't go inside myself. I get all the free advice I need from the family psychic. Junie, my mother, is convinced she can see into the future. I grew up knowing that I would marry a dark-haired man who was either a stockbroker or a banker. Either alternative distressed my mother, who tends to sew extra cash into the binding of quilts. But Junie felt I needed to know my destiny in order to prepare for a more disciplined, ordinary life.

Of course my very real husband, the Reverend Wilcox, has hair somewhere between gold and red, and where to store our extra cash is seldom an issue. Nor did I give birth to the three predicted sons, divorce after four years, or move to a commune to teach Japanese. My oldest sister Vel is still waiting for the man with royal blood who will sweep her off to distant lands, and my youngest sister Sid is thrilled with her job as a country club event planner. She harbors no plans to become either a taxidermist or lion tamer.

So I'm not a fan of psychics nor am I a believer. But on this subject, I'm in the Emerald Springs minority. Because without fail, everyone who has mentioned Joe's ability to see into the future has spoken in hushed, reverent tones. Joe has accurately predicted pregnancies for childless couples, new jobs for the chronically unemployed, and college scholarships for B students. He's warned of real health problems and sent believers scurrying to the doctor. He's counseled men to bring flowers to their wives, and women to crank it up in the bedroom. Joe's kind of an old-fashioned guy — or at least I always thought so.

Me, I think Joe's real gift is hope. In almost every case, he's given his enraptured audience a reason to keep plugging. And on the health front, who among us doesn't need a little push to make that appointment for our annual physical?

So I'm a skeptic, but that doesn't mean I can't understand the power of suggestion. And Maura was correct. A lot of people were going to be disappointed that their annual opportunity to have Joe set their lives on a straighter path wasn't going to happen this year. The food bank would surely lose money.

"Is there anybody else who could do it?" Ed asked. "Anybody who's assisted him in the past and knows the ropes?"

Maura was still dabbing at her eyes. "Joseph always did it alone. He was the only one they wanted to see. He'd always finish up well beyond closing time. If people lined up before eight, then if he had to, he'd stay until ten."

Before he opened his mouth I saw Ed's solution in his eyes. I shook my head. "No. Nope. Nada. No chance. Not happening."

"Aggie, she'd be perfect."

"She," of course, was Junie.

"Aggie's mom likes to dabble in that kind of thing," Ed told Maura. "And she's got the clothes for it."

That part was true. Junie's wardrobe runs from outrageous to borderline illegal. She could assemble an extravagant gypsy costume from clothes she wore to the grocery store.

The thing is, Junie has already stirred some controversy in Emerald Springs. She's been a resident in the parsonage for four months and already she's appeared before our city council three times. Once to ask that they reconsider their planned sale of twelve wooded acres at the edge of town to a developer anxious to build a shopping mall. The next month to bring in a petition on the same subject signed by five hundred Emerald Springs residents. The signatures were collected door-to-door, and now Junie knows the life stories of a lot of my neighbors.

Last month she made her third trip to present the council with a quilt designed and made by the many local quilters who flock to our parsonage for quilting lessons. The quilt was a poignant rendition of a forest in ruins. Even Brownie Kefauver swallowed hard over the mama squirrel trying to rescue her babies from a felled tree.

So Junie has fans, and Junie has foes. For her part, she loves everybody. I know she would never predict a bout with cancer just to terrify somebody who opposes her on this issue, but not everybody knows Junie the way I do. Nor do they know that they have nothing to fear from her divinations.

I shook my head again. "Ed, Junie's already made a few enemies. She might make a few more if she's sitting behind a crystal ball."

"Do you have another idea?"

This was a polite way of asking if I had a better one. I didn't. I shrugged.

"Then we'll ask her," he told Maura. "That will be one less thing for you to worry about."

I didn't have time to concoct another protest or a better solution. There was scuffling of feet outside the kitchen doorway, and Tyler scooted in. At twelve Tyler is lanky and unformed, but there's no question he'll be a handsome young man. He has brown hair that's a compromise between his mother's blonde and his father's mahogany, and brown eyes he owes to his dad alone. I think he'll eventually be tall, but that's hard to tell. I know he'll be handsome, because he has the bones for it. And if in the end he looks like either Joe or Maura, he'll be a winner.

Tyler's had his share of problems at our middle school. Ed's told me some of them; Deena, our twelve-year-old, has told me others. Most revolve around a couple of insulin reactions in full view of his classmates. Once in the middle of a test a teacher refused to heed Tyler's plea to let him eat the snack he always carried for an emergency. Tyler's blood sugar dropped so precipitously that he ended up slugging her, and the medics had to be called. A second incident occurred at a soccer game, and now Tyler, an affable, intelligent kid, was regarded by some of his former friends as a social liability. He wasn't the only diabetic child in the school system, and both students and teachers had gotten some much needed training after the incident in the classroom. But kids are kids, and in middle school, different is different.

Now I wondered how Joe's disappearance was going to affect this boy's life. And his blood sugar.

"How are you doing?" Ed asked Tyler.

Tyler has a great, no-braces smile. It blinked on and quickly off again as he greeted us both.

"Is Dad on his way home yet?" he asked Maura when he'd finished the formalities.

"Not yet," she said.

Tyler looked as if he hadn't bathed since Joe left home. His hair was oily and un-combed. His clothes were wrinkled, as if he'd been sleeping in them all weekend. If Maura thought Tyler was unaffected by Joe's absence, she was wrong. And the fact that she hadn't noticed said a lot about her own state of mind.

"How come?" he asked pointedly.

She looked to us for support. Ed didn't say a word. How much Tyler was told was up to his mother.

"Your dad's taking a few days away from everything and everybody," she said at last. "He works too hard, and he just, well, kind of crashed. You know?"

Tyler didn't respond.

"He's got a hard job," Maura said. "He needed some time to think it over and figure out what to do."

"Then why didn't he tell me he wasn't coming home?"

"It was a last-minute thing. You can

understand that." She made it sound like he ought to, and Tyler gave something of a nod.

"Can I talk to him?" he asked. "Can I call him?"

"No, he really wants to be alone to think. We should respect that."

"But it's Mayday! today."

"I know, and the timing is really bad. We can't tell people the reason he's not home. So we're going to make up a story. You'll have to play along. Then when Dad comes back, he won't be in trouble."

Tyler looked as if he knew he was being sold a bill of goods. I figured when we left, the questions would fly fast and furiously.

Ed seemed to be thinking the same thing. He held out his hand to Maura, then to Tyler. We said our good-byes, then we took the winding brick sidewalk back to our car and climbed in gratefully.

Ed was the first to speak. "She'll need help."

I hated to think about it.

"Joe's the grown-up in that family," Ed said. "Maybe he just likes it that way, or maybe Maura simply abdicated responsibility early in their relationship. I do know Joe's been the one who's managed Tyler's diabetes. Tyler's old enough to know how to handle diet and everything else, but he'll still need somebody keeping tabs on him."

"That will have to be Maura."

"No question. But Maura may need a friend, Aggie, to help her through this. I can check on her periodically, and catch up with Tyler whenever I see him, but she's going to need more." He stuck the key in the ignition, then he looked at me. "Does she have any friends like that?"

I wanted to believe that she did. Surely there were other women just like Maura who met regularly in their sunny, well-scrubbed kitchens and traded recipes and household hints. The Village might be full of them.

Ed started the engine. "The thing is, she's not going to be comfortable telling anybody else what's really going on."

"You aren't asking me to befriend her, are you?"

"No." He pulled out to the street and started toward home. We had gone straight from the Columbus airport to see Maura. I was looking forward to a shower and lunch, not to mention a hug from my girls.

"Maura and I have nothing in common," I said. "I'm not sure what we would say to each other."

"She could teach you how to fold contour sheets."

I punched his arm. "Did you get the feeling she's more worried about what people will think than she is about Joe? I mean, he could be lying somewhere so sick he can't even get to a phone. Or worse."

"It's hard to tell what other people are feeling. But I'm sure she's experiencing everything the rest of us would. And we don't know anything about the state of their marriage. They looked wonderful from the outside, but so does a house of cards."

"Joe was lying to her. No matter how we put it."

"That's going to be hard to deal with."

"Tyler worries me most of all." I thought about that, and it was my undoing. Wherever my friend Joe was, he would be worrying about his son. If I couldn't find Joe, at least I could make sure Tyler stayed safe until Joe returned. If he returned.

I looked straight ahead. "I guess I could check on her. Make sure she's handling this all right."

"You'd be a good role model, Ag. Maybe you're staying home with the girls, but you're still an independent woman. Could be Maura will pick up some confidence."

"And Joe will come home, see the new improved model, throw away his three-inch heels, and live happily ever after."

"I wish the world worked like that."

Didn't we all.

4

Junie wore a black pleated skirt that was long enough to hide all traces of her bright purple toenails. This was too bad because the purple exactly matched her hip-length velvet tunic, which in turn was nearly hidden by an assortment of gold and silver chains heavy with suns, moons, and stars. Her blonde hair was covered by a silk scarf hand painted with symbols from her favorite tarot cards, and peeking out below the scarf were gold hoop earrings large enough for an old-fashioned game of ring toss. She was sorry she hadn't had time to dig through all the clothes in her camper, which was parked at the side of the parsonage, and assemble a really *good* costume.

We had persuaded her that no one would find her wanting.

My girls flanked Junie in the back seat of our van. Six-year-old Teddy wore a sweatshirt and jeans in preparation for the pony rides. Her older sister Deena, in a green ribbed hoodie and capris, was dressed to fit in with her friends, who would all be at Mayday!

"I still could have gone with Tara," Deena said for the third time.

"I'm sorry our early return ruined your plans," I said yet again.

"I don't know why your coming back had to change anything."

"Because Tara lives on the other side of town, and this saves her mother from making the trip. You're going to see her the minute you get there. Shape up, okay?"

I didn't have to glance behind me to know that Deena was pouting. I'm not sure exactly *what* plans Ed and I had ruined by turning up on our own doorstep earlier than expected, but clearly something was afoot. Of course now that she's finally twelve, Deena never wants to be seen with us, but this seemed a little more emphatic than usual.

"I might get tired of riding the ponies," Teddy said. "And throwing darts at balloons."

"There are lots of things to do at Mayday! You can win a cake at the cakewalk, or play bingo for prizes, or get your face painted."

"I might be bored." She sounded worried.

"I'm sure some of your friends will be there."

"If you get bored, precious, you can tell fortunes with me," Junie said.

"I don't know how."

"Well, you can sit under the table. We'll put a cloth over it, and you can hide. Then every once in a while you can lift the table and make ghostly noises, like there's a spirit haunting the tent."

Teddy giggled. I don't think she realized Junie wasn't teasing.

Ed — who did realize — tried to intercede. "Junie, she could scare somebody into a heart attack."

"Don't worry, I'll read their palms first to be certain they don't have health issues."

Now that we had substantially contributed to Junie's delusion that she could see the future, we would never again be able to have a semi-rational discussion about her abilities. I was silent. The best way to nip the table scheme in the bud was to make sure Teddy was happily occupied elsewhere during the fair.

"Do you believe in spirits?" Teddy asked her grandmother.

I settled back, content that the ensuing conversation would hold Teddy for the remainder of the ride. I just hoped Ed wouldn't get involved, or we might never make it out of the car.

I didn't really want to go to Mayday! Normally I would be more enthused, but with Joe missing and Maura making up stories to cover for him, the whole event just seemed out of kilter. Still, as we parked in the grass where men wearing orange armbands directed us, I hoped for the best.

The Helping Hands Food Bank occupies a five-acre spread not far from the land parcel Junie wants to protect. Nobody can complain about the food bank's treatment of their property, though. True a large utilitarian warehouse built from recycled materials sits at the back of the lot where a smattering of trees once resided. But most of the trees were used in the construction of an administration building that resides closer to the road.

To one side of that attractive two-story building a one-acre community garden is already green with lettuce and peas. The garden serves two purposes. It provides a place to grow food for local families. Some gardeners eat everything they produce, but more often the surplus is distributed at the food bank. It also serves as a demonstration garden to encourage families who have room at home to add to the food supply. In the summer volunteers give instruction, seeds, and leaf mulch to anyone willing to till his own soil.

Some distance away, on the other side of the building, the aforementioned leaf mulch forms a pyramid.

The administration building itself houses more than offices. The downstairs is a store that provides clothing and household furnishings to families with limited incomes. Local social service organizations give coupons that are treated like cash, and families can choose what they need from good-quality donations, some crafted especially for the store. Although the food bank is a partnership among three counties, all administration tasks are performed here.

Today tents were set up on the expansive grounds between the parking area and the administration building. The scope was well beyond the typical elementary school fair. Although there were no mechanized carnival rides, I saw inflatable games, including a moon bounce and rock-climbing wall. May is too cold for a dunk tank, but we had our very own fun house — or more accurately a fun tent — complete with silly mirrors, mazes, and overzealous clowns who have catapulted more than one child into therapy.

To one side a small stage buzzed with

activity as the sound system was checked for upcoming performances by local talent. A ring for pony rides would do a brisk business, and the midway with its combination of homemade and rented games would soon be packed with kids trying to win prizes their mothers would quietly dispose of next week.

This year the weather was nearly perfect. A few silvery clouds drifted overhead to remind us this was an Ohio spring, and shrinking puddles left from last week's showers dotted the parking area. A breeze with occasional strong gusts whipped between tents, but the sun wasn't taking no for an answer. The temperature was sweater-mild. I gave the girls money to buy tickets for the attractions and watched them take off for the ticket booth, hair streaming behind them. Teddy would wait for us by the roped-off entrance. For the rest of the afternoon Deena would pretend she didn't know us.

"Do you know where they want me?" Junie asked.

I gave her costume the once-over again, just to make sure there was nothing I'd missed that would add exponentially to her growing reputation. While I'm dark-haired and thin enough to fit everything from my midriff down into a comfortable size eight, my mother is blonde, blue-eyed, and plump.

Junie is convinced she was Hapsburg royalty in a previous life. The fact that now, given a babushka and a shapeless sack of a dress, she can pose for a portrait of a sixteenth-century Eastern European peasant is karma she must bear.

Today Junie's fortune-teller getup wasn't that far from a shapeless sack and babushka.

"Agate?" she prompted.

"We'll scout it out together," I promised. The three of us picked up Teddy inside the gate. Ed was immediately waylaid by the president of our church board, a nice man who never quite knows when to quit. I signaled that Junie and I were heading off to find her tent, and we left him there.

"Just as soon as I get Junie set up, you and I can do whatever you want," I told Teddy.

"I'll be making a list." She pushed her tortoiseshell glasses farther up her nose, as if to make sure she took in every possibility.

A quick perusal of the grounds didn't turn up the fortune-teller's tent, and since I'd only been to Mayday! once, I couldn't count on my memory. I looked for somebody who might know and spotted the manager of the warehouse. I had been introduced to Chad

Sutterfield at Joe and Maura's party, and seen him a few times since, this being the small town it is.

I flagged him down, and we walked over to greet him. We were still a little early. In another half hour the grounds would be mobbed.

In case he didn't remember me, I held out my hand. "Chad, Aggie Sloan-Wilcox. We met at the Wagners' Valentine's Day brunch."

"Right, your husband's their minister." He shook my hand and nodded to my mother and daughter. "My parents used to go to your church when I was a teenager. I was unrepentant."

Chad grinned wickedly, and I thought he wasn't kidding about the last part. From what little I know, he has that reputation. Chad is uncommonly easy on the eye, with the rakish charm of Harrison Ford and a similar rangy build. He has brown hair and eyes and what looks like a Florida tan. Most noticeably he seems completely comfortable with himself and his place in the world. That latter is an indefinable essence that can't be taught, and I'm afraid women are drawn to it like mice to peanut butter. It doesn't matter if there's a trap under all that yummy goodness. We are helpless to resist — or so we tell ourselves.

From my best friend Lucy Jacobs I've heard that Chad is a ladies' man, but everybody seems to like him, even the women he's kissed good-bye. His family is rich, and he's generous and exciting to be with, although possibly just a shade too pleased with himself.

Maybe in the end women get tired of peanut butter and don't mind a healthier diet. I'm in my midthirties, and so, I guess, is Chad. From what I remembered, no woman has stuck with him long enough to be a wife.

I introduced Junie and Teddy and explained our mission.

"Yeah, I heard Joe can't be here. That's a shame. But we're glad to have you Mrs. Bluebird. I know you'll be a big hit."

"You can call me Junie. And Bluebird is my chosen name, not one on loan from a husband."

He looked puzzled. I thought it better not to explain that Junie had chosen Bluebird because she was certain that in a prior life — well before she joined the Hapsburgs — she had also been a bluebird. As the story goes, there had been a fight with an evil rat snake and numerous unhatched eggs. I try not to think about it.

From the corner of my eye I saw Maura approaching. Her expression was unclouded, and she greeted people as if Joe was somewhere on the grounds repairing the sound system.

She joined us, a sunny smile lighting her lovely face. "So, is this your mother, Aggie?"

I made the introductions again. Maura beamed at Junie. "You are so kind to take Joseph's place today."

She turned to Chad. "I suppose you've heard?"

"No details. What gives?"

She was still smiling, but I thought I noted a different approach here, something more cautious and thoughtful. "Oh, he's in New Jersey taking care of his mother. I'm afraid she's" — she looked down at Teddy, then back up at Chad — "quite ill."

"That's a real shame." He shook his head in sympathy.

"We all know the timing's bad, but these things can't be helped. So Junie's agreed to help out. Aren't we lucky?"

I thought Maura might not think so when the complaints began to come in, but I'm a firm believer in miracles.

"I suppose you don't know when he'll be back," Chad said.

"Not right now, but I'll keep everybody informed."

"Because I have some things I need to talk to him about. Food bank stuff. Would a call be a problem?"

"He asked me to relay any messages, Chad. He needs to focus on his parents."

"I never realized Joe was from New Jersey."

"Born and bred. And there's no one else to help. A very small family."

I weighed what was happening here. Was it good that Maura had pulled herself together and was managing this conversation with such aplomb? Or was it bad that she was developing something of a talent for fiction?

I had no idea. That's the problem with not believing the world is black-and-white.

Chad was making sympathetic noises. "So what can I do to help?"

"Well, I spoke to Hazel," Maura said.

The ironic lift of his brow said it all. I was guessing *nobody* spoke to Hazel Kefauver unless the circumstances were this dire — or unless they were somehow locked together in the trunk of a car.

"As Food Supply Manager we both think you ought to do the opening speech," Maura continued. "I know it's last-minute, but do you think you can come up with something? You're more or less second in command."

"More or less," he said with a grin.

She remained unruffled. "Will you do it?"

"Of course. Anything for Helping Hands."

He said a few cheerful words to Teddy, who was not bowled over by his charm. I swallowed a lump of maternal pride.

Chad led Junie and Teddy off to show them the fortune-teller's tent. It turned out to be the farthest away, in front of the warehouse, behind the midway, and under a thick grove of trees. I planned to collect Teddy in a few minutes and try to keep her busy elsewhere.

Maura waited until they were out of earshot. "I guess I did the right thing by asking him."

I started with praise and edged into advice. "You did it very well. I just wonder if you ought to take him into your confidence. It looks like he's going to be in charge for at least a day or two, and it's going to be clear something's up when you don't give him a number for Joe."

"I'll worry about that when it happens. Maybe Joseph will be back by evening. We don't know."

"You haven't heard anything?"

She gave a minimal shake of her head.

"I gather you don't think Chad's trust-worthy?"

She looked at me, eyes clear and un-troubled. "Joseph thinks he's trustworthy, and that's all that matters."

I felt the urge to educate her, to stir up any traces of independence that hadn't completely been extinguished. "Maura, Joe's not the only one with instincts and opinions. I think if you really believed Joe was right about Chad, then you would have told him the truth. So maybe you have some concerns?"

She examined me, as if she was trying to decide if *I* could be trusted. Then she looked away. "Joseph always believes the best about everybody. But I just wonder . . ." She glanced back at me. "What if Chad wants Joseph's job? Wouldn't this be exactly the right moment to make a grab for it?"

She seemed embarrassed at such a nega-tive sentiment, and color suffused her cheeks. "Is that being too harsh? Am I just reacting to this *problem* we're having at home?"

At least she hadn't said "little problem." I rested my hand on her shoulder. "Maybe something's happened in the past to make you worry about Chad. Maybe you're simply reacting to something you've seen or heard about him. That's good, isn't it? That you paid attention?"

She seemed less embarrassed. Perhaps the encouragement was taking, because she continued, "Of course the food bank is Joseph's territory, not mine. But I've always wondered if Chad is waiting for him to move on so he can swoop in and become the director."

"Then I'm sure you made the right decision."

"Do you think so?"

I was glad I was here to give her a shot of confidence. "Absolutely. You have good instincts and you're using them."

She looked pleased. "I'd better move along and talk to people like nothing is wrong. I'm good at talking to people."

"You're very good at it." I held myself back from chanting "Go Maura!"

We parted company and I looked for Ed. He was still talking to our board president and motioned me over. Tom Jeffrey teaches math at Emerald College, the excellent liberal arts college that lifts Emerald Springs out of rural obscurity. He's a nice, average-looking guy, a bit stuffy, but earnest enough to take his position seriously.

"Tom's just given us passes to the VIP

tour," Ed said in welcome. "There's a reception afterwards."

"I'm on the board," Tom said. "You can hear a little more about what's going on."

For a moment I thought he meant what was going on with Joe. Then I realized he was talking about Helping Hands.

Ed gave a slight nod, invisible to anyone not married to him.

"Great," I said. Maybe I would pick up something that would help explain Joe's disappearance. Or maybe I'd just pick up something deliciously chocolate at the reception to make up for having to hobnob with Hazel Kefauver.

We took our leave and started toward the fortune-teller's tent. "Thanks for agreeing," Ed said. "Tom's been trying to get me to join the food bank board since I got to town. I just couldn't get out of this."

"Why haven't you joined?"

"Hazel."

"I've heard she gives Joe a lot of trouble. Do you know anything about that?"

"Tom was telling me a little. Hazel's a big proponent of organic food, whole grains, macrobiotic diets. She wants the food bank to refuse donations that don't fit a narrow profile she's drawn up. Apparently she says that beggars can't be choosers, and the

84

people who need help should learn to eat whatever they're lucky enough to be given." Ed's tone grew steadily icier as he spoke.

"Ouch."

"She's probably not quite that vindictive, but that's what you get when you take away the smiles and the flowery language."

"I've never seen her smile, and she wouldn't know a rose from skunk cabbage."

"Joe's been able to thwart her because nobody else on the board agrees with her. But she has a lot of clout in the community, and they don't want to cross her if they don't have to. So it's been a difficult dance."

"Could that explain why he vanished? Joe just got fed up?" I thought about it. "Forget that. He wouldn't leave Tyler just because he couldn't stand Hazel."

We were in sight of the fortune-telling tent now. I hoped my mother was settling in. I hoped I could drag my daughter out.

Ed stepped out of the way of a trio of giggling middle schoolers. I recognized them as some of the Green Meanies, a group of girls of which Deena is a part. But Deena wasn't among them.

"Tom also said Hazel put her foot down about a number of things at Mayday! this year," he said. "She claims the costs were too high even though they make a lot of money to offset it. So she cut out one of the popcorn machines and a couple of the food vendors —"

"Oh, if only they'd served buckwheat groats and mashed turnips."

"She also cut out a couple of games on the midway and a trio of professional mimes who were always crowd-pleasers. Claimed they could get local mimes from the high school to do it for free, but Tom says not to expect much. The new guys kept talking to each other during rehearsal."

"I feel a headache coming on. Tell me you aren't joining the board."

"I'm not joining the board. I'm going to be polite and interested and say no if they ask me again."

We had drawn within ten yards of the tent when I realized that we were about to run smack-dab into the topic of our conversation. Hazel Kefauver and her mayor husband were standing just outside the tent flap. And wonders of wonders, they were talking to my mother.

"That headache?" I said. "What's bigger than a migraine?"

"A stroke."

"If I have one, can I just sink to the ground right here?"

He took my arm. "She's *your* mother."

I didn't point out that had this been Ed's mother, Nan, she and Hazel would have faced off by now, one-upping each other with the names of important people they counted among their acquaintances.

When we reluctantly approached the circle Junie was regaling the Kefauvers with plans for the tent. "I've got my tarot cards, candles, incense, and an Indian print table-cloth."

"I'm sure that's all well and good," Hazel said, "but the important thing is to move people through quickly. Joe refused, and we could have made a lot more money if he'd just told his customers they were going on a trip or having a surprise visitor and turned them right back out again."

Hazel was large enough to block the entrance to the tent if she so desired. She was muscular, with a snapping turtle jaw that looked lethal to me. Her hair was a drab brown cut short to expose a head shaped like a football helmet. She wore a gray suit that would have been more attractive on her husband, sensible lace-up shoes, and a glare.

"I'll certainly remember that," said Junie, no stranger to the troublesome. She had sweet-talked her way through craft and Renaissance fairs for decades. She has a wonderful way of drawing the positive from everyone she meets. I was just afraid that this time, she'd met her match.

"We're glad you stepped in," Brownie said. Today his bow tie was a natty yellow stripe. Personally, I think he's trying to draw attention from his receding hairline and protruding ears. Or maybe Hazel sits on his chest and forcibly knots them around his throat.

"Yes, we're glad you stepped in," Hazel repeated. "But it's beyond the pale that Joseph Wagner didn't come himself."

"I can see you're stressed about that," Junie said soothingly.

"Anybody would be. The nerve of that man."

Ed stepped up, and the Kefauvers saw and grudgingly made room for us. They aren't members of our church. Hazel has voiced her dislike of a religion that doesn't tell people exactly what they should do. We pray for her minister.

"Mayday! looks impressive again," Ed said. "The food bank is such a valuable contribution to the community."

"Yes, well it's more valuable since I took over. You have no idea how much money the previous board spent. Shameless!"

I detected less vehemence in her tone than

the words suggested. She seemed to be struggling to crank up her rhetoric, but not quite succeeding. Now that I was standing beside her, I noted that she looked pale and tired. Normally her skin is an angry flush, as if her blood pressure is about to establish record highs. Today she merely looked gray. I wondered if she had succumbed to the unusual spring flu that was making its rounds through the schools. It wouldn't stop her, though. Hazel would run the world from her deathbed.

"I've seen a lot of areas of the country that have nothing similar," Ed continued, undeterred. "Helping Hands is something we can be proud of." He turned his gaze to Brownie. "In fact, I hope the city council will reconsider its cuts in the budget and fully fund their portion. It would be a great example for the other counties. We should be the leaders since the food bank is right here."

"There's too much waste already," Hazel said, before Brownie could answer. He looked grateful. I suspected this was the way their relationship always worked.

"Better a little waste than people who need food going without it," Ed said.

"We have people taking food who don't need it. I'm convinced of it, and I'm going to stop it. The regulations need to be stricter. I can tell you there are some other big developments in the wind for Helping Hands. I'm going to make sure that nothing is hidden anymore."

"Why don't you let me see your palm," Junie said, "and I'll tell you if you're about to get your heart's desire. We can't always be certain, can we, that we're on the right path?"

Before Hazel could refuse, Junie lifted her hand and turned it to see Hazel's palm.

I glanced at Ed. For the first time since we'd approached the Kefauvers he was smiling. I wondered what he hoped Junie would tell Hazel.

Hazel looked as if she wanted to snatch her hand back. But Junie, soft and cuddly though she is, has traveled the country back and forth subduing recalcitrant RVs, putting up and taking down vendor's booths, and raising three scrappy daughters. Hazel might best her if they arm wrestled, but not by much.

"First your heart line . . ." Junie looked up and smiled. "You're a sexy woman, Hazel. You sly thing."

Brownie looked astonished, and Hazel was outraged. "I really don't believe in this nonsense!"

"And you have a strong will, but you have a softer side. You take on these projects, like the food bank, because deep inside you want so badly to help the less fortunate."

"Hmph!" Hazel sputtered, and she tried to jerk her hand away, but Junie wasn't quite finished.

"And you have a marvelous life line," Junie said. "I think you'll live to be ninety. Maybe older. That's a lot of time left to do good works." She let Hazel take back her hand. Then Junie smiled. "Was that quick enough for you, dear?"

I always love my mother. Right now I loved her a little more than usual. I tried not to smile.

Hazel turned to go, but Junie touched her hand. "Just one more thing? Your hand is like ice, and your skin is much too dry. I'd recommend a sweater and having your circulation checked. We don't want you catching your death of cold. There's still a nip in the air."

"There's nothing wrong with my circulation," Hazel said haughtily.

"Then maybe there's something wrong with your heart. I'd consider the possibility."

They were gone before Ed spoke. "You know, if you weren't my mother-in-law, Junie, I think I'd adopt you."

Together we leaned over and kissed her cheeks.

5

Since I was certain Teddy would be bored silly by a VIP tour, I promised she could stay with Junie if she promised not to raise the table. In the hour before we met the other VIPs, Ed, Teddy, and I knocked down bowling pins with baseballs and reeled in plastic fish, cheerfully accepting our candy bar prizes. Holding hands we watched Teddy make three circuits on a pony named Snapper.

While Teddy and I waited at the end of the line for circuit number four, Ed wandered off to try his swing in the batting cage. It was Teddy's last ride since the tour was due to start in fifteen minutes.

She nodded toward the cotton candy vendor. "Miss Hollins is over there."

Jennifer Hollins is Teddy's first grade teacher, and our relationship has been less than stellar. My attempts to be a supportive, thoughtful parent have been met with skepticism. Recently I've kept the lowest possible profile, but now, as she headed our way, I was trapped.

"Good afternoon, Teddy." She leaned over to look Teddy right in the eye. In her loose, flowered dress, Mary Janes, and brown hair fastened on both sides with barrettes, Miss Hollins didn't look much older than my daughter.

"I'm riding ponies."

"I don't blame you. I'd ride them, too, if they'd let me."

Teddy giggled. She liked her teacher, and I thought the feeling was mutual.

Miss Hollins straightened and smiled at me. With a year of teaching under her belt, I think she was finally starting to feel a bit more comfortable with parents, too. "Are you enjoying Mayday!?"

She would be surprised at my real answer. I hedged. "It's a lovely day for it, isn't it? We couldn't have ordered better."

"I'm glad I ran into you two. I have some good news."

I was in the mood for good news. I smiled expectantly.

"Teddy's going to be the star in our end-of-the-year play. She's been chosen to play Cinderella. What do you think, Teddy?"

Teddy is a hard child to impress, but at

this news, she positively glowed. "I get to wear the glass slipper?"

"You certainly do. But you have to promise not to break it."

Teddy giggled.

I'm not a hard parent to impress. I was glowing, too. Who doesn't want to see her child so delighted? Teddy gets lots of praise for her quick little mind, but how many times in her life will she be the star of a fairy tale?

Miss Hollins read my expression accurately. "Just so you know, it's not your mother's Cinderella. The fairy godmother only gives suggestions, and at the end, Cinderella has to rescue Prince Charming from a dragon before they can marry, then she teaches him how to clean the castle."

"You're kidding."

Miss Hollins smiled, too. "Uh-huh. Although we have changed some of the dialogue to make it a little less oppressive."

I laughed. Maybe Jennifer Hollins and I were over the hump. She'd developed a sense of humor, and I'd developed the ability to keep my lips sealed. She said goodbye to Teddy and wandered off. Teddy was next in line, but she was so happy, I was afraid she might float right off Snapper.

After she finished her ride and gave Snapper an apple slice, I took her by the hand and started toward Junie's tent.

"No lifting the table," I warned again.

"What if Junie asks me to? Who should I listen to? She's older than you are."

"I'm directly in charge of your future."

"But if it weren't for Junie, you wouldn't even be here."

This was not an argument. It was a philosophical discussion. I'm surrounded by them and somewhat immune. I explained that Junie would expect her to do what I asked her to, that after all, Junie herself had taught me the value of following a mother's advice, and thus if she followed my advice, she was also following Junie's. That was complex enough to give her food for thought and me an interval of silence.

We were almost at the tent when I saw Deena. I was surprised to find that she wasn't with any of her girlfriends. I was particularly surprised to find that the *boy* she was with was Tyler Wagner, a cleaner, neater version of the one I'd seen earlier that day.

"I didn't know Deena and Tyler were friends," I said.

"Deena said that if I saw her with Tyler, I should pretend I didn't."

"Hmmm . . ." So Deena hadn't been as

unhappy to have her parents drive her to Mayday! as she had been to have us here at all.

I remembered suddenly that I was twelve the first time I fell in love. My heart did a double flip-flop. I wasn't ready for this. She was just barely twelve. A baby. Our entire future flashed in front of me. A decade when she rolled her eyes every time I tried to give her advice about men. Another when she came home regularly to tell me her heart had been broken. Then another decade when she rolled her eyes every time I tried to give her advice about her children.

I wanted to grab my daughter by her strawberry blonde braid and yank her back to yesterday.

"I'm going to pretend I don't see her, too," I said, although I wanted to follow them around the grounds quizzing Tyler about his intentions.

"Is pretending like lying? How do you tell the difference?"

That discussion took us to Junie's tent. There was already a short line outside, and I heard discontented mumbling that Joe wasn't telling fortunes. Considering everything, it seemed like a bad sign people were disgruntled *before* they went inside. Imagine how they would feel when Junie finished with them?

I dropped Teddy off with my mother and hoped for the best.

When I got to the warehouse Ed was with the rest of the guests waiting by the door. To my surprise I found Detective Kirkor Roussos chatting with him.

"Solved any more murders lately?" he asked when I extended my hand.

Roussos and I have an odd relationship. Since arriving in Emerald Springs not quite two years ago, I've been involved in two murder cases. Both times I've figured out whodunit just in time to get myself in serious trouble. Nevertheless, I did figure out who the bad guys were, and I think Roussos more or less respects me for that.

Roussos is whipcord lean and gorgeously Greek. I'd have to be dead not to be impressed. He's also smart, cynical, and occasionally witty. He's one of those guys who makes me glad I'm happily married. Because if I weren't, I could be in trouble.

"Not lately," I said, when he shook my hand, noting the faded jeans and nubby silk sports jacket that were more or less his uniform. "But if you need my help, you know where to find me."

"How could I forget? I've worn a path to your door."

"Trust me, it will grow over if you just stop suspecting my family of murder."

"You're sure? You're not addicted to detective work?"

I glanced at Ed, who seemed to be hanging on my answer. And what could I say? I had just trooped all over Manhattan trying to find out what happened to Joe Wagner. Only that time Ed was one of the gang.

"You just keep the murder rate in check, and I'll be fine," I said. "Helping with homework and gutting houses keeps me plenty busy."

"I'd hate to get too close to you if you had a crowbar in your hands." He sent me half a grin, then turned to talk to a couple of men who had just wandered up. I recognized one of them as our chief of police, and another as a member of the city council, who was often the only voice of reason.

Chad came out of the warehouse and everybody turned expectantly. He began with his most fetching grin and a few jokes. Then he launched into an apology for Joe. He delivered it with such charm and good humor that by the time he finished, I don't think anybody really cared whether Joe Wagner was in New Jersey or Hong Kong.

"Maybe Maura was right," I told Ed as we all marched into the warehouse. "Chad's something of a smooth operator, isn't he? Could be he wants Joe's job."

"Every second in command wants to be first. Chalk one up to Maura for noticing."

With both of us cheering her on from the sidelines, Maura would be so self-actualized by the end of the week she could run for president.

I tried to concentrate as Chad showed us how and where food was stored. He gave statistics about where the food came from, how much from local farmers, how much from community food drives, how much from grocers and wholesalers worried about expiration dates or outdated packaging. We saw the kitchen where volunteers prepared meals for the elderly and homeless and a small classroom where schoolchildren came to learn about world hunger and the way food is grown and distributed. We saw the office in the back, where all supplies were carefully accounted for and donations were logged and acknowledged for the IRS. We saw the garage where two trucks used in the transfer of food were housed, and the tool room where the community garden supplies wintered over.

I was impressed by how clean and orderly everything seemed, and I had to give Chad his due.

He kept moving, and we visited the administration building to see the store. He showed us the new and brighter paint, and the way shelves had been rearranged to better show off the merchandise. I recognized several baby quilts that Junie and our church needleworkers had made and donated. Some lucky families would be able to wrap their new babies in handcrafted warmth.

The administration offices and conference room were excluded from the tour. I imagined that Chad had little to say about what happened there. But by the time he walked us over to the VIP tent, I thought everyone was impressed by the food bank and by Chad himself. I was even more worried about Joe.

"Please enjoy our hospitality," Chad said as he ushered everybody into the tent, which had been set up beside the warehouse, out of Mayday! traffic.

Clearly the food bank valued their VIPs. I had hoped for a plate of brownies, but there were tea sandwiches and delicate pastries, platters of fruit and cheese, and best of all a chocolate fountain with cubes of pound cake, fresh strawberries, and other assorted goodies.

"I like this VIP stuff," I told Ed. "If I'd

known there was a chocolate fountain in my future, I wouldn't have squawked so loudly when I discovered what you planned to do with your life."

That was meant to be a joke, but Ed wasn't paying attention. I followed his gaze to the table. My first glance had stopped at the fountain. Now it stopped at the punch bowl, where his was riveted.

"That looks like the Women's Society punch bowl." He glanced at me. "Why would our church punch bowl be at Mayday!?"

I understood why Ed was looking at me for the answer. The punch bowl and I have a history. Not exactly *this* punch bowl, since its two predecessors more or less collapsed into a million pieces. But since the last time, I've sworn off relationships with cut glass. I stay ten yards away. I have nightmares about Waterford crystal.

I held up my hands. "If it's ours, I had nothing to do with it. Nothing."

"If you want punch, let me get it, okay?"

"I would die of thirst rather than get too close."

"Don't look now, but the chocolate fountain is right next to it."

"Then I'll stand on the opposite side. I promise."

I looked over and realized that Sally Berrigan, a member of our church and Women's Society, was standing to one side of the table with a small group of volunteers, looking proudly at their handiwork. Sally is involved in almost every social justice organization in town, and they're all lucky to have her. She always gets things done, and obviously had been instrumental in creating the spread before us.

I walked over to her as everybody descended on the food and gave her a hug. "This looks yummy."

Sally beamed. She's an attractive older woman in a no-nonsense, Ivory soap sort of way. You only have to look at Sally to know you're in the most capable of hands.

"I wanted the VIPs to feel good about their trip to Mayday! Of course if Brownie Kefauver bites his tongue instead of my cucumber sandwiches, I won't be sorry."

I knew the context. Sally ran for mayor in the last election and was soundly defeated. Her platform was thoughtful and well considered, which apparently was the problem.

I looked over my shoulder and saw that indeed, the Kefauver family had arrived. They hadn't been on the tour since Hazel knew everything she needed to about the way the food bank worked — and planned to throw her axe into those gears anyway.

"That woman," Sally said softly. "You have no idea how much trouble she caused with this reception. We had everything planned, then she came in and slashed the budget."

I tried to soothe. "Well, it looks like you did a wonderful job." I hesitated. "You even thought to borrow the church punch bowl."

"Not because I wanted to. We had everything set to rent from Quite the Party, and Hazel cancelled our order. She said we would have to borrow whatever we needed. So we did, with a lot of effort. And the chocolate fountain? We had one on order that came with an attendant. They aren't as easy to operate as you might think. But Hazel decided we could learn."

"It looks great. You learn fast."

"Yes, and as long as the bees don't find it, we don't have strong winds, we got all the lumps out of the chocolate, nobody trips over the cord, and the fountain is perfectly level, it should work just fine."

"Wow."

"Oh, and the final blow? Hazel refused to let us purchase the chocolate that's made especially for it. We had donated chocolate available, so she insisted we find a recipe ourselves and use it."

The chocolate fountain was beginning to look a shade less yummy.

Sally must have read my expression, because she put her hand on my shoulder. "It tastes perfectly fabulous. You just add vegetable oil based on the pounds of chocolate you need, but you have to melt the chocolate first and do some adjusting to get it flowing. Then you turn it off and on again every twenty or thirty minutes to reprime the pump. I won't go on . . ."

"I'm wondering why you didn't get Hazel to do this herself, since it was her idea to change the order."

"Hazel and chocolate? Not a chance. Her views on what foods are acceptable for human beings are way out there. Only food in its purest form. She claims she eats nothing but nuts, whole grains, fruits, and vegetables. Of course . . ."

Sally's eyes were sparkling. I knew that look. Sally was listening to her better side, trying to stem the flow of gossip. But I wasn't above pulling a brick or two out of that dam.

"You don't think she really follows the diet?"

"You're a vegetarian, aren't you?"

"I don't expect other people to follow the

lettuce-lined path."

"Well, the rumor is Hazel doesn't practice what she preaches. She's a junk food junkie. I'm told she's a hopeless chocoholic, and get this . . . she smokes!"

I envisioned Hazel, the food Nazi, rolling a tobacco leaf and smoking it "in its purest form."

"People have seen her smoking?" I asked.

"People have smelled it. I'm one of them. She tries to cover it up, but she's not successful. I get the feeling maybe she smokes half a pack at a time whenever she can get away with it. I think she more or less stores it up until she can go off on a binge by herself again."

This was a character flaw that improved Hazel's resume. She almost sounded human. Imperfections have their place.

"But of course she would never admit it," Sally continued. "So she rails against the evils of chocolate and lets the rest of us do all the work. She forgets the rest of us have busy lives, too. In fact, the minute I'm done here, I'm heading out of town."

"Somewhere fun?"

She looked at me as if I needed my consciousness raised. "A conference on urban renewal for small cities."

In her own way, Sally is as single-minded

as Hazel.

I told her again how lovely everything looked, then I wandered over to sample the wares.

Chad Sutterfield was standing by himself at the end of the table, so I went to chat with him after I filled my plate. I planned to save the chocolate fountain for dessert. I wanted to look forward to it.

"You did a great job on the tour." I offered him one of the tiny spinach quiches that had just been put out, but I guess it's true what they say about real men. He shook his head.

"You'll have to tell me how those are. We have thirty boxes in the warehouse freezer."

"What will you do with them? They don't seem like the kind of thing families are looking for when they come to get groceries. 'I'd like dried milk, canned tomatoes, a pound of cheese, and a box of fancy appetizers?'"

"One day next week we'll probably include them in our meals for the elderly." He watched me take a bite and smiled when I nodded my approval.

"You get all sorts of odd things like this?"

"We're always surprised what people think we might use. Once we got a hundred pounds of ground ostrich meat."

"What did you do?"

"They say it's really healthy, so we couldn't see disposing of it. Our volunteers made spaghetti. I won't tell you where we served it. Maybe you ate some."

"Nope. I'm a vegetarian, brought on at least partly by too many meals of mystery meat in school lunchrooms."

"I could tell you some hair-raising stories about string beans."

"Leave me some illusions."

A couple more people wandered up to thank Chad for the tour, and I wandered off to find Ed. After his warning, I was going to make him serve me a glass of punch. I might drink half a dozen glasses just to make a point.

I got close to the table just in time for disaster to ensue. The tent flap blew open, in itself nothing to cause a problem. But the same strong gust of wind that had sent it flying swept across the chocolate fountain. I remembered what Sally had said and jumped backwards just in time. Unfortunately, others nearby weren't so lucky.

Brownie, who had been dipping a strawberry, was now as chocolate as his name. And Hazel had been sprayed with enough dark chocolate to indulge in clandestine licks for a month to come.

The Kefauvers jumped back, sputtering.

"Turn that thing off!" Hazel screeched. "Who's responsible? Who's the incompetent who's responsible!"

Brownie took her by the arm and pulled her away from the scene. She was too busy peeling chocolate off her chin to resist. But she continued to screech more abuse as she peeled.

If you've never seen a chocolate tornado, you've missed something special. Chocolate flew everywhere. Everything for several feet in diameter was thoroughly coated. Sandwiches, pastries, and the punch bowl. As if that wasn't enough of a problem, the chocolate that wasn't spraying the table was bubbling out of the fountain in bursts, as if it was taking shots at the people trying to move food out of harm's way.

"Unplug it," Sally commanded, and two men I'd never met dropped to their knees, crawled under the table, apparently bumping heads judging from the profanity, and managed to make a simple job unbearably complicated. While they struggled with the cord, chocolate coated everything in sight.

Ed came over to watch from a safe distance. "Tell me you had nothing to do with this."

"Oh, ye of little faith."

"What happened?"

"Sally was just complaining about how hard the setup was. I guess they didn't get it right after all." I looked up at him. "I'd built up to the chocolate fountain, you know. I have an active fantasy life, and I was dragging it out. I was just about to indulge. Does this seem fair to you?"

"I'll buy you a funnel cake."

"Maybe I could get a little closer and open my mouth. I can always wash my hair."

"Hazel!"

I wondered what Hazel had done now. I hoped whatever it was, it didn't involve Sally Berrigan and hands around the throat. Hazel was probably stronger, but Sally had more friends.

I turned to see Hazel facedown on the ground to our left. Hazel is a difficult woman and hard to like, but I knew she wasn't the kind of person who would faint for attention.

"Ed . . ." I grabbed his arm. "Something's got to be wrong."

"She was furious." He started forward.

I wondered if in her rage, Hazel had gone after Sally or somebody else, and they had shoved her and she'd fallen.

But now Brownie was kneeling beside his wife, shaking her. "She was okay. She was okay a minute ago. Then she gasped and . . . then, then she fell."

Once the tour was over I hadn't noticed Roussos, but he must have been with a crowd of VIPs closer to the tent door. Now he pushed past us and joined Brownie on the ground.

"Help me turn her over," Roussos ordered.

"Maybe we shouldn't. Maybe she hurt her back or her neck or —"

"We're turning her over now."

Used to following orders, Brownie pushed as Roussos got on the other side and pulled. I put my hand to my mouth. Hazel looked awful. And the chocolate splattered all over her cheeks and neck didn't help.

Roussos put his fingers against the side of her throat. He kept moving his fingers, as if he was feeling for a pulse. I knew he hadn't found one when he tilted her head back so her jaw dropped open, and he felt inside her mouth. He was checking to be sure her airway wasn't blocked.

"Somebody get the medics," he shouted.

He turned back to Hazel, positioned himself to blow air into her lungs, and began.

I was at his side in a moment. "I can do the chest compressions."

"Stay there just in case." He breathed again.

I watched in horror. Hazel's chest rose with each puff, but she wasn't breathing on her own. Just as I was about to repeat my offer, there was a noise from the door, and one of the emergency medical technicians on Mayday! duty rushed in.

I stepped out of the way, and he said a few words to Roussos, did a quick assessment, then took over. Roussos stood above them watching. I don't think he realized he was shaking his head. Roussos never gives anything away, so I knew the news was as bad as it gets.

I don't know how much time passed. The fountain was unplugged, people were asked to leave, and finally the ambulance that had been parked at the front of the grounds arrived.

As the only clergy on site, Ed stayed to comfort Brownie, and I stayed with him. Ed didn't tell Brownie to keep his chin up or not to lose hope. Because it was clear to us at that point that there was no hope for Hazel. Hazel Kefauver was gone, and all the hope in the world wasn't going to bring her back.

6

So *this* is how I got elected to scrape chocolate out of every crevice of the Women's Society punch bowl.

After Hazel met her maker in the VIP tent, Sally Berrigan was a wreck. Sally, who was one of the first to discover a body on the parsonage porch back in the fall, has yet to develop a tolerance for death. May that continue.

By the time the ambulance carried Hazel away and something approaching order was restored, Sally had to leave for the conference in Washington. Ed and I had taken turns comforting Brownie and Sally, switching partners regularly. Sally had to be convinced that the mishap with the fountain — for which she unwisely blamed herself — hadn't contributed to a heart attack or stroke and killed poor Hazel. And let's be honest. By the time she calmed enough to see reason, she was in no shape to be handling an antique punch bowl worth more than the average annual pledge to our church.

There's a history that goes along with the punch bowl. My mother procured it to replace our previous casualty, and afterwards she enumerated its fine points to me. American Brilliant Cut glass, made between the years 1886 and 1914, is highly collectible, and even in its time, a luxury item. Each piece was created by a team of craftsmen, and there is nothing comparable on the market today. Our bowl looks like a series of interlaced fans with a sawtooth rim. It has aged well, with only the faintest wear on some of the teeth. Junie endeared herself forever to the Women's Society by replacing their ordinary pressed glass bowl with this one.

With all that history, despite being upset myself, I was the chump elected to take the punch bowl back to the church to be sure it was sparkling clean and stored away before anybody missed it. Sally claimed no one else had nearly as much invested in doing the job right.

Of course no one else had been at least partially responsible for the demise of the other two. I may not be required to confess regularly, but I do understand the concept of penance.

Since the kitchen of the Consolidated Community Church has a sink large enough to accommodate the punch bowl, early Monday morning I borrowed Ed's keys from our kitchen key basket, carefully boxed and toted the bowl to the back door of the church, and let myself in. Ed was home with Junie and the girls making breakfast, and I would have preferred to be at our kitchen table working on a second cup of coffee. But even though Monday is normally a quiet day at church and Ed's day off, I knew that later in the morning the building wouldn't be quiet at all. Our annual rummage sale is scheduled to take place at the end of the week, with bag day after the service on Sunday. Today marked the beginning of the sorting season.

Last year's sale was an education. Apparently the rummage sale is a litmus test of sorts. If you still feel friendly toward your fellow congregants when the sale ends, then you have evolved into a higher state and may be called on to give sermons instead of simply listening to them.

My kindest instincts tell me that almost every person who volunteers is normally friendly and patient. I don't know why sorting and sizing old tennis sneakers and grandma's support hose turns docile lambs into hungry wolves. But I know, having been in charge of the toy room last year, that by the end of the sale, I was ready to shake every parent or child who tried to get a bargain on a leaking kaleidoscope or hotel-deficient Monopoly game.

I guess the sale means too much work, too many people with too many ideas about how things should be done, and too many items that should have gone in the trash in the first place.

Of course since rummage pays some part of my husband's salary, I don't make these sentiments known.

The most stalwart of the rummage sale strike force are members of our Women's Society who have been running Tri-C's sale for years. While they complain enthusiastically that our new members don't help, they criticize them when they try, drastically cutting the field of new volunteers.

So the ladies of the Society are still the ones who arrive first and depart last, and this morning I was afraid if I arrived too late they were going to walk in the kitchen and find me chipping hardened chocolate off their punch bowl. Never mind that Sally Berrigan was responsible, and Sally is president of the group. With Sally safely out of reach I couldn't point my finger. The obvious solution was to finish the job before anyone could see.

Our parish house kitchen is informally expansive, a mishmash of donated utensils, pots and pans, and ancient dish towels. China cabinets line the walls, filled with serviceable crockery used most often for monthly potluck suppers. I let myself in and carefully set the box with the punch bowl on the island behind the sink. Once I found the detergent, I filled the largest sink with warm water.

While I waited, I noticed that the cabinet where the glassware is kept was being emptied. Glasses lined the counter below it. The same was true of the cabinet where cups and saucers reside. I wondered if January, our sexton, planned to scrub the shelves and put in new shelf paper. It was certainly needed.

While the sink filled, I opened cupboard doors, noticing other changes as well. Apparently some group or other had taken on the kitchen as a service project, and I was delighted to see it. Shelves had been organized. The pantry where the coffeemakers hang out together was clear of stems and baskets that hadn't fit any appliance in residence since 1952. I just hoped we weren't making room for more mismatched finds from rummage sale donations.

I lifted the punch bowl out of the box and was ready to set it in the water when I realized that as I'd wandered, two cars had parked in the small lot behind the church. Now as I watched, women got out of each. Fern Booth from one, Ida Bere and someone I didn't recognize from the other.

Had I made a list of people I didn't want to see, Fern and Ida would have topped it. Between them, the two women share the unofficial position of Consolidated Community Church Critic. Fern specializes in ragging on the minister and his family, and Ida specializes in herding everyone to whatever moral high ground she's chosen for the month. What a team.

Many people in the church would understand if I calmly explained that the punch bowl had been on a field trip to Mayday! when a gust of wind spattered it with chocolate — just about the time the mayor's wife fell dead on the ground a few yards away. They would believe I'd only been a prisoner of circumstances and was now doing my sacred duty by cleaning and putting it in the closet.

Fern and Ida were not two of those people. I pictured an interrogation room, a bright light shining in my weary eyes, pleas for water denied.

I pictured them sentencing me to another year in charge of the rummage sale toy room.

I'm ashamed to say I followed my instincts and took the easy way out. I slipped the punch bowl back in the box, folded the flaps so no one could see inside, and set the box under the sink behind a plastic wastebasket filled with sponges and dishcloths. Then I pulled the plug, dried my hands, and made my way to the front of the church. When I heard the back door open, I slipped outside.

Unless ants found the punch bowl and drew attention with squeaky sighs of ecstasy, the bowl was safely hidden for the moment. More important, I was safe from explanations and a week of hard labor matching dominoes and testing batteries.

I could have gone home, but since I was already out and dressed, I decided to tick off the next item on the day's to-do list. I circled back to the parsonage and gunned the motor on our minivan so Ed would know I was escaping. Then I backed onto Church Street and started toward the Village. I was on the way to Maura Wagner's house, where I would be plied with calories, caffeine, and enough sugary false cheer to make up for the chocolate I'd missed yesterday.

Although Hazel hadn't been far from my thoughts, passing City Hall brought her death back to the forefront. Ed and I moved to Emerald Springs for a variety of reasons, but one of them was a desire for peace and tranquility. At heart Ed's a scholar, torn between a desire to practice ministry or to write weighty tomes about historical ministers and their contributions. Emerald Springs seemed the perfect compromise, a small, established church in small-town America, with a liberal arts college that possesses an excellent library, a healthy congregation with an endowment large enough to pay him an adequate salary, and a decent school system for our daughters.

Ed believed there would be time in his schedule for prayer, contemplation, research, and writing.

Ed is not always right.

Two murder investigations in the past year have provided snags in that scenario. That's two more than anyone expects in a lifetime, so theoretically, we're due for some peace. Unfortunately, the last few days had me worried about our future. Joe's disappearance? Disconcerting, but perhaps if all concerned are lucky, nothing more than a bad case of the flu or a temporary emotional meltdown.

Witnessing Hazel's collapse and death? That's harder to put a positive spin on. Seeing her on the ground brought back memories. I didn't really know Hazel, and what I knew about her wasn't particularly positive, but I feel truly sorry her life ended, and ended the way it did, smack-dab in the middle of affixing blame for the chocolate fountain mishap.

Junie is big on final moments. She believes they epitomize everything about a person's life. And as you might imagine, my mother thought Hazel's last moments were sadly significant. Last night she listened as I recounted the story, then she shook her head.

"You watch, precious. That poor woman will come back as an exterminator or a telemarketer. She'll be forced to spend her next life listening to homeowners scream threats at her until she develops some humility."

Of course this heartfelt prophecy comes from the same woman who only an hour before Hazel's death had promised her a long, sexy life. Since that prediction hadn't quite panned out, I was hoping Junie was going to be two for two on the subject of

Hazel Kefauver. I couldn't picture our mayor's wife in a khaki shirt and cap, tank and sprayer in hand — although let's face it, there isn't a termite or rat that would stand a chance against her.

I pulled up in front of the Wagners' house, got out, and marched resolutely up the walkway. Today the rag dolls were dressed like Morris dancers, with brightly colored ribbons, hats, and vests. I was surprised Maura hadn't set up a maypole on the lawn to add to the ambience.

I saw Maura right after Hazel's collapse. Like everyone else she was shocked. Maura had experienced too many upsets this weekend, but judging by the dolls, she was soldiering on.

Maura answered before I could knock. Today she wore the lilac equivalent of yesterday's outfit, although to give her credit, this sweater did have tiny cables running up the front.

"Oh, Aggie, I didn't expect you." Her smile was PTA chairman perfect.

"I thought I'd stop by and see how you're doing."

She seemed almost puzzled, as if she couldn't imagine why that might be an issue. "I just got Tyler off to school. Would you like to come in for some coffee?"

"That would be nice. How's Tyler doing?" I now had a bigger stake in knowing, since he and my daughter seemed to be keeping company.

She let me in. We got all the way to the kitchen before she answered. She motioned me to a seat at the table while she bustled around the way she had yesterday. Today it looked as if our calories would be delivered in the form of freshly baked muffins.

"Tyler's okay." Maura stacked plates on a tray and poured two cups of coffee from a full pot. I wondered if she set it to brew automatically whenever the doorbell chimed.

She turned with the tray in her hands. "I made sure he did his testing and shots. I'm not as much help as I should be, I guess. I hate needles. They scare me to death. I did natural childbirth just to avoid them."

We were trading confidences. Now it was my turn. "I did hypnosis when I had Deena. A woman in the church was taking classes and wanted to practice on me. Ed claims I clucked and flapped my arms like a chicken whenever she told me to."

"Ed was *there?*"

"For both girls. Joe wasn't?"

"Oh, I didn't want him there. I wasn't at my best."

I've yet to meet the woman who is at her best when she's ten centimeters dilated. Hypnosis or not, had I felt strong enough during either delivery, I would have gotten off the table and wrung Ed's neck. Still, for most of it, having him there meant everything. To both of us.

"What did Joe do while he waited?" I asked, sliding into one of the reasons I'd come. "Without family to hold his hand? Or maybe there was *somebody?* A cousin, a great aunt?"

"Nobody."

"That's going to make it harder . . ."

"What?"

I hadn't meant to say that out loud. I shrugged, but Maura was on to me.

She passed me a cup, then set the tray with sugar cubes and cream in front of me. "You're going to look for him, aren't you? You're going to try to find Joseph."

How could I hide the truth? Maura was my best source of information. Even if she thought she knew very little, she must know *something* that would help.

"I'm going to do what I can. But I don't know how much help I can be."

She lowered herself to the seat across from me. "He needs to come back. This is where Joseph belongs. He's made a good life for us here."

Okay, I thought I'd settled this with myself yesterday. Nobody knows how they'll react in a brand-new crisis. Still, I'm pretty sure that if Ed just up and disappeared, I would be worried sick. I would be bugging the police and calling every hospital in the state, sure something awful had happened to him.

Because why else would Ed be gone?

Maura was worried, too, but I wasn't sure she was worried about Joe. She seemed more worried that he might be choosing to stay away.

I reached across the table and stopped her in the middle of cutting muffins into quarters and fanning them out like the petals of a daisy. I slid my hand over hers and squeezed.

"Were you and Joe having problems, Maura? Because I get the feeling you think he might just be holed up somewhere, refusing to come home."

She gave a small unconvincing shake of her head.

I sat back. "I can't help unless I know what's going on."

"Nothing's going on. It's just that . . ." She shook her head again. "Well, Joseph's been working long hours lately. And we fought about it. I felt . . . feel that he should

125

be here with his family in the evening. I keep a lovely home, make delicious meals; he should be here to enjoy them. I finally told him. Do you think that's what drove him away?"

I wondered how anybody could be this naive, or this out of date. Maybe June Cleaver worried that Ward was so tired of the Beaver's antics he planned to divorce her, or Harriet Nelson was afraid Ozzie might leave the family to escape Ricky's singing, but I seriously doubted it. Some of those traditional fifties housewives are still alive and well in our Women's Society, and I can tell you they are sharp, gutsy women, not at all afraid to demand their rights. Maura was a mystery to me. I was growing more convinced it was now *my* job to help her get up on her feet and walking.

"That sounds like a perfectly normal argument," I said, feeling my way. "Not at all the kind of thing that drives people apart."

"I just keep imagining he's angry at me, and that's why he doesn't come back. If I could do it over, I wouldn't say a word to him."

"Why *was* he working such long hours?"

"I never asked."

Joe is such a personable guy, I couldn't imagine it would have taken more than a

"So what happened at work today?" to get the whole story.

I tried a different tack. "Do you happen to know where in New Jersey he grew up?"

She offered the muffin plate, and I took a quarter. Every piece was exactly the same size. If I'd had time to dissect them and count crumbs, I was sure I would find them equal.

"I don't think his childhood was happy," Maura said. "When I asked about it, he was vague. Joseph's always vague if he doesn't want to talk about something, and I learned not to pin him down. I think they moved a good bit. I got the feeling his father couldn't hold down a job. But that was just a guess."

I felt a touch of remorse. Maybe Joe was vague about work, as well. Maybe when Maura tried to find out how things were going, he clammed up. And didn't we have proof that this generous, open guy kept secrets?

I made a mental note to find out what had been going on at the food bank to keep him so occupied into the evenings. And I repeated yesterday's note to myself not to be so hard on Maura.

"If you think of anything he might have told you, will you let me know?" I asked.

"Of course. I appreciate your help, Aggie." She smiled, and this time the smile was genuine and warmed her face.

"Just two other things, then I have to go. Do you have copies of your credit card bills or recent receipts? I thought maybe I could track his movements in New York and make some calls."

"Joseph paid all the bills. I never even opened them."

"Do you know where he filed them afterwards?"

She bit her lip. This time she actually looked chagrined. "No. He may have paid them at work. I think he did a lot of family business on the computer there."

"So he did all the paperwork?"

"We each had our roles. I guess that's unusual these days, but it worked for us. I never paid a bill, he never cooked a meal."

"Will you look around and see if you can find any records? Of course if you do, you might want to be the one to make those calls."

"I'll look, but I'm sure there's no reason you shouldn't see them."

"Good." I got to my feet. "Oh, the last thing? Do you have any recent photos of Joe? Just in case?"

She looked relieved. "Finally, something I can help with."

On my way out we stopped in the living room, and Maura opened an album on the table. I could see it was one of those cleverly done scrapbooks, with stickers and pages that folded out, and little mementoes glued in place. She thumbed through to the end and lifted a photo from a silver paper frame that had held it in place.

She handed the photo to me. "I have a lot more. I'll get them together for you. But here's a start."

We both stared at the photograph. Joe was looking up at us, a big, hunky Italian guy with the world's greatest smile.

"The house feels empty without him." Maura looked up at me. "You'll try to find him, Aggie? Everybody says you're good at figuring things out."

I wasn't sure that anything I figured out was going to make her life happier, but I nodded.

Outside the ribbons of the Morris dancer dolls were fluttering in a light spring breeze, and the morning sun was smiling in the sky. I could almost feel the gaze of friendly neighbors peering through windows to be sure all was well on the street.

Here in the Village, with its charming houses and well-tended yards, it was hard to imagine that the rest of the world wasn't

129

exactly the same. Husbands never disappeared. Chocolate fountains never splattered. Women, even angry women, never died at charitable events. Standing here I could see why Maura found the real world confusing.

Suddenly I wasn't quite so sure this neighborhood and those neighborly gazes were completely benign. Despite the smiling sun I got a chill down my spine. It was time to move on.

In my van again I headed toward the Victorian to see what the newest carpenter on a growing list had accomplished on our renovations over the weekend. I pulled onto Bunting Street and parked, telling myself I should sit a moment to admire what Lucy and I have accomplished.

The house that will be Junie's quilt shop was designed and constructed in Stick Victorian style at the turn of the twentieth century. Although it was easy to miss before we began our renovations, the house has always been well proportioned and gracious.

When Lucy and I got our first glimpse, the exterior was a nondescript beige. For the update, Junie suggested a color that falls somewhere between a muted mauve and lavender. Junie's psychic ability may be questionable, but her color sense is extraordinary. Now the front porch is spruce green, the shutters black, and the considerable amount of trim is a warm cream or soft rose. The effect is charming without drawing negative attention to itself on a street with a mix of residential and commercial buildings.

The tired, overly disciplined evergreens were dispensed with last month to be replaced by a variety of blooming shrubs and beds of perennials. Junie always wanted to tend a garden, and now she'll have one. Once the forsythia and Japanese magnolias that will block out the parking area have grown tall enough she has plans for a patio with a fountain in the back. She envisions an annual summer tea on the lawn for her best customers, and many additional happy hours with her granddaughters.

Junie will love being the proprietor of a quilt shop, and she'll love living here — if Lucy and I can only make it happen. The problem is that we never planned on doing anything as extensive as this project, so we quickly reached the point where our own efforts weren't enough. We were knowledgeable and talented enough to do simple flips, and we even assembled a list of contractors in our price range who were capable of doing required rewiring and plumbing. But despite following every lead, we have yet to find a crew who can install a kitchen, build attractive shelves and counters for merchandise, and change the basic configuration of the rooms upstairs, which will be Junie's apartment.

The first team we hired installed a bathroom countertop backwards, so the backsplash nestled against our belly buttons. The second framed in a closet on the wrong side of what would be Junie's bedroom so that the biggest window could be curtained by caftans and poodle skirts.

Two more failures followed these, both companies recommended, both incapable of swinging a hammer without error.

Now we're praying — Lucy in her bat mitzvah Hebrew and me in Unitarian-Universalist — that our fifth try will be the last. Hank Closeur, of Closeur Contracting, seems knowledgeable and receptive. Best of all, he and a couple of his men will be moonlighting, working on weekends and evenings, and giving us a price break because of it. We don't want to stretch Junie's budget any tighter than we have to.

I realized I was sitting in the van pretending to view with pleasure the progress we had made when in reality, I was just afraid to go inside and discover more mistakes. Junie is a welcome guest in our home, but she's ready to move on to this new phase of her life, and Ed and I are ready to pack the boxes.

Conquering my sense of dread, I made the trip up to the front porch and peered in the window first. Nothing seemed amiss in the front of the house. In fact, from what I could tell, nothing was different. That didn't bode well.

I unlocked the door and stepped inside. Sometime toward the end of the last century the downstairs had been remodeled so the floor plan was open and inviting. Luckily Junie liked it just the way it was, envisioning bolts of fabric in what was once the living and dining area, books and patterns in what had been a small kitchen, and notions in the study. Lucy and I had hired a crew to help demolish the kitchen and haul everything away but the fridge, which would eventually go in what was now a mudroom, for the employees to use. Another crew had refinished all the red oak floors. Now it was time for shelves along the walls, an island built to Junie's specifications, and a checkout counter in the front hallway.

Hank's first assignment was the island, where fabric would be laid out and cut, old quilts would be spread to determine what repairs could be done, and new projects shown off to the quilt store staff and customers. Junie said the island would be the heart of the room, a focal point for anyone walking in the door. All well and good, but Hank's vision of the island was clearly quite different. Somehow, despite every caution, despite chalk marks on the floor exactly where Junie wanted the island to go and plans and materials that were sitting on the other side of the room, Hank or someone on his crew had begun to construct it just a few feet from the fireplace. In fact, so close to the fireplace that circling the island would be impossible for any woman with hips.

And Junie definitely has hips.

There was, as always, good news and bad. The bad news was the placement. The good news was that they'd done so little work on the island I could probably pry out the poorly driven nails anchoring it to the floor and move it myself. With one hand.

I have a problem with technology. In our troubled relationship I'm more or less the jilted lover, constantly pleading for explanations and one more chance. I'm convinced if I try harder, read enough books, I'll win technology over.

My newest attempt to please is a cell

phone. These days I'm away from home enough to need one, and Ed insisted. Seems I've had too many close calls lately, never mind I've never met a murderer willing to wait while his victim-to-be dials 911. Still, my daughters have almost lost hope I'll ever be cool, and this was a stopgap measure. So last week I bought a nuts-and-bolts version and the cheapest wireless plan I could find, and attempted to join the twenty-first century.

Anyone can punch in numbers, even the technologically challenged. Now I fished for the phone resting in my pocket and made the attempt. I punched in Hank's number, which is the numerical form of Closeur. Words instead of numbers are a plague on the universe, and I was so slow, so careful, that the first two times the call didn't go through. The robot operator got tired of waiting and cut me off.

I finally connected. The phone rang twice, then somebody answered. Unfortunately, that somebody answered in Chinese, or at least that's my best guess. I apologized in English and hung up. I hoped I'd reached San Francisco and not Beijing.

The fourth time was a charm. I was mastering this. Pocket calculators next, then iPods. Someday e-mail without Deena loading the program and retrieving my messages.

I waited until the woman who answered got Hank to the phone, then in my most professional manner I told him everything that was wrong. Just as he was about to answer, the line went dead.

I know there's a redial function on my phone. With a manual, a glass of wine, and Deena sitting close beside me, I'm sure someday I'll find it.

I found a pad and pen and wrote Hank a note detailing everything I'd said on the telephone. I left it on what passed for carpentry and hoped that the next time I saw this room, the damage would be undone and a beautiful new island would be standing between our chalk marks.

Clearly on top of everything else, technology has addled my brain.

My girls wake up early to get ready for school. Brownie Kefauver wakes up earlier. At least he did on Wednesday morning when his frantic pounding sent me toddling down the stairs in my fuzzy slippers and Ed's plaid flannel bathrobe. I was yawning when I unlocked the door, and my mouth stayed open when I saw who was waiting on the other side.

"Well . . . hmmm . . ." Having just dispensed with the vocabulary I feel most comfortable with before seven a.m., I opened the door wider and silently ushered him in.

By the time he sidled through the doorway, my brain was slowly cranking up. "Mr. Mayor." I don't think I'd ever called him that before. Maybe it was left over from an old episode of *Spin City.*

"Mrs. Wilcox, I need help."

I nodded, because nodding is tough to

screw up. I held a finger high, wordlessly asking him to wait, and went to the bottom of the stairs. "Ed." Since that emerged as a croak, I tried again. "Ed!"

Ed came down to the landing. Somehow he'd had the presence of mind to throw on sweat pants and a T-shirt. Of course I was wearing *his* robe, and my peach chenille wouldn't have suited him at all.

Although I guess it would have suited Joe Wagner.

"Brownie," Ed said, coming down to join us. "What can I help you with?"

I figured Brownie must have come about Hazel's funeral. The Kefauvers attend the Methodist church that nestles up to the Emerald Springs Oval, only a brief stroll from the parsonage. I knew the church was in the middle of a renovation project, and we had wondered if their sanctuary was ready for a funeral as large as Hazel's. Now I guessed Brownie wanted to use our church instead. To be polite he might even ask Ed to say a prayer or lead a responsive reading.

But none of my foggy musings prepared me for his next words.

"It's not you I'm here to see." He turned to me, dismissing my husband. "Mrs. Wilcox, I need your help."

I glanced at Ed, wondering how he was

138

taking this. No hogger of the limelight, he merely looked intrigued. His expression changed as Brownie continued.

"Hazel was poisoned."

I turned back to Brownie. Only then did I notice what he was wearing. Gone was the bow tie, perhaps because it was too early to insist that fingers tie or clip, but more likely because he was wearing a yellow polo shirt. With the buttons undone. I was surprised I'd recognized him.

"Poisoned?" Ed asked.

"That's right!" He ran his hand through what hair was left. "And I know, at least I'm pretty sure, or almost sure at least, that the police suspect me."

Silence thrummed through the parsonage. Even the clocks forgot to tick. I cleared my throat when it thrummed too long. "Why?"

"Because they always suspect the husband, that's why!"

"Somebody told you this?"

"Please, Mrs. Wilcox, I know how they work. Plus they asked if they could look through the house, just to see if they could determine why somebody would want her dead. But they did more than look. They went through her things. They even carried away some of our household cleaners, some supplies from the pantry and garage —"

"Aggie. Call me Aggie. And let's sit down."

I led him to the sofa, and to his credit, he was still calm enough to remember that he had to bend his knees and lower his butt to the cushions. Once he did, he rested his head in his hands.

"Did you just find out?" I asked.

"Last night, and I haven't had a wink of sleep." He looked up, still a little, nondescript man, but now that he wasn't dressed like Pee-wee Herman, he looked real and surprisingly vulnerable. I sympathized with all he had been through.

"Did they say how? What? When?" I asked.

He shook his head. "They refused. And I probably won't know until they charge me with murder."

"You don't know that's going to happen."

"Hazel was a wealthy woman. And now every penny will come to me. Can you think of a better motive?"

Not really, but I could think of other possibilities. Hazel Kefauver was universally disliked. Perhaps not hated, but certainly not the first person anybody thought of inviting to a backyard barbecue. If indeed she'd been murdered, then somebody had been angry enough to dispatch her to wherever it is people like Hazel go.

"You need means, motive, and opportunity," I told him, trying to help. But even as I said it, I realized the opportunity part was a done deal. I mean, Brownie *lived* with her. And means? Well, that depended on whatever poison killed her, and it sounded as if this was something the police were keeping to themselves.

"I saw the way Detective Roussos was looking at me when he came to tell me the autopsy results," Brownie said.

Roussos. No surprise there. The police chief wouldn't get within a hundred yards of this, not until everyone was sure Brownie was the murderer, and he rushed to take credit. No, for the moment, our chief would stay on the sidelines and turn this over to someone without political aspirations.

"Roussos always looks like that," I said. "I bet he gazed accusingly at his mother from the cradle. She probably had to hire a nanny. Did he say somebody poisoned her? Or simply that she was poisoned? Can you remember?"

Ed spoke from across the room. "Aggie, may I see you a moment?"

I'd forgotten he was standing there. I patted Brownie's hand. "I'll be right back. Think about what Roussos said."

Ed was waiting in the kitchen. And clearly

he wasn't here to make coffee. His arms were folded, his eyes narrowed.

"You're helping him."

"Well, sure." I smiled innocently. "I mean, if he'd come to ask you if he could use the church for the funeral, *you* would have helped. Right? It's the same thing."

"I thought we had a deal."

"What deal is that?"

"You said you were going to stay out of murder investigations. Stay out. Remember?"

"Oh . . ." I nodded, as if I finally understood. "I'm not investigating a murder. I'm just trying to see if I can help Brownie prove he's not the murderer. Surely you can see the difference?"

"No."

"This is our mayor, Ed. You don't honestly think I should tell our mayor I can't help him because my *husband* thinks it's a bad idea. That'll reinforce his value system. What kind of message is that?"

"An honest one. An intelligent one."

I love my husband. I know he's reasonable, not controlling, and that he has my interests at heart on those rare occasions when he tries to talk me out of something. He knows the same thing about me. But this time I had to set him straight.

"I'm going to hear what he has to say. Then if I think I can help, I'm going to. But I'm not going to put myself in danger to protect Brownie Kefauver, if that's what's worrying you. I've learned that lesson."

"You've made up your mind, haven't you?"

"I haven't had a chance to make up anything, not even our bed." This time *I* narrowed my eyes. "But you have to trust me. Apparently I've found something I'm good at doing, and within limits, I plan to continue. You've been fine with me looking into Joe's disappearance. This isn't that different."

"Joe wasn't murdered."

"We don't know that." There, I'd said it, and I saw from his expression that Ed was worried about this possibility, too.

I went on before he could respond. "I don't want to have a fight with you every time I leave the house. I'll be careful, and I'll be smart. Give me some credit."

Since it was clear he was going to mull over at least some part of what I'd said before he answered, I went back into the living room and took my seat again.

I'm not sure Brownie realized I'd been gone. He spoke as soon as I was seated. "Roussos said she'd been poisoned. That's all he said. Nothing else."

"There are accidental poisonings. It would help if we knew with what." I decided to check with my detective nemesis to see if he would at least tell me if the police suspected foul play or carelessness. But I was guessing the first. Roussos would probably have told Brownie if Hazel's death seemed accidental.

"Were you and Hazel together all day Sunday, before she . . ."

"I wasn't out of her sight." He said this as if it hadn't been his choice.

"What about the day before?"

"Saturday? She was away for part of the week visiting her sister. She came home Friday evening. On Saturday we did some shopping, then a little yard work. She went to the library, and I took a nap until she got home."

I pictured Hazel rousing her husband from a sound sleep. Perhaps insisting on callisthenics or a round of tofu smoothies to get his blood flowing vigorously.

"And then?" I prompted.

"Dinner with friends. An early night. Sunday we went to church."

"I noticed Hazel's color wasn't good when I saw her at Mayday!" Now I wished I'd said something. Would she have listened? Would she have asked the medics to look her over? Would she have slugged me?

"I guess I wasn't paying much attention," Brownie said. "She just looked like Hazel to me."

I could see he wasn't going to be any help figuring out when the poisoning occurred. Hazel was lucky he noticed when she fell on the ground.

If you can call dying luck.

I touched his arm. "Just a couple of other things. Will anybody have reason . . . Let me rephrase. Have you given anybody reason to think that you might have done away with Hazel yourself?" I flinched at my slang. "I mean, have you been seen in public fighting? Have you confided to anyone that you wished you had a way to get Hazel out of your life?"

He didn't deny the possibility, which surprised me. In fact he squirmed, which was answer enough. "I'll think about that."

"And the last thing?" I waited until he was looking at me. "Why me? I mean, you have all the money you need to hire a real detective. So why did you come to me? I'm nothing but an amateur."

"I've heard you're nosy, and know how to find things out. And you discovered who killed Gelsey Falowell."

"Yes, well . . ." I didn't like the nosy part.

"But why not a professional?"

"Because the police will find out if I hire somebody. And maybe I'll look even more guilty, like I'm pretending to get them off my case. Besides, I'm the mayor. What would it say about our city if I act like I don't trust the police enough to let them do their job? I can't throw money at this. I can't ask a pro to get on board. For now, you're all I've got."

It wasn't exactly a ringing endorsement, but I guess it had to do. It even made a weird kind of sense. Hiring a detective might look like Brownie didn't trust the cops. And that really wouldn't be good for the local morale. Hiring me? Who would take that seriously?

"I'll give this some thought." I stood, and he followed a moment later. "I'll be back in touch," I said.

He didn't add anything until we got to the door. Then he turned to face me. "I didn't kill my wife. And I don't know anybody else who disliked her enough to want her dead."

Anybody *else?*

"I hope you'll help me." He held out his hand. Shaking it was a little like cleaning a fish. But at least Brownie's eyes were just worried, not staring blindly into forever.

"I'll talk to you soon," I promised as I closed the door.

Ed spoke from behind me. "Do you really think Joe was murdered?"

I turned warily. He didn't look spitting mad. "Coffee?"

"It's brewing."

I followed him to the kitchen and plunked down at the long table that bisects the room. Our parsonage is a hulking Dutch Colonial. The rooms that should be large are not, and the ones that should be smaller for efficiency — like the kitchen — are large enough to hold Sunday services. The house has character, though, and we're learning to feel at home here.

Outside I could hear the plunk of our morning newspaper as it bounced off the sidewalk before merrily playing hide-and-seek in the bushes. Moonpie, our silver tabby, jumped up to the chair beside me, gauging my mood before he tried for the table. I narrowed my eyes, and with feline disdain he began to lick himself, waiting to leap, I'm sure, the moment I looked away.

"I don't know if Joe was murdered," I said, keeping my eyes on the cat. "But doesn't this open up a nasty possibility? The last time anybody saw him, he looked pale and ill, remember? And Hazel looked like death warmed over before, well, you know. They're both connected to Helping Hands. What if he succumbed to the same poison, and he's just lying somewhere unclaimed or unnoticed?"

"I'm afraid somebody will notice soon. Mother Nature will make sure of it."

I fished around in the drawer of the phone table behind me. I could just reach it if I tilted my chair on its hind legs, something the girls are repeatedly warned not to do. Out for revenge, Moonpie jumped on my lap and both of us nearly went over. I set him on the ground more gently than he deserved and got up to find what I was looking for.

"Maura gave me this." I waved Joe's photo at Ed, before I set it on the table.

"What are you going to do with it?"

"Eventually the police are going to have to know he's missing. If Joe doesn't call or come back, she'll have to make a report."

"But for now?"

"I'm not sure. How can you search for somebody if you're supposed to pretend you know where he is? I've got a photo and nobody I can show it to."

Junie wandered in, followed by Teddy. I could tell immediately that my mother had helped Teddy pick out her outfit. My sober little first grader wore a blue velvet dress with white lace trim, a rhinestone bracelet, and jewel-encrusted flip-flops Junie had bought and decorated for rainy day dress up.

"Well . . ." I nodded. "You look like Cinderella at the ball. You're sure you want to climb to the top of the jungle gym in that outfit?"

"She's trying to get in character," Junie said.

"I need a crown."

Deena wandered in. "She can't go to school like that. Everybody will laugh."

"When you were in first grade, you went to school dressed like an astronaut." I noted that today she was going to school in her best jeans and an eyelet-trimmed T-shirt with nothing printed on it. She looked adorable. That frightened me.

Teddy lunged for Moonpie, who waited until the last possible second to evade her. Moonpie's quite the tease. Teddy righted herself and saw Joe's photograph on the table. "Who's that?"

Junie, who was dressed like she belonged in Cinderella's court, peered down at the table. "Oh, look at that. It's the man who came into my tent and wouldn't step out of the shadows."

A cold chill ran through me. "What do you mean?"

She lifted the photo. "Remember, Teddy? I asked this man if he wanted to have his fortune told and he refused?" She held it out. "Did you see him?"

Teddy spoke in a deep voice. "I don't want my fortune told. I know better than anybody else what's in store for me."

This time I felt frozen in place. The voice wasn't Teddy's. It sounded like an adult male. It *sounded* like Joe Wagner.

"Well, now we know why our precious was chosen to be Cinderella," Junie said, tucking a lock of Teddy's hair behind her ear. "That's exactly what he sounded like and exactly what he said. Isn't she marvelous?"

I knew my daughter was a wonderful mimic. And I knew she had a nearly photographic memory. But used this way? I wasn't all that glad to have heard the demonstration.

"Teddy, did you see this man?" I asked.

She shook her head. "I was under the table, but I never raised it off the ground," she said in her normal voice.

"She didn't," Junie confirmed.

"You're sure this is the man?" I asked my mother.

Ed came over to view the photo and then

Junie. "You're absolutely sure?"

Junie considered. "It was dark in the tent because of the deep shade from all those trees, especially around the edges, and he slipped in and out again so fast I hardly got a look at him. He never got close to me."

"So you're backing down?"

She shook her head. "No. I can't say so with 100 percent certainty, but I'm guessing this was the man I saw. I'm almost sure."

"I can't believe it." Two hours later I was standing at the Victorian, admiring the perfect skeleton of Junie's main island. Lucy Jacobs was standing beside me, tilting her head, as if that would help her envision the finished product.

"I was over here on Monday," I said, choosing to leave out the part about my cell phone. "Everything was screwed up. I called Hank and told him, but he never called me back, and he hasn't answered any of my other calls. I thought he'd quit on us. But look at this. He got it right, and he wasn't even supposed to come back until the weekend. Somebody finally got something right!"

"You're not just imagining there was something wrong on Monday?"

"No, look." I walked toward the fireplace

and pointed. You can still see where they were putting it, although they've really patched the floor nicely. I was worried."

Lucy shook back her red curls, partially confined in a green bandana. Luce is a size four and looks great in everything, even the ragged jeans and knee pads she'd donned today. In a few minutes we were set to tear out the layers of vinyl flooring in the upstairs bathroom. A few weeks into this project she cancelled her membership at the gym. She can't pick up guys at the Victorian, but she might be a size two before we finish.

"Well, false start maybe," she said, "but it looks like Closeur's a keeper. And I wasn't optimistic. Some of my clients haven't been happy with stuff he's done for them."

In her other life Lucy's a Realtor, so she has a lot of insider information. This works well for both of us. She finds houses that won't sell because of simple cosmetic flaws and owner stubbornness, and we buy them together, do the bare minimum to sell them, and put them back on the market. Our first successful flip consisted of clearing out junk and simple updating. We expected to do basic updates on the Victorian and turn it around quickly, too, but Junie had seen the house and fallen in love. Now it was up to us to turn it into a quilt shop.

We trooped upstairs together, patting each other on the back for finding somebody who could actually move our project toward completion. I thought if all went well, Junie might be able to move into the apartment by June and start stocking her shelves for an opening in early autumn. She had already infiltrated the local quilting guild. She'd taught her favorite pattern at one of the winter meetings, and now she was holding a Wednesday night class in the parsonage dining room. Every Wednesday the group seemed to grow larger. It was past time to move them into the new classroom area in the Victorian's basement before Junie started selling yard goods out of our bedroom.

The bathroom in question had several layers of vinyl flooring over a hardwood subfloor, and if we tried to install yet another subfloor and layer of tile over these, Junie would have to duck her head when she stepped up and into the room. We had already, with great effort, removed two layers. Today we planned to remove the final one. The wallpaper was already history, the walls painted a periwinkle blue, and if we were lucky, we would be able to save the hardwood, sand, and refinish it ourselves. But we weren't counting on it, and tile was a nice second choice.

We had already determined that the vinyl wasn't contaminated by asbestos, and which way the floorboards ran so we could cut the vinyl in the same direction, hopefully minimizing scarring.

"You're up for this?" I asked.

"I've got until five. I have a showing this evening."

"Let's get moving."

We divvied up the floor, repeated our plan of action out loud so we were working together, then started carefully cutting away strips of flooring and scraping them up with putty knives.

"Well, I've got news for you," I told Lucy.

I could almost hear her holding her breath. Lucy loves gossip more than selling houses. And she loves being right in the thick of it.

I proceeded to tell her in slow, agonizing detail about Brownie's early morning visit. The thing about Lucy is that she likes gossip, but if I tell her she can't repeat something, she won't. She's that best friend you always wanted in high school, the one who wouldn't steal your boyfriend, copy answers off your test paper, or talk about you behind your back. Now she just listened. Raptly.

"You've got to be kidding!" she said, once

154

I finished.

I sat back on my heels. This was not going to be a fun job. My arms were already sore from pulling up the flooring, and I could see there was going to be a lot more work once that was done. Lots and lots of sanding ahead, and tile was looking better.

"I'm not kidding. Hazel was poisoned, and Brownie's sure they suspect him."

"Is there any truth to it?"

"I'm sure he's right. He's the one who benefits most from her death."

"You mean because he inherits everything?" Lucy paused. "Or because he's finally rid of her?"

"Whoa there." I couldn't turn to see her face. The bathroom was spacious enough — for a bathroom. But I was more or less stuck between the toilet bowl and the sink. "What do you mean 'finally'?"

"What do you think I mean? Theirs wasn't exactly a marriage made in heaven, Aggie. I mean, you've seen them together, right? She kept the little guy on a leash. Like a cocker spaniel." Lucy paused. "But you know, even a little dog will bite if it's mistreated."

I wished I could see her face, but if I tried, I'd suffer whiplash. "Are you telling me he could have done it?"

"No, but I'll tell you what I do know.

Hazel wasn't the only woman in Brownie's life."

As a matter of fact this was old news to me, although everything had happened so quickly this morning, I hadn't thought about it. "You mean Keely?"

"Among others."

"Get out of here! You mean multiple affairs?"

"I don't know if we can call them affairs. Our friend Keely was getting paid, wasn't she? Maybe the others were — are — too."

We had met Keely Henley in the fall. Once upon a time she had served drinks at Emerald Springs's most notorious bar, Don't Go There. On a research trip Lucy and I talked to her about another murder, and along the way I learned that she had a "relationship" with our mayor. Since it hadn't been relevant I'd simply filed it away under "hypocritical politicians." Now, suddenly it mattered.

"Is this what you know, or what you've heard?" I asked.

"Know, as in personal experience with Brownie?"

"Lucy!"

"I have it on pretty good authority. I sold the Kefauvers' housekeeper a condo, and when her offer was accepted, we went out

156

to celebrate. Three mudslides later Dora pointed out a woman on the other side of the room and said she was sleeping with the mayor. Of course I'm sure if I'd pursued that conversation after the mudslides wore off, she would have denied it. But I don't think she and the vodka were making it up. And I've heard rumors, too, about other women."

And then there was Keely.

"Ick."

"Yeah, the ick factor's pretty strong," Lucy said. "But even though it doesn't excuse him, Hazel couldn't have been fun to live with."

"Which is why divorce is legal."

"Okay, but fun or not, Hazel was the one with the money and the power. I'm betting Brownie was happy enough to use both, even if she did come with the package. So he got his kicks elsewhere, or maybe he slept with other women just to get back at her. Like that spaniel, again, peeing on his owner's Persian carpet."

"I hope you don't enlighten the police about this, or use that simile. At least give me a chance to prove Brownie *didn't* do it first. A day or two would be nice."

"Silly, I'm sure the cops already know the whole story. A lot of people know. It wasn't a well-kept secret. Remember, you stumbled on Keely without breaking a sweat."

"He's a dead duck, isn't he?"

"Well, now he's got the money and power without her. And poisoning? He's such a little sneak, it would be just like him."

"Thus ends the first meeting of the Brownie Kefauver fan club."

Lucy pretended to rap a gavel on the floor, although it was only a putty knife. "Why did you tell him you'd see what you could do?"

I had been asking myself the same thing since I left the house this morning. I had no ties to the Kefauvers. And I thought as a mayor Brownie was inept and dishonest. Emerald Springs might even be better off if he was behind bars. There was just one problem.

"I don't think he did it." I backed out slowly on my hands and knees so I could see her again. "Call me nuts, but I don't think so. I don't think he has the courage. And I think he's genuinely confused and upset about everything that's happened. Not sad, maybe, but upset."

"He could be upset because he knows he's a suspect."

"And that's another thing. Anyone with a brain — and he fits into that category, if barely — would know that an autopsy would find poison. He must have okayed one, right? Her death didn't really look suspicious, so I'm not sure an autopsy was absolutely required. And Brownie would know he was going to be tops on everybody's list of suspects, so if he wanted her dead, wouldn't he simply hire somebody to do it when he had a clear alibi? This just seems too obvious to me."

"So you're involved because you sense injustice? Super Aggie? Get a clue here. There are no tall buildings to leap in Emerald Springs."

Lucy didn't know about Joe, and despite trusting her completely, I didn't feel I had the right to tell her yet. So I couldn't explain that deep down I had a suspicion Hazel's death and Joe's disappearance were linked. Especially now that my mother and daughter were convinced they had seen Joe Wagner at Mayday! just about the time Hazel Kefauver died.

"Ed doesn't want me anywhere near this," I said. "He's afraid three times won't be a charm." Considering everything else she had said, I almost expected Lucy to take Ed's side, but she shook her head.

"How's he going to stop you? You've obviously already started and come up with some conclusions. And you'll be careful, right? We'll be careful."

I liked that "we." "That's not much to go on."

She smiled her brightest smile. "Okay, let's get more. Let's make a list of all the people who might have wanted Hazel Kefauver dead."

"You're really going to help?"

"Try and stop me."

Lucy left at five, first wiggling into a short black dress and heels that were high enough that if she hadn't already told me, I could have guessed her new client was a man with potential. Shortly afterwards I left in my ratty jeans and work shirt, clutching a list of people to talk to, including the local tile dealer. After all our work, the hardwood floor wasn't worth saving.

Lucy planned to cozy up to Dora, Brownie's housekeeper, and a few people at the courthouse. I was going to follow up on Hazel's work as a volunteer, particularly at the food bank. Then we were going to get together somewhere fun for a girls' night out with murder and margaritas on the table.

I don't like being on the outs with my husband. I decided to make black bean

160

burgers as a dinner treat. We could throw them on the barbecue, play badminton with the girls while the burgers cooked, and try to ignore my involvement in another murder. Tonight when we were alone I would promise to stay on the periphery of the investigation. Ed's a reasonable guy and he's worried about Joe, as well. I thought I could convince him to accept the inevitable, particularly if we went to bed late enough that nobody would bother us.

I swung by Krogers on the way home to pick up buns and an extra can of black beans. I was putting my groceries in the car when I realized that the lush brunette with pigtails who was walking toward the edge of the lot was none other than Keely Henley. I dropped the second bag on the floor and slammed the door, starting after her before I could even figure out what to say.

Keely was taking it slow, and I was puffing like I was training for a marathon. I caught up to her easily.

"Keely?"

She whirled — which couldn't have been easy considering how tight her shorts were — then she grinned. "It's you. Where you been keeping yourself?"

This was a nicer reception than I'd expected, although in all fairness, I *had* more or less saved her life last time we spent a day together.

"I've seen you once or twice, but only in the distance," I said. "How have you been?"

"Me? I'm a different woman. Ever since, well, you know."

I did know. I just nodded.

She moved a little closer. "I got religion again."

Put that way this sounded like something she was being treated for with penicillin or strong mouthwash. But Keely looked so pleased, I was pleased for her.

"I guess you're not back at Don't Go There?"

"No. It don't fit who I am now, you know? I got a new job, at Way Too Cool."

Way Too Cool is an ice cream parlor that opened a few months before in our downtown. Junie and the girls came back with good reviews. I'm waiting for the weather to warm up a little more before I dive into a strawberry sundae. A true Midwesterner, I'm not.

"Do you like your new job?" I asked.

"It's okay. Nobody yells at me or nothin' like that, although come to think of it, I guess sometimes the customers yell. But at least nobody's trying to kill me."

In the scheme of things, this was an

improvement. Still, I thought maybe Keely needed a little help moving into her new role. In her tight yellow shorts and a black halter top cut almost to her navel she looked more like dessert than the person serving it.

Her rosebud lips turned up in a smile, and her big blue eyes were shining. "You doing okay? You up to anything special?"

I considered what to tell her, but before I could say anything she put her hand on my arm. "Do you know what I heard today? The guy who told me don't lie, either. That Brownie Kefauver? You know, the guy you told me was the mayor?"

"He *is* the mayor."

"Uh-huh. Yeah, now I know that. But anyway, his wife dropped dead at Mayday! You know about Mayday!?"

"I was there."

"You were? I was, too, only not there when she, you know, dropped dead like that. I was dishing up ice cream at Way Too Cool's stand. Just chocolate and vanilla, on account of it being too complicated to bring every-thing."

I was nodding hypnotically.

"Anyway, she just keeled over." Keely shut her eyes and dropped her head to her shoulder to illustrate. Then she opened her eyes. "And now they're saying it was murder. Somebody poisoned her."

This certainly made it easier for me to ask Keely questions. But I felt sorry for Brownie. I wondered if there was anybody left in the county who hadn't heard.

"I did know that," I said. "And I remembered that you knew him . . . pretty well."

Now she was nodding.

Encouraged, I went on. "Here's the thing. Some people are going to suspect Brownie of being the one to murder Hazel. And I just wondered what you thought of that. Does it seem possible to you? Knowing what you know?"

"That's easy. He would never do nothing like that."

I was surprised she was so convinced. "Mind telling me why you think so?"

"Because he's one of them guys who can't stand up for himself. You know? And having a wife made it real easy to do whatever he wanted and still get away after he zipped up his pants."

I winced. This was more graphic than I'd hoped for. "So he could use being married as an excuse?"

"Not that he really needed one, you know? I mean nobody was asking him to stay around. At least nobody I knew."

"It sort of sounds like there were a number

of, umm . . . women in his life?" I hesitated. "I'm sorry, Keely, but it would help me to know if you're still, umm . . . involved with him?"

"Another easy question. I got religion, remember? I got morals now. I only sleep with a few guys, and I don't let them pay me, unless they want to take me out to dinner."

"Well, that's . . ." I fished for the right adjective. "Great. Really great."

"It's too bad about Mrs. Kefauver, you know, but I gotta say this. Some people won't be sad she's dead."

I was still congratulating myself on selecting *great* from among its more judgmental competitors and almost missed Keely's last sentence.

"Really, why not?"

"I know her. She's not . . . she wasn't a nice lady."

"It sounds like maybe she found out you and Brownie were, well, you know . . ."

"Nothing like that. No, she used to come into Way Too Cool. That's how I know her. She liked to say she was the mayor's wife, like that entitled her to privileges, that's how I know it was her."

"Was she rude?" This wasn't hard to imagine.

"She was rude, and she was sneaky. See, she used to come in right when I was closing up. She'd sneak in the door just as I was shutting it. Then she'd insist I give her a double scoop of chocolate ice cream, even if I'd already started to clean out the freezer or close out the register. The nerve of her. Course, now she's dead and that takes care of all her nerves, doesn't it?"

I winced again. "I imagine that upset you and the other employees."

"She used to do it when I was alone. Just me. Never when anybody else was around. You know what I think? I think she was one of those secret choco-hallways."

Seconds passed. "Chocoholics?"

"That's what I said. You know, like an addict with his meth or his crank? That was her, only it was chocolate ice cream. And you know what else? After all the trouble she put me to? After me being nice enough to let her in — on account of my boinking her husband before I got morals — anyway, in spite of all that? She never once gave me a tip. She gave me nothing but attitude. So that's why I say not everybody'll be sorry she's gone. I'm going to try, on account of getting religion and loving everybody, but it's not going to be easy."

I was fairly certain this was the longest

speech I'd ever heard Keely give.

"You've been a big help." I held out my hand and she shook it solemnly. "Are you still making birdhouses?" Keely had a surprising talent for constructing birdhouses that looked like houses in town, then selling them to homeowners. I had been quite impressed when I'd seen one in the Kefauver yard.

Of course that was before I realized what else Keely was selling Brownie.

"When I can," she said modestly.

"I'm still waiting for you to make one for the parsonage."

"I might do that. And I'd do it cheap for you."

We said good-bye, and I started back to the van. I hoped the black bean burgers would make up to Ed for the time I'd be spending on Hazel's death in the coming days. With the cat out of the bag — I apologized silently to Moonpie for that imagery — Brownie needed my help more than ever.

8

The funny thing about marriage? You don't always have to see eye to eye. Black bean burgers didn't soften up my husband on Wednesday, but by Friday night he was resigned. He took me out for spaghetti and cheap red wine and asked me to keep Roussos in the loop when I investigated. As apologies go, it was a winner. He didn't even spoil it by asking for a promise.

Late that night, hours after spectacular makeup sex, I sat bolt upright in bed, clutching the spring leaf quilt Junie had made for us, my heart pounding.

Ed sat up, too, and rubbed my back. "Nightmare?"

"Uh-huh." I didn't tell him that my terror had nothing to do with Joe or Hazel. Or even that it hadn't been a dream, but a revelation.

He pulled me gently back against him, wrapped his arms around me, and fell sound asleep. My eyes were wide open.

I had forgotten about the punch bowl.

Actually, it wasn't as simple as that. I had remembered twice, once yesterday and once the day before. But both times I remembered too late in the morning or too early in the evening to find the building empty. I certainly had plenty of opportunities to wash it on Thursday, because I did an obligatory tour of duty in the toy room cleaning and pricing. Today I was slated to work wherever the committee needed me.

Unfortunately, it seemed that everybody in the church was also there on Thursday. The kitchen or the parish hall was filled with people finishing preparations, then yesterday the sale started. I had planned to wait until everybody went home, slink over, and tackle the punch bowl late in the evening. Then Ed appeared to sweep me off my feet and whisk me to Joe's Spaghetti House.

I am a Spaghetti House slut. Now I was paying the price for slavish devotion to cheap Chianti and marinara sauce.

I shifted just enough to see the clock without waking my husband again.

Would anybody report me if I was seen sneaking in or out of the church at four a.m.? I could imagine clutching the punch bowl in my arms, refusing to give it up as local cops surrounded me. This isn't as theatrical as it sounds. The local cops really have very little to do. Our force is sort of a Midwestern version of the one in Mayberry, with Barney Fife and his lone bullet. With nothing more exciting on their schedules, they could turn a punch bowl into an international incident.

I decided to wait for the rosy fingers of dawn or the moment Ed turned over. Whichever came first.

Two hours later, the sun and Ed made their moves, and I slipped out of bed, already exhausted but anxious to end the drama. I pulled on the same jeans and shirt I'd worn last night and tiptoed downstairs, where I added shoes and finger combed my hair. On my way out I stole Ed's keys from the key basket in the kitchen.

Outside the sky was brightening rapidly. I took off for the parish house, and let myself in. I couldn't believe I was actually alone. As dedicated as our rummage sale vigilantes are, they weren't at church yet. I pictured them at home eating hearty breakfasts, doing push-ups and jumping jacks to make it through the first wave of eager bargain hunters.

I plugged the sink and started to fill it.

Then I opened the cupboard under the sink to get the detergent. I'd squirted a healthy amount and was watching it bubble when I realized that I hadn't noticed the box.

I squatted again and pushed things from one side to the other. The wastebasket with its sponges and dishrags was still there. So was a coated wire drainer, a plastic bag stuffed with plastic bags, an extra bottle of detergent, and a trio of assorted cleaning products.

But no box. No punch bowl.

For a moment my life flashed before my eyes. Craft fairs with my mother and sisters. Carefree weeks of forced marches and target practice in my father's survivalist compound. The day I met Ed. The birth of my children.

I wondered when the Women's Society rode me out of town on a rail if I'd be allowed to bring our photo album.

I plopped seat first to the floor and put my head in my hands. Too many early mornings and not enough sleep. I tried to think. The room was torn apart last time I was here. Somebody had been cleaning and organizing.

I opened my eyes and looked under the sink again, since the doors were still open. Did it look different? I wasn't sure, although

I thought that last time there might have been more clutter. Everything now in residence actually belonged there.

January.

January Godfrey is our sexton and, like Junie, something of an old hippy. He is organized and conscientious, and best of all, he minds his business. January isn't paid enough to spend every waking hour reordering our existence, but after he's done with the basics, he has a habit of moving through the buildings, thoroughly cleaning and clearing one room at a time until he finishes and begins all over again.

I rose and saw that the cupboards, which had been torn apart the day I tried to wash the punch bowl, were now cleared of junk, scrubbed clean, and sporting new shelf paper. Best of all, the mismatched glassware was gone. Darn, I'd miss those jelly glasses and Dollar Store tumblers, but I bet they were going to be replaced with something better.

I stood and wiggled my toes to restore circulation. I would feel better when I knew for sure, but I guessed that in the process of cleaning and clearing, January had found the punch bowl, washed it, and returned it to the Women's Society sacred closet. He would have done it carefully and with respect. I had nothing to worry about.

Of course I *would* worry until I asked him. But for now I had to take this on faith.

I pulled the plug and left the building. Like everybody else I needed a good breakfast and a quart of strong coffee before I faced the thundering herd.

Ed knows that working in his church office is impossible during sale week. So although he visits in spurts to lend moral support, he hightails it home to his study immediately afterwards. Today he was torn between coping with the rummage sale mob and his two daughters. Deena and Teddy won, and he agreed to stay home with them while I worked the sale. Junie planned to be gone all day hunting for old quilts, treadle machines, and interesting storage bins at our local antique malls. I just hoped that soon there'd be a real shop where she could install them and begin to decorate.

Two scrambled eggs, whole wheat toast, and a pot of Juan Valdez, and I was ready. By the time I left again the street outside the church was lined with cars, and the sidewalks were growing crowded as people waited for the doors to open. I smiled my apologies as I pushed my way to the head of the line and waited to be snatched inside.

Somebody asked if Tickle Me Elmo had visited our toy room, but I pretended not to hear.

Yvonne McAllister was in charge of assigning tasks, and she stood close to the door with a clipboard and walkie-talkie. After thirty years of more than two packs a day, she recently quit smoking. Now, every time a door slams or somebody gets too close, she snarls. Since Yvonne is a renowned pacifist and a real sweetheart, nobody pays attention, which is the problem with being the peaceful sort on a bad day.

"I've got a job for you," she said, cutting right to the chase. I noticed that her reed-slim body was rapidly plumping out, and I was afraid I knew what she had substituted for cigarette smoke. Yvonne is a vegetarian, too. Unfortunately sugar is more or less a vegetable.

She pointed toward Ed's office, which is right off the reception area leading into the parish hall. "We've got a situation."

"Somebody's holding Norma hostage?" Norma is the church secretary, a perfectly nice woman who talks faster and louder than a Bible salesman. Ed's trying to train her, but I'm pretty sure that something essential is missing between her brain and her vocal cords. Organ donation may be our only salvation.

Yvonne didn't smile. She shifted weight from one foot to the other, then back again, and she stared at me as if I were growing scales.

I stood a little straighter. "I know where Ed keeps his stash of granola bars."

"With chocolate coating?"

"I can check and see."

She looked a little cheerier. "As we were about to close the doors, Brownie Kefauver came in last night, carrying a box of Hazel's things."

"Yikes." This was not what I'd expected to hear. *Situation* at a rummage sale means that somebody forgot to get enough change, or the crew making sloppy joes for the luncheon added too many onions.

"Somebody took pity on him," Yvonne said. "It certainly wasn't me."

"I guessed that."

"They told him we'd be happy to sort and price whatever he had and get it out on the tables today. I guess they thought he was so overwrought, he couldn't *stand* to look at Hazel's belongings because of the memories. Maybe they didn't even realize that the box in his hands wasn't the only one."

"I'm guessing that wasn't the case."

"See for yourself." Yvonne walked over to

Ed's office and threw the door open. She did it with such vigor, it bounced against a bookshelf. I stepped inside and saw that the room was piled with boxes. There must have been twenty or more.

"I think he's removing every trace of Hazel from his life," Yvonne said.

Maybe Yvonne isn't at her best these days, and her outlook is a little different without a screen of cigarette smoke. Maybe like most of the people in our church, she doesn't want a mayor who makes decisions based on whether they benefit his supporters. But I couldn't fault her for her conclusion. Brownie was deleting Hazel from his memory bank.

I needed to have a little talk with Brownie about the appearance of guilt. Sooner rather than later.

I crossed the room and unfolded the flaps on the closest box to reveal a stack of badly folded skirts. "What would you like me to do?"

"Ed's office is the only room in the building that's not being used for the sale. But I don't feel comfortable letting just anybody else inside. Will you go through these?"

I felt like a kid in a candy shop. And I was hopeful that the best chocolate was hiding somewhere out of sight. "Is it just clothes?"

"Handbags, shoes, coats. I think that little turd went through her closet and threw everything in these boxes."

I ignored the *turd* and my own disappointment. "I'll find those granola bars. Right away."

"I would appreciate it."

"And I'll go through the boxes as fast as I can and get the stuff to the right tables."

"You do that. I'll make sure nobody bothers you."

I wasn't sure that was necessary. I'd hoped for the contents of desk drawers and filing cabinets. But maybe I'd get an idea or two about the woman from handling her things. Besides, even this was better than pumping up basketballs and dressing Bratz dolls.

If I had only a tenth of the psychic powers Junie claims for herself, I could easily figure out who murdered Hazel Kefauver. In the hour it took me to sort the contents of the boxes, I probably handled everything Hazel had worn in the past decade. Unfortunately, I didn't get a single vibe about who might have poisoned her, but I did learn a lot about the woman.

Had Hazel been invited to shoot pheasants in the Cornwall countryside, she certainly had the clothes. She liked good quality wools and tweeds, in neutral or muted colors. She preferred long sleeves, skirts well below her knees, and serviceable underwear. Yes, Brownie had also gifted us with Hazel's bras and panties. What a guy.

Most of the clothing was well used. I doubted she rarely treated herself to impulse buys. In her favor, she seemed to live by the standards she demanded of others. No waste in Hazel's closet. Nor had she cared if a garment suited her. Clearly vanity was never an issue.

She also took care of her things. Despite Brownie's sloppy packing, I could see the clothes were neatly pressed. There was a faint medicinal odor to the wool, perhaps some sort of herbal sachet to keep moths away. And just a hint of tobacco smoke — which lent credence to that rumor I'd heard.

The handbags and belts were more of the same. Good quality but utilitarian, wearing down at the edges. Inside the handbags, there was nothing of interest, not even tissues or gum wrappers. I wondered if Brownie had emptied them or if Hazel meticulously removed every item when she changed to a different style. I was betting Brownie had checked them for cash.

Yvonne hadn't realized just how much Brownie wanted Hazel out of his bedroom.

Not only did we have the wardrobe, we had the costume jewelry, the library, and the knickknacks. The first two took up the smallest box. There was little jewelry. Brownie had probably taken the good stuff to the pawn shop, and given us what he couldn't sell. There were a few practical watches, a couple of chains and pendants, a brooch or two. Nothing that would make anybody draw an extra breath at the jewelry table.

The books were more interesting. Self-help, mostly, with titles like *Free Your Inner Superhero, Even the Scarecrow Had a Brain*, and my personal favorite, *Ruthless or Toothless: You Decide.*

I could understand why Brownie was in such a hurry to get rid of the books. I don't think they were meant to be Hazel's nightly reading. I pictured her standing over Brownie as he finished his bedtime quota.

The knickknacks were in the last box. I was a bit surprised Hazel had collected china commemorating events in the life of the British royal family. Princess Margaret and Princess Diana on their wedding days, the queen staring at the world from a china beaker. Maybe Hazel had thought of herself as one of the Windsors, exiled to dismal little Emerald Springs, where no one knew how to make a proper curtsy. What surprised me more was that Brownie included the china in the boxes along with everything else. I doubted any of it was a priceless collectible, but had he sold these pieces he might have made enough to have his bedroom repainted a color Hazel had despised.

I put that box to one side, debating how to handle it. Since I wasn't sure that Brownie was now — or had ever been — in his right mind, I felt an urge to protect him. I decided to consult with Fern Booth, who was in charge of Aunt Alice's Attic, where all dishes and collectibles were sold. That seemed to be the right thing to do. And heck, it couldn't hurt my standing with the Tri-C Critics to let Fern make the decision whether to give the box back to Brownie or sell the contents and run with the money.

I was reboxing clothing to carry it to the appropriate tables when I realized I hadn't checked pockets. Today women's clothing is all about slim lines, so pockets are often excluded. But nothing here was right off the runway, and there were pockets galore. I decided to check a few to see if she was a pocket stuffer.

She was.

Thirty minutes later I had built several small mounds on Ed's desk. Sixty-four dollars in small bills and change. Keys. Shopping lists and receipts. A gold bracelet with a broken clasp. A compact and comb and an assortment of other items I didn't have time to catalogue. I could feel time ticking away, and I knew if I didn't get the clothing out to the appropriate tables, it had no chance at all of a new life in someone else's closet. Frankly I didn't think it had much chance anyway.

I rummaged through Ed's desk and found a padded envelope. I swept everything except the money inside, sealed it, and stuck it in a desk drawer with a note scrawled across it. I would go through the envelope later and figure out what to do with everything. Some of it, like the bracelet, should go back to Brownie. The rest could probably be tossed.

I put the money in my wallet because it would make the perfect excuse to lecture him on the danger of making his feelings about Hazel so abundantly clear just days after her death.

I was carrying the box of skirts into the social hall when I saw Maura in the children's chapel where the garden shop was set up. Still lugging the skirts, I caught her checking the root system on an African violet.

"That's a pretty one, isn't it?" I said. "I think it's one of May Frankel's. She has a wonderful collection."

"I have the perfect window. Just enough light. I've been looking for the right plant."

I lowered my voice. "How are you doing?"

"Getting along. I have something for you, but I didn't think to bring it. I'm so busy . . ." She looked dejected. "I never realized just how much Joe did now that I'm doing everything alone."

If Joe returned, I wondered if he would be more appreciated at home. Of course I had no real way of knowing what the situation was before he left. Maybe Maura routinely stuffed him with homemade pies and gratitude, but somehow, I didn't think so.

"I'll stop by tomorrow and pick it up if I can," I said, curious to know what she had unearthed.

"You look like you could use some help." She nodded to the box.

Since it was now more or less my job to help Maura cope, I weighed the alternatives. If she helped me deliver the boxes, that might begin to integrate her into the life of the church and make her feel part of the community. On the other hand, this *was* the rummage sale. Volunteers had been chewed up and spit out for less. Tyler needed at least one parent at home.

I nodded my thanks. "I appreciate the offer, but you've got enough on your plate. Just stay and enjoy. I can take care of this."

She looked grateful, but I gave her points for trying. I was beginning to think Maura had potential.

We said good-bye and I finally got rid of the box. In fact, except for the china, I got rid of all of them in the next fifteen minutes.

I was just about to take the china upstairs to Aunt Alice's Attic when I saw January Godfrey going outside for a smoke. I decided to follow him and make sure my punch bowl theory was correct.

I've never been able to figure out how old our sexton is. He has the lithe body of a runner, although considering the cigarettes, it's doubtful he has the lungs. His long hair is white, but his face is unlined. He can converse knowledgeably on any topic and has given Ed more than a few ideas for sermons.

As for how long he's been at the church? Well, a lot longer than we have. In fact, I think January has outlasted half a dozen ministers. Since his memory for church history is extraordinary, January's the one we go to when we need information about something that happened in the past. If

January saw it or heard about it, then he'll remember every detail.

I found him in the bushes, on the far side of the parking lot from the parsonage, a cigarette perfuming the air. He was wearing his signature faded jeans and T-shirt. Today the shirt was a souvenir from the Rolling Stones Steel Wheels Tour of 1989. As January's shirts go, this one is practically brand-new.

January looked too comfortable. I wanted to shake him and demand he tell me about the punch bowl, but he's a hang-loose guy, and I knew I had to ease into it.

I managed a strained smile. "How's it going? Are you ready to quit your job yet?"

He laughed. "Don't let them get to you."

"They'll all turn back into pumpkins at the stroke of midnight. I've seen it happen."

We chatted a little. He has a deep voice that makes everything he says sound important. Most of it is.

I finally got down to business. "January, Sally Berrigan borrowed the church punch bowl for Mayday! and it was splattered with chocolate. She asked me to wash it and put it back . . ." I told him the rest of the story, trying not to make myself sound like a pathetic wuss.

He chuckled. "What could Fern Booth

have done to you, Aggie?"

"I didn't want to find out."

"Well, did you get it washed? Don't leave me hanging."

This was not what I wanted to hear. "No! It disappeared. I was hoping you'd washed it and put it back when you cleared out the kitchen."

"I didn't clear out the kitchen."

I slapped my hands across my chest, more or less the way an undertaker might place them in a casket. "Don't tell me that."

"Some of the proceeds from the rummage sale are supposed to go toward replacing the old glasses. The committee boxed them for the rummage sale and ordered new ones. You'll like them."

"January, you didn't find the box under the sink with the punch bowl in it?"

"Too bad, huh? I think I might have saved you a lot of trouble."

Somebody had found it. The punch bowl was no longer there.

My brain was racing frantically. "Who was on the kitchen committee, do you know?"

"Oh, you're not going to like this."

He recited the list, and he was right, I didn't. Fern Booth was at the top, and Ida Bere was right behind her. The day I'd seen them coming up the walk? Probably to box

185

up the old glasses for the sale.

I tried to piece together my future. "Okay. Then one of them probably found it and washed it, and it's back where it belongs. They'll confront Sally about this the moment she gets back, and she'll tell them the last time she saw the punch bowl, I was carrying it to my car after Mayday!"

"Then you can tell them what happened, Aggie. Get a grip, okay? We'll go look in the Society's closet. I've got keys. You'll see it's fine, and if it ever comes up in conversation you can throw yourself on their mercy."

"January, how long have you been here?" I demanded.

"Okay, it *will* come up. But the only thing you did was store it under the sink until you could get around to washing it. You can leave out the part about seeing Fern and running off with your tail between your legs like a little sissy."

"I'm a middle child. I try to make everybody love me. And besides, you're supposed to give me support and comfort." I looked down at his hand. The cigarette was burning away, but the only thing he'd done since I arrived was flip the ash on the ground and grind it into the dirt with his foot. He'd never once lifted it to his mouth.

"Why aren't you smoking that?" I asked.

"I haven't smoked a cigarette for ten years."

"You just let them burn to ash?"

"I'm not ready to go cold turkey."

"You come out here to escape, don't you? You time these breaks when you have to get out of the building."

"I take more of them since Norma Beet became secretary."

"Maybe I'll take up cigarette holding, too."

"Better than taking up target practice." He threw the cigarette on the ground and mashed it with his foot. Then he picked up the butt, like the good guy he is, and put it in his pocket.

"Let's go check that closet," he said.

We went in through the back way. I smiled at passersby and pretended that standing over January as he opened the sacred Women's Society closet was no big deal. But it *was* a big deal. Because although the sterling silver tea and coffee service was there, and the serving platter that more or less matched the punch bowl was there, and everything else that belonged there was *there,* the punch bowl was not.

"Holy smokes." I leaned against the wall a moment, and closed my eyes.

January hovered over me, shielding me from view. "You say it was in a box, right?"

"Uh-huh."

"I bet somebody took it out and set it on the counter without opening it. Maybe it got mixed up with the boxes of glasses they're selling."

My eyelids flew open. "You think so? But somebody would have opened it by now and seen what was in it."

"If I were you, I'd trot right up to Aunt Alice's Attic and see."

"What, and tell Fern Booth how badly I screwed up?"

In fairness to January, he only clucked like a chicken twice. "Just peek in the boxes, if any are left."

I remembered Hazel's china collection. I had planned to carry it up there anyway. I'd be greeted with smiles. Maybe they'd last long enough for me to poke around a little.

"If you hear screaming from the second floor?" I said.

"I'll bring the fire extinguisher. You jump to one side when I aim it in their direction."

I patted him on the arm and went to fetch the collection of royal faces gracing my husband's study.

Upstairs I tiptoed past the toy room, terrified I'd be reeled in to restring tennis rackets. But the toys seemed to be doing fine without me. In fact, no one even seemed to notice I *wasn't* there. I wondered how my massive contribution could so quickly have been forgotten.

Aunt Alice's Attic took up the largest religious education room on the second floor. Half a dozen people milled around under the hawkeyed gaze of Fern Booth. Four tables were set up with china and glassware. Another four had what were loosely termed *collectibles.* Pottery from airport gift shops, a few leather-bound books, a Wedgwood teapot with a cracked spout, packages of lace-trimmed handkerchiefs, a basket with embroidered hand towels and crocheted doilies. The list went on.

I saw immediately there were no chocolate-coated punch bowls. I didn't know how to feel.

Fern saw me and started in my direction. I swallowed. She looked angry, but she often does. I told myself not to run.

"Isn't it a little late to be bringing donations?" she demanded.

Fern has salt-and-pepper hair cut with geometric precision around a face as square as the trapdoor of a gallows. I think she's training her eyebrows to meet in the middle to perfect a permanent scowl. But she really doesn't need that extra touch.

189

I forced a smile. "I'm sorry, but these just came in last night and actually, there's something of a problem with them. I came for your advice."

If possible, she looked even more suspicious. This time I couldn't blame her. I'd never asked for advice before and probably wouldn't again.

I explained the situation, setting the box on the nearest table as I did and opening the flap so she could see what we had.

"Do you think we should sell them or give them back?" I practiced my most ingratiating voice. "I'll let you decide."

She took moments either to consider or crank up her attack. But when she spoke, she almost sounded pleasant. "I think you'd better ask the mayor. Then, if he says he still doesn't want them, we'll put them in the Society closet and keep them for the sale next year. Do a little advertising in the newsletter so we get the best price."

Her solution was not only kind, it was sensible. I didn't know what to say. This was a new side of Fern.

"You don't agree?" She more or less bellowed the words.

I jumped. "No, I agree. That's exactly what we should do."

"Anything else?"

Here she was, all buttered up, or as close as I was ever going to get. I just couldn't ask her about the punch bowl. I could not spoil the first pleasant moment we'd experienced together.

So I hedged, or beat around the bush, which sounds like a double affront to gardeners everywhere. "Just wondering how you're doing up here. Did you get anything great to sell this year?"

"Just the usual." Her tone changed to something less cordial. "Why? Are you looking for something for the parsonage? Did we forget something?"

At the accusation, I felt grounded again, back in familiar territory. I was almost grateful. "Nope, we're doing fine. I love collectibles, that's all."

"Well, we've done well enough here. The money will help us buy that new glassware."

"January told me about that. Sounds like such a good idea." I counted my heartbeats and made myself wait until ten had thundered by. "What did you do with all the old glasses?"

"We boxed them up. Every single box was sold."

"Wow, just like that, huh? How did you find room in here once you set all those glasses out on the table?"

"We couldn't do that. Do you see enough room? We just taped up the boxes and sold them that way. We stacked them over by the door and left one open so people could see what was inside. But we didn't want anybody picking through each box and switching glasses around, not for the price we were giving them. Why?"

"Oh, I just wondered who needed entire boxes of glasses."

"Mabyn bought a couple of boxes. And Dolly Purcell bought one for her grandson's new apartment." She narrowed her eyes. "Aren't there enough glasses in the parsonage? Or maybe you think you have too *many?*"

"We have exactly the right amount. To the glass. To the ounce."

"Well, you should have gotten here sooner if you needed more or better."

I should have gotten here sooner, all right, because I was pretty sure the mystery of the missing punch bowl was at least partly solved. I wondered who had bought the box with the punch bowl inside, thinking they had just gotten a bargain on mismatched tumblers and juice glasses? If that person was a member of the church, I was pretty sure she would realize the mistake, bring it back, and explain what had happened.

But if she wasn't? All bets were off.

"I'll let you know what the mayor says about this china," I told Fern. "Thanks for your advice."

She went back to frowning at customers, and I went home to see how much a one way ticket to Papua New Guinea would cost. I hoped there was enough money in our checking account for Ed and the girls to come with me.

I had one other choice. In addition to finding Joe Wagner and discovering who had poisoned Hazel Kefauver, I could find the missing punch bowl. If I decided against New Guinea, I needed to hang out a shingle.

9

The Consolidated Community Church is a multiple-choice congregation. When the time comes to seek a new minister, the search committee investigates candidates from several denominations for a wider pool of possibilities. Luckily for them Ed wanted a quiet church in a quiet place and the rest is history. He's the third Unitarian-Universalist they've called in their long history, but they're still getting used to the idea of ministers who prefer asking questions to answering them.

Unusual or not, Ed's sermons have become increasingly popular. Sundays are anything but quiet at Tri-C these days. Last month the board voted to begin holding two morning services in order to fit everyone inside our historic but limited building. Now the day starts with choir practice, then first service and religious education for the children, a break for social hour, and a sermon discussion upstairs in our parish house for members who prefer arguing to chatting about the weather or the state of the union in our social hall.

Another social hour follows the second service, with another discussion and usually an informal meeting in the children's chapel for anyone interested in finding out more about the church.

This Sunday, in addition to everything else, we had a bag sale of rummage leftovers that began at noon. When Ed finally got home, he would be weary enough that I could tie him in a knot and hang him in the coat closet.

By the time I wound my way through the first social hour, the second service, and a stint cashiering for bag day, I was nearly as tired. But I wasn't so tired that I couldn't stalk my prey. I was busy all morning developing a list of punch bowl suspects. First I captured Dolly Purcell, an eighty-something member of the Women's Society, and pinned her to the wall.

Okay, perhaps not. But I did engage her in scintillating conversation of the James Bond sort.

Okay, perhaps not.

What I did instead was ask Dolly if she bought anything exciting at the sale. She was one of two names Fern had given me, and like all optimists I hoped Dolly was going to deliver. Unfortunately this was not to be. She told me all about the box of glasses she gave her grandson Paul, and how she and Paul stacked them in his cabinets together. Strike one.

I did get the names of another member who also purchased glasses. Dolly remembered because she almost lost her own box to none other than Ida Bere, who wanted two for herself. She claimed Ida tried to persuade her to give up her box because Ida planned to use the glasses for meetings of a new organization she had formed to protest the release of butterflies at weddings and other special occasions.

I really didn't want to know more, but I thanked Dolly and went in search of Ida. In Ida's defense, she is worried about all sorts of things that really matter. War, poverty, hatred, discrimination. I bet when she was born sixty or so years ago, she emerged carrying a sign demanding better pay for hospital employees. I'm sure the delivery room nurses were grateful for her intervention.

Anyway, Ida, who has lent her compact body and steely gaze to many a cause, is also prone to go out on the limb on a moment's notice. I didn't know if this was one of those causes, but I vowed to stay as far away from it as I could.

I saw Ida just as she was leaving. Since it's a little hard to detain somebody in our doorway at lunchtime, I caught up with her outside.

"Ida . . ." I sprinted beside her to match her determined stride. "The rummage sale's looking like a real success. I know you worked hard on it."

She glanced at me, but her mind was elsewhere, most likely in Mexico with the monarchs. She sped up, so I sped up, too.

"The sale's always hard work," she said. "None of this comes easily."

"True, but it's a great way to build a community." Although frankly, I wasn't quite sure the rummage sale was meeting that goal.

"There won't be a community of *any* sort unless this world of ours gets down to business and fixes the things that are wrong."

I wanted to tell Ida to take a deep breath, but I was pretty sure if I did she would complain about air pollution, which would lead to a discussion of ozone depletion and global warming. All to be feared and addressed, of course, but on a lovely Sunday morning I was hoping for a brief reprieve.

"Do you have any tips for new rummage salers?" I asked.

"Like what?"

I celebrated my first piece of luck. She'd practically invited me to ask questions. "Tips on how to organize donations. For instance, did you find anything unusual that was hard to place?"

"What do you mean unusual?"

"I heard you and Fern cleaned out the cupboards in the kitchen. Was it hard to figure out what to do with everything?"

"No, I just wish I'd grabbed a couple of boxes of those glasses right off the bat. Of course that wouldn't have been fair."

I broke in before she told me why she needed them. "Oh, you didn't get any?"

"Just one box. I needed more. I got half juice glasses. And I needed bigger glasses." Then, just as I was striking her off my list of suspects, she got her revenge.

For the next ten minutes I was forced to stand in the parking lot while Ida regaled me with stories of butterfly woes all the way from the tropical rain forest to Canada. By the time I got home, I was so depressed I wasn't sure the punch bowl or anything else really mattered.

Half an hour later Junie came home from the sale with six brown bags stuffed with other people's junk and my two daughters. She peeled me off the sofa, and when I told her what was wrong, she made tea plus an order for three butterfly bushes for her new backyard and two for ours. Junie always knows how to make the world a better place.

Ed arrived with the padded envelope I'd left in his drawer and dropped it on the counter for me. I ladled vegetable soup from my slow cooker, made sure Ed chewed and swallowed, and put him to bed for a nap. While I tidied up I checked Ida and Dolly off my mental list, put a star next to Mabyn's name, and added another parishioner from whom Ida had not been able to wheedle a box of glasses.

I had promised Lucy I'd meet her at the Victorian at two to see what Hank and his crew were doing. When we hired Closeur Contracting, Hank consulted his calendar and promised to spend this entire weekend working at the house. Three or four men scrambling to finish a job can do an amazing amount. By now I was hoping they had finished the island, roughed in the new kitchen, tiled the bathroom, and started patching the walls and ceilings upstairs where demolition had taken place.

In work clothes I took off for the Victorian. I was alone since the girls and Junie were going to spend the afternoon cutting up fabric she'd bought at the sale. She had promised to teach the girls how to make something called penny rugs. Afraid of another long explanation, albeit a cheerier one, I'd asked them to surprise me and escaped.

On the way I drove by the Kefauver residence. I was running late, but if I could find Brownie, I had time for a terse lecture on the fine art of staying out of jail. I halfway expected to find a priest in the midst of an exorcism ritual. But there were no vehicles in the driveway, including the Kefauver Lincoln, and no lights visible from the street. I put Brownie on my to-do list for tomorrow.

When I arrived Lucy was standing in the middle of the downstairs. Sadly, she was the sole occupant. Hank and his guys were nowhere in sight.

Before I could work up to a tantrum, Lucy put a finger to her lips. "Not a word. You're going to love what they've done."

Try cranking down from an undelivered tirade. Moments passed before I could breathe. "They were here?"

"Not when I got here a little while ago, but obviously they've been here this week-end. Look at the island." She stepped to one side, and I saw it was finished. And what a beauty it was. In fact Closeur Contracting had gone the extra mile on trim. This was high-quality custom cabinetry.

"Oh, it's wonderful," I moved closer so I could stroke the varnished oak and open the drawers, which glided effortlessly. "Somebody really knows what he's doing."

"And they measured and marked for shelves on the walls. Look."

Again, I was impressed. The shelves were actually going to go on the walls where they belonged. Not in the bathroom. Not inside the fireplace. And somebody had thought to use a level so that bolts of fabric would remain upright.

"I can almost see fabric here." For the first time in my imagination the place began to look like a quilt shop.

"Let's check out the second floor. We don't have a lot of time alone."

"You're meeting some man here? It's the guy you were dressing up for on Friday, isn't it? You're going to spread a blanket in front of the fireplace and open a bottle of some vintage I've never even heard of. You have truffles in your purse. And Camembert."

"At what point in your marriage did you start indulging in these fantasies about the lives of other women?"

"Hey, I love my life. It's just that I love yours, too."

"You love what you *think* my life is. It's not as much fun as your imagination. There's a reason most of the guys I meet aren't married."

"I could look around for you. I've done pretty well by my sisters." Both Vel and Sid were in touch with men they had met in Emerald Springs after their visit over the Christmas holidays. I didn't know what the outcome would be, but I still patted myself on the back.

"With my luck, you'd find me some handy psychopath," Lucy said. "You're a wacko killer magnet."

"No fair. You've been with me every step of the way. If you hadn't helped me catch them, those guys would still be roaming the streets."

"Well, there are plenty more where *they* came from, so stay out of my love life." She started toward the stairs as I began a mental list of men to introduce her to.

"There's no *guy* coming," Lucy said halfway up, "but I ran into Joe Wagner's secretary Cilla Hunter. Have you met her?"

I told her I hadn't had time to do any investigating at Helping Hands.

"Well, she told me something interesting

that I thought you ought to hear."

"Luce, do you know everybody in Emerald Springs?"

"Close enough."

I wondered what Cilla Hunter had to say. Now I wished I had told Lucy the truth about Joe.

"Will you look at this?" Lucy stopped, and both of us admired what had been done.

The upstairs was finally beginning to look like an apartment. We walked through the new doorway that had been framed in at the top of the stairs. Traces of the old walls had almost vanished, and new walls were taking shape. The two bedrooms that had been combined to make a living area looked as if they had always been configured that way. What would soon be a kitchen at the far end, open to the rest of the room, was neatly framed in, and the counter that separated it from the living area was exactly the right height. There was room for a small table by the closest window, which looked over neighboring yards. Hank or one of his men had even thought to write measurements for the appliances and cabinets on the walls so Lucy and I could make our order immediately. Best of all, the measurements looked like standard sizes. That would speed things up enormously.

"Winners. We actually chose winners." I punched Lucy on the arm. "We're good, girl. Really, really good."

"Do you think they're working at night? They've done so much, and they aren't here."

"Who cares? They're doing the job. I want to check the bathroom."

The bathroom floor was still gouged wood, but the tile I'd picked had been delivered and was sitting in the middle of the room. We set a few squares on the floor to see how it would look and agreed it was exactly what Junie had asked for.

The doorbell rang, and reluctantly we both went downstairs. I hoped the visitor was Hank Closeur so I could tell him how pleased I was. But a tall, striking woman about our age stood on the porch. Her dark hair was cut boyishly short, scraped back from a freckled face, but in tight jeans and a red babydoll camisole she had a figure no one would mistake for anything but a woman's. The subtle scent of jasmine wafting in my direction confirmed it.

Lucy introduced us. Cilla Hunter had a handshake that felt like the beginning of an arm wrestling match. We invited her in and did the thirty-second tour, but clearly, she hadn't come to discuss architecture.

I saw no reason to stand around and make awkward conversation when I could be pumping Cilla for information about Hazel and the food bank. I suggested we sit on the back porch stoop and enjoy the day. We walked through what had been the kitchen and grabbed soft drinks from the old refrigerator as we passed.

Outside we settled ourselves against the railing or leaned back against the steps. I looked over what would be Junie's garden and yearned for the butterfly bushes to arrive. I wondered what Hank would charge to build a covered porch here so she could enjoy her garden on rainy days, too.

"Cilla, tell Aggie what you told me today," Lucy said.

Cilla popped the tab on her Dr. Pepper and more or less poured it down her throat. Everything about this woman seemed larger than life. I liked her already.

"I don't want this going any further," she warned when the can was half empty.

"You can trust Aggie. And she knows the Wagners. She and Joe are friends."

I had expected this conversation to be about Hazel. I was surprised, but not as surprised as when she began to speak.

"I think Joe Wagner's in trouble. Either that or he's missing."

I looked at Lucy, who raised one delicate auburn brow.

I opened my Sprite and managed to spray my blouse. "What makes you think so?"

"The story that's going around says Joe's off taking care of his dying mother. Only I happen to know he's an orphan. He told me once he doesn't have any family at all. I know I remember it right. It seemed so sad."

"Okay." I nodded. "So what do you think's going on?"

"I don't know, but I wonder if we ought to go to the police. Mrs. Kefauver's dead. Maybe something terrible's happened to Joe, too."

"Or maybe he's just taking some time off."

"Aggie, if that's the truth, why would his wife lie about this?" Lucy demanded. "Unless maybe she had something to do with his disappearance."

"Maura?" I nearly blew Sprite out my nostrils. Cilla helpfully pounded me on the back.

"Well, she's spreading lies," Lucy said when I was breathing naturally again.

I could see Cilla going to the police. She struck me as someone who got things done. If she thought Joe was in trouble, she would march right up to the station and make sure she was heard. I had to level with her, at least a little.

"Joe *is* missing," I said. "Maura called Ed last weekend when we were in New York. Joe was supposed to be at a meeting there, but he never came home."

"Funds for Food," Cilla said in her musical alto. "He goes every month."

I didn't contradict her. Nothing would be gained by telling the whole truth.

"We were able to trace him to a club he'd visited," I told them. "People there remembered him and said he wasn't feeling well and left. Nobody saw him afterwards. But he did call Maura. The problem is he used his cell phone and the call was breaking up. She doesn't know what he said, and there haven't been more calls."

"And she hasn't phoned the police?" Cilla said. "She probably doesn't know how to dial the damned phone!"

Since I'd thought something like that last weekend, I couldn't fault Cilla, but I did have to defend Maura.

"Look, she's trying to protect Joe. That's all. She's afraid if she tells the truth, that he vanished right before the most important work event of the year, his job won't be waiting when he returns. She thinks he may have had something of a breakdown and needs some time to recover." I caught Cilla's eye. "Does that sound reasonable?"

She considered. "Maybe."

"Have things been tough at work? Maura said he was working late a lot." I chewed over the next sentence, but in the end, I decided I had to ask. "Or were things tough at home? That you know of anyway?"

"Joe never talked about home. Oh, he talked about Tyler a lot. He's so proud of that kid, but he never said anything much about Maura or what their life was like." She took another swig. "Joe's the best guy in the world. He's 100 percent responsible. I just can't see him walking away on the weekend of Mayday! Something's happened to him. I just know it."

Here was the angst, the fear that was missing when we talked to Maura. Cilla was clearly more emotionally involved with Joe than his own wife. I know people react differently, express themselves differently, but this seemed like a clear signal that Cilla was too fond of her boss and that Joe's marriage hadn't been a bed of roses. Either he and Maura were so estranged she hardly missed him, or she was simply not a woman who felt much for anyone. I was betting on the first, because the Maura who had begun to emerge in our last encounters was a warmer, smarter Maura than I had known before.

Lucy took her turn as detective. "How about work?"

"Work's been a bear." Cilla slapped her empty can on the step beside her. "Hazel Kefauver — may she rest in peace and never wake up — was making it impossible to get anything done. She was always after him about something. Electing that woman chairman of the board was the worst thing that ever happened to us. She was trying to single-handedly dismantle everything Joe worked so hard to build. He had to work extra hours just to keep her at bay."

There was an edge to Cilla's voice that was sharp enough to amputate a limb. No question Hazel Kefauver had been on her personal hit list.

"What kind of things did they fight about?" I asked.

"Everything. Nutrition. Donations. Policy. Hazel had strong opinions about everything. She more or less wanted the food bank to be there for emergencies only. She thought if a family came in more than once or twice, then it was clear they weren't working to help themselves and ought to be cut off. And when people did deserve food, she wanted them to eat the way she dictated. She said if they were hungry enough . . ." She didn't finish and didn't have to.

I remembered a story I'd heard about donations of powdered milk to an African village. Milk hadn't been part of a normal diet, so the villagers had used it to whitewash their huts. I didn't know if this was true, but it was a powerful example of how not to help others.

"The best way to make a difference is to let the people who need the help make the decisions," I said. "And I bet your clients aren't voting for wheatgrass juice."

"Our clients aren't *voting.* Hazel scared away two men who were representing the homeless on the board. Or I should say she angered them so much they left in protest. Joe was furious. I've never seen him that angry."

I smashed my empty can, and both women jumped. "When was that?"

"Not long ago. The last board meeting." Cilla counted. "Two weeks?"

"Was the feeling mutual?" I rubbed my balled fist on the leg of my jeans. I'd enjoyed smashing the can, but I was paying the price. "Did Hazel dislike Joe as much as he seems to have disliked her?"

"Hazer — that's what we called her when she wasn't around. The Old Hazer, may she rot in hell. Anyway, Hazer wanted Joe out of there. She was always snooping in his office when he wasn't around. I couldn't really kick her out, but I made sure she knew I was watching. I caught her once sitting at my desk going through his papers, and I told her if anything turned up missing I would report her, even if she fired me. But she had keys to the building, so God knows how many times she was there when I wasn't. Way too often things were disturbed on my desk."

"This wasn't a good job situation," Lucy said. "Poor Joe Wagner."

"I don't think he was happy." Cilla looked at me. "And I don't mean just because of Hazer. I don't think he was happy at home. There, I've said it, and I'll say this, too" — her eyes glistened suspiciously — "She doesn't deserve Joe. Maura, I mean. He's something special, and he needs somebody who realizes it."

I didn't look at Lucy, but I knew what she was thinking. That's what happens when you have a best friend, even when you're not in high school anymore.

Both Lucy and I know the sounds of a woman hopelessly in love. Cher expresses it perfectly in "Song for the Lonely." But for all kinds of reasons, I wasn't going to sing that now.

211

■ ■ ■ ■

I stopped by the Wagners' on the way home. The dolls were dressed as if they were on safari, with the male doll carrying a butterfly net. I hoped Ida Bere didn't live in the Village.

Maura let me in and led me to the kitchen. The house smelled peachy today; every surface glistened. I wondered if she ever slept.

Tyler was chatting nearby, and when I didn't hear another voice, I realized he was probably on the telephone. I'm still young enough to remember having similar conversations at his age. *Uh-huh. Not really. You think? So how come?* I recognized Tyler's end of the conversation as the standard guy responses. I was pretty sure there was a girl on the other end doing most of the work.

I was afraid I knew which girl it was, too. My fingers itched to turn on my cell phone and call home to see if our line was busy. But the possibility I might accidentally dial the White House was the cure I needed.

"I can't stay," I told Maura, who was wearing sunny daffodil gold, "but you said you had something you wanted to give me?"

"That's right. I'll get it."

I didn't sit, since I really did want to get home and check on my daughters. Okay, just check on one, but boy, did I want to do that immediately.

Something was baking in the oven and I peeked through the door. I hoped it wasn't something that was going to send poor Tyler's blood sugar through the roof.

She came back carrying a manila folder and held it out to me. "I did what you asked. I searched through Joseph's papers to see if there were any bills or receipts that might lead to finding him. But he must pay the bills and file them at work, and I didn't find a single receipt that wasn't for groceries or Tyler's insulin."

I took the folder. "So what's this?"

"I don't know. It's a bunch of newspaper clippings. I found them on the top shelf on his side of the closet, in a shoe box where his boots are supposed to be. Don't you think that's odd?"

I leafed through the yellowing newsprint, but at first glance nothing jumped out at me. There seemed to be a variety of stories, and a couple of ads. I did note that they had been clipped in such a way that I couldn't tell what newspaper or newspapers they had come from.

"May I take these home and check

through them?"

"Of course, but bring them back. I don't want Joe to know I was snooping."

"Um, Maura, if you weren't snooping, *that* would be worth keeping from him. He's missing. Looking for him isn't a bad thing."

"I suppose." Her eyes were sad. Her lips actually drooped. "This is so hard. I don't know what I should do and what I should wait for *him* to do. Tyler reminded me he always goes to camp in August. It's a special camp for diabetic kids. Anyway, I know a lot of paperwork has to be filled out. Only I don't know where it is, or where Joseph keeps Tyler's medical records. When he comes back I'm going to give him a piece of my mind."

"Well, that makes sense. You're entitled." I looked up. "Can you call the camp and ask how far along the application is?"

"And what do I say about Joseph?"

"Just tell them he asked you to take over."

"I guess I could." She hesitated. "And I could call the doctor and ask for copies of Tyler's records, too."

I patted her arm. "You have to be proactive. Do anything you can, and if Joe complains when he gets back, sock him."

She giggled, and I felt pleased I'd been the cause. I guess it's nice to be needed.

"If I'm going to be proactive, I have a favor to ask you," Maura said.

I wasn't sure I liked that as much as the giggle. "If I can help, I will."

"I'm worried something's going to happen to Tyler at school when I'm not at home to catch the call. When Joseph's here, it's not a problem. The school calls him, and if he's out, they call me. But now I need backup. Plus if I run into a problem some afternoon and can't be here when Tyler's expected, somebody needs to make sure he tests and does his shots. You wouldn't have to do them, you would just have to be sure they got done."

"So you'd like me to be available?"

"Would you mind, Aggie? I have friends, but they aren't the sort of people I can ask. They're just into other things. I'd like you to have our key, just to be safe."

Despite myself, I was flattered. "I can do that. I'll be glad to help."

"If you're going to help me, then I need to help you, don't I? That's the way this works."

I was doubly proud of her. "Let's exchange house keys. If I run into an emergency and my girls need help, I can call you."

Okay, so I wasn't as trusting as I sounded. For a variety of reasons I felt completely safe doing this. One, I had both Junie and Ed as backup. Plus Lucy, and mothers of Deena and Teddy's friends and close friends from church. My girls were never going to feel abandoned, and Maura was never going to be called on to take responsibility for them.

Two, half the people in the church already seemed to have parsonage keys. Once I walked in my own house to find an older man who didn't look familiar checking our furnace. Apparently he'd been watching over it for years and felt it was his right to walk right in anytime he wanted to change the filters. I've been trying to convince Ed to change the locks.

"I like that." Maura smiled with real warmth. "Let me get you a front door key."

While she was gone I fished in my purse for my own key. I could put one of our spares on my chain when I got home. Or I could ask furnace guy to fork his over.

She returned with a key chained to a hand-beaded elephant. The beads were bright red and blue, and I guessed that Maura had taken an entire afternoon of her life to craft this keychain. "It's darling." I took it and turned it over. "Did you do this?"

"African trade beads. I love working with

them. I'm glad you like it. It's yours to keep."

I was touched. I thanked her, and she seemed pleased. She walked me to the front door and once we were out of the kitchen I heard Tyler say. "Yeah, I don't like language lab, either." Then, "No way!"

"I think Tyler might have a girlfriend," Maura said as she opened the front door to usher me out.

I stopped on the porch and turned, avoiding the butterfly net as best I could. "Does he talk to you about it?"

"He's never talked a lot. He's a quiet boy."

I didn't counsel her to ask Tyler about the girlfriend. My relationship with Maura was tentative enough already. I didn't want her to begin thinking of me as an in-law.

10

Maybe it was the heavy burden of so many questions to answer. Or maybe it was pawing through all that germ-laden merchandise in the toy room. Or maybe it was just my usual spring allergies. But when I woke up the next morning I didn't want to raise my head off the pillow. The ceiling was as much as I wanted to see of the world. My nose itched, my eyes watered, and overnight my joints had gone on strike. I felt as washed-out and worn-out as one of Hazel Kefauver's sweaters. In the rummage sale of life, I would be relegated to the bargain table.

"Ag?"

I turned and saw Ed standing over me, dressed in sweats.

"Is our will up-to-date?" I croaked.

"Not feeling too hot?"

"What time is it?"

"The girls are at school. Junie's over at the Victorian working on her garden. I was going for a run, but if you need me . . ."

I pushed up to rest on my elbows. "I'll be fine. At the most I'm getting a cold. It's Monday, right?"

"That's what the paper claims."

"What are your plans?"

"Something tells me they aren't going to include you. Don't worry, I'll entertain myself. I might head over to the college and do some research."

Ed could easily spend a delightful day off in the stacks. I felt not an iota of guilt.

I levered myself up another inch. "Go ahead and enjoy yourself."

"Then I'll run in that direction. Will you feel good enough to pick me up later?"

I managed a nod. "Thanks for seeing the girls off."

"Teddy's back to her regular clothes."

I felt no remorse for the loss of my princess. Cinderella belonged on a stage, and Teddy belonged on the jungle gym.

"She seems upset about something, though," he said. "Do you happen to know what?"

"Not a clue." Just like the rest of my life.

"Maybe you'll have better luck talking to her than I did."

"I'm sure if I work at it all day, enough sound will come out of my throat for a conversation."

"I'll get a pizza for dinner. Just laze around and feel better."

He kissed me on top of my head, afraid, I'm sure, to risk contamination. Then he disappeared through the doorway.

I sat up a little straighter and saw that he had left orange juice and a slice of buttered toast beside the bed. "Thank you," I called after him.

"There's coffee in the pot."

I figured the juice and toast and a shower might give me enough strength to get that far. And sure enough, half an hour later I installed myself at the kitchen table where the newspaper was already spread.

The *Flow* is short on national news and shorter on world news. But anyone who needs to know how much money Grant Elementary raised with their recent bike-a-thon, or how many times Brownie Kefauver said "huh?" during the city council meeting, can find that and more on our pages. For bigger news Ed and I rely on the *New York Times.* That's usually my first stop, but today I went right to the *Flow* and turned to the obituaries.

Hazel Kefauver's photo stared out at me, a younger, more attractive woman than the one I'd known. The younger Hazel had been blessed with abundant curly hair, and at that point in her life, still remembered how to smile. I wondered when she had forgotten and become the judgmental, rigid woman who died in the VIP tent.

I read a detailed account of Hazel's life. She and Brownie had been married for twenty-four years, just missing their silver anniversary. Her parents and a brother had passed away before her. There hadn't been children. I wondered if this had contributed to her dissatisfaction with life. Or had she chosen not to have them because children are naturally rebellious and messy, and she wouldn't have been patient with either?

All this seemed to indicate that Brownie would be Hazel's sole heir. Perhaps she had left something to charity, even the food bank, but from what I was learning about her, I wasn't optimistic. At best Hazel would have attached so many requirements that the money was virtually useless. No one in need would be any richer now that she had passed on.

I noted that the funeral was planned for this afternoon and that somehow the Methodists had managed to make their sanctuary acceptable for the service. If I hadn't been so happy with Closeur Contracting, I would have begged the minister for the name of their crew.

The telephone rang and I heard my mother's voice on the other end. Junie had left me herbs for tea. I was to drink the resulting brew no matter how it tasted to build up my resistance to whatever I was coming down with. She would stop on the way home this afternoon and pick up a salad. Our dinner was beginning to sound like a feast.

Dutiful middle child that I am, I got up and put on water to boil.

I was feeling marginally better, but not good enough to leave home to order cabinets or get quotes on appliances. I had no reason to cook and no energy to work on the cupboard I was refinishing for our dining room. Reading about Hazel had given me the start of a headache, so a novel was out of the question.

I made the tea, added a dollop of milk to cool it, and held my nose. Even with nostrils pinched, Junie's brew tasted like radiator scrapings. But my mother knows her herbs. If this ailment could be beat into submission, the tea would be the knockout punch.

And speaking of punch, the time was perfect to track down the punch bowl. I was alone, and I wasn't good for anything else. Despite every urge just to head back to bed,

I headed for the telephone and the church directory. Mabyn Booth was first on my list, but she wasn't home. Mabyn is Fern Booth's daughter-in-law, and at Christmas-time I'd helped her get something of a handle on their relationship. Now I realized that episode had parallels to my new relationship to Maura. I wasn't sure how I had suddenly become a mentor to two different women in our congregation, and where that might end. I needed some serious training.

On the best way to stay out of other people's business.

My second call was to the woman Ida had mentioned in her butterfly rant. According to Ida, Doris had practically snatched Ida's second box of glasses right out of her hands. Of course I knew that in any battle of that type, all bets were on Ida. I imagined poor Doris had already been halfway to the cash register before Ida got there.

Doris was home, cordial, and one more dead end. She was, however, delighted with her glasses, which she had set up in her basement bar. I hung up wondering why all these women, none of whom seem to have serious financial problems, didn't just head to the nearest discount store and buy glasses in a pattern they chose at a price they could afford. What was it about this "bargain" that had set them off?

And where in the heck was the biggest bargain of all? The American Brilliant punch bowl?

I'd struck out. Next I was going to have to confess my sins to somebody and beg for help. The problem was I didn't know who.

I tabled the search until I could talk to Mabyn. My headache was getting worse, and I was in no condition to make decisions with such grave consequences attached.

I was putting the directory back in the drawer when the telephone rang again. I claim no special knowledge of universal laws, except one. The telephone always rings when you don't feel like talking. I believe with every fiber of my being that telephones are close genetic relatives to cats. A phone can sense when you're not feeling well and perform accordingly. After a meal Moonpie always chooses laps according to the degree of indigestion. Unable to leap on unsuspecting abdomens, the telephone rings incessantly.

Ours was still ringing. I answered with no enthusiasm.

"What is *wrong* with you?" Lucy asked at my lackluster tone. "Deena's got a whole year before she turns thirteen, and Teddy probably won't take calculus for another year or two. Celebrate while you can."

"I woke up feeling like leftover French toast."

"Poor baby. What's on your calendar for the day?"

"Either a nap or checking out some odd newspaper clippings that Maura found on Joe's side of the closet."

"I'm heading to Give Me a Break. Latte or a mocha? I'll treat."

"I haven't combed my hair. You won't hold it against me?"

"Cut it like Cilla's. You'll never have to comb it again."

Twenty-five minutes later I was still gazing in the hall mirror trying to figure out whether anybody would notice a transformation from medium brown bob to George Clooney casual, when Lucy walked in.

"If I looked like Cilla, I could pull it off," I said.

Despite the minutes that had passed Lucy knew what I was talking about. "She's an Amazon, isn't she? So gorgeous. Do you think Joe knows she's in love with him?"

I pictured the two of them on stage at the Pussycat Club. Joe as Cher, Cilla as Sonny. I thought with a lot of makeup tricks, she might be able to pull it off, although she would always be better looking.

Lucy handed me a steaming mocha topped with whipped cream. The largest size. If Junie's herbs hadn't cured me, this would speed the process.

"So what about these newspaper clippings?"

Between turning my head one way and the other in front of the mirror, I'd gone upstairs to get the clippings out of my dresser drawer. Things had been too chaotic when I returned yesterday to spend any time looking through them. Now I led Lucy to the coffee table where I had spread them out. We took a seat on the sofa in front of them and began.

"What are we doing?" Lucy asked.

"Just read them all, and I'll do the same. Then we'll see if there's anything that jumps out at us."

"Like what?"

"I don't know. Look for a common thread."

The first article I picked up concerned a car dealership in Burlington, Vermont, that had awarded salesperson of the year to a woman named Henrietta Clay. There was a photograph of Henrietta and the owner of the dealership with the rest of the sales staff and a customer or two fanning out behind them.

"Maybe Joe Wagner kept a collection of the most boring articles in the universe," Lucy said.

"What was yours about?"

"Bank of Boston is giving free booklets on Finding Financial Security in the Twenty-First Century."

"Let's hop a plane." I told Lucy about good old Henrietta.

We read another batch in silence. "A PTA in Dedham, Massachusetts, raised money to fight illiteracy by holding a used book sale," I said. "And I have a real estate ad for a new development. If this is what housing costs in the Boston area, I'm glad Ed didn't take the church he was offered there. We would have lived in a furnished room."

"Some hairdresser in Quincy won a prize for cutting the most heads of hair for charity on Valentine's Day," Lucy said. "They called the event the Cupid Cut-a-thon."

"Think she could make me look like Cilla?"

"You're forbidden to cut your hair until you feel 100 percent well."

"You have noticed the one similarity, right?"

"New England," Lucy said.

I leafed through the others just slowly enough to see that all but one mentioned

Massachusetts or Vermont. There were more articles that seemed of no relevance, an obituary, an interesting piece about custom window seats. I wondered how a window seat would look downstairs in the Victorian under the bay window. I'd have to check with Junie, but I thought maybe her customers would like a place to sit and look at fabric or pattern books, and we could build storage underneath.

The odd duck was an article about a man in Florida who was convicted in a Social Security scam and sentenced to a stint at Leavenworth. I read it out loud. The date, like the name of the paper, was gone. But the article mentioned a law passed the previous year that had made it possible to increase the length of his sentence. I did the math and figured the article had been published three years before.

"I bet Simeon Belcore isn't a happy camper about now," I said. "Leavenworth can't be much of a vacation spot."

"Shame on the guy for stealing money from Social Security. That's a privilege only the United States Congress should enjoy." Lucy looked up. "Did you say Belcore?"

"Uh-huh."

"I saw that name." She shuffled through papers. "Here, in the article about the hairdresser. One of the men who was shorn for charity was named Belcore. Ben Belcore."

I picked up the article about the PTA and felt a tingle that said we were on to something. Either that or I had moved on to chills and fever. No Belcore was mentioned in the article, but on closer examination I saw the link.

"There's a Belcore in this photo. I can't tell from the text if he's a tutor or a non-reader, but it says Z. Belcore." Z. Belcore was standing behind somebody else, and he was wearing a cap. No clues there.

We checked everything else. Except for the real estate ad, there was a Belcore in every clipping. A Belcore built custom window seats. One of the lucky souls in the photo of customers receiving Bank of Boston booklets was named Belcore. Even the obituary mentioned Belcore. It was the deceased's sister's married name.

"Wow." I set my last clipping on the table.

"What do you think it means?" Lucy asked.

I was thinking and didn't answer. Something was nagging at me. Maybe if my mind had been slogging along at its usual rate, I could have figured out what it was. But I wasn't at top form. I just knew there was a key to this, and I was missing it.

Ignored, Lucy began her personal analysis out loud. "It's unlikely Joe just happens to know a lot of people named Belcore and he's gathered a stack of clippings about them. That's too weird. Unless he's related to them somehow. Maybe his mother was a Belcore, and these are cousins. But didn't Cilla say Joe was an orphan? Without any family?"

"Fairheart." The frazzled ends of two clues finally connected. I felt a jolt of electricity. "Josephine Fairheart." I looked at Lucy. "Belcore is Italian for fair heart."

She wrinkled her unlined forehead, just for me. "And this is relevant why?"

"Joe was going to New York every month to perform at a club there. His stage name was Fairheart."

Lucy's eyes widened. "Aggie, you said *Josephine* Fairheart."

I had and wished I hadn't. But it was time to go all the way. So far Lucy had been a big help, and she would be more help if she knew the truth. "You have to keep this to yourself, Luce. It's Joe's business and not ours to judge." Then I proceeded to tell her about Joe's extracurricular activities.

"You went to the Pussycat Club without *me?*" She leaned forward and slapped me on the knee. "I can't believe it!"

"What, you wanted me to fly you in for the night? Ed and I had been checking leads all day, and we just stumbled on it."

She pouted. "We could have had such fun."

"And if I'd been with *you,* we would have squeezed out a few minutes to watch the entertainment. I was cheated." I told her quickly about Dorothy and what she'd told us. "I got a couple of makeup tips, too."

"For a small-town minister's wife, you do pretty well for yourself."

I lowered my gaze like the modest woman I am. "It's a gift. So now, how do we find out what connection Joe has to all these people?"

We batted around ideas for the next ten minutes. Maybe the adrenaline was stronger than whatever I was fighting off, but I started to feel a bit better. We discussed and rejected a plan to track down whoever we could from the articles and ask them point-blank about Joe, explaining he was missing. Joe had gone to some lengths to hide these clippings and perhaps his relationship to these people. We had no idea why or what can of worms we might be opening if we outed him.

We considered looking up Z. Belcore in

Dedham, or Ben Belcore in Quincy. We could ask Z if his reading skills had improved, or query Ben about his haircut, but what good would that do? How did you move from haircuts to a missing man in Ohio?

Lucy leafed through the clippings again, and so did I. I stopped at the obituary, and a plan began to form, based on another bout of sleuthing we had done together.

"You remember the time you called that Realtor in Kentucky and pretended you were interested in vacation property?"

"I know, I thought about calling the Realtor who's handling the development in that real estate ad and asking if this development has any connection to the Belcore family. Think I should?"

That wasn't where I'd been headed, but it wasn't a bad idea. "And what will you say if he says yes?"

"*She.* I'll probably tell her I'm looking for a house and have some notes from a friend, but they don't make any sense. Then I'll ask her to enlighten me. And I guess I'll ask exactly what the connection is and go from there."

"You frighten me. You just came up with that?"

"Aggie, I make cold calls all the time. I've

developed the fine art of finding out what I need in as little time as possible. That's all."

"Some people would say you aren't exactly telling the truth."

"Am I hurting anybody?"

That was a moral dilemma best left to Ed. "So while we're discussing your abilities, could you do something with the obituary?"

"Like what?"

"Well, the guy who died had a sister who's married to a Belcore. A Mrs. Dan Belcore in Braintree. Maybe you could call and pretend to be somebody from a life insurance company? You could say the payment's due on a policy for one Joseph Belcore, and he gave their address as a backup."

"Good story, but why them in particular? Why not one of the other Belcores?"

"Because I think we'll have better luck getting gossip from a woman. Not to stereotype, but if there's a story, maybe she'll be less wary. She's married to a Belcore, she's not one by birth. She's probably not as protective."

"You think *I'm* devious? And what's this about me doing the calling? This is your idea, you call."

I wheedled. "I'm not nearly as talented or experienced."

"If you're going to stick your nose in other

peoples' business, you need to be." She took pity on me. "I'll go first. You work on your patter. And don't forget this is a good cause. Joe Wagner may be in trouble somewhere."

"Situational ethics."

"Get over yourself, Aggie."

Lucy dialed the number on the real estate ad without taking even one extra moment to work on her spiel. I was torn between awe and horror as somebody answered, and she was off and running.

She hung up a few minutes later. "Here's what we've got. We're lucky to be living in Emerald Springs because those prices in the ad? That includes next to nothing. Everything is an upgrade. Like toilets and, floors, I don't know how —"

"Dispense with the real estate, okay? What did she say about the Belcores?"

"Creative Construction is building all the units. It's owned by a man named Jake Belcore and his sons. Apparently there are a lot of sons, too. And even though she was trying hard to cover it up, I don't think she's too high on them. She said the date to take possession listed in the paper has been moved back. There were some problems."

"Lovely. Did she say what they were?"

"No, she downplayed, of course. She was trying to sell me a house."

"Nothing else?"

"She did mention Jake Belcore was ill. She used that as a reason for the delay. But she said he's doing better now and things are back on track."

"Could Joe be one of Jake's sons? Or a nephew? And why would he lie? She said lots of sons. That would mean Joe has lots of family."

"Some of those Belcores in the clippings might be sons. So now it's up to you to find out more for us. Ready to make your call?"

"Not with you listening!"

"Fine, I'm going to the bathroom. I'll wash my hands for fourteen seconds, like we're supposed to, and I'll comb my hair. Then I'll go in the kitchen and see if you have anything worth drinking in your refrigerator. But when I'm done rummaging, I'm coming back."

Making the call to information for the phone number of Dan Belcore in Braintree was easy. I jotted down the number and took a deep breath. The hard part was coming up, but I knew Lucy wouldn't be gone forever. I dialed.

A woman answered. She sounded middle-aged and tired.

I realized I hadn't invented an insurance company. I didn't want to use a real one in case the Belcores got suspicious and made some calls of their own.

I cleared my throat. "My name is Agate Sloan, from the Consolidated Community Life Insurance Company of Ohio." I had always thought the name of our church had better uses. I felt a thrill of pride. Next I'd be cracking safes and socking money in overseas accounts.

"Is this one of those phone solicitations? Are you trying to sell me something? I'm on the do-not-call list, you know. I could have you arrested."

I winced. "I'm not trying to sell you a thing, Mrs. Belcore. I'm trying to find a Joseph Belcore. Mr. Belcore has a policy with us which is about to expire. All our premium notices were returned, so it seems he's moved and forgotten to give us his change of address."

I was doing okay, but my stomach was tied in knots. On the other hand, she sounded less tired now, almost perky.

"Joseph Belcore? Why are you calling me? My husband's name is Dan."

"This was the alternative address he gave us."

"Joseph gave you our address?"

For a moment I forgot to speak. There *was* a Joseph Belcore. Of course *their* Joe could be someone else. Joe isn't an uncommon name. But still.

I realized she was waiting. "Yes, and I got your phone number from information. Can you give us his new information so we can send the premium notice right out? It's a sizeable policy, and we don't want it to expire before he does." This was a touch of life insurance humor, but apparently she missed it because she didn't laugh.

"I can't believe Joe would give our address. We haven't heard from him in years. Nobody has. There was that business with the FBI. Then he just disappeared off the face of the earth. Poor old Jake's never gotten over it."

"I'm sorry. The FBI? That sounds like something we might need to know about."

"I don't see why. It blew over after he left. Personally I think somebody made it go away, if you know what I mean."

"What went away?"

"I don't know, except that nothing was ever proved. Still, you have to wonder why Joe took off. I always wondered if he got fitted with a pair of concrete shoes, but now you're telling me he's alive? And he gave you our address? But how could he have? We just moved into this house in April, so no way would he have it. You're saying he gave it to you since then?"

"No. No, our letter to your old address came back, but it had a forwarding address from the post office. I just decided to look you up and call because it's quicker than sending out the letter again."

I was amazed how fast I had come up with that. Apparently I was born for this. What a shame.

Mrs. Belcore tsked sadly. "Well, you found us, but we can't help you find Joe. Nobody in the family even talks about him anymore. Not when I'm around, anyway. It's hard on Jake. He misses Joe something awful."

I could only think of one other thing to ask. "Would you mind telling me how long Joseph Belcore has been missing?"

"Maybe fifteen years, I'm not sure. He was a college student. The only brother to go, you know. Jake was so proud. Then Joseph comes home for the summer, the you-know-what hits the fan, and he's gone. Forever."

"It's a sad story," I said, and meant it.

"Yeah. And Jake's not getting any younger. If you track down my brother-in-law, you tell him to get himself back here to make things right with his dad before he passes on."

"I'll be sure to tell him. Thanks so much, Mrs. Belcore." I hung up before she could think to ask me to repeat my name and the name of the company I was with.

Applause sounded from the doorway. "A star is born," Lucy said.

"It's no wonder so many people get ripped off. Once she warmed up I could have gotten her bank account and PIN numbers."

I told Lucy everything Mrs. Belcore had said. Lucy sprawled on the sofa beside me and listened raptly.

"What's your gut instinct? You think it's the same Joe Belcore?"

"Why else would he have the clippings?" The thrill of discovery was dying now, and I just felt sad for an old man who had lost his son. I also felt sorry for the young man who kept in touch with his family by clipping articles about haircuts and bank booklets.

I turned so I was half reclining, my knees to my chin. "If Joe left his family to escape arrest for some crime he committed, then maybe he left Maura and Tyler for the same reason."

"I missed something. Who wanted to arrest him this time?"

"Junie saw Joe's photo a couple of days ago. She's almost sure she saw him at Mayday! She says he came into her tent, but he left without having his fortune told. The light wasn't bright, and he didn't get close. But Teddy was there, and you know Teddy. She did an imitation of the man's voice . . ."

"And it sounded like Joe?"

"Afraid so. Exactly."

"You think Joe killed Hazel Kefauver? That maybe he pretended not to come home when he was supposed to, then he sneaked into Mayday! without anybody knowing he was there, poisoned her without being seen, and left again? Half the town was there, Aggie. Somebody who knew him would have spotted him. Does your story make sense?"

"Put like that, no. But nothing makes sense to me. I just can't believe Joe's a murderer."

"I could point out that you also liked the last two killers you caught."

"So much for my instincts, huh?"

"What's up next? We've got some idea who he was and where he came from, but no idea where he went."

"Roussos might be able to find him. The problem is that Maura hasn't reported him missing. And she's not going to report it because she's afraid he'll lose his job. Besides, now, with all this other stuff lurking in Joe's background, Roussos is going to be immediately suspicious."

"So you're not going to tell him?"

"No, but I am going to see him. Tomorrow, if I'm feeling better. I want to find out whatever I can about Hazel's death. I owe it to Brownie *and* to Joe."

"And you think you can waltz in there and just ask him? And he'll tell you everything he knows?"

"I'm hoping for some hint gleaned from body language and eyebrow position."

"You could take me with you to get my impressions."

I tilted my head. "Why? The man isn't your type."

"And my type is?"

"Rich guys who do what you tell them to."

She didn't deny it. "That doesn't seem to be working out so well."

"I told you I'd make a list."

"Put Roussos on it somewhere."

I wondered if Lucy was kidding. I wondered how much more information I could get out of him if he was dating my best friend. Then I wondered how quickly the information would dry up once they broke it off. Lucy always broke it off.

"I'll leave your business card on his desk," I promised, "and a map to your condo. "Is that subtle enough?"

"Remind me again why we're such good

friends?"

"There aren't enough hours left in the afternoon."

11

The next morning I felt perky enough to get up early and greet the girls with banana pancakes. As an apology for sleeping late the day before I even topped them with butter and real maple syrup.

I was also anxious to talk to Teddy. Starting about three yesterday afternoon chaos had reigned in the Sloan–Wilcox household. Deena's transportation to her riding lessons fell through. Since I much prefer she hang out with horses than boys, I dragged myself to the car and drove my daughter and three friends out into the country.

The trip back might have been a good time to quiz my youngest daughter about her long face, except Teddy asked me to drop her off at the Victorian with Junie to help plant the hardiest annuals in the front beds.

By the time I picked up Ed at the college and everyone else got home, ate dinner, and began homework, our washing machine hose sprang a leak and flooded the basement. Unfortunately, thirty minutes before, Ed had headed for the hospital to make a pastoral call. The girls, Junie, and I bailed and mopped and by then, nobody was in the mood for a serious conversation.

Maybe it was Junie's tea, but this morning I was up for doing some gentle probing. And I was hoping a bit later I might be up for a tête-à-tête with Roussos, too. I wasn't at all sure one subject would be easier to crack than the other. Teddy keeps a lot to herself. If she isn't ready to share, neither thumbscrews nor promises of her very own pony can make her talk. Not that I have direct evidence. Since I have no teenagers, thumbscrews aren't at this time part of my parental repertoire.

Deena arrived first. Today she wore turquoise, a sparkly T-shirt with a bold orange Z blazed across it, and knee-length pants with the same Z on the pocket. Sid sent the outfit for her birthday, and Deena likes it so well I've been afraid she might never risk putting it on.

"I like your hair that way," I said. She had twisted shoulder-length locks on both sides and fastened them in the back with a gold barrette. Last month she asked to have her ears pierced, and we agreed that if she still wanted this at Christmastime, that would be one of her presents. I imagined there were a thousand similar queries in my future, most a lot more troubling.

"Can Tyler come over and do homework with me some time?"

There it was, out in the open. I couldn't believe my luck. "You seem like good friends."

"Not *good* friends. Friends."

I heard the warning note in her voice. If I went any further, the conversation would be shut down.

Teddy arrived to defuse the tension. Unlike her sister, Teddy looked as if she had dug through Junie's rummage sale finds for her outfit. She wore purple corduroy pants that were too short and an old flannel pajama top. The only shoes downstairs were chartreuse rubber rain boots. I was afraid they were part of the wardrobe plan.

"Is this Cinderella before the ball?" I asked, debating whether to send her upstairs for another try or to tough this out.

She promptly turned around and left. I heard her retreat up the stairs.

"Well, you said the right thing." Deena poured too much syrup on her pancakes.

"What do you mean?"

"She doesn't want to be Cinderella anymore. She's trying not to dress like Cinderella. So now she'll change into something better."

I thought this might be a compliment. I felt an urge to run upstairs and scrawl it in my journal. Except that I don't have a journal and the pancakes would burn.

"You can certainly have Tyler over," I said. "But he probably has to go home first to check blood sugar."

"There's nothing wrong with that!"

I bristled silently, testing and discarding responses until Deena was ready for a second helping. By then I realized that although I was the only person in the room, my daughter wasn't talking to me.

"So who's been telling you there's something wrong with Tyler taking care of his diabetes?" I slid another pancake on her plate.

Before Deena could answer Teddy came hurtling downstairs again. This time she wore brown cargo pants and a short sleeve sweatshirt with butterflies appliqued on the front. I beamed. She could pass out literature for Ida Bere.

"So, Teddy," I said, glancing at the clock, "how are things at school?"

She flopped down across from her sister

and rested her chin in her hands. "Will you talk to Miss Hollins and tell her I don't want to be in the play?"

"No." I set her plate in front of her. I'd created a Mickey Mouse pancake to make her smile, but Mickey didn't do the trick.

When she didn't reach for the syrup, I passed the pitcher. "Teddy, if you don't want to be in the play, you have to talk to your teacher yourself."

"Nobody's been *telling* me," Deena said. "But some of the other Meanies think it's sick, sticking himself like that."

"She won't listen to me," Teddy said. "But she would listen to you."

One weighty conversation at a time was a lot to handle. With two coming at me from different ends of the table, I felt like I was at Wimbledon.

"I hope they're not giving Tyler a hard time," I told Deena.

"It's not fun. It's supposed to be fun." Teddy hadn't picked up her fork.

"Why isn't it fun?" I asked.

Deena finished her last pancake and stood. "Everybody acts like they're going to catch it. Like I'm going to catch it if I hang out with him."

"Surely they know enough —"

"It's not fun because it's dumb." Teddy

picked up her fork and stabbed her pancake. "Do I have to do dumb things just so I'll grow up and be a good person?"

I needed help. "Ed!" I went to the bottom of the steps. "Breakfast is ready. Right now!"

"No, it's like a test," Deena was telling her sister when I dragged myself back into the kitchen, head pounding. "That's how the whole school thing works. You do stuff you don't want to do until they flatten you. Then when you're, like, the height of that pancake, they let you graduate."

"You're making that up."

"Nope. You'll find out."

"Teddy, your sister *is* making that up." I faced my older daughter. "Are you worried about the way people look at *you* or the way they look at Tyler? Because you don't want other people's immature perceptions to influence your choice of friends."

"Half the Meanies are treating me like I've got some fatal disease."

The Green Meanies are an informal group of the more popular girls in Deena's class. It still mystifies me that Deena has so easily fallen in with them, without social climbing, angst, or tears. Most of the girls are normal, good kids, a few are lifelong friends material, and a few will probably do something they'll pay dearly for before they graduate from high school. I like them all, although I'm less certain about some of their mothers.

"Imagine how they treat Tyler," I said.

"When I'm a teacher, nobody will have to be in a play." Teddy held up the entire pancake and bit off Mickey Mouse's ear. I winced.

I needed to know more, was about to insist on it, when Ed made an appearance.

"Girls, you're running late," he said. "I have a meeting across town, I'll drop you off if you want."

Chairs scraped the floor and both girls took off upstairs to brush their teeth and get books.

I grabbed Ed by the shoulders and shook him. "Where were you when I needed you?"

He kissed my head and wrapped his arms around me. "You'll always need me, Ag."

An hour later I was dressed and in the van. Late last night I'd gotten a telephone report about Hazel Kefauver's funeral from Yvonne. I called Yvonne when most people were already in bed. Now that she's trying to quit smoking, I knew she was getting little sleep. She was so grateful to talk she gave me a play-by-play that probably lasted as long as the service. The hymns, the readings, the sermon, which had praised Hazel as a dutiful child of God who spent her all too short life in service to others.

With the funeral behind him, I hoped I would find Brownie at home this morning. I swung by his house on my way to the police station, but once again the cream-colored Lincoln wasn't parked in front of the house. On the off chance the car was in the shop, I got out, walked up the herringbone brick path to the door, and rang the bell. No one was home. Since my phone call hadn't been returned, either, I wondered if I was going to spend my time hunting the mayor when I should be hunting the murderer of the mayor's wife.

Our police station is downtown, in a disreputable building with twenty-four-hour parking meters and carpets held together by duct tape. Next month the station will move to the new service center complex on Gleason Road. I had hoped all murders within our city limits would cease until I had better surroundings in which to badger Detective Roussos, but that was not to be.

I parked on a side street and hiked over to the station, first stopping at Give Me a Break for their largest black coffee and a latte. The black coffee was for Roussos. I don't think he's a foamy milk, shot of vanilla syrup kind of guy.

I guess I'm getting something of a reputation. I walked into the reception area and the cop on duty, who I had never seen, lumbered to his feet and said he'd get Roussos. Before I even opened my mouth.

I perched on a hard plastic chair and slid my hands up and down the sides of the cups to make sure every inch of my palms suffered second-degree burns.

By the time Roussos came out, either the coffee had cooled or I'd lost all feeling in my hands. I stood and held out the appropriate paper cup. "The way you like it."

"I can't take bribes." He took it anyway.

"Darn, now I'll have to find another cop who'll look the other way when I set up that roulette wheel in my living room."

"You're not here to chat, are you?"

"What would *we* chat about?"

"Anything except what I think you're here for."

"You could take me back to your desk and find out."

"Let's go for a walk. I need to stretch my legs."

The area around the station's not the most scenic part of downtown, but the day promised to be a pretty one. There was a small park just a block away, and we headed in that direction. Birds sang from telephone wires and pansies winked and nodded in sidewalk planters. The air smelled like spring, even if it still indulged in a nip or two every time the wind whipped around a corner.

"So, you came to see me for a reason?"

There was no beating around the bush with this guy. And there was a personal line we didn't cross. I was very married, and he was very not. So that cut down on the banter enormously.

"I've heard through the grapevine — like almost everybody else in town — that Hazel Kefauver was poisoned. You're treating the death like a murder?"

"You feel like you have to be involved in every suspicious death in Emerald Springs? For what reason? I forget."

"I was there when she died, remember?"

"Yeah, well so were a lot of other people. And not one of them has asked me to share what I know."

"How shortsighted. Aren't you glad somebody's on top of things?"

"Not one bit."

"Aren't you interested in what I saw that day?"

"I saw what you saw. And we talked to people at the scene, remember?"

"Did I happen to mention that I spoke with Mrs. Kefauver maybe forty-five minutes before she died, and I noticed she looked washed-out? I remember thinking maybe she was coming down with that flu that's been making the rounds. My mother says her hands were like ice and as rough as sandpaper. So whatever killed her might have been ingested earlier in the day."

"We'll keep that in mind."

"What did she ingest?"

"Nice try."

"You can't tell me? It's a secret?"

"It's an open investigation, is what it is. You aren't family —"

"Then you're telling family?"

"We're keeping some details to ourselves."

"Is there anything you can tell me?"

"Yeah, stay out of this."

I glanced at him. "Don't you need my help?"

"Don't flash those dimples at me."

"You weren't even looking."

"Been there, done that. If you keep trying to get yourself killed, we're going to have to assign a cop to follow you around twenty-four seven. And the city budget won't stand for it."

I imagined Roussos slinking along behind me everywhere I went. I had to smile. "I don't think *Ed* would stand for it."

"Then do your hubby a favor and back off."

I thought of Joe and I thought of Brownie. Even if Roussos's advice was sound, I wasn't willing to follow it. However, it didn't sound like I was going to get any help from this quarter unless I told him why it mattered to me.

We reached the park. A mom and three preschoolers had taken over the swings, and two teenage boys were shooting hoops on the basketball court. I tossed my empty cup into the trash can.

"You know Joe Wagner's a member of our church, right?"

"No, I didn't."

"Well, he is. And the food bank means a lot to him. Hazel's death right there at Mayday! could have a negative impact on their donations."

"And so you promised him you'd solve the murder when you're not running car pool and selling Girl Scout cookies?"

"I solve murders because it's a pleasant little break from the hard work of real life. After a day of doing what I do, we'd have to scrape you off the sidewalk."

He grinned. I knew he'd been razzing me. Beneath all the barbs we respect, even like each other.

The grin disappeared as quickly as it flashed sunshine in my direction. "Where is Joseph Wagner, anyway? We really need to ask him some questions."

"I'm sure you asked his wife, right?"

"They don't make them vaguer than Maura Wagner. I'm not sure that woman knows where *she* is."

"Joe's the mover and shaker in the family."

"So where's he moving and shaking these days? Mrs. Wagner gave me a phone number in New Jersey, but nobody answers."

I wondered how Maura had come up with a number for Roussos to call. A friend on vacation?

I felt my way. "Joe's not having an easy time of it. I imagine he's too busy, maybe too upset, to be answering phone calls." That was most likely true, wherever he was.

Roussos finished his coffee, without taking his eyes off my face. Then his cup followed the path of mine. "We'd better start back."

"I'm actually parked that way." I nodded behind me toward Give Me a Break.

"You know something about the Wagners you're not sharing, don't you?"

"You know something about what killed

255

Hazel that you're not sharing."

"They pay me not to share. Nobody's paying you." He frowned. "Tell me nobody's paying you."

"I can tell you that."

"Do you know where Joe Wagner is?"

I considered. I'd struck out on the poison, but maybe all wasn't lost. "I don't know why you care. Isn't Brownie Kefauver your prime suspect?"

"What makes you think so?"

"Motive and opportunity. Although I don't know about means since you won't tell me exactly what killed her."

He didn't answer. Roussos is a master at keeping things to himself, but I thought I saw a flicker of something in his eyes, enough to almost confirm that Brownie was, as I'd expected, their focus.

"I don't know where Joe is," I said. "If you have a phone number, you know more than I do."

"Yet you're looking into this murder because you're worried about him and the food bank?"

"It's amazing, isn't it? All these little threads that weave the tapestry of life."

He shook his head. "Stay out of the investigation."

"Which one, Hazel's murder? Why Joe's

not answering the telephone? Why I have to bring you coffee because nobody at the station can make a decent cup?"

"I mean it, Aggie."

"I know you do, Kirk."

He went his way; I went mine. I think he was muttering.

I'd already had fruitless conversations with both my daughters and now Roussos. It wasn't even nine thirty. This was a brand-new record. As if to make sure that *fruitless* was the word of the day, I saw Mabyn Booth and her daughter Shirley coming toward me.

I told myself I was lucky. Now I could find out about Mabyn's rummage sale purchases. But I knew the news wasn't going to be good. How could it be, unless the universe was finally about to take pity on my good intentions?

I didn't run, although I was tempted. I stood my ground and flinched as Mabyn and Shirley drew closer, waiting for the next blow.

Mabyn shifted Shirley so she could give a friendly wave. "I got your message, but it was so late last night I didn't want to call you back. You must have left the house early this morning."

"An errand day." I said hello to Shirley,

now a contrary two-year-old. She glared at me. Mabyn is a charmer, and her husband is a regular nice guy. But Shirley skipped an entire generation of genes and seems to be a clone of her grandmother. I was glad Mabyn and Howard had years ahead in which to modify the worst of Grandmother Fern's traits.

"So what's up?" Mabyn asked.

I couldn't think of a way to ask about the boxes of glasses without an out-and-out lie. Mabyn wouldn't believe I was checking to see if everybody was happy with their rummage sale purchases, even if, for the most part, this was true. I mean, whoever opened the box with the punch bowl was probably very happy, a state I wished to correct.

I settled on a bigger piece of the truth. "I heard you bought a couple of boxes of glasses at the rummage sale."

"Uh-huh, I did."

"Have you opened them yet?"

"No, I just stuck them in the basement. I'm taking them over to the Munchkin Theater next week. We serve punch after rehearsals, and we've had complaints that paper cups are environmentally unfriendly. I've signed on to do their PR. It's something I can do with Shirley in tow."

Munchkin Theater was a children's theater

group that Teddy had evinced some interest in joining. From what I'd gleaned during our disjointed conversation this morning, I doubted Mabyn would be promoting my daughter anytime soon.

"Will you do me a favor?" I lowered my voice. "Will you open the boxes and look inside before you take them to the theater?"

"Sure, but why?"

"If I tell you, I'll have to kill you."

She laughed. "Do I need to paw around in them?"

"Nope, if you see glasses, feel free to take them to the Munchkins."

"Someday you'll tell me?"

"You bet. Oh, and please don't mention this to anybody, especially your mother-in-law."

"There's very little time in my conversations with Fern to mention anything. *She* is the mentioner."

I nodded in commiseration. "My mother-in-law lives in Boston and thinks transportation to Ohio is conducted by riverboat and covered wagon."

"She never visits?"

"She came for Ed's installation, but that didn't change her mind. She asked us to do all the visiting in the future. She gets palpitations when she has to leave New

England."

"I'll trade."

I laughed, but now I wondered if Nan, who for all her faults did know Boston up one side and down the other, might be able to find out something more about the Belcore family scandal for me. I'd have to give that some thought.

We parted company, and I felt fairly secure that my secret — at least what Mabyn knew of it — was safe for the moment.

I had one more errand before I drove over to the Victorian to meet Lucy. I was close enough to City Hall that I had time to take a slight detour. I wanted another crack at finding Brownie.

Emerald Springs City Hall has nothing particular to recommend it. The building is three stories of ordinary tan brick, with narrow slits for windows, like Moonpie's eyes before he jumps on his favorite catnip mouse. The roof is flat enough to almost disappear, if not to cave in during a winter blizzard.

I looked at the directory in the entry hall and took stairs to the second floor. Brownie's office suite sat at the end, and even from a distance I could see that the walls were paneled in walnut and the floors carpeted in thick maroon plush.

I entered and nodded to the secretary who sat at a Louis XIV desk outside what was obviously Brownie's office. That door was closed, and I heard voices from inside.

I stopped in front of the desk. "I was hoping to see the mayor."

"Do you have an appointment?"

I wondered how Brownie had gotten this babe past Hazel. She was exactly the kind of va-va-voom siren who walked into the private eye's office in a Mickey Spillane mystery. Blonde, stacked, and always trouble. This one was also too young to have any work experience.

"No appointment." I made a guess. "You must be new."

"My first week."

I *really* had to talk to Brownie. "What happened to . . ." I snapped my fingers, as if I couldn't remember the former secretary's name.

"Maude? Oh, she retired."

Before or after Hazel's death? And did it matter? Brownie needed arm candy sitting outside his office like he needed a Miranda warning. Va-Va-Voom was a neon sign.

"Brownie told me to stop by." I glanced down at my ragged fingernails, which compared unfavorably to Va-Va's red talons. "Is he tied up in a meeting?"

She shrugged. "There are people in there. I don't think they had rope."

I *so* hoped she had a sense of humor, but I was desperately afraid she was serious. "Any idea how long they'll be?"

Fortunately, she didn't have to answer another question, since I was afraid I had already unfairly taxed her. The door swung open and Brownie walked out with the police chief and several overweight men in suits. Brownie's eyes widened when he saw me. He wore a three-piece suit and a bright red four-in-hand tie with matching pocket handkerchief. My heart sank.

"Excuse me," he told the others. "I won't be a moment."

He extended a hand to me, then he gripped my shoulder and marched me to the other side of the room.

"What are you doing here?" He sounded frightened.

I had come to give him some much-needed advice. But clearly I couldn't do it with all these people watching. "I need to talk to you."

He nodded, even as he whispered, "Not now."

I realized my real mission was hopeless, but at least I could get one question answered. "I found some items of Hazel's in the clothing you donated to the rummage sale."

He raised his voice a little, to be overheard. "Yes, dear Hazel would have wanted her things to go to charity."

I smiled and lowered my voice to a whisper. "Not *that* fast, she wouldn't have. And do you want me to bring you what I found? I found keys, money —"

"I don't want —" He stopped himself. "How much money?"

No surprise he didn't want *that* going to charity. "I'll give it to you later. But there were some other things, like china —"

"Just throw them away. Give them away. I don't want them." He raised his voice again. "I'm too distraught."

I lowered my voice even more. "Be careful. People watch what you do."

He looked perplexed. The men had been talking among themselves, but now their conversation ended. Two of them were looking our way.

I held out my hand and we shook. Then I left. Brownie was under enough scrutiny as it was.

12

I arrived at the Victorian a few minutes before Lucy. I hadn't expected to find anyone working since Closeur Contracting only agreed to work on weekends and occasional evenings. Still, the work had been progressing so well and quickly that I wouldn't have been surprised to see a Closeur pickup outside.

Unfortunately, there were no trucks, ladders, or toolboxes on the porch, but I was surprised to see a light upstairs and a window open. Junie had been here with Teddy yesterday, and I guessed that after a bathroom break or a tour to investigate the renovations, the light and window had been forgotten.

I unlocked the door and called for Lucy, just in case she had arrived by foot and gone upstairs. There was no answer, but just as I was about to step over the threshold, I heard a door close.

Window open. Gusts of wind. Bedroom door slamming shut. Perhaps I could have accepted this as an explanation if the door *had* slammed, not clicked quietly. And *if* the sound had come from upstairs.

It hadn't.

I froze in place. The sound had come from the back of the house right here on the first floor, not far from where I was standing. I was fairly certain someone had been inside, then left by the back door. I wondered if I sprinted through the house and into what had once been the kitchen, flung open the back door, and screamed "I got you!" who I would catch.

Nobody, it seemed, because I was still rooted to the spot.

"What are you doing, Ag?"

"Yikes!" Uprooted at last I whirled to see Lucy right behind me.

"You didn't hear me?" She sounded incredulous. "Are your ears plugged from that cold?"

I shook my head and held my finger to my lips, actions that required more coordination than I seemed to have. My finger landed on an earlobe.

"I heard somebody inside," I whispered. "The back door closed when I opened this one."

"Why didn't you check it out?"

"You wanted me to confront whoever it was by myself?"

"You said you heard the door close, as in, hel–lo, whoever it was had already left!"

"Maybe. But maybe they were just coming in."

"What, to find you standing here like you're playing statues?"

I stepped aside and ushered her past me. "Be my guest, oh brave one. Are you carrying Mace?"

We were still whispering. She rummaged in her purse and came up with a small cannister. "I've always wanted to see if this works."

"You might get your wish. Just don't spray me."

"Tiptoe," Lucy said.

"Really? I thought I'd do my fe-fi-fo number and clump over there like the angry giant!"

We tiptoed, and without patting myself on the back, I will say that those years of ballet we'd both endured as children hadn't been a complete waste. We were as light on our feet as the fairies in *Sleeping Beauty*. Tchaikovsky would have wept.

No one was in the kitchen, a relief so great that *I* almost wept. I peered out the back door, and Lucy peered out the back window. Of course by then whoever I'd heard was long gone.

I breathed a deep sigh of relief. Lucy jammed the Mace in the pocket of her blazer. "Let's check out the house and see if anything's been disturbed."

We each grabbed a soft drink, then, together, we began our search.

The downstairs looked the way it always had, but upstairs I put my hand on her arm and stopped her. "What do you notice?"

"Just tell me."

"Smell. The bathroom's been tiled."

She frowned. "Yesterday?"

"Nobody was here yesterday except Junie."

"Then I guess Hank came last night."

I pulled my cell phone out of my purse and handed it to her. "Let's find out. Call Hank. Dial his last name."

"And there's a reason you can't do it?"

I just looked at her.

"You're hopeless." She shook her head, turned on my phone, and punched in the number.

Lucy reached him, which surprised me. I think either Hank forgot to check caller ID, or none of my other calls had gone through, which was more likely.

"Hank, this is Lucy Jacobs. Aggie and I are over at the Victorian on Bunting Street . . ." She stopped talking and just listened for a full minute. She finally answered. "Hold on a moment would you?"

She covered the receiver. "He hasn't been here since the day they started building the island in the wrong place. He's apologizing. He says he'll try to get here this weekend and see what he can do about fixing it."

We stared at each other. "Let *me* fire him," Lucy said. "I know it's your phone, but if I hand it over to you, who knows what will happen."

I nodded magnanimously. She uncovered the receiver. "You're fired, you son of a —"

I covered my ears. I uncovered them when she closed the phone.

"Well, that went well," I said.

"So who's been remodeling the house?"

I didn't know, but I did know that we'd yet to check the basement or attic. Clearly we weren't on the trail of a fiend. How many people have a mystery contractor? Our guy wasn't breaking and entering. He was building and entering.

"Maybe we should just go away." I walked over to the bathroom and pushed the door open wider. Tile adhesive perfumed the air.

Sure enough, the tile wasn't yet grouted, but it had been perfectly laid. "Do we really want to catch him before he finishes? We'll never find anybody this talented again."

"We have to figure out what's going on here. We'll finish looking through the house."

We struck gold in the attic. Somebody was living here. Hidden behind boxes Junie had moved here from her camper, we found a sleeping bag, neatly rolled and tied, a small camp stove, a store of dried food, and copies of *Field & Stream* that had been well thumbed through. Behind a couple of pieces of old furniture salvaged from the house, I found a backpack with a few toiletries, a towel, and some work clothes. Size forty-two.

"A big homeless guy?" Lucy asked.

I thought of my experiences with the homeless. They never seemed to travel this light because they were carrying an entire lifetime with them. This guy had packed for a short camping trip.

"We have to talk to him," I said. "I don't think we have a thing to worry about. He clearly means us no harm. He's doing a great job here. If nothing else we definitely owe him wages."

"How do you propose we arrange that?"

"We could leave him a note. We know he reads."

"That might scare him away."

"Then we have to confront him."

"How do you propose we do that?"

The answer seemed all too clear. "We have to come back later tonight and catch him. We can enter through both doors so he doesn't escape the way he did today."

"And you think Ed will be in favor of this?"

"I think Ed will believe that you and I have gone to a movie."

"Now you'll spend the rest of the day trying to figure out how to word that so you aren't exactly lying to him."

But I'd already come up with a scheme. "Nope, I'll just tell Ed there's a movie you and I have always wanted to see, and I'll be home late. I just won't mention that those two thoughts aren't necessarily connected."

"I think we may have created a monster."

I let Lucy worry. After all, I was learning these skills from her. But of course I was going to tell Ed the truth, the whole truth, and nothing but. I just hoped I didn't have to tell him before we confronted the Victorian's new resident. And the chances were good. Because I happened to know that Ed had a board meeting tonight.

■ ■ ■ ■

Lucy and I made a list of what still needed to be done, although we had no idea who would complete the work for us. I was hoping that once confronted, our attic dweller would agree to stay and finish the job. We could move in some furniture to make him more comfortable, set up a microwave and toaster oven, and stock the fridge. I wanted to keep this guy.

Since it was lunchtime, she followed me home and we made omelets to eat with blueberry muffins Junie had baked for yesterday's breakfast. Afterwards, while Lucy washed the pans, I cleared the table. Still vaguely sneezy, I opened a drawer to rummage for a pack of tissues and saw the envelope of Hazel's things that had been stuffed inside.

"When's your next appointment?" I asked.

"I need to go back to the office at some point to do a little paperwork. Why?"

"I found a clue, Nancy Drew," I sing-songed.

We settled in the living room with big cups of spiced tea, and I opened the envelope, having given Lucy all necessary information while it brewed.

"So Brownie said he didn't want any of this, without even knowing what was here?" Lucy sounded skeptical.

"Except the money. Don't you think if he was really guilty, he'd want to see every scrap, just in case?"

"Unless there's nothing he could have left behind."

"He's not behaving sensibly." I told her about Va-Va-Voom and the four-in-hand tie with matching handkerchief. "Next up, hair plugs," I said.

"Is he *trying* to look suspicious?"

"Would he know how?"

"Brownie was more or less the lap dummy, and Hazel was the ventriloquist. Who knows what he'll be like without her running his life."

This was an interesting thought. If we could keep the little guy out of jail, then watching what he made of himself in the years ahead might be interesting. I was betting he'd ditch the mayor's office lickety-split. He would need lots of free time to deplete Hazel's family fortune.

I ripped open the envelope and dumped the contents on the coffee table, which was getting something of a workout these days. First Joe's past, now Hazel's.

"You couldn't throw away the old tissues?" Lucy asked, wrinkling her nose. "You thought we'd need to check DNA?"

"I missed a few, okay? I was working at top speed."

Lucy got up and came back with a plastic grocery bag. She dropped the tissues inside, along with an empty package of cough drops, a tube of lipstick, and an Estée Lauder metal compact with just a residue of powder.

"Now that you've tidied up, can we get down to business?" I began to stack papers. Lucy took my cue and assembled everything else into piles. There was more than I'd remembered.

"Okay, what have you got?" I asked.

"A gold-plated bracelet with a broken clasp. It's not worth much, but you could sell it at next year's rummage sale."

"Try not to bring that up, okay?"

"Keys, a comb . . ." She dropped the comb in our trash bag. "A leather organizer, a book of stamps, a pocket calorie counter —"

"Hazel was on a diet?"

"Or pretended to be."

I told her what Keely had said about Hazel's addiction to chocolate.

"Living proof." Lucy held up one miserly square of a chocolate bar, then dropped that into the trash bag, too.

I retrieved it, pinching the wrapper between my fingers and avoiding the chocolate. "Maybe we shouldn't be so hasty. She was poisoned, remember?"

"You think she was poisoned by a chocolate bar?"

"Let's not take chances." I set it to one side, although it looked so old I doubted it had come from recently worn clothing. "Anything else?"

"I wish."

"Except for the extremely remote possibility that we have the murder weapon in our possession, nothing seems particularly helpful. Except maybe the organizer." I picked it up and thumbed through, hoping for a calendar filled with information like "Met with So and So today who wants to murder me." Instead I saw that the organizer was from 1999. Apparently, Hazel had only rarely cleared out her closet. I gave it to Lucy, who dropped it in the bag.

"Okay, your turn," she said.

"You take half, I'll take half." I handed her a stack of papers.

"This feels familiar. Didn't we just do papers?"

"Those were Joe's, and a good detective knows repetition is part of every case."

"I'm beginning to worry about you."

We worked in silence, but by the time we finished, only one thing had really jumped out at me. Hazel had folded several pages of handwritten notes about food bank supplies into her pockets. I remembered Cilla saying she was convinced Hazel had been out to get Joe. Hazel had spent a lot of time poking around his office. I wondered what Hazel had hoped to find and if this innocuous listing of ears of corn and sides of beef had been part of it?

"Is this evidence of some food bank problem?" I asked, handing it over to Lucy. "Or are these just some notes Hazel needed as board chairman?"

"Who knows? We'd have to talk to somebody there. I could show it to Cilla."

"Of course if something is going on, Cilla could be part of it."

"We do have Hazel's keys, you know. Didn't Cilla say Hazel had keys to the offices?" Lucy jingled the ring enticingly.

"What, you mean break in and go through their files without having any idea in the world what we're looking for?"

Lucy's eyes were shining. "Now you're talking like a detective."

"No way. Not happening. Not going there. Better to take a chance on Cilla. The way she feels about Joe, I doubt she would ever do a thing to jeopardize his job."

We were interrupted by my mother, who came in the front door carrying a cardboard box that nearly didn't fit through the opening.

I jumped to my feet to help guide her, taking the box out of her arms. I looked down and saw neatly folded fabric that looked vaguely familiar. "What's this?"

"Felted wool. For the penny rugs the girls and I are making."

"Oh. You went to buy fabric?" The closest store was miles away, which was part of the reason Junie's quilt shop was bound to be a success.

"No, precious, I've been at It's a Wash all morning. I didn't want to use your machines for felting. It's messy."

I set down the box and picked up a folded square. "Why does this look familiar?"

"I bought bags of wool skirts, pants, and blazers at the rummage sale. Maybe you saw them when you were there. The girls and I took them apart, then this morning I washed the pieces in hot water and put them through the hottest cycle on the dryer. Heat shrinks everything and tightens the weave. Now the fabric won't ravel when we cut and stitch it."

Hazel Kefauver's skirts, pants, and blazers. Shrunk almost beyond recognition.

Junie sounded delighted. "I'll dye most of the fabric because the colors are unbelievably dreary. But you have no idea what this would have cost anywhere else. It was high-quality wool, quite a find. I'm so glad I moved here."

I kissed her cheek. "Aren't we all?"

"Oh, I did find one odd thing in a pocket. I've been meaning to give it to you. Can you wait a moment?" She started upstairs.

"Is that fabric what I think it is?" Lucy asked.

"No point in telling Junie and spoiling her fun."

"You missed something in a pocket?"

"I told you what a hurry I was in."

Junie returned and held out her hand. Resting on her palm was a small plastic object about an inch square.

I saw why I had missed it. "What is it?"

Lucy was peering over my shoulder. "It's a photo card for a digital camera. Tell me you know what a digital camera does."

"Of course I do. I just don't choose to use one myself. My little Brownie box camera works great. When I can load the film." I took the photo card and turned it over. "I'm assuming this didn't go through the laundry?"

Junie picked up her box of fabric. "No, I found it when I was cutting up a skirt. It was caught in a seam. You girls have fun."

"Luce?" I held out the card once Junie was gone. "What equipment do we need so we can see if there's anything useful on this?"

"A computer and a few minutes."

"Let's go."

Ed is not technology challenged. He has a USB universal media hub plugged into our computer, something he hadn't — for obvious reasons — bothered to tell me. Lucy found the correct slot and inserted the card. In less than a minute we were looking at a strip of three photos. Lucy clicked on the first one.

"Can you tell anything?" I squinted at the photo. I guessed it was a dark city street with a collection of streetlamps. The photo was blurry, as if Hazel or someone had moved the camera when she shot it.

"I think those lights may be signs," Lucy said. "Neon signs. But they're impossible to read."

I leaned closer to the screen. "Could be. Let's go to the second one."

Lucy went back to the strip of three and clicked the second. This photo was a little clearer. We could tell that buildings sat one on top of each other, some were brightly lit, some were darker. This was not Emerald Springs. We don't have this much neon in the entire town.

"Cleveland?" I guessed. "Cincinnati?"

"Hard to tell. Can you read that sign?" She pointed to a corner of the screen.

I leaned closer again. "Pizza?"

"I think so."

"I'm sure Sam Spade could do something with that, but I'm at a loss."

"Such an amateur." Lucy went back to the strip and clicked on the third photo.

This time we didn't need Sam Spade. Hazel had finally gotten the hang of her camera. Maybe she'd figured out how to use her flash. Maybe she'd realized that she had to set up the lens or a filter for night-time photos. But whatever it was, now Lucy and I were staring at the outside of the Pussycat Club in New York's East Village. The pink neon cat with enough wattage to light up the entire downtown of Emerald Springs could not be argued with.

"Hazel knew," I said. "She was at the Pussycat Club. She knew about Joe. She must have followed him there."

Lucy sat back, still staring at the photo on the screen. "Now I guess the next question is did Joe know about Hazel? And did he kill her before she could tell the world and destroy his life?"

13

Nan called before I had a chance to decide whether I should ask her for help. Generally Ed's mother calls when there's little chance her son will be home. I'm not sure this is a snide refusal to believe ministry really is a job with long hours, or just that her conversations with Ed — who refuses to be hooked by guilt or any other negative emotion — are less satisfying than conversations with me. I'm hooked almost every time.

"Agate, this is your mother-in-law. Ed's mother?"

I wondered if Nan thought I had more than one husband. "How are you?" I was so pleased with my tone I risked another sentence. "I thought you were heading for Martha's Vineyard this week."

"That's *next* week. Perhaps I'd better send you a calendar."

I dropped into a chair and picked at a hangnail with malicious intent. "I'm afraid you've missed Ed again. He's at church all day on Tuesdays." I did not offer to send *her* a calendar, chalking up a point in the mature adult category.

"I just called to see how my granddaughters are doing."

"They'll be sorry they missed you, but of course, they're in school." I subtracted my point, so unfortunately, we were even again.

"How is Teddy's little play?"

I could fault my mother-in-law for many things, but never for forgetting the details of her granddaughters' lives. Nan follows them from afar, but she does follow them. In her own way, she's fond of my girls, and they are as fond of her as children can be of someone who continually tries to mold them to her specifications.

"She was thrilled to be picked for Cinderella," I said, and didn't add that Teddy was less thrilled now.

"I'm sure you were surprised. There must be many little girls in her class who wanted the part."

I was silent a moment, thinking about what she'd said. Had Nan inadvertently fingered the problem? Had Teddy lost friends from jealousy? Or had she been so pleased with her own good fortune that now they thought she was stuck-up? The perils

282

282

of first grade. I wanted to wring my hands, but I was too busy with the hangnail.

"And Deena?" Nan probed.

I recited what I could. I didn't tell Nan about Tyler, afraid she might call Deena and deliver a lecture on the importance of eschewing the opposite sex until she's been admitted to an Ivy League university. Nan lives in terror that our decision to send both girls to a public school outside New England has doomed them to universities like Johns Hopkins and Northwestern and a life of mediocrity.

I asked Nan to tell me what she was doing, and she reciprocated. As our chats went, this one was remarkable. I was so encouraged I decided to broach the subject of Creative Construction. At the next lull, I went for it.

"We have somebody in our congregation who's loosely connected to an old Boston scandal. You're so well informed, I wonder if you've heard anything or seen anything in the papers there." I proceeded to tell her what I knew about Creative Construction, then I waited.

"Agate, you know the worst people. How can this help Ed move to an *important* church? Don't people expect more from you?"

This was the big zinger, the reason she'd lulled me into submission with pleasantries. Okay, maybe not, but now that she'd well and truly hooked me, I could feel her preparing to reel me in.

"The more I know, the more I can help," I said so sweetly my saliva crystallized. "You don't want your only son consorting with criminals, do you?"

"Ed?"

Did she have more than one son? I was beginning to wonder if I had inadvertently married identical twins.

"Knowledge is security," I said. "It sounds like you know something about these people."

"Those people are in and out of the news. And it's my civic duty to stay informed, as is yours."

"Well said." I sat on my stinging finger and clenched my jaw instead.

"There were rumors about the Mafia being involved in Creative Construction and money laundering. No one ever seems able to prove anything, though. Of course they're from Charlestown, not the North End." As if that esoteric bit of geography said everything I needed to know.

"It must be a fairly well-established company to set off rumors. I mean, let's face it, lots of businesses have connections to organized crime, and they don't make the papers."

"They've done some rather large projects, several quite visible."

I had gotten more information than I'd expected. And I hadn't even needed to visit the Internet.

We discussed Martha's Vineyard, the need for Deena to do good works — not for the moral uplift but for her college application. Nan suggested Deena begin her own charitable foundation, and I promised to take it under advisement.

I hung up, more pleased than usual with my mother-in-law. Then I went to check Ed's closet, just to be sure there weren't two identical sets of everything.

My plans for the evening never came up in conversation. Unbeknownst to me the church board had planned a potluck supper, and Ed only came home long enough after office hours to cook a pot of brown rice. I knew it would be returned untouched to our kitchen later in the evening, except for Ed's own portion. I'd seen this before. Ed is oblivious.

The rest of us made tacos, and the girls started on their homework. Junie had promised that if there was time after they finished, she would take my daughters to our local craft store to choose dye for their penny rugs. I had finally given up and asked what they were. Penny rugs are small decorative pieces consisting of a base fabric covered with felted wool appliqués.

Having Junie in the house is like having a camp counselor, except that the crafts are far superior, and she's convinced her own ghost stories are true.

Lucy arrived at nine, after sunset. She wore black from head to toe, a nice touch. I wore the wrinkled blue T-shirt and pants I'd had on all day. I doubted we were going to find Johnny Depp grouting our tile.

Junie got a quick rundown of my plans, the tops of my daughters' heads were kissed, and I sailed out to Lucy's cherry red Concorde.

"Put the top down and we'll go cruising for guys," I said. "Or we can dance at the sock hop and drink chocolate malts at the soda shop."

"Or drive off a cliff like Thelma and Louise."

"On second thought, keep the top up."

Lucy pulled out of the driveway. "Someday I'm really going to own a convertible. Then you'll have to fantasize about something else."

"My fantasy life is so rich and deep, nothing can throw a kink into it."

"So what's your fantasy about our mystery man?"

"Somebody down on his luck and so grateful for a place to stay that he's paying us back the only way he knows how."

"Why would such a talented carpenter be down on his luck? I could keep him busy for the next year, and he could charge what he's worth. He could easily afford a nice apartment."

"I wonder if we're crazy to confront him like this."

"What's the alternative? The police?"

"You wanted more time with Roussos."

"Maybe so, but Roussos would haul him in. Even if he let the guy go afterwards, the damage would be done."

I thought so, too. And I couldn't ask any man I knew to come with me as bodyguard without involving Ed, and the moment Ed heard what we were planning, he would call Roussos.

Life is a circle.

"I have my Mace," Lucy said. "If he gets too high-spirited, you can flip him over your shoulder, or whatever it was you learned from your father."

287

"Make fun of my childhood. Go ahead. The next time you need somebody to load your assault rifle, you'll have to find a new best friend."

Lucy parked at the end of the block, and we both got out. We were slightly more subdued. For all the reasons Lucy and I discussed, I wasn't really worried. But I would be glad when I was proved correct.

"Okay, I'll take the back door," I told her, "because that's where he'll head when he hears you turning the key."

"Why you?"

"Because he doesn't stand a chance against me."

"Size forty-two."

"The bigger they are, the harder they fall. Remember?"

"I put the police on speed dial. I can get them in seconds."

"Just don't jump the gun with the phone or the Mace."

We were close enough now that it was time to split up. I pointed to the neighbor's yard, an older woman we'd gotten to know well. She was off on vacation this week. I knew because I'd promised to take in her mail. Now I threaded my way through the yard and squeezed through the row of lilacs that separated the two houses. I stayed as close to the back of the house as I could to avoid being seen through a window. Then I waited until I heard Lucy unlocking the front door. I grasped the back doorknob and started to insert my key.

I wasn't even close to target when the door flew open, and a large figure pushed through. I didn't have time to step aside. We went down together. Just two steps, but it felt like we were rolling down the staircase of the Statue of Liberty.

"Oomph." I tried to scramble to my feet and push him away. Our legs tangled, and I kicked and rolled to the side. He leaped to his feet and started across the yard at a fast lope.

The back lights came on and Lucy came down the steps in pursuit. I got to my feet, and got my first good look. Our intruder was almost out of the circle of light, just moving into the shadows at the back of the yard, but I'd seen enough to know who we'd caught.

"Joe Wagner!" I got to my feet and started after them. Lucy was just a few steps ahead of me.

The man didn't slow. My ankle had twisted during our fall, and I wasn't going to get far fast. I tried my last and best shot at stopping him.

"Joseph Belcore! You stop right this instant!"

Our guy stopped so suddenly that Lucy nearly collided with him. She backed away, and I hobbled in their direction, my heart pounding.

We had found Joe Wagner, or rather, he had found us. I didn't know how to feel. Grateful he was alive? Happy I no longer had to search for him? How about worried that we had been crazy to flush him out of hiding?

Because why would Joe Wagner have secreted himself in the Victorian without letting anybody know where he was, unless he had something terrible to hide?

"You know Joey?"

I stopped and stared, and my jaw probably hit my collarbone. The man moving toward us and into the light, the man who had asked the question, wasn't Joe Wagner at all. Yes, he was tall, with Joe's broad shoulders and general build. And his face? Well his face was like looking at Joe's, only Joe in maybe ten years. The nose was straight and the cheekbones high. He parted his hair on the same side, and it had the same casual wave. But the hair wasn't jet-black, it was laced with silver, and the olive skin crinkled around the eyes and drooped just a little under the chin.

I realized he was waiting for an answer. He was still poised to turn and run, his weight on the balls of his feet.

I shook my head to clear it, but the image when I opened my eyes again was exactly the same. Joe, only *not* Joe.

"I know Joe Belcore," I said. "But these days he goes by the name of Joe Wagner. You're his brother, aren't you? *One* of his brothers?"

"Where is Joey?"

"We don't know and we'd like to," Lucy said.

He didn't move. I pointed to the house. "You know, if you come inside, maybe we can figure this out together. We're afraid something may have happened to Joe. We could use your help."

He still looked undecided. God help me, I resorted to guilt. "Of course, if you don't care about him . . ."

The man stood very still. I wasn't sure we had a chance of keeping him there. Then he sagged.

"We'd like to pay you for all the work you've done for us," Lucy said, to sweeten the offer and take the sting out of my words. "And we want you to finish it. That was our only reason for coming tonight. We didn't know who you were."

"I just want to find my brother."

"Then we'll tell you our story, and you tell us yours," I said. "Maybe we can work together and make that happen." I turned and started back to the house, because what else could I do? Wrestle him to the ground? Nothing in my background had prepared me for that.

I wasn't sure Joe's brother would join us, but when I opened the door and held it, he followed Lucy inside.

Reuben Belcore — known simply as Rube — liked tacos. Five minutes of stand up conversation in the Victorian had convinced us we could have a more productive and comfortable talk at the parsonage. My offer of a home-cooked meal, even if it consisted of leftovers, helped Rube make the leap from suspicious to merely watchful.

He followed us in a rusted pickup truck that had seen a decade of use. The camper that fit over the truck bed had met with misfortune on the trip from Boston and he'd had to scrap it. I told him this was actually good fortune since eventually the mishap had brought him to us when he needed a place to sleep. But our connection wasn't pure coincidence. As he scarfed tacos, accompanied by fruit salad and two of Junie's fabulous brownies, he told us why he had installed himself in the Victorian.

"You kept showing up." He nodded to me, too busy eating to spare his pointer. "You were with the lady who took Joey's place as fortune-teller —"

"You know about that?"

"I heard about Mayday! when I got to town. I heard Joey told fortunes. He was always good at that. Once I was in the joint waiting for my trial, and he told me I'd get off and I did."

"The joint?"

"Just a misunderstanding."

I thought about everything I'd learned about Creative Construction. "Work-related misunderstanding?"

"They're always work-related."

My gaze locked with Lucy's.

Rube went on. "So I saw you with that new fortune-teller —"

"My mother," I explained. Junie and the girls were still out shopping.

"Then the next day I saw you with Joey's wife, when I was watching their house. He knows how to pick 'em, doesn't he?"

That was a question best left unanswered. "So you saw me with Maura?"

"Right, but you didn't see me because I

didn't want you to. When you left I decided to follow, just to see if maybe you had some important connection to him. You went over to Bunting Street, and when you left the old house, I went inside, just to see what was up."

"And you got inside how?"

He laughed. "You're kidding, right? You think those locks are secure? You know what a bump key is?"

"It's a key that'll let you into almost any house you want to get into," Lucy said. "I bought a set on eBay last week. But go on."

He looked pleased, as if he'd found a coconspirator. "When I got in I saw the note you left your contractor. I liked the house. I decided if I stayed there, maybe I'd find out more about Joey, and I figured you'd never catch on. And it was more comfortable than sleeping in my truck."

"What about all the work you did?" Lucy asked. "Great work, by the way."

"I'm no criminal. Maybe I let myself in and that wasn't strictly legal, but I figured I owed you for giving me a place to stay. Besides, I could tell you needed the help. Those other guys never showed up. And at night I didn't have anything better to do. I had my truck, I had my tools . . ." He shrugged in finale.

"Until today we thought they were doing the work."

"I was going to leave you a note before I left for good, telling you not to pay them. Baboons!"

I got the drift if not the precise translation. "Amen."

So now we knew why Rube had chosen our Victorian, but we still didn't know why he was here in Emerald Springs. Before I could ask, he ate his last brownie, dusted off his hands, and finished his third cup of coffee.

"Tell me what you know about Joey." He leaned across the table. His eyes were as black as olives, and they gave absolutely nothing away.

"You have to go first, so I'll know what to tell you."

He chewed the inside of his lip, as if considering. "It's not a good story."

I was sorry I had to hear it, because I didn't want anything to ruin my opinion of Joe Wagner. Discovering Joe was a part-time drag queen was campy and exotic, but entirely harmless. I didn't want to find out he was also a criminal.

Rube took my silence for permission. "I guess you have to know. But it doesn't put me and my brothers in a very good light."

I felt marginally more optimistic. "Go ahead and get it off your chest, Rube. Maybe you'll feel better."

"My father Jake's been married a lot. He's not so easy to live with, if you know what I mean? Wives died or divorced him. I kind of lost count."

"My mother's been married five times," I said.

He seemed to appreciate the comparison. "Something must be wrong in the Belcore gene department, but Pops only has boys, not a girl in the bunch. An even dozen. We didn't all grow up in the same house. Some of us lived with Pops, some lived with our mothers. But nobody moved too far away. So we spent a lot of time together, got to know each other. And one thing we all knew? Pops didn't have much patience, and what he had he saved for Joey, the baby."

"That's tough."

"Yeah, we all thought so. *Now* I can understand. Joey's mother was sort of the love of Pop's life. She was young and a real looker. And smart? Too smart for Joey's good, because she figured out early that living with Pops wasn't what she wanted. So she took off and left Joey and Pops behind. Joey was smart like her. I had a reading problem so I barely finished high school. Simeon? He had a social problem, if you know what I mean. He wanted something, he took it."

Simeon probably wasn't having much luck taking what he wanted in Leavenworth, but I nodded.

"Anyway, everybody but Joey had a problem or an excuse. Some of us are just lazy good-for-nothings. Or were, I ought to say. We improve with age, like good Chianti, huh? Anyway, Joey didn't need to improve. Straight As, good on the football field, responsible, you name it. He got a scholarship to college and decided he'd study business. Pops started talking about letting Joey take over the company when he retired."

I could see how this might upset the others, who had probably paid their dues in Creative Construction the old-fashioned way. Knowing that someday Joe was just going to waltz in clutching his college degree and start ordering them around? The situation had all the earmarks of a disaster.

"So is that what happened? Your father retired and Joe took over?"

"The summer after Joey finished his third year, Pops got sick. Cancer, if you want to know. The doctor said he didn't have much of a chance of beating it, and he'd probably pass away quick. Everybody was all broke up. Maybe Pops wasn't the best father, but he was all we had. Then Simeon reminded us that when Pops was six feet under, Joey would be lording it over us. He said he'd seen a will, and Pops was leaving everything to Joey. Of course Joey was supposed to keep all our interests in mind, but what good would that do? Joey didn't like something? Out we'd go."

He looked longingly at his empty coffee cup, so I got up to pour him another, glad I'd made a big pot. I offered a refill to Lucy, but she shook her head. She was clearly enthralled.

"I think anybody would feel upset with that situation," she said. "And your father probably never intended for Joey to take over while he was so young and inexperienced."

Rube took a long sip, then he licked his lips. "Here's the rest. Quick and clean. We set Joey up for a fall. It wasn't hard because he was so green and so honest himself. We shifted some figures here, emptied a bank account there. Joey was working in our office that summer. We fixed the books to show profits we never made, then we fixed them some more to look like Joey had skimmed all the excess into his own pockets. Simeon did most of the work. He knew how to make things happen." He sighed. "Somebody should have paid attention to that. It got him in big trouble later."

"Go on," I encouraged.

"When we showed Joey what we'd found, he denied it, of course. But what could he do? How could he insist he was innocent? All the proof was right there. So we told him we would make it go away because he was our brother, and we had to protect him. But we told him he had to leave for good, that we couldn't trust him anymore around the company or the family, and if he stayed in Boston, we'd be obliged to tell Pops what he had done and our poor dying Pops would be obliged to turn him in to save everything he had worked so hard to build. Joey was young, and he fell for it."

"You mean Joe didn't know he'd been set up?"

"Not then. I'd guess he's figured it out by now, wouldn't you?"

I guessed he had. "What about your father?"

"They did some long-shot operation, and he came through fine and dandy. You can imagine we got worried about then. See, we'd thought Pops would die before any of this came to light. But we went ahead and stuck with the story we invented. We told him Joey just disappeared, and nobody knew where he'd gone."

"And he believed that?"

"About that time we were bidding on some jobs against another firm that was *connected,* if you know what I mean. We told Pops we thought maybe they'd messed with Joey or took him as a warning that we should back off. We pretended like we did everything to find him. Pops was recovering, and he didn't have the strength to go looking himself. He finally accepted that Joey was gone. For years we thought Joey would come back and rat us out, but he never did. Pops still misses him terrible. He went on to marry and have one more son, but he's never forgotten Joey."

I thought about everything Nan had told me this afternoon. The Belcore family was some piece of work. Maybe Joe was lucky to have escaped — although I doubted he felt that way.

"What about Joe's mother?" Lucy asked. "Are they in touch? Could Joe be with her?"

"For a long time nobody knew where she'd gone. But she's the reason I knew something had happened to Joey after I traced him here. When that fellow at the food bank announced Joey was with his dying mother? See, when we decided we had to find him, we were finally able to track his mother down. She's living on the beach in Ft. Lauderdale with a new husband and kids, healthy as a horse, and hasn't heard from Joey since the day she walked out."

Lucy was full of questions. "If Joe has figured out by now that his own brothers framed him, why *hasn't* he gone home to tell your father?"

But I thought I knew. Joe was ashamed. Ashamed that he had let his brothers get the better of him. Ashamed that he had abandoned his dying father to keep from being arrested. Maybe even ashamed that he had never figured out how to make things right again. He's the most responsible person I've ever met. Something like this would eat away at Joe Wagner, but it wouldn't necessarily spur him to act irresponsibly.

"I bet Joe decided there was nothing to be gained by exposing you and your brothers and breaking your father's heart all over again," I said.

Rube hung his head a moment. "That's what I think, too."

"So why are you here?"

"We had a family meeting two years ago. We knew we couldn't go on like this. Pops is getting old, and he deserves to end his life with Joey beside him. At the very least he deserves to know what happened, and what we did. And we need to tell Joey we're sorry. It's weighing us down."

"And everybody agreed to this?"

"Simeon couldn't be there. At the meeting, I mean. Dan thought maybe we should just keep going like we had been, to keep from hurting Pops even more. But the rest thought it was time to end the lies, so we started looking for Joey. He did a good job of hiding himself. He changed his name, moved out of New England. It took awhile, but we finally got the lead we needed, and my brothers sent me to talk to him and see if I could bring him home."

"Your timing sucks," Lucy said.

"Tell me about it." He looked at me. "Tell me about Joey."

So I did. I told him everything I knew about Joe, about how much he was loved and admired in Emerald Springs, about his work at the food bank and what a good father he was to Tyler. Then, without mentioning the particulars of the Pussycat Club, I told him the rest.

I was just getting to that possible siting of Joe at Mayday!, a siting I now thought I understood, when the side door opened and my girls came running in, followed by their grandmother. I hadn't heard the car drive up.

Junie walked in, took one look at Rube, and grinned. "You found him!" Then she frowned. "Or maybe not."

"Is this the man you saw in the tent at Mayday!?" I asked.

She nodded. "But he's not your Joe, is he?"

I had noticed from the beginning that Rube sounded almost exactly like his brother when he spoke. Between that and my own reaction when I first saw him, I had already guessed that Rube was the man Junie and Teddy had identified as Joe. When he mentioned seeing me at Mayday! with Junie, I'd been almost sure.

Now my emotions were mixed. I was glad Joe hadn't been at Mayday! when Hazel died, because that put him farther down the list of suspects. But now there was no proof that Joe Wagner — or rather Joe Belcore — was still alive.

"Do you have to go back to Boston anytime soon?" Lucy asked Rube.

"I'm not going back until I know where my brother is."

She looked at me, and I nodded, sure what she was going to say next. "Will you keep working on the house while you're here?" she asked him. "We'll make it worth your while."

"You trust me after everything I told you?" I answered. "Aren't you the same man who's been working for us for free?" I held up my hand when he tried to speak. "The man who decided he had to right a very old wrong and came here to do it?"

"We've changed. All of us . . . most of us. I know I have. I won't let you down."

Junie put her hand over her heart. She hadn't heard much of the story, but she had heard enough. "I love happy endings."

And so did I. Unfortunately this wasn't an ending. It was just another curve in the road. I hoped someday Joe Wagner could sit in this kitchen and shout "the end" to enthusiastic applause. But at this point, I was afraid that was a long shot.

14

By Thursday morning whatever bug I'd harbored had been squashed by Junie's herbs or my own determination. I was no longer limping, and Ed was still speaking to me. I felt so lucky I considered buying a lottery ticket at the grocery store checkout, but I spent the money on a candy bar and enjoyed the immediate reward.

I was vacuuming cat hair off the sofa, one of the more futile jobs in the universe, when the telephone rang. It was Teddy's teacher.

Determined to hold on to my good mood, I took the phone in the kitchen and flipped on the burner under the teakettle.

"I have a feeling this is about Cinderella," I said.

Miss Hollins's voice did not warm at my conciliatory tone. "Did you give Teddy permission to drop out of the play?"

"Absolutely not. Why, did she ask to?"

"She didn't ask. She insisted."

I could have told Teddy this was not a woman who responded kindly to orders. I wished my daughter had asked me, but of course, I had told her she had to handle this on her own. I winced.

I got down my favorite mug. Clearly I was going to need newborn lambs frolicking in an English meadow to get me through the conversation. "Did she say why?"

"She refuses."

"I don't know either, but my mother-in-law suggested that perhaps some of the other little girls are jealous, and they're giving Teddy a hard time. Do you think there might be something to that?"

"I don't let students in *my* classroom behave that way."

Now *this* was the Jennifer Hollins I remembered, the brand-new teacher with a chip on her shoulder. Before I could think of a response that wouldn't get my daughter into deeper trouble, I heard her sigh.

"At least I try not to," she said in a softer voice.

"Nobody expects you to be everywhere. But that's just one guess. Do you have any?"

"I wish I could read their little minds."

"Welcome to the club. What did you tell her?"

"I told her we were counting on her, and

she has to continue. Can I count on *you* to reinforce that?"

I considered. "I agree with your strategy, but first I need to find out what's going on. Maybe this is stage fright or something a first grader shouldn't have to tough out."

"She seems to love performing. I don't understand it."

"Is there a good time to call you after I've had a chance to talk to her?"

I jotted down the information and hung up. I had dodged a bullet, but only just. If Teddy didn't want to tell me what was wrong, there was nothing that could make her. Then what could I do? Insist she remain, without having all the facts? Side with Teddy against her teacher?

In the living room I sat with my lambs and my Earl Grey and thought about all the puzzles in my life. Teddy was just one. Despite solving the mystery of the unpaid carpenter, I was no closer to finding Joe or Hazel's murderer or even Brownie for a moment of pleasant confrontation.

On top of that, the punch bowl was history. Now I was sorry I hadn't bought that lottery ticket. Because it was going to take a big win to buy another bowl for the Women's Society, at least one as nice as the one that had disappeared.

Silently I debated which problem I should tackle after I finished my tea and the sofa. I was fresh out of punch bowl leads, had struck out finding Brownie on the way home from the store this morning, and my calls to Joe's beach bunny mama had so far gone unanswered. Not that I expected to learn anything new from the woman who had deserted him.

Halfway through a mental inventory of clues and leads, I realized that I had never talked to the food bank staff. Despite knowing that Hazel had poked through Joe's desk before she died, Cilla was still the only one I'd interviewed. Hazel had followed Joe all the way to New York and the Pussycat Club. So what had she hoped to learn? Performing at the club was hardly grounds to fire him. What else had she been looking for?

I got up to find the lists I'd recovered from Hazel's pockets. An idea was slowly percolating, and I knew just the man who might help.

Halfway to the desk drawer I looked down at my black jogging pants. They were covered with cat hair.

Maybe I couldn't find Joe or the punch bowl, and maybe Hazel's murderer was still at large, but at least I had found the solution for removing all traces of Moonpie from our sofa cushions.

When I got to the Victorian, Rube was hard at work. "Come see the tile," he said, when I walked through the front doorway. "I hope you like the grout."

"We'll be so glad to have it finished, we'll go with almost anything." I followed him upstairs and indeed did approve of the grout, which he had matched to the darker tones in the marbleized tile.

"You get those cabinets ordered?" he asked.

"They should have them here next week." Luckily, Junie hadn't asked for custom cabinetry, but a basic medium-grade maple that our local dealer could get from his warehouse. Rube planned to add some decorative molding and a simple island topped with granite. Everything was finally taking shape. Junie was so optimistic, she was spending her days on the telephone to fabric manufacturers.

"I've got something for you to look at that has nothing to do with the house," I said. "Can you take a moment?"

He put his hands in the small of his back and leaned into them, like a man who has bent over one too many times. "I could use the break."

The house was more comfortable now than it had been. Yesterday I had moved in a small table, as well as two director's chairs, an inflatable mattress, and a toaster oven. Lucy had temporarily furnished the front porch with an inexpensive plastic patio table and chairs, and tonight she was bringing a microwave and a stand to set it on. We had stocked the refrigerator so Rube could choose to heat food here if he wanted. It wasn't home, but he seemed happy.

We sat together on the porch and listened to birds and the occasional swish of tires on Bunting Street.

"I've been thinking about Joe." Rube already knew about Hazel's death, but now I told him what Cilla had said about Hazel going through Joe's desk and files. "On top of that I think she was trying to track Joe down in New York before he disappeared. She was out to get him."

I fished in my purse and pulled out the supply lists and handed them over. "These could be nothing, or they could have something to do with Joe. What do you think?"

He looked over the papers, reading slowly and moving his finger along with the words. I remembered what he'd said about a reading problem. Rube was just a bit too old to have benefitted from learning disability testing. In his day, kids with problems simply got lost in the system.

After a few minutes he handed back the papers. "How come you wanted me to see these?"

I couldn't find a tactful way to tell him. "Because I get the feeling you've had some experience on the wrong side of the law."

He grinned at me, looking so much like Joe I had to find another place to rest my gaze.

"You think the food bank's in trouble?" he asked.

"I believe Hazel thought so. And if it is, then maybe Joe's involved some way or the other."

"He's in charge. If there's a problem, it's on his watch. Maybe somebody is taking advantage of him, the way we did."

"I hate to say this, but if Joe has a fault, that would be the one I'd bet on. Even after, well, you know. He trusts and he forgives, which on the surface sounds great. But I think maybe he does both too easily."

"Okay, if I was going to rip off a food bank . . ." He caught my eye again and winked. "Just hypothetically."

I'd learned a lot about Rube since Tuesday. He was a vice president at Creative Construction, in charge of project performance, although the company was in financial turmoil and no one was taking home much money. He was divorced with two sons, but he had a new woman in his life, although for now his emotional life was wrapped around finding his brother.

I smiled to let him know I was in on the joke. "So what would you do? Hypothetically?"

"Well, one trick? Almost every nonprofit organization has a tax-exempt number, right? So if somebody wants to make a lot of money and not play nice with the government, they just have to get that number, buy goods wholesale without paying tax on them, then sell at regular prices. Do it without alerting anybody, and they could make a lot of money fast."

I could see something like that happening at our church. I made a note to warn Ed. "Okay, that's good. What else?"

"Phony employees. I know a guy who set up a phony consulting firm, and the checks went straight to his house. Nobody caught on for years. The guys in accounting never talked to the guys who were supposed to be getting consultation. They just paid the bills."

"That might be hard to do in a small organization where everybody knows what everybody else does."

"Yeah, could be. But you said the food bank works in three counties?"

I saw what he was getting at. The distance between the Helping Hands complex and the satellite food banks in connecting counties might make that kind of deception easier. "They could ask for funds to use locally, I guess, and pocket them."

"Hey, you might get good at this."

"Oh great, another inappropriate talent." I imagined the church board hiring a security guard to follow me around during social hour, arming the ushers when the collection plates were passed.

"No harm in thinking like the bad guys," Rube said. "It keeps everybody safer."

"I don't need hypothetical as much as I need specifics. What do those lists suggest to you?"

He shrugged. "Just a guess, but maybe not all the donations are going into the warehouse. Maybe she was afraid the food was being sold on the black market. Simple, but maybe not so easy to prove."

"A black market for food?"

"If I was going to rip off a food bank, that's the way I would do it. Think of it this way. You own a little restaurant, and you're struggling all the time to make ends meet.

Some guy comes to the back door with a case of canned peas —"

"You have no idea how much I detest canned peas. Make it tomatoes."

"Canned tomatoes then."

"You ever notice the smell when you open a can of peas? Or the color?"

"Get your imagination back on track, okay?"

"I got it. It's an Italian restaurant. We'll call it Pedro's Pasta —"

"Pedro is Spanish. It's Pietro, and don't interrupt again. This guy's standing at the door of Pietro's Pasta and Pizza Parlor with a case of tomatoes. Now maybe Pietro buys his tomatoes wholesale for say, sixteen or seventeen dollars. But this guy says he'll sell this case to him for ten. Plus he's got five or six more cases to sell at the same price. So Pietro's saved maybe thirty-six, forty dollars, just by saying yes. The guy tells him they fell off a truck. Pietro doesn't want to know what truck. He pays cash and that's that."

"You sound like you know what you're talking about."

"You don't think guys at construction sites aren't tempted to do the same thing? Pilfering and reselling? As long as they don't take too much too openly, who's going to know?

Who's going to care? It's the price of doing business."

"Not at a food bank."

"When the money's not coming out of your income, do you care half as much if stuff goes missing? You're not trying to turn a profit. That's why they call it a nonprofit."

"I'd like to think most people who work for nonprofit agencies do it because they care about the people they serve."

"Not everybody."

"This still sounds like small potatoes to me. How much money can somebody make off a case of tomatoes here and there?"

"But it's more than tomatoes, isn't it? From the snooping I did when I was looking for Joe, I'd say a lot of food goes through that program. What's to keep somebody from getting a few sides of donated beef, removing the porterhouses and T-bones, the rib roasts, and selling them on the sly? Who would know once a cow's been ground into hamburger? I can't say for sure, but I'd guess that depending on how widespread the scam, somebody could make a whole lot of money over a period of a year or two."

All the discussion about small potatoes, Pietro's tomatoes, and porterhouse steak had made me think about dinner. Rube went back to work and I decided to go to the grocery store. DiBenedetto's on Robin Street, to be more specific.

At Christmastime my sister Vel introduced me to our little Italian grocery and to Marco DiBenedetto, one of those guys who makes it clear where the great Renaissance sculptors got their inspiration. I had hopes for Vel and Marco. She had visited me twice since then, and I was almost sure it wasn't my charms or Junie's that had drawn her to Emerald Springs. I also knew Marco had visited her in New York last month when he was attending a food industry trade show.

The outside of DiBenedetto's is plain, almost dreary. But the inside is like a trip to a market in Tuscany. Fresh, ripe vegetables laid out in attractive designs. Cheeses I've only dreamed of trying. The store isn't large, and nothing is cheap, but everything is selected with an eye to quality. Our local gourmets keep DiBenedetto's in business.

Thursday is fresh pasta day, which was only part of the reason I was here. Every Thursday two DiBenedetto aunts rise at dawn and crank out miles of linguine and acres of flat lasagna strips that are nothing like the dried ones with the ruffly edges from the chain groceries. Thursdays at DiBenedetto's has become a ritual of sorts. I take a number, then while I'm waiting to be called, I buy everything I need for the sauce of the day. The whole family looks forward to Thursday night dinners.

Today the aunts had outdone themselves. In addition to the usual, they had made gnocchi. I looked at my number, then I listened for the next one to be called. There were ten people between me and the dwindling supply, and I hoped that half of them got tired of waiting. I even checked the floor, just in case somebody farther up the line had thrown a number away — even though that wasn't exactly fair or kind. Fortunately for my better self, everyone thought gnocchi was worth waiting for.

I steeled myself to accept linguine and went to choose vegetables to go with it.

Marco found me among the lettuces. I refrained from asking when he planned to marry my sister.

"Aggie." He clapped his hand on my shoulder, and I very nearly swooned. Although he and Joe Wagner are big Italian guys, Marco has an edge in the rugged good looks department. There's just something about his eyes and his smile. Nothing I could ever adequately describe.

We chatted. Marco has two little boys, and we compared notes. Then he helped me choose an eggplant and three succulent zucchini. I told him I was planning a sauce for linguine since it looked like the gnocchi would be gone before I got to the counter. He left and came back with a package from the back and confided that he always put a little extra aside for his favorite customers.

Being one of Marco's favorite customers was enough good news to take me through the rest of the day.

He walked me to checkout, and I dove into the other reason I had come. I told him about my conversation with Rube, although I didn't tell him the problem in question might be our food bank.

"My friend was just making a guess," I said. "But I wondered if you've ever seen anything like that here? Does it really happen? People show up with food you can buy at a discount as long as you don't ask where it comes from?"

"It definitely happens. Last week a guy showed up with a refrigerator truck of freshly slaughtered beef. The truck had a Texas license plate. I'm guessing cattle rustler."

"Really?"

He smiled, an awesome thing to behold. "We pride ourselves on knowing exactly where our food comes from, so we never buy through the back door, no matter how steep the discount. But it's still not unusual to be approached."

"How about locals? People you recognize?"

"That never happens. If locals are selling inventory on the sly, they'd be crazy to do it here. They're probably selling it three states away."

We said good-bye and I took my groceries out to the car. They deserved refrigeration, so I made a stop at home. I was heading out the door again when the telephone rang. No surprise there. I was sure the phone had heard me opening the door, ready to exit. From now on I would have to parachute from a second-story window.

My curiosity is insatiable. I could no more let it ring than I could stop myself from trying to find Hazel's murderer. Maura was on the other end.

"Aggie, do you have a moment?"

Unfortunately my lamb mug was in the dishwasher, and my hangnail was covered with a Band-Aid. I leaned against a counter, squeezed my eyes closed, and visualized waves at the seashore.

"I haven't heard from Joe," Maura said.

"I'm sorry. I hoped he would call by now."

"You haven't discovered anything?"

Of course I had. I considered whether to

tell Maura about Rube and Joe's secret past, but unless I really had to, or Rube insisted, I thought I would keep that under wraps. I still hoped Joe would come back and tell her the truth himself.

"Nothing that will lead us to him," I said truthfully. "But I'm still looking. I was just on my way to the food bank."

"Oh, are you going to be there all day? Because I need a favor, but if you're going to be gone . . ."

"What do you need? I'll help if I can."

"I have an afternoon appointment with Tyler's doctor. She's going over some procedures with me, so I'll be up-to-date. I thought I had to tell her Joe is missing. I guess this could have effects on Tyler's blood sugar so she wants to have a heart-to-heart. Oh, and we got the camp application all squared away."

I was impressed. Really, right before our eyes Maura was evolving. She had responded appropriately to a crisis and displayed admirable maturity. I felt a sliver of pride that I was helping her along that path.

I also wanted the name of a doctor who took this much interest in her patients.

I made the phone call easier for her. "Do you want me to pick up Tyler at school? It's no problem."

"Would you? I'll call the middle school and ask them to alert him. When you drop him at our house, just remind him he needs to test and do his shot."

"You don't want me to stay?"

"Well, I'll be home by four. He *should* be okay." She sounded hesitant.

"Not a problem. I'll hang around. He'll probably have stuff to show Deena, anyway."

"That's great. Thanks so much. When I gave you my key, I didn't know you'd need to use it so soon."

"That's what friends are for."

We hung up, and I sprinted for the door. As I was getting into my van, I thought I heard the phone ring again. I backed out as fast as the law allowed.

Cilla was alone at the file cabinet when I walked through the door of the Helping Hands executive office. Today she wore a tight blue T-shirt with black jeans and flip-flops. Her toenails were a glittery scarlet, and I noted a tattoo peeking under the hem of her jeans. I wondered if Joe had been attracted to her, or if there had been something sizzling between them? I'd come away from our last conversation sure that Cilla was in love with Joe. But did Joe know it? Were the two of them having an affair?

Somehow I didn't think so. Again, Joe was just too responsible.

"Cilla?"

She spun around and almost left a flip-flop behind. "Aggie? I'm sorry. You startled me."

"You were a million miles away."

"Worrying about Joe, I guess. Where the hell is he?"

"That's part of the reason I'm here."

The reception area was surprisingly roomy. The walls were a buttery cream, and both of the windows wore attractive plaid curtains that coordinated with a sofa sporting half a dozen needlepoint pillows. A rust-colored armchair sat catty-corner and all the bookcases, file cabinets, and end tables matched Cilla's oak desk.

"Wow." I walked over to the sofa and picked up a pillow. "Let me guess. Maura did these." The pillows featured fruits and vegetables and were beautifully designed.

"She decorated the whole room and bought the furniture." Cilla made that sound like one of many sins.

Except for the boxes stacked high around the edges, the room would be an almost perfect place to work. I had noticed more boxes in the outside hallway as well. I was surprised Maura hadn't draped them with handwoven tapestries.

I pointed. "Not enough room in the warehouse?"

"The temperature there's quite a bit higher than the temperature here. We can't afford to keep it as low as we should for some food supplies. Anything that needs to be kept cool but doesn't need refrigeration ends up in our offices. Sometimes here, sometimes the conference room, sometimes Joe's office." She inclined her head toward the closed door just beyond us.

"At least you always have snacks available."

"You'd be surprised what ends up in the office building. Fresh baked goods. Chocolate and other candy that melts."

"Yum."

"It goes out as fast as it comes in. Right now these boxes have day-old doughnuts to serve at a party for the community gardeners tonight."

"It seems pretty quiet up here." I had noticed there were more offices farther along the hallway.

"It's traditional for people to take time off after Mayday! Of course this year with Joe gone, that means the few of us who are still here are swamped. But you didn't come for chitchat, did you?"

I heard the message. She was busy, and I needed to get straight to the point. I joined her at the filing cabinet and opened my purse. "I found these papers in Hazel Kefauver's pocket." I explained about the rummage sale. "I wonder if you'd look at them and tell me why Hazel had them?"

Cilla took the papers and quickly scanned them. "I think this is her handwriting." She handed them back to me. "They look like something she copied, maybe from the warehouse files? Or maybe they're notes from a board meeting?"

"Why would she copy something like this?"

"Well, it looks like a list of donations. Maybe the board was discussing expiration dates or moving inventory around at a meeting, and she wanted the facts."

Since no one else was around, I felt free to continue. "Put aside your better instincts. Let's pretend Hazel really was trying to find some problem here. Right before she died she told me there were some big developments in the wind for the food bank. I got the feeling she wanted to expose a problem."

"I told you she was out to get Joe."

Unfortunately I had a photo at home to confirm that. "Maybe there was more to it. Or maybe Joe *was* involved in something."

324

"Don't you think I'd know? He's a straight arrow."

I didn't point out the tiniest little kink in that arrow, the monthly trips Joe had lied about to everybody.

"Okay, then think like Hazel," I said. "You find these figures and they seem important enough to copy. Why?"

She considered a moment, then shook her head. "I think you have to ask the guys in the warehouse. Chad will probably know."

"How do Chad and Joe get along?"

Something changed in her eyes. She had seemed perfectly open, but now some part of her was locking up for the afternoon.

She closed the file drawer just a shade harder than she should have. Then she went to her desk and squirted a few drops of hand lotion into her palms, as if to stall. I recognized the jasmine scent, which seemed to be an intrinsic part of her.

"I guess they work well together," she said as she rubbed her hands together. "Chad's something of a goof-off, but Joe knows how to make him toe the line without being obvious about it."

"I'll take this over to the warehouse then." I inclined my head. "But I get the feeling you're not fond of Chad?"

"I really can't say more. I don't want to

325

lose my job." She paused. "Not that I'll want the job if Joe doesn't come back. They'll probably make Chad director, and I don't want to work for him."

I persisted. "You don't like Chad?"

"He's not Joe. What can I tell you?"

I heard more than a simple preference. "How about why you'd *really* prefer not to work for Chad?"

She hesitated. "Okay. Because I think Chad has wanted Joe's job for a long time. Chad's doesn't pay that well, although I guess that doesn't matter because he comes from money. His parents are loaded, and they give him everything he wants. His salary is pocket change. You should see his apartment, his car . . ."

"Then why would he want a harder job?"

"Prestige. And the work might be harder, but a lot of it is public relations. He's good at charming people. It's second nature. What women haven't already gone to bed with him might flock to his door."

"Ouch. That sounds personal."

"Don't look at me. I've had the chance but not the inclination."

"Cilla, why should wanting Joe's job, which sounds pretty natural, make Chad a bad boss in the future?"

"I would always wonder if he helped the

process along."

"You mean you think Chad might have something to do with Joe's disappearance?"

With every sentence she sounded more disgruntled. "No, but he might have slipped a word or two to Hazel or other board members about problems here. And knowing him, he would do it in such a sneaky way they didn't even realize what he'd done."

"*What* problems?"

"I really don't know anything specific. I could even see Chad making stuff up, dropping hints to make Joe look bad."

"But you've never seen or heard him do that or heard Joe complain?"

She gave a single shake of her head. "I just know that in his personal life, Chad's a loser. He's a love 'em and leave 'em kind of guy, only by the time he leaves, the women are glad to see him go."

Now Cilla's tone bordered on bitter. I wondered if this was more personal than she had admitted. Or maybe she really was just being protective of Joe. But I could tell this subject had come to a close.

I wanted to get into Joe's office in the worst way. If he paid his bills here, as I guessed, he would pay them from his own computer and desk. Everything and anything personal would be filed there.

"I guess that's Joe's office?" I nodded toward the closed door.

"When he's here that door is always open. Joe has nothing to hide."

"Have you looked through his files? To try to find anything that might help us figure out where he's gone?"

"Then I'd be as bad as Hazel Kefauver. I keep that door locked and nobody gets inside."

I was tempted to ask Cilla to give me access, but as much as she wanted Joe to come home, she hadn't been as helpful as I hoped. She had appointed herself Joe's guard dog, and nobody was going to mess with Joe on her watch, including me. He would return and find everything exactly the way he had left it.

If he returned.

A buzzer sounded, and Cilla grimaced. "Darn. They need me downstairs in the store. They always buzz if they have a problem at checkout. Are we done?"

"Not quite, but I can wait a few minutes."

"It might be longer."

My gaze flicked to one of the end tables. "You've got magazines."

"Okay. Just make yourself comfortable. I'll get back as soon as I can."

I don't necessarily believe things happen for a reason. To me the world seems chock-full of incongruities. But occasionally, everything just falls into place. Call it the "tickle" fingers of fate, some cosmic force with an irrepressible sense of humor. Sculptors don't chisel that grin on Buddha's face for nothing.

I was just feet from the locked door of Joe's office. I had time alone. Along with Hazel's pocket money I was carrying her keys in my purse — on the off chance I ever saw Brownie Kefauver again.

I didn't let myself consider what to do next. If I had, I would have bolted to my van. From the weight of Hazel's keys I was guessing she'd had access to every room in the buildings. After a few heart-stopping moments of trial and error I found the right one.

In a moment I was inside Joe's office.

I closed the door and stood with my back to it. This room was as tastefully decorated as the reception area. Joe's desk was larger than Cilla's. Instead of vegetable pillows there were paintings of farmland with grazing cows. But the impression was indistinct, because in a moment I was racing to the filing cabinet.

The top file drawer had personnel records

and reports to the board for years past. I closed it and moved on to the second. This one was filled with files about other similar programs, and grant proposals.

I opened the third drawer. The first hanging folder was labeled "Bills," the second "Receipts."

I was overjoyed to see that credit card statements were neatly filed by month in the second folder. When Joe came back I would ask for organizational pointers.

I pulled the statements and started through them, listening as I did for footsteps on the stairs outside the reception area. With the door shut I wasn't sure I would hear Cilla's approach, but I really didn't want anyone who just happened by to find me rifling through Joe's files.

I started at the back of the file. The last statement on Joe's Visa card had only gone through the end of March. I found charges in New York. The Chelsea Inn, a couple of restaurants. I thought Joe had tried to conserve funds, since not one meal totaled more than fifteen dollars. On a handy pad I jotted down the names of every Manhattan business he had used, then did the same for February's statement. Joe also had an American Express card, but nothing interesting turned up on it.

I paged through the rest of the bills, paying special attention to his phone bill, but the bill was too old to help me trace him now. I couldn't find any long-distance calls to or from New York and guessed that he had used his cell phone for those. Maybe he paid the cell bill automatically, because there were no records here. I finished with a folder marked "Tax-deductible Receipts," but again, nothing turned up.

Time was passing quickly. Cilla had been gone for more than five minutes, and I knew that at the most, I had just a few more. I closed the drawer and opened the bottom one. What I wanted to see most of all were copies of bills Joe had submitted for reimbursement. My luck was holding. Halfway back I saw a folder labeled "Expenses."

I perched on the edge of Joe's desk and opened this folder. These were as neatly compiled as the credit card statements, with receipts or copies of receipts clipped to each page. I checked and rechecked the file and my relief grew.

At no time had Joe charged *any* of his New York trips to the food bank.

Once a month Joe left to attend meetings at Funds for Food. Only there was no Funds for Food. He could easily have charged every penny to the food bank and gotten away with it — at least as long as he got away with the trips themselves.

But Joe was a stand-up guy. He was living a lie, but he wasn't asking anyone else to pay for it.

This was an interesting ethical problem. Joe had lied, but if I was right, Helping Hands hadn't paid any price for it except his occasional absence.

More interesting was whether Hazel Kefauver had gone through these same records, made the same observations, come to the same conclusions, and realized something strange was going on in New York.

Was this what had brought her to the Pussycat Club? The fact that Joe wasn't charging the food bank for his trips? Had that been a red flag? From his credit card statements she would know the hotel he usually stayed in. She would know where he ate and shopped. Had she gone to New York to snoop, hoping to catch him in a lie that would be grounds for dismissal?

But if she learned the truth, why hadn't she told anybody when she returned? What else had she hoped to learn first?

My time was up. If I stayed even a minute longer, I would probably be caught. My hands were perspiring and the still small voice inside me, the one I was supposed to cultivate, was screeching like a hungry toddler. Letting myself into Joe's office was one thing, but lying about it? I *so* didn't want to go there.

I replaced the folder and crossed the room. I cracked the door and listened. I thought I heard footsteps. Go? Stay?

Go! I slipped through the door and saw, with relief, that I was still alone. I managed to lock up and pocket Hazel's keys just seconds before Cilla came through the doorway.

She looked annoyed. "I'm sorry. A volunteer jammed the cash register. It's easy to do because it's so old, but of course Hazel Kefauver told us we couldn't buy a new one."

"Not a problem." My heart was beating so fast I was afraid she could hear it. I spoke louder. "I didn't mind waiting. But I really ought to get out of here and let you get back to work. I just had one more question. This probably sounds silly, but did Joe get a lot of annual leave?"

"Yeah, a lot. The board could never give him the kind of raises he deserved, so they gave him more vacation time. It was no skin off their noses, because he never took it all anyway. He and Tyler used to go camping for a week in the summer, but that was about all. Maura didn't like to leave her garden for long. So if they went away, it was just overnight. She was perfectly happy staying in Emerald Springs and taking care of their house and yard."

I wasn't surprised. Not only had Joe not charged his expenses to Helping Hands, he had probably counted those days against his vacation time, even if they didn't show up on any records.

I flashed her a smile. "Okay, I'm done here. Thanks for your time."

"I'm sorry I couldn't be more help with those lists. I did think of one thing, though."

"What was that?"

"Well, Joe told me once that there are two kinds of people in the world. The kind that takes things at face value and trusts that for the most part, the world's a good place."

"He was talking about himself," I said.

She nodded. "Then there's the kind that examines every little thing, picking it apart, searching through the debris, because they're convinced that something terrible will turn up if they just look hard enough. Joe said Hazel was that second kind of person, that it was in her nature. He thought eventually she would dig up some problem or other here, because she wouldn't be satisfied until she did."

I was afraid I was that second kind of person, too, although I wasn't looking for something negative as much as I was looking for truth and justice. But linking my own actions to Hazel's made me wince.

"Joe sounds like he was pretty tolerant," I said.

"A lot more than I was. I wanted him to come out swinging and find a way to stop her, but he said no, that in the end one of them would just have to leave. It was only a matter of time."

"It's odd, isn't it? In the end *both* of them left. Only by different routes." I only hoped that someday soon, Joe would find his way home.

15

I found Chad Sutterfield coming out of the warehouse with two other men. I can always tell how serious guy conversation is by the amount of horseplay that accompanies it. Chad socked the guy closest to him on the shoulder. Then that guy — burly and bald — shoved the blond coming up behind them into a holly bush.

I discounted any possibility the trio were discussing war, avian flu, or the second coming. That left women, beer, and football, all of which can be discussed simultaneously in grunts and words of one syllable. There wasn't a drop of class prejudice in my assessment. Had they been walking across Harvard Yard in academic gowns, I would have guessed the same.

The men caught sight of me, and the high spirits dimmed. Chad left the others and cut across the grass to say hello. Like the other two, he wore a spring green polo shirt with the Helping Hands insignia embellished by a photo ID card hanging around his neck on a chain.

In the distance I could hear families laughing in the community garden. I wondered if our family should try to reserve a plot. But then what excuse would I have to visit DiBenedetto's to spy on Marco?

"Mrs. Wilcox." Chad held out his hand. "Can I help you?"

I could see this young man taking Joe's job. Chad had remembered my name. He had the good sense to greet and impress me with his manners. I just wondered why he hadn't already moved on to something better? Was this the big frog in the small pond syndrome? A guy who had leaped to the biggest lily pad Emerald Springs had to offer but knew he would be treading water and dodging bass and walleye if he headed for the Great Lakes?

We shook. "I was just on my way to see you. I was curious about something, and Cilla thought maybe you could help."

He glanced at his watch. "If it won't take long. We're due at a local farm to pick up some beef. And I never keep donors waiting." He flashed a grin. "We want them to love us."

I wondered who didn't love Chad. He had

everything going for him. And yet, here he was, working in a warehouse at a nonprofit organization during the years when he should be vaulting to the top of his chosen field.

"It can wait," I said. "Or I can ask somebody else. Unless everybody's going with you?"

"Phil O'Hara's staying behind. He's not much for talking, but he can tell you about the way we do things. Is it that kind of question?"

All my instincts told me to nod. I was no longer certain I wanted to pick this man's brain, and I wasn't sure why. Because he was good-looking and smart and this was a podunk Ohio town? After all, Ed and I lived here, as did any number of good-looking, smart, and supremely nice people.

Or was it because Cilla and Maura thought Chad wanted Joe's job? Of course he did. That made perfect sense.

Or maybe it was just something about Chad's smile, something that said there wasn't as much inside to back it up as there ought to be. Chad was in charge of the warehouse. I'd hoped to watch him closely as he scanned the lists, but now I wasn't sure this was a guy who would give anything away. Alerting him that I was on the trail of a problem probably wasn't as good an idea as it had sounded a moment ago.

"I'll check with Mr. O'Hara," I told him. "It's nothing important. I'm just . . . looking into some facts about nonprofits in general." Facts like how they were cheated and abused.

"He's inside. Just don't keep him up too long. I think he likes to nap while I'm not standing over him." He laughed at his own joke. I forced a smile.

We said good-bye, and I watched the three men climb into a van with the Helping Hands logo on it before I finished my hike to the warehouse.

The door was open, so I walked in and wandered a little before I saw a man in tan coveralls moving food from a platform cart to a deep row of shelves.

"Mr. O'Hara?"

He stopped, his hand, complete with canned goods, hovering in midair. Then he finished putting the cans on a shelf, dusted his hands on his coveralls, and started in my direction.

O'Hara was built like a stevedore, but his head was too small for his body, as if it had shrunk with age while the rest of him stayed fit. And he was old. I guessed well into the Medicare years. Too old to spend his days stocking shelves.

"Chad Sutterfield said I could find you here." I introduced myself and held out my hand. He shook without a word. "I was going to ask Chad about something, but he was in a hurry. He said you might be able to help."

He shrugged. Definitely a man of few words.

I explained about the rummage sale and Hazel's clothes. I was beginning to think I ought to print up the story to save my vocal cords. I pulled the lists from my purse and handed them to him.

"I found these in her pockets. And now I'm curious. Why do you suppose she would have had them? I'm just trying to understand what she might have been doing in the days before her death."

He didn't take the papers. "Why?"

Clearly it was a good question, with an answer I couldn't easily give. "It's a combination of things," I said. "Most of all, because I'm a friend of Joe Wagner's, and before I turn this over to the cops, I want to be sure it's not going to reflect badly on him."

I had chosen this explanation among many. If O'Hara didn't respond favorably, it probably meant he wasn't a supporter of

Joe's. If he wasn't, then how much could I trust his explanation, anyway?

He held out his hand. Now I wished I'd copied the forms first, but I gave them to him and hoped for the best.

He took his time, but there was so little to see, he finished the first page quickly. He looked up. "Nothing but a list of donations."

"Why would she have it?"

He shrugged.

I expected him to hand the pages back. Instead he went on to the second one. Now he really took his time. He held the list closer to his face, then he retrieved reading glasses from a pocket and read it all over again.

Finally he removed his glasses and pocketed them. He held the papers at his side and tilted his shrunken head.

"Can I keep 'em?"

"Why?"

"Need to check things."

I already knew enough about O'Hara to realize this was all I would get. "I don't think I can leave them."

He toddled off, as if he hadn't heard me. I followed behind, hoping I hadn't been dismissed. We ended up at Chad's offices in the back of the warehouse. This was quite a comedown from Joe's. I could see where spending days in this utilitarian space without Maura's comfortable touches could make him yearn for something more.

O'Hara went to the copier sitting on one side among other office paraphernalia and turned it on. I knew better than to chat. I waited in silence. He made copies and handed the originals back to me.

"How do you know Joe?" he asked, surprising me.

"My husband is his minister."

"Where is he?"

"I'm told New Jersey."

He gave a humorless laugh.

I had questions; he probably had answers. Never the twain shall meet. I thanked him and he shrugged. I left him in the office and found my way out.

Call me an optimist, but I thought maybe O'Hara and I were on to something. Hazel's lists had set off an alarm. I wondered what else Hazel had found and copied, and whether I'd only gotten a taste of the good stuff when I searched her pockets. Would he actually talk to me if I brought him more?

The time was right to swing back by the Kefauver residence and see if I could catch his honor for a little chat before I picked up the middle schoolers and Teddy. Maybe Hazel had kept records at home that would help me draw some conclusions.

I found a pack of cheese crackers in the glove compartment and called it lunch. Then I headed for Brownie's house. I was getting tired of chasing him. He had asked me for help, and by golly, I was going to give it to him whether he wanted it or not.

In that mood I turned on to his street and crawled the length of it behind a small moving van. I was unpleasantly surprised to find we were heading for the same driveway, and that somebody with a low-slung black sports car had gotten there first. No cream-colored Lincoln was in sight.

I parked on the street and started up the herringbone path. Somebody had to be here. I rang the doorbell and rapped sharply. If nobody answered, I planned to gnaw through the wood panels like a belligerent beaver.

The door swung open, and Brownie stood on the other side. Just beyond him in the hallway a woman in her late twenties was bending over a box, apparently to demonstrate the elasticity of a stretch lace thong under a microscopic skirt. She straightened, and waist-length brown hair swung like a curtain over her bare shoulders.

"I'm afraid I'm busy . . ."

Brownie drew a sharp breath as I pushed

him to one side and strode into the hallway. There were boxes stacked along the walls, and into the living room. "I can see that. Now you're going to be even busier."

"We're packing up the rest of dear Hazel's things. This is Diana Diva. I just hired her as my personal assistant."

My eyes flicked to Miss Diva, who had probably come into the world with a less exotic name. I wondered when and where the new one had first appeared in lights.

"You have a couple of choices," I told him. "You can start behaving like a grieving husband and give the police fewer reasons to suspect you of Hazel's murder. Or you can spend some time on the Internet checking out prisons where you'd like to serve your time. Be sure you choose one with a comfy death row. Ohio is a capital punishment state."

He blanched. "I don't know what you mean."

"Is that Miss Diva's car in your driveway? She needs to get behind the wheel and drive to Michigan."

"It's *my* car. The Lincoln had too many memories. And it's black because I'm in mourning."

I stood right on top of him, peering into his eyes. "Don't mess with me. Not if you want my help."

His gaze flicked between me and Diana, who was standing there as placid as a well-fed milk cow.

"Shall I call her a cab?" I asked. Emerald Springs has a brand-new fleet of two, most often sitting idly in the garage.

He slumped. "I'll do it."

"You owe me," Diana said, in a melodious voice, holding out her hand. "Severance pay."

I figured I'd go for broke. "And while you're at it, tell Va-Va-Voom her probationary period at City Hall isn't working out. Start looking for somebody's grandmother to act as your secretary."

"Her name is Rachel Rapture," he said haughtily.

Was there really an employment agency that specialized in rehabilitated strippers? Or were both these women just hanging out with Brownie until they got their big break in triple-X movies? I was afraid to ask.

He slid bills out of his wallet and handed them to Diana, then he left to make the phone call.

"I kind of liked this job," she said.

I really didn't want to know why.

Brownie returned and escorted her to the porch. Once she was gone, he came back with two guys in overalls and caps with the same logo as the moving truck.

Brownie looked harried. "I really am busy. These men —"

"Are going bye-bye," I finished for him.

"What possible harm can there be in —"

"Plenty."

He escorted the movers back to the door, more bills changed hands, and finally he shut the door behind him.

He stood with his back to it. "I just —"

"You just despised your wife and your life with her, and now you feel like a canary who's finally escaped his cage. The thing is, there are bigger, deadlier birds out there waiting to nab you. And the more you flaunt your freedom, the more you attract their attention."

"I didn't despise her."

"Let's not argue over my choice of words. She ran your life, and now you want to run it your own way. Unfortunately you need a few flying lessons."

"But I've told people and told people I'm donating her things because the memories are so painful."

"Brownie" — I shook my head — "take the sports car back and get a sedan. Leave the furniture and whatever else you planned to erase from your life until Hazel's murderer has been caught. Can't you see how this looks?"

"We were married a long time," he said at last. "And I never dreamed I . . ." His voice trailed off.

I finished the sentence silently. After all those years of an unhappy marriage, Brownie had stopped dreaming that someday he would be able to live the way he wanted. And now he could. He didn't want to waste another minute.

But his next words surprised me.

"I never dreamed I would miss her." He looked down at his toes. "I'm not even sure what I miss exactly. We understood each other. We made allowances. Maybe we were happy together, and we never even realized it."

I didn't know what to say.

He pushed himself away from the door and started toward the box Diana Diva had been taping for him. "I can't bring her back. I've just been trying to move forward."

"I'm sorry." And I was. For his loss. For my conclusions — at least some of them. For not always understanding what lies beneath the surface.

He began to pull tape in long strips from the box, as if he planned to reassemble what he and Diana had undone. "Have you found anything? Do you have any idea who might have murdered her?"

"I'm following trails. Hopefully one of them will lead somewhere. But while I'm here, I've got another. Did Hazel keep any records from her charitable work at the house? Specifically the food bank?"

"I emptied her file cabinet yesterday."

"Tell me the trash hasn't been hauled away."

"It's still in her office, beside the cabinet. Two cardboard cartons."

"May I look through them?"

"The police went through everything. I don't know what you'll find."

"Hopefully something they didn't."

He led me to an office off a spacious, dignified family room. The house reminded me of Hazel's clothing. Somber, a trifle shabby, but everything that was in residence had been expensive and substantial when purchased.

When Brownie comes out of mourning I hope he employs a decorator who doesn't object to a little color. Hopefully not one of the Fiona Fling or Alissa Arousal variety.

He left me alone, and I wandered a little first, enjoying the fact that this time, I was looking through files with permission.

Not much was left on the bookshelves. I

wondered if Brownie would temporarily reassemble this room or just leave it as it was. I lifted books out of boxes and perused titles. Classics, a few British mysteries, nonfiction about the royal family including a few fairly titillating exposes. Hazel did have a lighter side.

The contents of the desk were history. There wasn't so much as an old Life Saver stuck inside a drawer. The closet was empty, too. I went through the wooden file cabinet but it had been thoroughly cleared. That left the two boxes of files on the floor beside it.

I sat campfire style and started my examination. I suspected the cops had already taken everything they found suspicious, like death threats and blackmail notes, but I doubted they had found her charitable work as interesting. They probably hadn't been aware that Hazel was collecting evidence against Joe and/or the food bank. That shed new light on everything.

I resisted making assessments about Hazel's personality based on what she chose to file and systematically swept through the folders. I found a folder with travel brochures and articles about hotels and airlines. There was another with the names of local businesses and opinions jotted in the margins. She had files of best seller lists and book discussion notes, and the names of everyone who had ever sent the Kefauvers a Christmas card. She had sample menus from caterers, estimates from painters and plumbers, and bulletins from Ohio State University Extension.

The first box yielded nothing of interest, although I was tempted to ask Brownie if I could keep the bulletin on noxious weeds of Ohio — in case I ran into one on an isolated tree lawn late at night. Know your enemy.

Halfway through the second box I pulled out a folder marked "Food Bank Inventory." The folder was filled with computer-generated lists. They appeared to have been compiled by the food bank staff.

I set that aside and continued to look. The second to last folder was marked "Food Bank Donations."

Bingo. I breezed through this one, too. These notes were in Hazel's handwriting, much like the lists I had found in her pocket. Nothing jumped out at me, but I was pretty sure I needed to spread the contents of both folders on my kitchen table and see what I could make of them.

I got to my feet, rummaged through my purse, and took out the cash I had found in Hazel's wallet. I laid it on her desk and removed her keys as well. These were harder to part with, but in the end I dropped them on top of the cash and left them behind. Get thee behind me, Satan.

I retraced my steps to find Brownie unpacking boxes in the living room. I held up the files. "May I take these with me?"

"Unless you think I'll be arrested for giving away her papers."

"I'm sorry. But you did ask for my help." He looked bleak.

"I bet friends are inviting you to dinner, aren't they?" I said.

"I don't want to talk about Hazel and who murdered her."

"Good friends will be sensitive. Why don't you give that a try? You could use some company." I couldn't help myself. "Just not the bimbo variety."

He shook his head. I'm not sure at whom. I let myself out.

While I waited for school to end I went home for a sandwich. Then, with a mouth full of peanut butter, I gave Lucy a call and somehow managed to convey the story of my trip to the food bank and what I had found at Brownie's.

I finished the sandwich and explanation. "I'm going over the files tonight, want to join me?"

She sounded disgruntled. "You have all the fun, and you broke into Joe's office without me. After you said you weren't going to use Hazel's keys."

"You can be the burglar next time."

"I promised a client I'd drive him by a house he's interested in tonight. He wants to see what the neighborhood is like when the kids are home from school and moms and dads are back from work."

"What does he think? It's one wacky block party every night after five?"

"Barking dogs and baseball games on the street. Plus the house is in the general area of the parcel Junie's trying to protect. So he's also worried about bulldozers and chain saws. He wants to park by the roadside and monitor traffic. I'll get to your house as soon as I can."

I grabbed a bottle of water and Maura's house key from the key basket in the kitchen and went back to the van. At the middle school I got into the line of cars, SUVs, and vans waiting to retrieve children. I turned the radio to our oldies station and hummed "Billie Jean" as Michael Jackson provided the lead. I had to hum, because all these years later, I still can't understand the lyrics. Is he or isn't he the father of her son? Some detective I've turned out to be.

Tyler was waiting by the time I pulled into the circle in front of the school, and he slid into the backseat when he saw me. Next Deena came out of the building so quickly I thought maybe she'd been watching from inside. Was she afraid of being teased by her friends if she waited with Tyler?

Once they were both in the backseat — Deena waved away my offer of the front — they chattered like good friends. I drove to Grant Elementary, and we waited a few minutes until Teddy finished rehearsal. She came outside and took the front seat. I realized immediately there was no hope of a conversation. She was mute.

No place is far away in Emerald Springs, and in minutes we were at Tyler's. Maura's dolls were at their most bizarre. Both of them wore bird costumes, one in yellow, the other in red. A large nest made of twigs and string sat on the porch in front of them. I was almost tearfully grateful there were no eggs inside it. Had there been, we might have been treated to weeks of hatching rituals. I'm not sure I could have visited Maura again, knowing what was in store.

"Why do you have Big Bird on your porch?" Deena asked Tyler.

"My mom needs a life."

I opened my door. The kids followed,

although I had to pry Teddy from her seat.

"I told your mom I'd hang around until she gets here," I told Tyler. "But she asked me to remind you —"

"I know. Test and shoot. I can do it."

"Can I watch?" Deena asked.

I started to protest, but Tyler answered first. "Sure. It's no big deal."

He didn't unlock the front door, so taking that as a cue, I brought out the beaded elephant and unlocked it myself.

The house looked the way it always did. While Tyler and Deena discussed and performed the array of medical procedures, I got Teddy a drink of water in the kitchen.

"Miss Hollins called today," I said, handing the glass to her.

"I know." She looked glum.

"Honey, I can't help if you don't tell me what's wrong."

She drank the water and put the glass on the counter.

"Are the other kids making fun of you for some reason?"

She looked puzzled.

"Maybe they're jealous?"

"I don't know."

"Animal, vegetable, or mineral?"

"Let's go outside. I don't like it in here."

"Why not?"

She shrugged and lowered her voice. "I don't think anybody lives here."

"Of course they do, honey. It's Tyler's house."

"I don't think it's a real house."

We went to the bottom of the stairs and I called up to Tyler's room. Deena said they'd be down in a minute. I planned to hold them to it.

Outside Teddy and I toured the yard, which she liked better. White peonies sent their delicate fragrance into the air. Primroses were beginning to close up shop for the year, but there were still enough yellow and red blooms to satisfy. We ended at Maura's rose garden, which I guessed would be spectacular in another month when the blooms began. The roses covered the corner of the yard beside a storybook-perfect shed, which was sided and roofed with wooden shingles and trimmed with Victorian gingerbread. Tyler and Deena joined us while I peeked through the window.

"Your mother has an amazing garden," I told Tyler.

"She's an organic gardener. Everything's natural."

"What kind of stuff?" Deena asked.

"Manure, compost. Want to see our compost pile? Every scrap of leftover vegetables goes into it. She makes her own insecticides out of stuff like hot peppers and garlic. She wins prizes every year at the fair."

He opened the door to the shed and pointed. "That's dried blood. It keeps rabbits out of the garden."

"Yuck!" Deena said.

I could tell he was enjoying himself, the way males of the species do when they can nauseate the females, and I was enjoying yet another view of a woman who actually took Martha Stewart seriously.

"That's bonemeal," he said. "Ground-up bone. It adds minerals to the soil."

"This is so sick," Deena said. "I hope you don't eat stuff you grow with that."

"And this is fox urine. It keeps away whatever the dried blood doesn't."

"You're making that up."

We were admiring the sweet-smelling compost pile when Maura arrived. Tyler seemed disappointed, and I realized he had been hoping for more time with my daughter. I liked him. What wasn't to like? He was a nice kid with good manners and the ability to gross out little girls. At this age, what else was there?

Maura greeted us. I noticed she didn't hug her son, but maybe that was because we were there, and she didn't want to embarrass him. Tyler walked Deena to our car, but Teddy stayed glued to my side.

"Did things go well?" I asked.

"Just fine. Thanks so much for doing this, Aggie." Maura smiled at Teddy, who didn't smile back.

"We have to scoot." I turned my daughter toward the car and gave her a gentle nudge. "Wait with Deena, would you?"

Teddy walked off as if she were slogging through taffy.

"I've got to ask," I said, lowering my voice. "Detective Roussos tells me you gave him a phone number for Joe in New Jersey?"

"I had to do something. I asked a sorority sister who lives there if I could use her number. She has caller ID, and she's not answering any calls from this area code." She looked rueful. "Was that a mistake?"

I thought it was clever, although I didn't think it would work for long. Eventually, if he really wanted to find Joe, Roussos would send a local cop to the address linked to the phone number.

Maura seemed to read my mind. "If the police find out I've lied, I'll have to tell them Joe disappeared. I'm just hoping he comes back before they realize what I've done."

We started after Teddy. "Deena and Tyler seem to be friends," Maura said. "Emerald

Springs has been a good place to raise him. Even with the diabetes he's always been one of the gang. That might not be true anywhere else."

Maura had enough problems. I didn't want to tell her that some of the kids at the middle school were not as tolerant as she supposed. In fact, I wondered if in a bigger city, where there was more diversity in every way, Tyler's medical issues might be better accepted.

When we got to the car, Deena and Tyler were whispering. I was almost sorry to separate them. Already belted into the front seat, Teddy was staring straight ahead.

"This was no trouble," I told Maura. "Call me again if you need me."

"I think I've missed out on a lot by letting Joseph take on so many things alone. I like having a friend."

I gave her a quick hug, which seemed to surprise her. But she gave me a squeeze in return.

We were halfway home when Teddy put her hand on my arm. "That girl's in my class. Rene Marcus. Over there."

I pulled to a stop at the traffic light and looked in the direction she was pointing. I saw a girl Teddy's size getting into a car that looked as if it was held together by rust and mud. I glimpsed dark curls, bare legs, and sneakers.

"Is Rene your friend?" I asked.

"She wanted to be Cinderella."

I watched as the car pulled away from the curb, no working muffler to blunt the clanking of the engine.

"She *is* Cinderella," Teddy said. "Really. Only she never gets to go to the ball."

At last I understood the problem. "I think it's pretty swell you're worried about her."

"Somebody has to," Teddy said.

I'm afraid worrying about people is going to be Teddy's mission in life. Just like her father's.

16

Ed and I worked on dinner preparation together, and as he made the salad and I made the pasta sauce, I told him what I'd figured out about the Cinderella crisis.

"Will you talk to Teddy?" I finished. "She's having a moral crisis, and that's your bailiwick."

"What do you think she wants to do?" He stole a few sunflower seeds before he sprinkled the rest on his salad. Ed's salads are masterpieces of design, colorful layers that seem too pretty to toss — although that's never stopped either of us.

I threw a handful of chopped mushrooms into my skillet and turned the heat up higher. "I don't think she knows. But worrying about Rene is taking all the joy out of the play. She feels guilty she got what she wanted and Rene didn't. And she's figured out that Rene isn't as lucky as she is in her daily life."

"Doesn't it seem like she should have a few years when she's completely self-centered? I thought that was more or less the definition of childhood. She'll have the rest of her lifetime to worry."

Despite the words, I heard pride in his voice. "She takes after you."

"So you say, but who's the one in our family who's running all over Emerald Springs trying to save everybody in sight? You're trying to help so many people at once, I'm surprised you can keep them straight."

I didn't pick up even a hint of censure. "All of a sudden you sound pretty comfortable with this."

"Maybe I've been doing some soul-searching."

I let the mushrooms sizzle and put my arms around him. "At least you get paid for it. Nobody can say you're not doing your job while you're thinking about big moral issues."

He rested his cheek against my hair. "We all serve in different ways. I guess yours is offbeat, but who am I to critique my children's most important role model?"

I thought about that after the meal, when Ed took Teddy out for a heart-to-heart at Way Too Cool. I was still luxuriating in his support. I'd never considered what my girls were learning from my obsession with finding answers. But maybe there was more to this than being nosy. I really did care that bad people got caught and good people went free — although things were never quite that simple. I cared that justice triumphed because that enhanced my view of a world in balance. I liked helping people I loved or admired. I liked bringing closure.

I spent a full minute basking in the warmth of my own regard. Then I went upstairs and got the folders I'd brought home from Hazel's and spread the contents on the kitchen table.

Ed and Teddy came home, and he took her upstairs to supervise bedtime. Deena watched a tape of *Zoey 101,* then went up to read before lights-out. Junie wandered through the kitchen on her way to and from the basement where she was dyeing wool. Lucy was sitting in a car somewhere hoping the neighborhood dogs were off on vacation.

Nobody needed me. I took advantage of that.

It was past nine before I began to see patterns emerging. I had separated the lists by dates, pairing the donations list with the list of inventory that most closely matched it and paying particular attention to donations that Hazel or someone had checked with a red pen.

I found proof that some of the food had made it into inventory, but I drew a blank too often. A farmer donated a side of beef, but the only record I could find was forty pounds of hamburger added to a food bank freezer a few days later. Forty pounds? Had the rest of the beef been used right away by the meals for seniors or homeless programs? Is that why it hadn't been added to inventory?

A grocery store donated thirty crates of dried pasta because the packaging was updated. The warehouse inventory that week didn't show a one. Could thirty crates of pasta be used so quickly that none made it to a shelf?

I jotted notes on every donation that didn't appear. Three sheets of lined paper later, I stopped. This could go on all night. Maybe there were good explanations why donations weren't showing up on the shelves, and maybe there weren't. But the possibilities for abuse seemed endless. Even if the donations showed up temporarily, who was to say that from that point on, they reached their target?

Exposing fraud was going to take a lot more expertise than I had. A real exposé would take a forensic accountant. Clearly, I needed to get in touch with Roussos and tell him what I had learned and why it pertained to Hazel's murder. If he believed me, he would take it from there.

I hoped Roussos wouldn't shrug this away just because it came from me. Hazel had suspected abuse, and she had attempted to track down the culprit. Look what had happened to her.

I was glad I shopped for every single ingredient in our dinner myself and that Ed and I had fixed it with our own hands.

Passing the phone on my way upstairs, I thought about Phil O'Hara. I wondered if his observations would make Roussos take notice. Something on Hazel's list had caught his eye.

I couldn't help myself. I stopped and thumbed through the phone book. There he was. If I called him, he'd have to respond verbally, right? He couldn't count on body language to make his point.

Before I could talk myself out of it, I dialed the telephone. O'Hara answered immediately. I launched in after "hello," apologizing for calling him at home. Then before he could answer — which seemed a long shot anyway — I told him what I'd been doing this evening. I wondered if he had anything to add, because the figures seemed suspicious to me. And unless he could explain the discrepancies, I was going to have to show them to the police.

"Something funny going on," he said.

I waited, but that was it. "In other words, some of the donations aren't being used to feed the hungry? I'm not imagining it?"

"Nope."

I tried for clarification. "Then you're saying somebody's committing fraud?"

"Could be."

"Mr. O'Hara, how can you tell?"

The silence went on so long I wondered if he had hung up. Finally he spoke. "We got so low on beef a month ago, we were serving beans and rice to our old folks. Macaroni and cheese, all that carrot-eater trash."

I didn't take offense. "And I'm guessing you saw donations of beef on that list I showed you. For the same time?"

"Yep."

"Who do you think's cheating?"

"Chad Sutterfield. Miss Hunter and I showed him your list and told him so this afternoon."

I nearly dropped the phone. "You and Cilla confronted him?"

"She came down to talk to me and saw me with your lists. We discussed it. Soon as

365

he got back we asked him. I told him I knew about the beef. He tried to tell me I was imagining it."

"You know, Hazel Kefauver was murdered, maybe because she realized something was up in the warehouse. You'd better take extra care locking your doors tonight." And maybe I needed to hang up and call Cilla right away, then Roussos.

O'Hara gave a humorless laugh, just like the one he'd favored me with when I told him Joe was supposed to be in New Jersey. "You know where the food bank gets most of its venison?"

I made a guess. "You?"

"Yep. You ever hear this old joke? If vegetarians eat vegetables, what do humanitarians eat? Well, somebody tries to get in my house, the humanitarians are going to have a feast."

I hung up and swallowed a few times to make sure I still could. I was about to pick up the phone when it rang again.

"Aggie?"

I recognized Lucy's voice. "Boy, have I got a story for you," I said.

"Aggie, the food bank's on fire!"

For a moment I couldn't absorb this. And when I did I couldn't think of a thing to say.

That didn't stop Lucy. "I was in the neighborhood with my client. We were driving around when we saw the flames shooting into the sky and heard the sirens. We came over to check it out. We can't get too close, but it looks like the fire's in the warehouse. And it's some fire. I've never seen anything like it."

Ed might be coming to terms with my avocation, but when I told him why I was on my way to Helping Hands, he threw on jeans and a T-shirt and told me he was coming along. While I waited, I tried to reach Cilla, but no one was home.

The fact that nothing much happens in Emerald Springs means that when something does, it becomes a community event. The closer we got to the food bank, the denser the traffic. We finally parked some distance away and hiked in. I was glad when I realized we were moving a lot faster on foot.

As we drove I told Ed what I'd learned tonight. Now he questioned me as we jogged toward the scene. Flames leapt into the evening sky, and the air grew steadily thicker and smokier as we got closer. Showers of embers threatened to catch nearby woods on fire. I thought it was going to be a long night for our firefighters.

"This O'Hara character actually said he thought it was Chad Sutterfield who was ripping them off?" Ed asked.

"He confronted Chad. To his face."

"Did he say why he thought it was Chad?"

"Getting him to say that much was miraculous. He didn't provide me with reasons."

"Do you think O'Hara will talk to Roussos?"

"I think Roussos will make him. But I bet they call in an investigator who's trained in this kind of scam and can get all the evidence they need through the records."

"The books probably look fine. I'm sure the food bank has to have audits annually, maybe more often. It sounds like Hazel got hold of a list of donations before it was doctored. The investigator can use her list to go right to the donors and see if their own records match hers."

"I can't understand how Chad got away with it."

"More likely *they,* don't you think? Not Chad alone. Some of the employees must have been in on this with him."

"I guess. It would take a crew to pick up donations and store them in somebody's garage or barn, then haul them out of state."

"They were stealing food from hungry people. I hope they catch every single person who was involved."

We were about fifty yards away now. I could see the road was blocked by a couple of cop cars, and men and women in uniform were holding back the crowds on foot.

We slowed and I began to search the crowd around us. "I wonder where Lucy is, and I wonder if Roussos is here. I'd like to tell him what I discovered. What are the chances this fire is a coincidence? And if it is arson, Hazel's list could be the match that set it."

Ed shook his head. "Look at that."

We got as close as we were allowed to. In the distance the smoke was so thick I couldn't tell which buildings were burning. I thought about the hard work that had gone into making Helping Hands a thriving enterprise, the store where families were able to maintain their pride and still supply their needs, the garden with so much time and love invested.

My eyes burned, but not from smoke or soot. I unzipped my purse and rummaged for a tissue.

"One question answered," Ed said, nudging me. I looked where he was pointing and saw Roussos moving through the crowd toward the barrier closest to us.

I took off after him, and Ed didn't try to stop me. We wiggled through the crowd until I was in touching distance.

"Roussos. Kirk."

Roussos turned and frowned, but he waited until I was almost on top of him.

"Why am I not surprised you're here?"

"Do you know what's burning? I can't tell."

"The warehouse."

"Do you know if they can contain it?"

"They're hoping." He turned as if he planned to move on, but I put my hand on his arm.

"Listen, I have information you need."

"Can't it wait?"

"It's about the food bank. It might have something to do with this. Somebody set this fire, didn't they?"

I could see him debating with himself. Then he took my arm and pulled me up to the barrier through the crowd with him. Ed was right behind.

The cops doing crowd control let him through, and us along with him. The air was getting smokier, and the only light came from flames in the distance and headlights behind. I was in such a hurry to keep up I stumbled over a root and dropped my purse. Items spilled to the ground around it.

"I'm sorry. Hold on." I grabbed my wallet and stuffed it back in, followed by a pack of tissues, my keys, and Maura's, too, which had flown farther afield. I found a hairbrush and the original lists of Hazel's that had started me down this road. Even in the dim light, I was pretty sure that was everything.

We stopped about ten yards beyond the barrier, and Roussos waited.

I held out the lists and told him what I knew, starting with the way I'd come to find them and ending with Cilla and O'Hara's confrontation with Chad today. I explained what I thought had been happening and that even though it sounded petty, if these guys had been at it awhile, they had probably pocketed a lot of money.

"If Chad thought he was going to be caught, he might have done something crazy like set fire to the warehouse."

"And when were you going to tell me all this?" he demanded, taking the lists and tucking them in a pocket. "When were you going to turn these over?"

"I'm sorry, but I only figured it out tonight. I was about to call you, then I heard about the fire."

"For what it's worth, you're on the right

track." He turned and started closer to the fire. I followed, and after a moment, Ed did, too.

"What do you mean?"

"Food bank hanky-panky. We've been tracing it for a week now."

"The way I did?"

"We didn't have the benefit of your lists. I recognized the name of one of the warehouse assistants. I arrested him four or five years ago, and he served some time. It just looked to me like he was living a lot better than he should on his income. We came to an understanding."

"He admitted it?"

"He's given us some useful information."

"Did he tell you Chad Sutterfield was involved?"

Roussos didn't answer. I was more surprised he'd answered me at all.

Ed filled the gap. "Detective Roussos, don't you usually investigate homicides?"

"You think Hazel Kefauver's death had to do with the food bank, don't you?" I asked. "That's why you're here."

We were as close now as I wanted to be. I could see just enough to know that the warehouse was rubble, but so far the firefighters had managed to contain the blaze so the administration building was intact.

To me, it looked like they were getting control of the blaze, and maybe the offices and the store could be saved. I wondered how many months would pass while the food bank tried to start over and build an inventory, and how many people would go hungry in the meantime.

A couple of firefighters came toward us. I recognized the chief from his appearance at civic functions I'd attended.

The men took Roussos aside and spoke in hushed voices.

"We should go," Ed told me. "We're just going to be in the way, Aggie."

I knew he was right, although I sensed there was something more going on. Ed was correct. Roussos did work homicide. Yes, our police force was small, but I doubted Roussos was also the arson investigator. And why was the fire chief talking to him now? Hazel's death wasn't an immediate concern.

"They've found a body," I told Ed, grasping his arm. "That's got to be why Roussos is here."

He didn't contradict me, and he didn't try to drag me away.

Roussos returned. "You need to get behind the barrier."

"Just tell me. They found somebody, didn't they? Somebody died in there?"

He shook his head, but not in denial. Like a man who had better things to do than answer more questions.

"Who?" I asked. "Do they know?"

"At this point they're only making a guess."

I thought about the old man who had confronted Chad this afternoon with a copy of my list and the woman who had been with him. I knew O'Hara was all right since I'd talked to him only moments before I'd learned of the fire. But Cilla? I felt guilt like a dark cloak enveloping me. This was my fault.

"It's Cilla Hunter, isn't it?" I asked softly.

He must have seen my distress. I'm sure it's the only reason he answered.

"No. Judging by what's left of his ID card, they think it's probably Sutterfield. Just keep that to yourself."

17

Ed is doing too many memorial services, and I have too many connections to the departed. As I dressed for the service that would commemorate the life of one Chad Sutterfield, I considered the events of the past week.

Although an investigation into the warehouse fire continues, the outcome seems fairly clear. The police learned that Chad arranged an alibi with his current girlfriend, then took a route to the food bank that included parking his car in the woods and hiking in the back way. He set a fire in his office, then tried to leave. But the fire behaved unpredictably, and Chad was caught in his own blaze. The firefighters found his body close to an exit door, but not close enough.

The reason for the fire seems obvious. Chad hoped to destroy all the warehouse records, a feat he accomplished. Without a warehouse, and consequently without a job, he believed he could leave town without fanfare and start over somewhere else. With the records gone he thought that if Phil O'Hara or Cilla went to the police, it would only be their word against his. He didn't know that Hazel Kefauver had died with a complete set of records in her possession, and that I had found them.

Unfortunately for Hazel, it *was* likely Chad knew she suspected food bank irregularities. He probably realized it was only a matter of time before Hazel switched her suspicions from Joe to him. So Chad, Mr. Irregularity himself, possessed the best possible motive for poisoning her. It wasn't much of a stretch to believe that a man who was capable of burning down a food bank was also capable of murdering a meddling busybody who got in his way.

I'm not privy to Roussos's thoughts. But when I handed over all the food bank records in my possession and asked if he thought they'd found their murderer, he didn't deny it.

The mystery of the food bank thief has ended. Most likely the mystery of who killed Hazel Kefauver has ended, as well. The mystery of what happened to Joe Wagner? That case is still open, and I'm the only one investigating. Maura hasn't yet filed a missing persons report, not even after she learned what Chad had been up to. We've argued over this, but she's determined to leave the door open for Joe to return.

Of course that depends on whether Joe is alive and not another of Chad Sutterfield's victims.

As I slipped my rebellious feet into black pumps, Ed came into the bedroom. He was already dressed and I knew he hoped we could walk over to the church together.

"This is so awkward." I stomped, and the shoe finally conquered the foot. "I don't know what you can say about Chad to make anybody feel his life was worthwhile."

"It's not the easiest service I've ever done. But the Sutterfields were members here for years. And they need closure."

I reached for a tissue since the cold I'd so successfully shooed away had come back with a vengeance. "They need amnesia. This must be so hard for them."

"They're nice people. You'll like them."

"I guess just this once, the apple not only fell far from the tree, it rocketed into outer space."

"Every kid has a million different influences tugging at him."

As I blew my nose I thought about our

girls. Deena, who was experiencing her first crush on a boy and was suffering ridicule from her friends because of it. Teddy, who was so worried about her classmate Rene that she couldn't enjoy her own success.

And that reminded me that some crises in a child's life, at least, could turn out well. "Has Teddy told you how Rene's doing as Cinderella?"

"She's coaching her. Friday's the big day."

After talking to Teddy and learning that I had indeed been correct in my assumptions, Ed had explained to our daughter that she needed to go to her teacher and tell her exactly what she had told him. I hadn't been as confident that things would turn out well, but Miss Hollins leaped into the role of the Fairy Godmother and waved her magic wand.

"With Teddy as coach, Rene will know every line and nuance," I said.

"Teddy could surprise us all and head for Broadway instead of Harvard Divinity."

"Either way she'll have an audience. And right now, yours is waiting." I went to wash my hands and stuff my purse with more tissues while he straightened his tie. I grabbed a silvery gray shawl Junie had knit for my birthday, and I was ready.

Junie and my daughters were cutting

fabric behind closed doors, so we called good-bye and started across the alley. The Sutterfields had invited the people they were closest to during their Emerald Springs years as well as some of Chad's colleagues and friends. They had decided against a eulogy, knowing there was little that could be said about Chad's life that would stand up under scrutiny. Instead there would be an opening prayer, Ed would do several readings, then there would be a period of silent contemplation during which anyone who had known Chad could stand and say a few words. Ed was prepared to say a few things himself, and I knew he had labored over them.

We entered through the parish house and passed through the social hall where a small reception would take place after the service. A local caterer was setting out sandwiches, and the coffee urn was heating. Luckily, the woman had brought her own punch bowl and glasses, and I wondered if this was automatic or because someone had realized ours was missing. My day of reckoning was approaching. Sally Berrigan was due back in town this weekend, and I would have to tell her what had happened.

I saw that somebody, probably Chad's parents, had set up framed photographs on a cloth-draped table to one side of the room. They had chosen photos of the boy and teenager. Elementary school Chad in a Cub Scout uniform. Middle school Chad on horseback, beaming into the camera. A teenage Chad about to run into the waves on a beach vacation. Missing were all traces of the man he had become.

I turned away because my eyes were filling with tears. Chad looked so ordinary in the photos, so much like the boys my girls are growing up with. I could picture any of them in the same places and clothing, beaming into the camera and their long, happy futures.

Crying wasn't going to help anybody. I had no tears for Chad, but for his parents? I could only imagine how they felt.

I left to wait in the church. Esther, our wonderful organist, had chosen Bach's Fugue in C Minor as prelude music, which set a mood of quiet gravity. People entered in clumps. I was surprised to see Maura, but I realized she was probably standing in for Joe, who despite everything Chad had done, would have come to show support for Chad's family. I was even more surprised to see Cilla.

I recognized a few other people who worked for the food bank, but most of those in attendance were older members of our congregation who had known Chad as a boy. Few of his contemporaries joined us. I wondered how many friends he actually had. The alibi girlfriend was nowhere to be seen.

Ed outdid himself on the service. The mood was thoughtful, nonjudgmental, kind. Although I was worried someone might bring up the circumstances of Chad's death, those people who did get up to speak told anecdotes that cast a warm light on the younger Chad. Mostly people sat in silence and took comfort in each other and in Ed's words.

When my attention flagged, *I* took some comfort in the number of people sniffling and coughing along with me. Spring had shared its germs without discrimination. I didn't feel great, but at least I wasn't alone. At one point Maura, in the midst of a coughing spree, got up and left for a few minutes. I wondered if the dolls on her front porch would play doctor and nurse until she felt better. I wondered if I could borrow them.

We left after a final prayer and Bach postlude. By then I was feeling wrung out, but I didn't want to desert Chad's parents. I decided to make a brief appearance, issue my condolences, then go home the back way.

Cilla was standing to one side looking at the photos of Chad when I arrived in the social hall, so I joined her. Almost everyone else was in line waiting to speak to the Sutterfields. I didn't want to barge in. I was also trying to avoid Norma Beet, Ed's talkative secretary who was there to make sure the caterer knew where to find everything. The caterer would really earn her fee today.

"I didn't expect to find you here," I said.

Cilla rearranged a photo, bringing it forward, as if to show it better, then another to more evenly distribute them on the table. I thought this was simple nervous energy and no desire to sugarcoat or showcase Chad's life.

"I wasn't going to come, then I realized I needed to say some kind of good-bye," she said. "I probably knew him as well as anybody did."

I gazed at the photos, shown to better advantage now that she had repositioned them. "He looks so happy, doesn't he?"

"I think he was one of those people who *was* happy most of the time. It just never occurred to him that the rest of us needed to be happy, too."

"Rest of *us?*"

Her hands dropped to her sides. "I don't know why I'm telling you this, but I lied when I said I was never involved with Chad. I made the mistake of being flattered by his interest a few times. I guess I'm still ashamed I fell for his line. Chad liked beautiful women without too many brains." Her gaze flicked to the doorway then back to me, and her expression changed. "Now *she* would have been his perfect mate."

I realized Maura had just walked in, but before I could respond, Cilla grimaced. "Although who am I to talk? *I'm* the chump who went to bed with him."

"Don't be so hard on yourself." I didn't warn her not to be so hard on Maura, either, although I hoped Cilla would stay away from Joe's wife. Maura didn't need more problems.

"I'm going to head out," she said. "I don't know what I would say to his parents."

"Go home and have a good cry."

"Did you hear the cops arrested Brian Sage and Will Novotny? They were fencing food with Chad."

I remembered the two employees I'd seen with Chad. "Bald, heavyset guy? And a middle-aged blond?"

"His cohorts." Cilla gave a short nod to

Maura, who was strolling in our direction, then she said good-bye and left.

"Have you spoken to the Sutterfields?" Maura asked after greeting me.

"I was waiting until the crowd thinned."

"I'm not going to try. I'd rather not be insincere, and after everything it would be hard to pretend I'm sorry he's gone." She bit her lip, and her gaze flicked to the photos. "What if Chad had something to do with Joe's disappearance, Aggie? I know the police think he killed Hazel. What if Joe . . ."

"Let's not go there." But I was beginning to lose hope that Joe was coming back, and the same thought had crossed and recrossed my mind.

"I know you think I should go to the police."

"Are you considering it?"

"This week's been awful. Even the people who believed Joe was off with his parents don't believe it anymore, not after the fire and everything else. They're all wondering why he doesn't show up and take charge. I don't think I can keep this to myself much longer."

I was relieved to hear it. "Then you'll talk to the police?"

"If I haven't heard anything by the weekend. Yes. I'll tell them everything. I guess I have to."

"I'll go with you if you like. Or Ed will."

"We'll see." She put her hand on mine. "Thanks."

After Maura left I joined the Sutterfields and waited for them to finish with a couple of our older members. Then I told them how sorry I was for their loss.

We were almost alone by then. The mourners who had stayed were getting refreshments. Ed joined me.

"You must wonder how this happened," Mrs. Sutterfield said. "And what kind of parents raise a son who strays that far."

She was an attractive woman in her late fifties, trim, blonde, and tan. Her clothes were expensive and in good taste. Even now she carried herself like a country club debutante, but her eyes were red-rimmed and haunted. My heart ached for her.

Ed knew what to say. "Chad was an adult and responsible for himself. However it happened, he was your son, and you loved him. Don't take on guilt that doesn't belong to you."

"He was our only child. We waited years for him to arrive. We wanted to make him happy, and we gave him everything."

Mr. Sutterfield, who was an older, visibly prosperous version of his son, put his arm around his wife's waist. "We realized our mistake a few years ago. Chad kept coming to us, insisting we bail him out of this and that. We realized we had to cut him loose and let him learn from his mistakes, or he would never become a responsible adult. So he's been on his own ever since. We thought he was doing well. We just had no idea he was —" He shook his head.

I felt so sorry for them. It must have been hard to deny Chad anything, especially when the things he wanted had been so easy for them to supply. Sometimes mistakes made from love are the hardest to face. I was afraid the Sutterfields would spend the rest of their lives reliving theirs.

I was just about to leave when I realized I'd left my shawl in the church. I told Ed I would meet him at home and took his keys to retrieve it.

The church wasn't locked. Esther had remained to practice for the Sunday service, and the empty sanctuary echoed. I stood in the back and enjoyed another fugue. We were lucky to have such a talented organist and the old tracker organ that filled our sanctuary with such majesty.

I clapped when she finished, and she turned and beckoned me forward. "I wanted to talk to you."

I found my shawl on the way to the front and draped it over my shoulder. "What did I do now?" I asked, only half joking.

"I was here when the caterer arrived. She wanted to use the church punch bowl to save her from hauling her own back and forth. We couldn't find it. I just wondered if you knew where it was."

"Why does everybody associate me with the punch bowl?"

Esther just gazed at me, as if she was sure I could make that connection by myself. She's incapable of accusing looks, but her pale blue eyes — a close match for her silver hair — were assessing me.

"Okay, here's the story." I launched in, glad to bare my soul and ask for advice. I had run out of leads.

"So, will they string me up, do you think?" I finished. "Or sentence me to hard labor?"

"You should have come to me before. I'm good at finding things."

I knew that was true. Esther comes away from garage sales with priceless treasures for under a dollar. Tell her you wish you could find a piece of sterling to fill out a place setting, and she'll find it within a month at a price you can afford. Not in a catalogue, not on eBay, but in somebody's attic or under a pile at the local flea market.

Still, I'd never considered asking her to find the punch bowl, because it hadn't seemed quite the same. The punch bowl was missing due to my own carelessness.

"Do you have any ideas?" I asked.

"Well, I was helping in Aunt Alice's Attic that first day, you know. I used to run it all alone but I let Fern take over a few years ago. I'm still the one who figures out what qualifies as treasure, and this year I did morning duty. Who have you checked with?"

I felt too achy to leap with joy, but I was beginning to take heart. I recited my list.

"You missed somebody. Did you talk to Betsy Graham?"

The name was vaguely familiar. I could picture a dark-haired woman, short, midfortyish, energetic. "The name never came up."

"Betsy's not at church a lot these days, because she and her husband are renovating a little cottage out on Lake Parsons, and weekends are the only time they can work on it. They've about finished now. I was out there a few weeks ago to see it. Anyway, she was buying all kinds of things to furnish it at the sale. I remember she bought several boxes of glasses."

"Wouldn't she notice she has the punch bowl by now?"

"She might just be piling everything up

until all the little details are finished on the cottage and they can move in."

"Thanks, I'll look her up in the directory."

Esther frowned in concentration, as if she was visualizing Betsy's whereabouts. "No, you probably won't find her at home. I'll give you directions to the lake. You can drive out if you can't reach her."

I rummaged through my purse, past my keys and Maura's, past my wallet and a wad of tissues. I scrawled the directions on the back of a receipt.

"You won't mention this to anybody? I'll have to come clean if Betsy doesn't have it. But if you'll give me a short reprieve?"

"My lips are sealed. It's your show, dear."

I refrained from hugging her. The best thank you gift I could give Esther was a clean bill of health.

"I'll let you know," I promised.

"You don't have to. I know you'll find it there." She went back to Bach, and I went back to the parsonage to wonder if she was right.

18

Ed made carrot and ginger soup for our dinner and put me on the sofa with a tall glass of orange juice and a box of tissues. Deena brought me one of Junie's crocheted afghans, and Teddy made a get well card with crayon drawings of Moonpie gazing wistfully at Pepper and Cinnamon, her guinea pigs. The guinea pigs, which in real life have no expression whatsoever, were clearly gloating behind the bars of their cage. I wondered what Moonpie had done to deserve Teddy's scorn, but I felt too lethargic to ask.

Junie set a steam vaporizer several feet from the sofa, then cranked it high enough to make sure everything in the room would be dripping by dinnertime. Black mold was on the bedtime agenda.

"Herbal tea on the way," she promised.

"I'll pass on the tea," I croaked.

"No, precious, you won't."

I closed my eyes. Nobody woke me until the soup was ready, but of course, before I was allowed to eat it, I was treated to Junie's home brew. She added enough honey to send all the worker bees in local hives out on strike, but at least the honey made the herbs tolerable.

After dinner, I was allowed to choose whatever I wanted to watch on television. I settled on *Surgery Saved My Life* on the Discovery Channel and watched my squeamish family scatter. I closed my eyes, victorious, and slept until bedtime.

Feverish and awake through the night, my mind raced in unpredictable directions. I kept thinking about Chad and Chad's parents, trying to reconcile the happy boy in those photographs with the young man who so recklessly destroyed the hopes of so many. The photos were a slide show in my head. How does a parent prevent a child from becoming a monster?

I imagined an older Deena leaving her selfless Peace Corps boyfriend to shack up with a greedy brain surgeon who owned a stable of racehorses in Lexington. I saw Teddy in Cinderella's golden coach scattering moldy bread crumbs to a starving crowd of homeless children.

I dragged myself out of bed and took a

handful of over-the-counter meds guaranteed to either bring my brain back online or send me peacefully to an easier world.

The next morning as everybody tiptoed through the halls with elephantine grace, I slept in. By the time I could sit up, I was fairly certain I had survived to live at least one more day.

Ed came in with a tray. "Feeling any better?"

My eyelids were stuck halfway. I was afraid my voice had been extinguished. "Ergh . . . galumph . . ."

He seemed perfectly satisfied. "How clever of you to get sick first, so you could get it over with. Everybody's on extra rations of vitamin C until you're well enough to take care of us."

"I'm . . . moving away."

"Sorry, but you'll owe us. Are you up for scrambled eggs?"

Surprisingly, I was, and for the toast that went with them. And the pot of Lady Grey tea — who may or may not have been related to Earl but who certainly knew her way around a teapot.

Ed came back up for the tray and perched on the edge of our bed. I noted the sizeable distance but refrained from reminding him I had breathed on him all night long.

"You're planning to take it easy today, right?" he asked. "The girls are gone, and Junie's going to be out all day. I can work here if you think you'll need me."

I had an errand I had to do. The punch bowl crisis had finally come to a head. Either I solved it with a trip to find Betsy Graham, who had not answered any of the calls I'd managed last night, or tomorrow I told Sally the truth.

"I'll be fine." I gave him my prettiest dimpled smile, spoiled somewhat by my nose choosing that moment to salute Niagara Falls.

He looked relieved. "I've got a pile of meetings, but you can always reach me on my cell. I'll leave it on."

I blew hard, then harder. "Don't worry about me. I'll be fine."

"I'll come home at lunchtime —"

"Not necessary. I can heat soup. It will do me good to move around."

"Don't overdo." He stood and took the tray.

I blew him a kiss so he wouldn't have to come any closer. "Thanks for everything."

I got up and took a shower, and when I came out the house was empty. I threw on whatever was in the front of my closet, looking down once I'd finished to note I was wearing an orange and yellow striped shirt, lavender capris, and lime green sneakers. Maybe I could paint my face and juggle bowling pins to throw Betsy off guard. Then while she was still dazzled by my performance, I could rush into her cottage and steal the boxes.

By the time I got downstairs I thought I'd probably live. I didn't feel any worse than I had at the memorial service. Maybe I'd sink with the sun again, but until then, I was well enough to see this through. I wrote Ed a note in case he came home and worried I might be vacationing on a slab in the Emerald Springs morgue, then I locked the house and took off for Lake Parsons. I gripped the wheel and turned up the radio as loud as I dared, to make sure I didn't get sleepy at the wheel.

Lake Parsons is a forty-five-minute drive through rolling farmland. The lake itself is small and marginally scenic. Houses crowd the waterfront and spill back along side roads. The biggest draw is a policy that welcomes every feasible type of watercraft capable of skimming the surface, with no restriction on size. At the height of summer vacation, Parsons is an earplug-friendly community. In May, however, I could appreciate the rippling surface and the large evergreens that still cast shadows on remoter coves.

The Grahams' cottage was situated on one of those. I gratefully followed Esther's directions as the road looped back and forth, teasing me with views of the water, then catapulting me back along deserted streets.

At last I pulled up to the right cottage and gathered my strength. The house was small and sided in cedar shingles with a screened porch stretching along the front to offer views of the lake. If my geography was correct, the sunset would be beautiful here.

I got out at last, girded somewhat for the confrontation, and dragged myself to the front porch. I rapped twice and waited. A Pontiac was parked in front, and I counted on somebody being home.

The woman I had visualized yesterday came out on the porch. When she saw me her eyes widened.

"Aggie? Aggie Wilcox?"

I didn't remind her of the hyphen, or my decision to retain my identity as someone other than Ed's spouse. She could have called me Bozo. I just wanted to sit down again.

"How are you, Betsy?" I smiled and felt my reserves of energy seeping away.

"What on earth are you doing all the way out here? Not that I'm not delighted to see you." She opened the door and ushered me into a cozy living room paneled in knotty pine.

Without waiting for an invitation I fell to the sofa. "I'm so sorry to barge in like this. But I'm desperate."

Then, without fanfare, I launched into my story, starting with Mayday! and moving right along at a snail's pace. My talent for editing was on hiatus, along with clear nasal passages and any hint of energy.

Betsy perched on the edge of a chair and listened patiently. When I finally finished I was afraid I was going to witness the spectacular sunset myself. But she had allowed me my say.

Now she shook her head. "I feel so bad. I could have saved you all this trouble. I've just been so busy, and I haven't been back to town in weeks, and the phone service out here is spotty. The phone company keeps insisting nothing is wrong, but we can't get to the bottom of it because every time I try, the phone goes out."

"You have the punch bowl?"

"I do. But I didn't know what it was when I bought it, of course. I was stocking the cottage cupboards. I grabbed a couple of boxes of glasses thinking they'd do me awhile until I could find something I really liked. Then I . . . I ummm . . . looked inside one day and realized, well, what was there. And I've been trying to, you know, get it back into the closet."

I wasn't sure if my spinning head was making hash of this, or if there really was something odd about Betsy's explanation. But I didn't care. I could get the punch bowl and take it back to church. Thanks to Esther, another mystery was solved. If my luck held Joe would come home unharmed, dress the front porch dolls like Sonny and Cher whenever he felt the urge to perform, and never leave Emerald Springs again.

I got to my feet. "I'm just glad you have it. And I'll be thrilled to reimburse you for the glasses you didn't get. May I take it now?"

"Oh, of course. And you don't need to worry about the glasses. I feel bad enough that you had to drive all the way out here."

She started toward the back of the house, and I followed her. The kitchen was small but charming. I could imagine tasty meals at the oak table as motorboats and Jet Skis roared by on Lake Parsons.

Betsy went into a small pantry and returned with a cardboard box. She set it on the table and unfolded the flaps. There, nestled in a flannel sheet, was the punch bowl. Gleaming and lovely, without a smudge of chocolate.

"That's a beautiful sight," I said.

She looked relieved. "I'm so glad you're not angry, Aggie. And I do apologize."

"Let me take it to the car and get out of your hair. And thanks for washing it. I'm sure that wasn't any fun. But at least the chocolate coating wasn't my fault."

"Let me carry it for you. Are you feeling okay? You're a little flushed."

On the way out we talked about spring allergies and colds, about how much she liked her cottage, and how some of the residents were trying to get the local township to pass a law limiting horse power on the lake, but nobody thought they would win.

I opened the back of the van and Betsy put the box inside. I started to fold the flaps over the top of it, but my hand faltered. I stared at the bowl, then with Betsy still standing beside me, I lifted it out of the box and turned it around, then around once more.

Betsy shifted from foot to foot.

I carefully returned the bowl to the box, folded the flaps, and faced her.

"The church punch bowl had deeper sawtooth edges, and a couple of them were worn. This is so close. You must have searched every antique store for a hundred miles."

"I'm about to apologize again."

I closed the back of the van carefully, then I leaned against it. "So what happened?"

"Aggie, I feel awful about this. I really hoped nobody would notice. I figured if nobody noticed, nobody would be upset. And this is a gorgeous antique, same time period, almost exactly the same as the other one. It's every bit as valuable."

"I can tell."

"I dropped the darn box. I thought it seemed awfully heavy for a carton of cheap glassware, but I never even considered something else might be inside. I was carrying it in and I tripped over our threshold. We'd been working on it, and it was loose, and I just went down with the box in my arms. I could hear the glass shatter. After I nursed my pride and my bruised knee, I opened it to see if anything had survived. And I saw what I had done."

"You must have felt terrible."

"You don't know the half of it. Or maybe you do? You've had a couple of bad weeks over this, too."

"So you decided to replace it?"

"I thought about coming clean and giving a big donation so the Society could pick out another one, but I knew people would be upset, not just with me, but about what had happened. Plus, I figured they would be upset with whoever had put it in that box in the first place."

"I'm *sure* you're right about that."

"So I started looking. I put together what I could and sent out photos to a bunch of dealers who specialize in the American Brilliant period, and one of them came up with this. It's so close. I really didn't think anybody would notice. It has the fans. Everything but the edge is nearly identical. Unfortunately, it took the dealer awhile to get it here. He wanted an independent evaluation for insurance. It just came a few days ago. I was going to bring it to church this weekend and leave it in the closet."

I stared at her; she stared at me. Then we both started to laugh.

"What a pair of doofuses," I said, when I could speak.

"You've got a good eye. I bet not one other person will catch this. Most of the time when people expect to see one thing, they don't notice it's something else entirely. But if you decide the truth has to be told, blame me for everything."

"I think I need to pay for half of this. The mix-up was my fault."

"Not a cent. It's my donation."

I told her I'd give her a hug once I was well again, she told me about a shortcut out to the main road, and I left.

I smiled for the first ten minutes of the trip. Little by little the smile disappeared. In the same way my mind had latched on to little things through the night and gnawed them to the bone, it was latching on again.

Betsy had said that when people expected to see one thing, they rarely noticed it was something else entirely. I wasn't sure why that resonated so deeply now. I thought my temperature was spiking again. Maybe if she'd said that ice cream was cold and should be eaten with a spoon, I'd be worrying about that now. But I didn't think so. Something was struggling to be heard, some piece of a puzzle I hadn't paid enough attention to, and Betsy's words had brought it back.

I thought it had to do with Chad's memorial service. And maybe with my feverish dreams.

By the time I parked behind the church and went around to get the punch bowl my legs were limp linguine. The closet was beckoning, and I was absolutely thrilled to be finished with this episode in my life. I had decided that once I felt better, I would tell Sally Berrigan the story, and leave it in her hands. I suspected she would see no harm in forgetting the entire saga since she was the one to write the first unfortunate chapter.

Halfway up the walk I realized I didn't have the keys to the closet. I wanted to bang my head in frustration, but nothing could convince me to wait even one more minute. I headed for the front of the church and Ed's office. Norma Beet was sitting at her desk, and her eyes behind cat's-eye glasses brightened when she saw me. She got to her feet and sent her chair spinning when she stumbled backwards. Norma forgets that her substantial tummy goes everywhere ahead of her, in this case straight into her desk.

I could see she was going to ask about the box. I headed her off. "Is Ed here, Norma?"

"No, he was here." She launched into a moment-by-moment replay of my husband's day.

Norma is harmless, and except for the incessant chatter, she's an excellent secretary. I think she's something of a project for Ed, who's sure he can teach her to say less and more at the same time. Ed's all about transformation.

I've learned to interrupt, although it doesn't come naturally. I balanced the box carefully on the edge of her desk and waved my hand to stop her. "Would you mind opening the Women's Society closet for me? I've got the punch bowl."

I said this so naturally, so casually, that she didn't even blink.

"No problem. Follow me."

She continued the recital on the way. Ed would have nothing left to tell me tonight, but I didn't care. Norma was going to open the closet.

Most of the time when people expect to see one thing, they don't notice it's something else entirely.

I told the annoying voice inside my head to be quiet so I could hear Norma, a demand I had never expected to make.

We reached the closet, and she opened it. I set the box down carefully. Lightning did not strike. An earthquake didn't rumble through the building. The ceiling didn't cave in on top of it.

I stepped back; Norma locked the door. That was that.

Norma wasn't finished. I stood there quietly exultant and listened as penance.

"You have an amazing memory for detail,"

I said, when she stopped long enough to draw another breath. "You remember every nuance of every moment. I don't think I've ever met anybody who pays that much attention to everything around her."

Her mouth dropped open. "Really?"

"Really, it's amazing. How do you do it?"

"What can I say? I grew up on a wheat farm in South Dakota, a place where nothing big ever happened. When I was little I realized that the only things around me that ever changed were little things. So I started noticing them. That way time didn't seem to stand still."

I was touched. And didn't that explain a lot? Here was a woman with almost total recall. Growing up, had anyone been interested enough in details to listen to her observations? Maybe Norma was just making up for lost time.

"I wish I paid half as much attention to things as you do." My poor overheated brain was trying to tell me something, and I stopped a moment. I realized what it was.

"Listen, Norma, something's bothering me. Maybe you can help. Would you mind trying?"

She looked so pleased. I had never realized that under the glasses and the extra pounds and the hair that got gradually darker at the tips from a bad dye job, that Norma had the makings of an attractive woman. She had great skin. A beauty queen's nose. And a pretty smile.

I rushed on, glad that I'd made her happy but not taking any chances she'd start to chatter again.

"At the memorial service for Chad Sutterfield, his parents placed photographs on a table in the social hall. Childhood photos of him. Do you remember?"

"Sure. I was in there to make sure everything ran smoothly."

I didn't even have to cut her off. She was waiting for me to continue. This was fun. A real conversation.

"Well, I keep thinking that something went wrong," I said. "But I don't know why I think so, or what it might have been. I keep seeing those photographs in my mind. They just keep nagging at me. Am I imagining it?"

"Maybe you're thinking about the one that disappeared."

I waited, on full alert now. "Disappeared?"

"Right. The picture of him on a horse. It was there when I left for the church, and it was gone when I came back. I noticed somebody was over there moving photographs around to cover up the gap. That pretty woman with the short dark hair? The tall one who smells like jasmine?"

Cilla. I remembered now that Cilla had repositioned the photographs, as if she was trying to keep her hands busy when she was feeling so many strong emotions.

Cilla, who'd disliked Chad to the point of hatred. Cilla, who had gone to bed with Chad before she understood what kind of man he was. Cilla, who was certain that Chad wanted Joe's job.

"Why would she want that photo?" I asked out loud, although I didn't expect Norma to have an answer. "A memento?"

"I don't remember any way she could have hidden it. She wasn't wearing a jacket. She was wearing a sundress, remember? Navy, with lighter blue flowers down the front? Nothing to disturb the line of it, no pockets."

"Maybe she got rid of the picture before we got there?"

"No, I'm almost sure I came back before she did. A minute or two before the service was over. I was worried about the caterer."

"Did the Sutterfields say anything about the missing photograph?"

"They were so upset, I doubt they even noticed. Of course, maybe they removed it themselves when I wasn't there. But I don't think so, because they had people around them all the time." Norma's eyes brightened. "We can ask January if he found anything in the trash."

"You mean like a photo or frame?"

"He emptied the trash after the service."

"Is he here?"

"No, he's gone home. Would you like me to call him?"

Norma was definitely improving, but I hated to sic her on January. On the other hand, I didn't have another drop of energy left. I was running on fumes.

"Would you?" I squeezed out my last smile. "You'll call me if he has anything interesting to say?"

"I sure will."

She chattered as she saw me to the door, but I had a new appreciation for Norma, and even this didn't spoil it.

"Thanks for letting me help," she said before she closed the door.

"The pleasure is mine." And now I was vaguely ashamed. Because in the same way I had decided Maura was hopeless, from the beginning, I had discounted Norma, too.

I told the voices in my head to take a rest. I hadn't been as generous toward Norma as I should have been, but in the future I would try harder. Meanwhile I had found and returned the punch bowl. I had discovered why I'd been bothered last night by a mental slide show of Chad Sutterfield as a boy. And I had made a connection between Cilla's actions at the memorial service and the disappearance of the photograph. Pretty good for somebody who was looking at life and death through a head filled with seaweed.

I started for my van, for home, for my bed and a long, dreamless nap. I got the house and the bed. I even got the nap.

But dreamless wasn't in the cards.

19

Early Friday afternoon I saw my doctor. My memories of the night before were vague. When I slept, I slept sitting up. Breathing was hard enough that I considered going cold turkey. Ed kept me pumped full of liquids and Tylenol to keep my temperature down, and we had conversations about whether I should go the doctor in the morning or the emergency room right away. But a call to the hospital reassured us that a virus with flulike symptoms was making the rounds, and we were already doing what we needed to.

The doctor prescribed heavy-duty cold and cough meds and took a chest X-ray. I was ordered to bed before my symptoms degenerated into pneumonia and told that under no circumstances was I to go to Teddy's play tonight and contaminate the audience.

Ed brought me home, promised to fill the

prescription after a late afternoon meeting, and settled me on the sofa with a thermos of juice, the phone, and the television remote. Junie would be home not long after the girls arrived. I wasn't to do anything but get better.

My head hurt too badly to read, and despite feeling giddy with exhaustion, I couldn't sleep. I kept the television off since even on good days I've been known to contact alien life-forms simply by pressing Menu or Mute on the remote.

This left puzzles to solve, and not sudoku or the *Flow*'s daily crossword. The puzzle of why Cilla might have taken a photo from the memorial table. The puzzle of when and how. Whether she had told me the truth about her feelings for Chad. How or if she was involved in the fire or Chad's death.

When the telephone rang I still wasn't getting close to an answer. Norma was on the other end. She had talked to January, and yes, he had seen a picture frame and glass in the trash but no, he couldn't tell her where it had originated. He thought it might have come from one of the restrooms.

I called Lucy, but I got her voice mail. I pressed the number to page her and got a window cleaning service. When I called back to leave a message, I was offered a time-share in Cancun. At least that's my best guess, judging from the mariachi band in the background.

Cilla and I weren't yet friends. I decided to take a chance on losing a future filled with shopping trips and daring hair appointments. I called information and let them dial the food bank.

I was transferred twice, but eventually Cilla picked up.

I went through the polite formalities. I suspected she was hoping I had information to share about Joe, because she almost sounded breathless.

"I need your help," I said cutting through the chitchat. "We've discovered something odd, Cilla, and you might know more than we do." I launched into the explanation about the missing photo of Chad on horseback and the discarded picture frame. Then I waited.

"I never saw it," she said.

"You were at the table when I spoke to you, rearranging the photos. I just thought —"

"What did you think? That I wanted a memento of that creep?" She paused. "Okay, it's not nice to talk that way about the dead. But you're seriously pissing me off."

"I'm just trying to figure out why the photograph was removed."

"I got there and noticed a gap. Call it nervous energy, but I just moved things around to distribute them better. And maybe to say a private good-bye, although it was more like good riddance."

I don't know why, but I believed her. Now I was sorry I'd made her angry.

I put my thoughts together out loud. "So we know that while we were at the service, somebody came in and took it. Because by the time you got there, it was already gone."

"Why do you care anyway?"

I didn't answer, because I was thinking back on the service and the people in attendance. Someone could have walked in off the street, of course, but now I remembered that one person in attendance had left for a few minutes in the midst of a coughing spell.

Maura.

"Aggie, I asked why you care!"

I pulled myself together. "Look, I'm sorry I ever wondered if you might have something to do with the photograph. I believe you. But you can help in another way. Can you tell me what kind of relationship Chad had with Maura?"

Now *she* was silent. I wondered if she was

planning how to slam down the receiver to best effect, or if she was simply thinking.

"I never saw any sign of friendship," she said at last. "I can't remember ever witnessing them in a private conversation, or even acting like they wanted one. They were polite. But . . ."

"Go on please."

"I think a strong suspicion Chad wanted Joe's job was one of the few things Maura and I had in common."

That was nothing new. "Okay."

But Cilla continued. "She kept an eye on him, you know? Like she didn't trust him. Maybe even more than I didn't trust him."

Still nothing new.

She wasn't finished. "And once she told me she married Joe because he only saw the good in people, but sometimes that meant he didn't see what was right under his nose."

"Those were her words?"

"It seemed a little odd, but I figured she was talking about Chad wanting Joe's job. Maybe she was suspicious all along that Chad was up to no good, and Joe wouldn't listen to her. You should ask her."

"I might." I thanked her and hung up.

Had Maura suspected that Chad was stealing from the food bank? Had she warned Joe?

Had she stolen the photograph?

I was contemplating these questions when Teddy arrived home. She knew better than to crawl into my lap, but she came into the living room and we gave each other pretend hugs from across the room.

"How was the play?" I croaked. "Did Rene remember all her lines?"

"She was good. And she was happy."

I was sorry I couldn't hug my daughter for real, because I was so proud of her. "Did you feel a little sad it wasn't you onstage?"

"No. Miss Hollins let me sit up close so I could help with lines if Rene forgot. It was almost like being in the play." She beamed as she lifted herself on tippy-toe. "And I get to be Cinderella tonight, so I kept remembering that."

I pretended to hug her again. Once we put Jennifer Hollins in the loop, she'd come up with the perfect solution to Teddy's dilemma. From the beginning, two performances had been scheduled. One this afternoon for the students, and one tonight for parents and friends. So Rene had been asked to play Cinderella for the matinee, and Teddy for the evening performance. Two glass slippers, two little girls happy with the decision. One young teacher showing what she was really made of.

And wouldn't it be great if all moral dilemmas were so easily solved?

"You can't go tonight can you?" Teddy asked.

"I'm going to have to watch the videotape. I'm so sorry."

"I'll talk extra loud so you can hear me."

Deena came home and without being prompted, helped Teddy get a snack. Then she came into the living room and stood where Teddy had. "Can I go to the library with Tyler in a little while?"

Since the library was on the oval, just a stone's throw from our house, I didn't see a problem. "I don't know why not."

"We're doing our final project together in science. We picked each other for partners." She paused. "Everybody knows."

I nodded, not sure what to say.

"The Meanies are so shallow." She started to leave, but even with a fever I couldn't let it go at that.

"Mind telling me what you mean?"

"Well, they were making fun of me. So I told them I like Tyler better than I like them, anyway. Except for Tara and Maddie, who are still okay."

Middle school seemed a little early to risk exorcism from the popular crowd. I was delighted. I thought the poor but worthy Peace Corps volunteer might still have an edge over the greedy brain surgeon. Even if the brain surgeon happened to have Kentucky Derby contenders in his stable.

"So, you and the Meanies are kaput?" I asked.

"No, now they're acting like it was all so yesterday. Carlene invited me to spend the night at her house next weekend."

"Well, sometimes when you stand up for yourself, things work out nicely."

"Really? I stood up for myself in English class. I told Mr. Sammons that the book he wants us to read is dumb, and we ought to be able to pick one that's interesting."

"I bet the *dumb* word didn't help your cause, right?"

"He told me to write an extra page about why the book didn't meet my high standards. So now I have more work to do."

"Win some, lose some."

She rolled her eyes, and I tried not to smile.

I dozed until Deena came back in to tell me she and Tyler were leaving and Teddy was upstairs trying to train the guinea pigs. I hadn't realized Tyler was going to escort Deena to the library. He came in to say hello. Once again I thought what a nice-looking boy he was with his brown hair and eyes.

They were gone, but for some reason every time I closed my eyes I pictured Tyler in different settings. At the beach. Repeating the Cub Scout promise.

On horseback.

When I gazed at the photos of Chad after his memorial service, I thought about the boys my daughters were growing up with, how ordinary they seemed. Just like Chad.

Now I realized where that association had come from. The photo of Chad Sutterfield in middle school, which was the missing horseback photo, had strongly reminded me of Tyler Wagner.

I sat up and ran my fingers through my rumpled hair. "You're an idiot, Aggie."

The resemblance to Tyler had been clear enough that after one quick glance I'd almost made the connection that day.

Chad Sutterfield was Tyler Wagner's biological father.

I rested my aching head in my hands. Maura had disappeared long enough to snatch the photo that afternoon. Now I realized why Maura might have the ultimate motivation for stealing it.

That very afternoon hadn't Cilla told me that Maura was exactly the kind of woman

Chad liked?

Another piece clicked into place. Now I knew why Betsy's comment about the punch bowl had pinged around my aching head with such vengeance. Betsy had said that most of the time when people expect to see one thing, they don't notice it's something else entirely. She had almost passed the new punch bowl off as the old one. It was still entirely possible that nobody else would ever notice the difference.

Maura had been married to Joe Wagner. She had given birth to a son. Tyler looked like neither mother nor father, but wasn't that true of many children? The combinations of genes produced something entirely unique? Expecting to see Joe's son, Joe's son was what people saw. Probably even Joe had been fooled.

But what if he *hadn't* been? What if Joe had discovered the truth and walked out on Maura. Maybe that was the garbled message from his cell phone. Maybe Joe was so furious, so betrayed, he was never coming home.

I dismissed this immediately. Even my poor fried brain knew this couldn't be right. Joe loved Tyler. He would never walk out on the boy he had raised as his own.

So how did this tie in? Tyler's parentage

was interesting, but what did it prove? I'd seen statistics that claimed more than 10 percent of all children are conceived outside of wedlock, unbeknownst to the fathers of record. If that was true, Joe was in good company. Maybe Maura's lies amounted to fraud, but I didn't think this was a crime that would interest Detective Roussos.

Then what about murder? The police thought Chad had died in a fire set by his own hand. But what if this wasn't true? What if Joe had set it out of revenge, trapping Chad inside?

I shook my head in frustration. What proof did I have things hadn't happened exactly the way the police believed? I couldn't imagine Joe Wagner committing such a heinous crime.

No, if I told Roussos what I'd learned, he would tell me it didn't matter. My theory was only that, and there was no real crime connected to it.

Of course there was another person in the triangle.

What if Maura had killed Chad because he threatened to tell Joe the truth about Tyler? Maybe Chad finally figured out that Tyler was his and demanded his parental rights.

I threw that away, too. Why would a man

as self-centered as Chad claim paternity, if with it came financial responsibility and child support payments?

No. If Chad was threatening to tell Maura, he wanted something in exchange for silence. A man who steals food from the poor and homeless is a man who won't blink at blackmail.

The telephone rang, and Lucy was on the other end. "You tried to call, didn't you?"

"The trumpeter in your mariachi band reported me, right?"

"Aggie, are you sick or just plain nuts?"

"As a matter of fact . . ." I launched into my woes, dispensed of them quickly, and moved on to my conversation with Cilla. I didn't feel comfortable telling Lucy my suspicions about Tyler. And she wasn't going to be any help figuring out Maura, because Lucy didn't know her.

"That reminds me," Lucy said when I finished. "Cilla called last night to say she thought she saw Joe poking around the ruins of the warehouse after work. But before she could get there to confront him, he disappeared."

I was surprised Cilla hadn't mentioned this to me during our phone call, but I guess I had upset her too much. "If the Joe sitings continue, we'll have to tell her about Rube."

"Knowing Rube, he was poking around for clues."

We talked a little about the house, then Lucy told me to take a nap.

I had to make one more call before I did.

I hated to involve Roussos at this point, but I had promised my husband I would keep Roussos in the loop. And I had a question I still wanted an answer to. Possibly enough time had passed and enough threads had been tied up that he would finally give it to me.

I don't know how long I waited before Roussos got to the phone. Teddy was still upstairs with Pepper and Cinnamon, and I'd had a three-Kleenex moment. But eventually Roussos picked up.

"Don't tell me you found a dead body in your attic," he said when he realized it was me.

"Like you'd be the one I'd call first."

"Yeah, I know. You'd only call me when the killer was standing behind you with a .45 and a machete. How about Joe Wagner? You got any leads on him? The man's warehouse burns down, and his warehouse manager dies in the blaze, but he doesn't come back, even for a day?"

"I can't help you there. But this is about the Wagners. Would you be interested if I told you I think Chad Sutterfield might have been the real father of Joe Wagner's son?"

He was silent a moment. "Okay, dazzle me. What makes you think so?"

I was encouraged. I played all the angles, pausing just once for a coughing fit. I finished on a gasp.

"And this would interest me why?" he asked. "We know Sutterfield started the fire in his office. That's a given."

"You're certain?"

"Without a doubt."

"I guess I can't interest you in buying this as a motive for Hazel's death?"

"Sutterfield killed Mrs. Kefauver because he was the father of Wagner's son?"

"I don't know. Maybe she figured it out. Maybe she was on to him, and he poisoned her. How was she poisoned? Was it something he might have put in her food?"

"You're getting better about slipping these questions in. I like it when people grow. Makes me feel all warm and fuzzy inside."

I felt awful, but I smiled anyway, although I hoped he couldn't tell. "How can telling me hurt now? You're so sure you have the murderer. And he's dead. So what's the big deal?"

He was quiet long enough to give me hope. "Nicotine," he said at last. "Ring any bells for you?"

"Nicotine? Like cigarettes?" I thought for a moment. "She was supposed to be a secret smoker. Could she have smoked so much on the sly that it killed her?"

He gave a humorless laugh. "Not likely."

"So how does somebody get poisoned by nicotine?"

"It used to be easier. They sold it over the counter as a pesticide until they banned it in the 1990s. I hear it was good for aphids. But just to make your day I'll tell you it takes less nicotine than arsenic or strychnine to kill somebody."

"So what, did somebody sit on top of poor Hazel and feed her cigarette butts?"

"We're not completely clear. Anything else you want to know?"

"Anything else you'd like to tell me? Like whether you're sure Chad killed Hazel Kefauver, or the jury's still out?"

"Sure, I'll tell you something —"

I knew that tone. "Right. Stay out of your investigation, I know. I'll get back in touch when I've figured out how all your pieces fit together. Be looking for a way to put me on the payroll."

We hung up simultaneously.

I dissected what I'd learned. I was left with the feeling that Roussos was still investigating. Not only to figure out how Hazel ingested enough nicotine to die from it, but because he wasn't certain Chad had been the one to supply it. He had actually shared the name of the poison, which surprised me, but I thought, perhaps, he'd done it to see if it rang any bells.

Just as important, he had listened carefully when I told him that I thought Chad was Tyler's biological father. My opinion? Roussos was still collecting evidence and looking for motives.

"Nicotine." I tried to imagine the ways a lethal dose of nicotine might be delivered. We had cigarettes and chewing tobacco. We had aids like the patch for people who were trying to quit smoking. Sid had told me about the nicotini, a drink for people who didn't want to get off their barstools and go outside to light up. Something about soaking tobacco leaves in vodka and adding flavoring.

Yuck.

Could any of these delivery systems be ramped up to poison Hazel? Was there any reason to suspect that Brownie had access to nicotine in a form that might have killed her? Or Chad Sutterfield? Theoretically, I'd gotten involved to help our mayor, but the investigation had taken on a life of its own.

Everything was jumbled in my head now. Joe's disappearance. Hazel's murder. The fire and Chad's death. Tyler's parentage. Nicotine?

For once I was sorry I was such an Internet idiot. There would be information about nicotine poisoning online, I was sure. But I didn't have the energy to go looking, nor did I want to deal with the consequences. Ed's computer is possessed. At the very least we need an exorcism.

I tried hard not to fall asleep, but when Junie came home, rhapsodizing about how quickly Rube was completing work on the Victorian, I shared a few perky sentences with her. Right before I closed my eyes.

20

Teddy looks wonderful in rags. As the official family seamstress Junie had made the Cinderella-in-the-ashes costume from fabric scraps and burlap. Since Rene and Teddy were the same size, Rene had worn it first. But I couldn't imagine anyone who could look more forlorn or pathetic than my own daughter.

I was so proud.

After dinner I enjoyed the bedraggled Teddy from across the room. "Promise you'll come home dressed like a princess so I can see that, too?"

"I wish you could go!"

To preserve the surprise, I hadn't been allowed to see my daughter in either costume. None of us had realized I wouldn't see her onstage, either.

I felt as sad as she did. "We'll watch the videotape, and you can tell me every little thing."

"I might never be a star again."

"You'll always be a star to me."

Teddy's not fooled by mushy mommy compliments. By the same token she's logical enough to realize that my coughing on the parents of her school friends won't win her any fans. Luckily she had her father, grandmother, and sister to applaud too loudly. By the time they left, she was reconciled to my absence.

I wasn't glad to see them go, but the silent house was more helpful than the medication my doctor had prescribed. I felt lightheaded, and the world and its problems seemed one galaxy away. I didn't have to converse. I didn't even have to think. I could lie on the sofa and doze until they returned. Since the parents were putting on a cookies and juice reception after the play, I figured I had a couple of hours to wallow in my illness.

The telephone woke me. I searched for it under the afghan, but my sleep-befuddled brain wouldn't quite connect the ringing with the proper quadrant of the sofa. By the time I located it between two cushions, I said hello as my caller was hanging up.

I was just as glad I was awake, because I needed to blow my nose again. Always the optimist, I thought if I kept trying, someday

I'd be able to use my nostrils for something other than storage. I reached for the tissues only to find that I'd emptied the whole box during other futile attempts.

I was thirsty, anyway. I sat up, then I got gingerly to my feet. If possible, the medication was making me woozier. I wanted my money back.

In the kitchen I yanked a bottle of spring water out of the refrigerator and scouted for a new box of tissues in the pantry. When nothing turned up there, I squatted to look in the cupboard nearest the door and found a stash. Bless Ed, he had prepared for the worst.

I got to my feet too quickly, and a wave of dizziness swept over me. I grabbed the counter to steady myself, knocking a stack of newspapers and the key basket to the floor in the process. Congratulating myself for not breaking anything, I waited until I felt steadier, then holding on to the counter with one hand I gingerly lowered myself until I could reach the basket. One by one I picked up the keys and dropped them back inside. The papers could wait until the gang returned.

I was upright again, setting the basket farther against the wall, when I realized that I had retrieved and replaced Maura's key along with extra copies of our car and van keys, and keys to the house.

I fished out Maura's and turned it over in my hand. I was almost sure that the last time I had seen the familiar beaded elephant, it was making nice with my wallet at the bottom of my purse. Who had removed it and put it back in the basket? I was tired and confused, but I was almost sure. Two days ago I'd seen Maura's key as I rummaged for something at Chad's memorial service. And since then I hadn't felt well enough to play musical keys. Proof? The usual extras were here, but my own set of house and car keys was still upstairs in my purse.

I tried to bring details into better focus. I remembered searching for paper to write down Betsy's address. Maura's keys had been right there in my purse along with my own.

Odd.

I tried to imagine any reason why Ed would have removed Maura's key and put it here. Or one of my girls or Junie? This seemed like a small thing, but a small thing that made no sense.

My purse was upstairs. I had dropped it beside the bed when I came home from the doctor's office. I wondered if I was clear-headed enough for a trip up the steps. The change of scenery might be nice. I could get into my nightgown and under the covers. When she came home, Teddy could still tell me about her success. And while I was up there I could . . . what? Check to see if the key weighting my hand was a mirage? That I was imagining the whole thing?

Okay, I was sick. The medication was making my head spin. But there was only one explanation. I was wrong. Somewhere along the way I'd dropped Maura's key in the basket again, and I just didn't remember.

I would not go upstairs and check for the obvious. I would not.

I was on my way.

I gathered up all my supplies. The new box of tissues, the spring water, the *Flow,* so I would look as if I wanted to be educated and industrious, even if I was sound asleep.

I made the trip without incident and dropped everything at the foot of our bed. Then I sat on the edge and pulled my purse to my lap. Out went the wallet, the pack of tissues, the notepad and pen. Out went my keys.

A beaded elephant winked at me in the light of the bedside reading lamp.

I lifted it out and set it in the palm of my

hand. Maura's, for sure. But this was not the key and keychain she had given me. There were three keys hanging to one side, one obviously a car key. And the elephant? Not red and blue, like the one downstairs in the basket, but red and green.

My head was swimming now. Why did I have two sets of keys to Maura's house? And why this second one with several different keys?

I had been to Maura's house, and used my key to let Tyler inside. I had hung around with my children and toured Maura's garden. Had I seen this keychain on a table or counter and thought I'd forgotten it? Then I'd put the right one in the basket when I got home, which left this one in my purse?

This seemed logical except for one thing. I didn't remember finding keys at Maura's. And I didn't think I would have mistaken this keychain for the one she had given me. The color was subtly different, yes. That I might have overlooked. But there were three keys here. Surely I would have noticed that.

I closed my eyes and smelled smoke. I saw flames leaping toward the sky. I felt myself stumble and nearly fall. My purse tumbled to the ground and the contents went flying.

My eyelids snapped open. "The food bank."

The three words brought on a coughing fit. When it subsided I tried to remember exactly what had happened the night of the fire. I stumbled while trying to keep up with Roussos. My purse had been unzipped, so everything went flying. Despite the darkness I found everything close by except Maura's keychain. At the time hadn't I felt lucky that I spotted it a short distance from everything else? I grabbed it in the dark and stuffed it in with my own keys.

And that was the last time I'd paid the slightest attention to it. I hadn't changed purses. I had left the keychain inside and never noticed the differences.

Maura had been at Helping Hands.

"When?"

Theoretically Maura could have lost her keys any time. She could have lost them at Mayday!, before or after. But unless she drove to the food bank with someone else, how could she have started her car and driven away? Did she routinely carry two sets of keys? Even so, wouldn't she have gone back and searched? The keys were lying on the ground in plain sight. I had seen them in the darkness.

And even if she had driven with someone

else, wouldn't she have realized the keys were missing when she got home and tried to let herself in? I was fairly certain no key was hidden outside the Wagner house, because Tyler had waited patiently for me to open the door the day I took him home. He hadn't looked under a rock or checked the pockets of one of Maura's dolls.

Wouldn't she have found a way back across town to search for the keys?

The logical conclusion? Maura had been at the food bank on the night of the fire.

Although I found my rapidly evolving theory hard to accept, puzzle pieces began to fit together. Maura was at the food bank the night of the fire, and so was Chad, who died there. If I was right, twelve years ago Maura had given birth to Chad's child. I knew Maura was afraid Chad was after Joe's job, but what else was she afraid of? Chad telling Joe the truth about Tyler? Chad having some sort of hold over her? Perhaps one that was growing increasingly hard to placate?

The police were sure Chad set the fire in the office. But for some reason, he hadn't been able to get out in time. Had Maura engineered that? How?

I had more questions than working brain cells. Maybe Maura knocked him out and he hadn't come to in time to escape? Seemed hard to believe. Chad was a large, healthy male, and Maura played the helpless little female to the hilt. But lately, hadn't I begun to suspect there was more to my new friend than met the eye? I'd seen the stronger woman emerging in a positive light, but could I have been wrong?

What about Hazel? The motive there seemed obvious. Hazel and Joe didn't see eye to eye. If Chad was a threat to Joe's job, Hazel, the board chair, was a bigger one. Maura loved her life in Emerald Springs. She loved being the spoiled wife of an esteemed community leader. She loved her house and garden and the hours she devoted to both. Emerald Springs was a small town with limited job opportunities. If Joe lost his job, most likely they would have to move away.

And finally, what about Joe? Had he confronted Maura about Chad? Had she poisoned Joe so she could stay in Emerald Springs without him, the respected widow of a murdered man? Still, if that was the case, why was she so determined not to tell the police Joe was missing? Was she waiting for the body to decompose so when they found him, they would find no trace of poison?

When it came right down to it, how would Maura know how to poison anyone?

My theory was elaborate. My headache was more elaborate. I really couldn't tell if I was making sense. I needed somebody to listen and tell me if I needed a nap or an immediate trip to either the police station or emergency room.

I dialed Lucy, and this time got her voice mail. I asked her to call me back immediately and hung up. I thought about calling my sisters, but there was too much to explain to catch them up to speed.

Just one more detail. One more clue, and I could call Roussos again. The key just wasn't enough. I had no proof Maura had dropped it the night of the fire, and not a bit of proof she was there when the fire actually started. I didn't want to alienate Roussos to the point that he no longer took my calls.

I crawled under the covers and kicked everything at the foot of the bed to Ed's side. When Ed got home I would show him my discovery. And I would tell him everything else. Ed was the soul of logic. Either he would tell me to stay off the cough medicine, or he would help me figure out what to do next.

I closed my eyes and saw roses. Big, dinner plate roses in clusters at the county fair. Roses in perfect health because they had been tended so lovingly. Maura's roses, fed with compost and ground-up bones, dusted with dried blood, protected by fox urine and homemade sprays made from botanical combinations. Maura, the organic gardener with a strong stomach.

Nicotine was an organic substance. What had Roussos said about it being a banned pesticide? Could it still be made at home? Was it as simple as buying a pack of cigarettes and soaking them in water? Hadn't Roussos said the pesticide had been used to kill aphids?

I knew enough about roses to know that aphids were a chronic problem.

One more clue, I had told myself. Now I sat up and dialed the police station. Knowing the nonemergency number by heart? That was almost more frightening than what I had to tell.

When the dispatcher answered I explained who I was and what I wanted, but this time I wasn't lucky. Roussos was gone, and she put me through to his voice mail.

I recorded what I had discovered since I'd last spoken to him and added my theories. Then I asked him to call me when he got the message.

I had done my duty. More than my duty. Maybe I had done enough to move the investigation in the right direction. And maybe Maura had an alibi as solid and polished as her pineapple door knocker. I really hoped so. But if she didn't, if she'd been involved in all these events, then I wanted Roussos to grab her and shake the truth about Joe out of her.

For now, whether he did or didn't, I was finished.

I closed my eyes and let the exhaustion I'd been fighting claim me. My house was locked tight; my family would be home soon. I was safe . . .

"Holy Nirvana." I sat up so fast the room did a little dance.

I had two sets of Maura's keys, yes. But I had forgotten something just as important.

Maura had *mine.*

I had no reason to think Maura could read my mind. How would she know I suspected she had joined the Emerald Springs Sociopaths Society? Yet, if anything I was coming to believe about her was true, Maura was smarter than any of us had given her credit for. And far more dangerous.

I was not safe in my own house.

I tried to think where I could go. Our neighbors are old, and I didn't want to share my virus with them. I could probably get myself to the church, but Ed had his keys with him so I couldn't get in unless January happened to be there.

I decided on our car. I could go outside in my nightgown with my pillow and an afghan, drive to a nearby street and lock myself in, then wait until my family came home.

Okay, I would never hear the end of it. But did I care?

Not so much.

All those summers with my survivalist father? The one lesson that had never changed from year to year?

Run.

I got to my feet just fast enough to be sure I didn't swoon and went to the closet for slip-on sneakers. Okay, no fashion statement with my nightgown, but I was going to tough that out.

I slid them on my feet and grabbed my peach chenille robe off the back of the closet door. I closed it and turned.

"Not exactly a match with those shoes," Maura said from the doorway.

I squealed. I probably would have anyway, even if I hadn't known what I did about her.

"I'm sorry. Did I surprise you?" Maura was dressed more casually than I ever remembered seeing her. Pale denim jeans, sneakers adorned with only a sprinkling of rhinestones and sequins, and a soft gray camp shirt with an appliquéd kitten curled on a pocket. She entered the room and stood at the foot of our bed.

I knew my best chance was to lie. And to do it quickly and flawlessly. I put my hand to my chest as if to check my heartbeat — that part, at least, was real.

"Well, yeah, you did. I bet Ed called you, didn't he? He wanted you to check on me. He's such a worrier." I stood perfectly still. I knew the moment I edged away from her, this game was up.

The game was up anyway. She shook her head, as if she was about to tell me that the PTA president wanted somebody else to chair the next book sale.

"Just so you know," she said. "I thought a lot about this. I wasn't sure you would put the pieces together. And even if you did, I wasn't sure you had enough proof to convince anybody. In the end though, when it came right down to it, you had my keys. And I was pretty sure that the minute you realized it, you would remember where and when you got them."

I tried to sound puzzled. "I don't know what you're talking about. Dropping keys isn't a crime."

"Aggie, you're like a cat with a mouse. You shake it and worry it until it's all played out. Then you leap. You've been shaking and worrying, and I realized the leap was coming. I really hate to do this, but you know, once you're on a roll? Killing people's not as hard as you think."

My gaze darted around the room looking for something to use as a weapon. I was bigger than Maura, although not by much. She looked soft and feminine, not anyone's concept of a bodybuilder. But I was dizzy, and all that childhood training wasn't going to help as much as it should. Not when the room kept spinning and spinning.

"I've already called Detective Roussos," I said. "I told him everything I figured out."

"Did you? And why would I believe that? You never pushed me to go to the police about Joseph. I would be *so* surprised if you went to them yourself. Not until you had everything you needed to convince that hot detective you're a super sleuth."

There was nothing in reach that would help me. The lamp was plugged behind the bed, and I thought if I grabbed it, I'd probably bring the mattress with it. There was a framed watercolor on the wall to my right that one of our parishioners had painted, but instead of glass, the framer had used acrylic. I couldn't shatter it over Maura's head. It would bounce. Our botanical prints had no glass at all.

I edged away from her, toward the dresser closest to the door. I had a hand mirror on the dresser. It was my best bet.

"So, if you're going to try to kill me, you might as well tell me how I fit into your murder scrapbook. I'm pretty sure you killed Hazel. I'm guessing some kind of nicotine solution, like something you make yourself to put on your roses?"

"Nothing that diluted. Nicotine sulfate. Last year one of the ladies in the rose society was moving into assisted living, so she cleared out her garden shed. She gave me a jar because I'd had so much trouble with aphids. She's been hoarding it since it was outlawed. Wasn't that convenient?"

Not for Hazel. I edged a little closer to the dresser and talked, hoping to keep her from noticing.

"How did you get Hazel to swallow the stuff? Didn't it taste like an ashtray?"

"Oh, that's the beauty of nicotine. It can also be absorbed through the skin. It said so, right on the label. I'd seen Hazel at Cilla's desk a couple of times, pouring over Joseph's records. Her hands were always so chapped and rough, and Cilla keeps her favorite jasmine-scented hand lotion there. Hazel would slather it on it like she owned the bottle. So Friday night I dissolved some of my treasure in an identical bottle and replaced Cilla's. The smell of the lotion is so strong, Hazel probably thought the tobacco odor was coming from her own hands. She smoked, you know. Every chance she got. Anyway, I knew Hazel would be in the office before the fair, because she was trying so hard to trap Joseph. She was so stupid, she thought he was the one fencing all that food."

"Wasn't that taking an awfully big chance? I mean, what if Cilla had gone in over the weekend and used the lotion herself?"

"Gosh, wouldn't that have been a shame?" Maura gave a humorless laugh. "That cow wants my husband. That would have been one way to deal with her."

I winced. "I guess your plan worked, huh?"

"I knew it would. Hazel had an extra incentive for visiting Joseph's office. Where do you think they were keeping the chocolate for the chocolate fountain? Hazel knew it was right there. So my idea was foolproof. I knew she'd lock herself inside, gorge on chocolate, look through records, and slather on the hand lotion. Wasn't she predictable?"

"And you replaced the lotion afterwards?"

"Easy as pie. I have Joseph's keys. I did it before Hazel keeled over. As simple as switching bottles at Mayday! when nobody was in the office but me."

"And you did this why? You knew Joe didn't have anything to do with stealing supplies. Hazel was no threat."

"You know, that's not going to help you, that mirror, I mean. Do you realize how pale you are? You look like you're going to fall over without my help. I saw Ed at the pharmacy this afternoon. He told me the doctor said you were one step from pneumonia. Right before he told me you'd be home alone this evening. I called to be sure they'd gone." She took a step toward me.

I held up my hands to ward her off. "Don't kid yourself, Maura. I may be sick, but I'll put up one hell of a fight."

"All that gardening makes me strong. You'll be surprised."

I was feeling worse by the second. "Why did you kill Hazel?"

"Because Joseph didn't want to fight her anymore. He told me he wanted out of the food bank and away from the stress. He thought maybe if we moved somewhere else we could start over as a family, too. Find more common ground." She laughed almost fondly. "We had everything right here. I don't know what got into him."

"You didn't want to leave? So killing Hazel seemed easier?"

"Safer, I'd say. Without Hazel, Joseph would be happy again. Things would be perfect, the way they used to be."

"Oh, right, perfect. With you passing off another man's child as his?"

She lifted one elegantly shaped brow. "You must have seen that photo before I got rid of it. I hope by the time Tyler's a grown-up nobody remembers what Chad looked like. That nasty old resemblance. Another good reason to kill him."

She was discussing this with the same lack of passion as if we were discussing china patterns. *That was another good reason to go with the gold rims instead of the silver bands.*

"Another?" I asked.

"We had a brief affair. Nothing important. But Chad's been asking me for favors ever since he realized Tyler was his. First, I had to persuade Joseph to hire him. Then Chad wanted to know Joseph's schedule every minute, so he could take advantage of it. I had to keep Joseph busy if Chad planned something that was going to take extra time, and I was always supposed to report back to Chad if Joseph got suspicious."

I was almost close enough now to grab the mirror. "The police are sure Chad set that fire."

"Oh, he did. When he realized he'd been caught, he decided to burn the records and leave town. But I knew that whether he was here or somewhere else, he would be after me for the rest of my life. So when I realized what he was planning, I waited. And while he set his little fire in the office, I set a bigger one in the rest of the warehouse. It was so easy to do. They kept gasoline in cans for their equipment. Plenty of fuel for a real bonfire. And you know what? I waited until Chad came out of his office, so he would die knowing it was me, then I lit one match. No more blackmail."

She shook her head as I grabbed the mirror. "What do you think? That I'm some kind of vampire? You hold that up and I'll shrivel at my own reflection?"

I whacked it against the top of the dresser and when it shattered, I grabbed the largest piece, slicing my thumb in the process. "Don't come any closer, Maura."

"Oh, Aggie, you're shaking. And now you're bleeding. I may not have to do a thing. You might just fall to the floor. That would be convenient."

I brandished the glass at her, as I backed

toward the doorway. "I think you killed Joe, too. All this talk about wanting him to stay at the food bank? I think he's dead, and you killed him."

"No, I didn't. I've been honest about Joseph." Again, she could have been reciting her grocery list. "I don't know where he is. It's very inconvenient. He left me to deal with this alone. I really thought I had it all worked out. Then I dropped my keys the night I set the fire. I realized after I hiked back to my car through the woods. And I knew right where I must have dropped them. But by the time I circled back, the fire was huge. I saw you with Detective Roussos and Ed. Then I saw my keys on the ground . . ."

"And you saw me pick them up." It explained so much.

"Then what do you know? There was that unfortunate photograph." She shrugged — right before she lunged.

I didn't know what Maura had planned, but I wasn't going to stay and fight with one shard of glass. I fled through the doorway and toward the stairs. Adrenaline buoyed me, but I wasn't as quick or steady as I would have been. I reached the steps just ahead of her, but Maura lunged once more and I went down.

I knew how to fall. Instinctively I bent my knees and elbows and rolled, tucking my head as close to my collarbone as it would go. I dropped the glass and used my hands to cushion the impact, but despite this, my head banged against one step then another as I tried to stop myself from rolling all the way down. I screamed as I went and hoped that someone would hear me.

I lay sprawled across the steps, head down, the world spinning around me. Maura tackled me, and despite my flailing, she shoved me against the railing. Then she pulled a hypodermic out of her pocket and uncapped it.

I struggled, or at least I thought I was struggling. But things were growing hazier. I could hardly breathe, and my entire body throbbed in agony. She jabbed me hard through my nightgown and into the back of my knee, and I screamed one more time. Before she could do another thing, I made one last effort to topple her.

"Maura!" a deep voice shouted.

She jumped away, and suddenly I was free. I could still feel the needle, but Maura was no longer attached to it.

I heard clattering on the steps. Just before the world went completely black I lifted my head.

"Rube?"

But this time it wasn't Rube, although it took me a moment to be sure. This man was younger. His hair was darker, his shoulders perhaps not quite as broad. And as I watched he grabbed his protesting wife by the shoulder and dragged her down the remainder of the steps to the floor below.

Joe Wagner had come home at last.

21

When the sun shines in Ohio, nothing in the universe is brighter. No sun is more talked about, fawned over, or allowed freer access to dusty corners. On the summer solstice, the Celtic Oak King, god of the waxing year, spreads his golden warmth over every inch of Emerald Springs one last time and chases away our darkest memories.

The Wilcox family had special reasons to enjoy this day. The Victorian was finally ready. Junie was moving in, and once she was comfortably settled, she was going to begin the arduous task of turning her lovely new space into Emerald Springs's only quilt shop.

For now, between loads, we were catching our breath on the front porch. Ed, my girls, Junie, and me. Frankly, these days, I can hardly get enough of them.

"Where shall we put your lovely penny rugs?" Junie asked my daughters, whom she had unofficially hired as decorating consultants.

The penny rugs had consumed the weeks since Maura Wagner was taken off to jail and I was taken to the hospital for observation and orange juice. The juice counteracted the insulin that had leaked into my system from Maura's syringe. I just missed receiving a massive fatal dose. Joe arrived before Maura could push the plunger. My worried girls had stayed close by my side in the intervening weeks, and designing and sewing the rugs had occupied us all.

"Your table." Teddy's design was composed of apple trees and bluebirds of brilliant reds, greens, and blues. Junie agreed that the penny rug, as long as two placemats and about as wide, would be perfect as her table centerpiece.

Deena's penny rug, about the size of a bathmat, was an exotic garden, with sun beaming brightly down on a field of wildly colored flowers. She opted to hang it on Junie's kitchen wall, and Junie told her the choice was perfect.

"There must be a lesson here," I told Ed, as the girls left to adorn their chosen territory with their grandmother. "Hazel Kefauver's somber old clothes reborn into a form that's bound to give everybody who sees them pleasure."

Ed pulled me to his side and squeezed my hip. "Don't tempt me to go all theological on you."

I rested my head against his shoulder. I was still waiting for words of recrimination, for the booming ministerial "I told you so," but Ed has been remarkably restrained since my near-death experience. Although sleuthing had moved me solidly into Maura's view, finding her keys had pushed her over the edge. I think Ed realizes that even if I hadn't followed a single lead, once I put those keys in my purse, Maura would have come after me anyway.

Maybe he also remembers that in the beginning, he was the one who nudged me into becoming Maura's friend.

Roussos had been less restrained. He arrived at the parsonage just ahead of my family where he found Joe trying to subdue a spitting, kicking Maura. In between bouts of abuse, Maura tried to convince Joe that if he would just let her kill me, all their troubles would be over. Roussos disabused her of that notion right before he called the EMTs to take me to the emergency room for observation. I think I was on the way to the hospital before he actually told me that if I ever interfered in another case, he would personally spring Maura from the state pen to do her worst.

Yeah, yeah. I saw the relief on the guy's face when he realized I was all right. Turns out he had gotten my message and decided the situation warranted more than returning my phone call.

From the beginning the arson investigators had realized that two different fires had been set the night the warehouse burned, due to finding two different accelerants. From this they had surmised that Chad wasn't the only naughty resident of our fair city. And because she was so uncooperative about Joe's whereabouts, Maura was on their short list of suspects. With the help of the New Jersey cops Roussos determined that the phone number she gave him was a sham, and from that moment on, Maura stirred serious interest. My announcement about Tyler's parentage had stirred it more.

Of course Joe's disappearance and Maura's cover-up were only peripherally related to the food bank crimes and fire. But Maura's desire to protect Joe, or rather protect his job so she could continue to dress her front porch dolls and blithely poison aphids, threw her under suspicion and brought Roussos to my door when I needed him most. This was an irony I relished.

So okay, I'm not as old a soul as I would like to be.

"Are you going to miss having Junie in our house?" I asked Ed.

"That's a loaded question."

"I'm glad she's not moving far."

"I know. Just far enough."

I knew Ed loved my mother, and Junie was as ready to have her own space again as we were to have the parsonage to ourselves. She had so many plans for her new shop. I wondered if Emerald Springs was ready for her — would our little burg ever be? The years ahead would be interesting.

"More boxes waiting." Ed glanced at his watch. "Tell Junie I'm making another run. Then we'll head to dinner."

Lucy was treating the whole family to falafel sandwiches. Since the evening promised to be beautiful, we planned to picnic at the oval and listen to our community band serenade us with a spirited, off-key summer concert, most likely heavy on the Beach Boys. I was into simple pleasures these days. Surprising how beloved they become when it looks like all those pesky little afterlife questions are about to be answered.

I kissed my husband, something I'm doing even more often these days, and watched as he backed the van onto Bunting Street. Before I could turn away, a dark sedan pulled into a parking space in front of the house, and in a moment both the driver's and passenger's doors opened. Joe Wagner and Tyler got out.

I hadn't seen Joe since the night his wife tried to kill me. Before the word could go out about Maura's arrest, he whisked Tyler away from Emerald Springs. Rube disappeared with him, although four days later, a crew of young, good-looking men with Boston accents and names like Nino and Tony arrived to complete work on the Victorian. Gratis.

There was still so much I didn't know, but curiosity is different from resolve. I'd had reasons to find out what was behind Hazel's murder and Joe's disappearance. But once I knew Joe was safe, I had no good reason to pry. My work was finished. Brownie was off the hook and grateful enough for my help that he had given our family a summer membership to the county pool. Maura was behind bars and hopefully no danger to anyone except a cell mate who disagreed with her choice of bedspreads or wall decor. Considering how close I'd come to either being reborn as a chipmunk or chatting with St. Peter, I had filed Joe and the Pussycat Club under "Life's Little Mysteries" and moved on.

Okay, not willingly. But I was working on it.

Now Tyler preceded his father up the sidewalk. Tyler is still young enough that he hasn't fallen prey to the slack-jawed, vacant-eyed expression of a teenager who doesn't want his feelings known. From his face I could tell this boy wasn't sure if he would ever be welcome anywhere again.

I couldn't ask if he was doing okay. Of course he wasn't. But I knew Joe would make sure that with time and patience, the wounds Maura had inflicted on their family would heal enough that Tyler could move on.

I knew better than to hug him, but I extended my hand and grasped his hard. "I'm so glad you're back, Tyler. Deena will be glad, too."

"Really?" he asked.

I heard a serious question, so I gave a serious answer. "She's been worried about you. We all have. You'll make her day."

He smiled. Tentatively, but that was a start. I pointed him through the door and told him to climb the stairs.

Joe and I were alone.

"Want to sit?" I pointed to the new wicker glider that Junie had placed on the porch as part of a comfortable grouping. I could already imagine her customers sitting here pouring over pattern books and comparing purchases. No one would ever want to leave.

Joe followed me to the porch. I noted new lines around his eyes. I thought he looked more like Rube than he had before his wife decided to start killing people.

"How are you?" I asked, once we'd settled ourselves.

"Taking this one day at a time." He rested his head against the back of the glider. "We've been in Boston. You probably guessed?"

"When Rube disappeared, too, it seemed likely."

"It was tough."

"I can only imagine."

"You know the whole story? How my brothers tricked me into leaving?"

"Rube told me. He was determined to make things right again."

"They're trying. And Pops?" He opened his eyes and smiled a little. "He was so glad to see me, he almost forgave them for what they did all those years ago."

"How did Tyler take to his new family?"

"They provide something to think about

besides his mother. He likes the cooking, and right now he can use all the hugs. We're moving there. I've already put a down payment on a little house around the corner from Pops and my little brother Benjamin. Pops isn't going to live forever. I want Tyler to get to know him and the rest of the family. They've made me general manager of Creative Construction. I'm supposed to whip them into shape."

"You'll really be missed here. Are you sure?"

He smiled a little, but he shook his head. "I couldn't go back to Helping Hands. I trusted Chad. He was good at what he did and even better at hiding the criminal stuff. Our jobs were defined in such a way that I didn't have enough oversight, but that's not an excuse. I should have figured out what was going on. I guess it was good training for the family business. Nobody's going to get away with anything in Boston. I'll be watching, but they claim that's what they need."

"Will you come back and visit?"

"Truthfully? Probably not. Tyler and I need to make a fresh start away from everything that happened." His eyes met mine. "You know about Chad and Maura?"

I nodded.

"I'm not going to tell Tyler. Not yet, maybe not ever. He's got enough to deal with. I don't want him to think he's lost me to DNA after losing his mother to prison."

"You've had a lot of shocks."

"That was no shock, Aggie. I've known since he was born that he wasn't mine. I just didn't realize he was Chad's. When Maura couldn't conceive we both went through testing. I discovered I had a condition that could probably be corrected by surgery, but by the time the doctor told me, Maura was already pregnant. So I was almost sure she'd had an affair. Then once I saw Tyler, it didn't matter. He was mine from the moment he snuggled into my arms. He'll always be mine."

"That's the way it should be."

"You probably wonder where I disappeared to all those weeks."

"Yeah, big-time. But I also know it's no longer my business."

This time his smile was more natural, more like the Joe I'd always been so fond of. "So what *do* you know?"

I recapped. When I finished he didn't look embarrassed, he looked impressed. "Well, you've got a reputation around here, and I guess you deserve it."

"A 'tar and feathers' reputation? Or an

'ask her for her autograph reputation'?"

"A 'be careful what you tell her' reputation. But for the most part, it's respectful."

"I'm surprised anybody gets near me. No one's safe."

"You don't cause the crimes, you solve them."

I couldn't help myself. If I have a reputation as a nosy broad, I deserve that, too. "So, where did you go that night at the Pussycat Club? Did your disappearing act have to do with Hazel?"

"In a manner of speaking. But I'll back up. I've learned some painful things about myself. In every relationship I've had, I've always been the responsible one. At home growing up, in later years on every job I took on, and finally in my marriage. I chose a woman who expected me to take care of her from the moment she got up in the morning, then we had a son with medical problems who needed to be taken care of." He didn't say this as if he felt sorry for himself, more as if it were a fact he'd recently come to grips with.

"That's *your* reputation."

"And well deserved. Anyway, it's not a plus. The load was too much to carry, and I didn't have any outlets. Then one evening, after a day of meetings in Manhattan, a bunch of guys decided to go to the Pussycat Club as a joke, and I tagged along. It was amateur night, when they pick a couple of guys from the audience, dress them up, and let them perform. You probably already know I got chosen, but when I went up on that stage, something happened. I could forget everything at home, everything at work, my lost family. I could pretend to be somebody else, some dame who didn't have to be responsible for anybody but herself. Changing sexes was part of it. I guess because my mother ran off when I was so young, I equated male with responsibility. But as a woman I could be carefree and funny and sing my heart out."

"Joe, this sounds like you've been doing a whole lot of thinking."

"I started drinking. A lot. After getting a taste of what life was like without all that pressure, I started looking for other ways to release it. Alcohol's one of those classic responses. I drank to put myself to sleep at night, had a beer too many at lunch to get through the day, had a couple with dinner to get through another night with Maura. I was miserable, but at the same time I was afraid to leave because of Tyler. I knew she would tell the courts Tyler wasn't really mine, and so my rights would be worth less to a judge than hers."

I rested my fingertips on his arm. "Anybody would be stressed out with all that on their plate."

"It built to a head. I got so I had to get away each month and perform. It was like a release valve, and without it, I knew I was going to explode."

I visualized this. Joe with the pressure slowly building. Hazel trying to destroy him at work, Maura doing nothing at home to help. I could see it happening, like a movie building to climax.

"Then the night you disappeared, you were onstage and Hazel walked in," I guessed out loud.

"That's exactly what happened. Right at the end of my second number I saw her come in. I don't think she realized who I was, but I knew if I went back out there, she'd figure it out. Everything just came together, except me. *I* fell apart. I retreated to my dressing room and knew I had to do something. There was a treatment facility in Pittsburgh that I'd heard good things about through some clients at Helping Hands. I called, and they told me they would meet me at the bus station if I could just get myself there. I called Maura and told her I couldn't go on the way we were, and I was checking myself into a clinic."

"But the call went haywire."

"I didn't know that. I never found out, because I chose Chad to be my go-between both at work and at home. I was allowed one phone call twice a week, so I called him. Religiously. And every single time we spoke he said just what you'd expect. He was thrilled to have more time to steal the food bank blind, so he told me things were fine at home and work. Maura was stepping up to the plate, and she hoped I came home soon. Everyone at work and on the board understood why I'd left so suddenly, and of course, my job would be waiting when I returned. And all that time he never told a single soul what was really going on."

"So you put the fox in charge of the henhouse."

"Then the fox vanished. Suddenly Chad's phone was out of service, and I didn't know what to do. Just as I was about to break down and call Maura, I saw a newspaper a visitor had left in the reception area and found out what had happened here. I left immediately."

"Cilla thought she saw you poking around the remains of the warehouse, but I thought she'd probably mistaken Rube for you. The two of you look so much alike from a distance."

"I'd learned enough about myself to know that I couldn't just go charging in and make everything right. Not at work, and not at home. First I had to figure out what was going on, then figure out who needed to respond. So I got a room outside of town and started making calls, pretending to be an insurance adjustor, and as you say, poking around. The story emerged pretty quickly."

"I guess the one thing I'd really like to know? How you managed to dash in at the last minute, just in the nick of time, and save my life. For which I'm grateful, by the way."

"My pleasure." He covered my hand with his. "I'm so sorry, Aggie. I know how you got into this. But I'm just so sorry you went through what you did."

"Hey, it could have been worse. You cut it close, but you got there."

"I was on my way to see Maura. I finally came to the conclusion our marriage was over and I had to take my chances with the legal system. There were enough people who would vouch for me as Tyler's primary caretaker. I thought I had a good chance of getting custody. So I went home to tell her.

I decided to knock on the front door, because I didn't want to let myself in and give her a nasty surprise. I got up to the porch, and one of those dolls she loved so much was in the way. I think it was dressed as a jockey, probably because the Preakness was coming up. Anyway, I knocked up against it, and the doll fell in front of the door. I bent to retrieve it, and while I was there I heard Maura call upstairs to Tyler. She said she was going out for a little while, and he could watch television until she got back."

He looked away, as if he was visualizing the scene. "The house was lit and I could see Maura through the sidelights. As I watched she filled a hypodermic from the supply of insulin we kept in the hallway table for emergencies. I was actually pleased. I thought she had finally started helping Tyler take care of his diabetes, and she was getting the insulin ready for him before she left. I remember thinking that was great, Tyler would finally have two parents who could handle things in an emergency, that maybe we could actually share joint custody."

He turned back to me. "Then she put the needle in her pocket. She got her purse and started toward the front door. I was confused. I thought about confronting her once she got away from the house and trying to have our talk somewhere private, but the needle bothered me. I wondered where she was going with it and why. So I stayed in the shadows, and when she left, I followed her. She went directly to your house and used a key to unlock your door, which seemed strange. I was pretty certain that if anybody in your house was diabetic, I would have been told, so the insulin made no sense. I didn't know what was going on, but I became increasingly uneasy. After a few minutes passed I decided to knock and confront her, and about then, I heard you scream. The door was unlocked. You know the rest."

"Man, that story is filled with a lot of 'almosts' isn't it?" I shuddered.

"She can't hurt you or anybody else where she is now. Although I guess that's not really true. Even when everybody else has forgotten her, Tyler never will."

"You'll help him through it."

"That's one responsibility I'll take on willingly."

Joe got to his feet, and I joined him. I heard a noise in the side yard and turned to see Tyler and Deena just far enough away that our conversation couldn't have been audible. As I watched, Tyler leaned over and kissed my daughter.

I heard the shrill whistle of years rushing past me. I was afraid Deena had just entered adolescence. She might be ready, but I sure wasn't.

I managed to pull myself back to the present and Joe, but it wasn't easy. "Are you heading to Boston tonight?"

"We just came to get a few things and talk to some Realtors."

"I've got a good one for you, if you haven't found another you like." As we walked down the steps I told him about Lucy, then I told him about everything Rube had done for Junie.

"The crew? Those are my nephews. The last time I saw most of them they were in diapers. But they're all in the family business. I have a lot of catching up to do."

We stopped at the bottom of the steps, and Joe whistled for Tyler.

"Ed's at the parsonage making one more trip with Junie's boxes," I said. "You'll stop and see him?"

"You bet. I want to say good-bye."

I leaned over and kissed his cheek. I thought Maura Wagner was the worst kind of fool. I wondered if Cilla would get herself to Boston once Joe had recovered a little. I certainly hoped so.

"You know," I said, before Tyler could join us. "There's just one more question . . ."

He smiled a little. "Go ahead. I knew it was coming."

"What about the Pussycat Club? Will you be performing there again? Because I heard you were really, really good."

"No, my days at Pussycat are over. It served its purpose."

"I know they'll all be sorry. Dorothy's going to feel like the Wicked Witch just flew in on a broom."

"Not to worry. I called her and told her she could have the coat. She'll recover."

Tyler came scooting around the house. Deena followed, and I thought that my confident, rational daughter looked like lightning had struck.

Joe and Tyler said good-bye, and arm in arm Deena and I watched as they headed for their car. Joe got to his door and turned.

"Aggie?"

I cocked my head in question.

"Did I mention that the little theater down the road from our new house is doing *La Cage Aux Folles* next fall?" He winked at me.

Deena and I watched them drive away.

"Life sucks," she said. "I mean, it really

sucks! How come he has to leave?"

"I think you'll see him again."

"No way. Tyler says they're never coming back here."

I didn't elaborate. But something tells me our family will need to schedule a trip to see Nan in, say, September or October? And while we're there? Well, let's just assume, I plan to take in the sights.

And the entertainment.

ABOUT THE AUTHOR

Emilie Richards is the *USA Today* bestselling author of more than fifty novels. She has received a number of awards during her career, including the RITA from Romance Writers of America and several from *Romantic Times* magazine, including a career achievement award. She has been interviewed on both television and radio, including stints as a guest on the *Leeza* show and *Hard Copy.* Visit her website at www.ministryismurder.com.